Exceptional Liars

By Marla Todd

ISBN: 978-1-7361473-0-6

♕ *Oscar Gray Publishing: Where all the cool cats write.*

Prologue

Also by Dr. Gregory Atkinson
Letting Go – A Marriage Guide for Beginners
Love and Loss
Love and Respect
Love and Trust
Living through Love

Excerpt from To Elizabeth with Love
By Dr. Gregory Atkinson

This book was written as a love letter to my wife Elizabeth Hobbs Atkinson. She was brutally tortured and killed by a man who had once been my friend. Her body was never found, but her legacy of love will still be here.

Liz and I met in the summer while working together at the Olive Branch Youth Christian Summer Camp in Pennsylvania. I was the director that summer and Liz was a counselor. We hit it off immediately with our passion for Christ and quick comfortable friendship.

I first noticed Liz's bright smile and easy laugh. I couldn't help notice her beautiful figure and grace as she moved with the children. She was sunshine and I was drawn to her warmth.

Within a week, we were inseparable. At the end of the summer I asked Liz to marry me. She was nineteen and I was twenty-six, both sure in our love for each other and commitment in Christ.

Marriage is an equal partnership in love and friendship, blessed by God as the perfect union between a man and a woman. When I met Liz, I finally met a woman who was my best friend and true equal. She was the one I could finally have that perfect union with.

The next six years were filled with such joy and passion I could have never imagined. We also had our share of tragedy, with three stillborn children and multiple miscarriages. Then, just as we had hoped that maybe God would grant us the blessed titles of Mommy and Daddy, the unthinkable happened. Liz was brutally murdered, in a cruel twist of fate by a man who called himself the Killer of Virtue.

According to the police report, my darling wife lost enough blood to kill her before she was stuffed into the back of a car. The evidence showed the massive loss of blood didn't kill her; at least not before she'd put up a valiant struggle for her life. Nobody knows if she died in the killer's car or was dumped unceremoniously in an unknown location. Nobody knows if she too, like the other five innocent victims, was dressed like a whore and posed as if ready for her next customer, waiting for the police or an innocent jogger or hiker to find her. Traces of clothing soaked with her blood, torn pages from her notebook and other artifacts were found in the woods, scattered by animals and weather, but her body was hidden much too well to ever be found.

From the day Liz vanished, I prayed for her return and for hope. The day she was pronounced legally dead, I lost all hope and thought I, too, would die. Only my faith in God and the love Liz and I shared kept me from going off into a black abyss of hopelessness and grief.

Not a day went by when we didn't say, "I love you". Not a day went by when we didn't hold hands. Not a night went by when we didn't completely celebrate our physical passions as man and wife.

Liz was sunshine, a joy to all who met her. She was my anchor. She was my best friend. No man had ever loved a woman as I had and still love Liz. No woman ever loved a man as Liz had loved me.

Perhaps one day I will marry again. I know Liz wouldn't want me to be alone, but another wife could never replace Liz. It will be different next time, God willing, if it is God's will for me to marry again.

My comfort comes from my faith and my knowledge that Liz is in a better place.

~ Gregory Atkinson

"Son of a bitch." I put down my glass of wine and threw the book across the room.

I'm surprised the bastard hasn't been struck by lightning. What a crock of crap and lies. Any poetic justice of my situation had gone down the drain at that moment. Greg is walking and talking and writing best-selling books about me and about our marriage...and I'm still dead... saved by a serial killer, no less. God save me and have mercy on my soul and on that abusive lying son of a bitch Gregory Atkinson. May he rot in Hell. But he did get his wish: I am in a better place.

A much, much better place.

Chapter 1

All of us Hobbs kids were exceptional liars, well, except my brother Jordan, who was a liar by default by his refusal to tell either lies or the truth. There were seven of us. Jordan was the youngest and had no discernable personality or identifying character traits except for his unusual refusal to talk, unless it was to speak about his love of the Lord and his belief that our brother Steve, now deceased, would soon come back as an avenging angel. The rest of us were quite talkative and also could quote scripture as fluently as we could lie.

Once upon a time, the fashionable and pious Belinda George met the successful, and widowed young father Douglas Hobbs. Like Hitler and Mussolini, they created their own empire complete with an army of children to worship the ground they walked on and do their bidding unflinching and loyal.

The eldest Hobbs child, David, was a serious and brilliant boy. His mother was our father's first wife Barbara Vanderhook, a quiet mouse-like woman who hung herself from the upstairs banister when David was five. She left a note saying that she could never love her strange, cold son. Part two of the note stated that she loved her husband (my father) too much even knowing that he saw her as a failure.

We didn't see much of David growing up, as his mother's will left enough money for him to be shipped off to an exclusive prep school two hours from our home.

In the meantime, my mother started to pop out her own large brood of children. First came Mark Douglas Hobbs, the favorite and most aggressive. A year later, the twins Bradley George and Katherine Belinda arrived. Bradley was almost as aggressive as Mark but had a charming manipulative side, which he used at every opportunity to his advantage. The sensitive, pretty, and evil Kathy spent her childhood trying to be our mother's favorite. Unfortunately for Kathy, Belinda's only favorite was Belinda.

Eighteen months after the birth of the twins, one cold January morning, Stephen Allen Hobbs came into the world, singing out songs of justice that continued until the day he died. Elizabeth Ann Hobbs came along ten months later in October. After my arrival, the lines were drawn and it was the real twins vs. the almost-twins.

Brad and Kathy were classic bullies in every sense of the word, worshiping their leader, Mark. Where Steve and I lacked in meanness and brute force, we made up in cunning and deception.

Another two years passed in the Hobbs household when Jordan Emmanuel Hobbs arrived. Unlike the rest of us, Jordan was quiet and uncharacteristically passive in nature. In contrast to the physical prowess of his elder siblings, Jordan was flabby and sedate. He could sit for hours while the rest of us ran, jumped and tumbled like we were training for the Olympic Ultimate Fighting Club.

I remember once when Steve and I had hidden in my parents' closet and heard them talking about us. I remember my mother saying, "I can't take it any longer. We should look into sending the children off to a boarding school."

"What about Jordan?"

"He can stay here."

"We'll keep the retard at home. What will everyone think of that? With the rest of the children here, nobody notices we have an imbecile on our hands."

That was the end of all talk of sending us away.

Jordan and David were both odd in the opinion of the five middle children. Both were quiet and passive; behaviors we couldn't understand. To his credit, David had a mean, cynical streak that we greatly admired.

Mother (as Belinda insisted we call her) was at first delighted in the status that seven children brought her, but what she gained in status, she lacked in maternal instinct. The seven Hobbs children were alternately ignored, neglected and both physically and psychologically tortured by our mother.

Our father demanded perfection; perfect behavior, superior grades, perfect musical pitch and a house that would put any military ideals to shame, and a complete devotion to God and the study of the Bible. Of course, there were consequences if we did not live up to his standards. Like mother, our father also believed in quick, harsh physical punishment to all infractions of his code of conduct. Luckily for us, we rarely saw the workaholic bastard.

Chapter 2

Food was always a big thing in the Hobbs household. Not that anyone cooked, because they didn't. It was the lack of food that kept the growing brood of Hobbs children hungry and always on the prowl. Mother didn't cook, so while we were young she used her charms to get good spirited women from our church to come help her out with the babies. There were so many of us toddlers, five children under the age of six plus a baby. Nobody could resist the lovely young mother in need.

As we grew older and started school, things changed dramatically. We ceased to be cute or interesting to Belinda. This was not the way she wanted to spend her time.

Not being one to spend money on anyone other than herself, our mother had a schedule of pot luck dinners at our church she'd take us to at least four nights a week. We'd bring a loaf of French bread and a grocery bag full of empty containers. In turn, we'd come home with cakes, cookies, pasta, salads, casseroles, fried chicken and whatever other leftovers from the groaning church tables that would feed us the remaining three days. The rest of the time we foraged from our almost bare cabinets and from the homes of friends. Our lunches came from the school cafeteria, so we always knew we'd be fed at least once a day during the week. Unlike the other kids, we never complained about the quality of school meals.

By the time Mark was eleven, we were also cooking for ourselves. Let me take a step back. My parents never ate with us. They went out almost every night for dinner or brought dinner for two in and ate it in the formal dining room without the distractions of the children.

One morning after Kathy got mad at me for calling her a stupid butt picking rat, she threw a skillet containing about a half-pound of bacon and several cups of flaming hot grease at me. With that little prank, all hot meals at home ended.

Five-year-old Jordan started to howl like a wounded dog.

Steve started to scream, "Her skin is coming off. HER SKIN IS COMING OFF!"

Brad ran over to look. "You're peeling like a snake. Gross."

I was hyperventilating and remember hearing myself making sharp, high-pitched noises after every breath.

Mark grabbed Kathy by the arm and dragged her to the corner. "Don't say anything to Mother or Father. You didn't do anything. Do you understand?"

"I can't lie. It's a sin. I don't want to sin," babbled Kathy, who by then was crying uncontrollably.

"It isn't lying if you don't say anything," said Mark, "Make them think Liz spilled the oil." He turned to the rest of us. "Liz spilled the bacon grease. That is the story."

"Fuck you, Mark!" yelled Steve.

"You're going to Hell for saying that," said Kathy.

"Fuck you, Kathy," said Steve. At age nine, Steve was enjoying his use of a new word.

Mark grabbed Steve by the head and started hitting him. Brad was pulling Steve away and screaming at Mark. Jordan climbed up on the table and started to recite the Lord's Prayer. Okay, it was more like screaming the Lord's Prayer at the top of his lungs.

I fell to the ground in pain and started to wail. My entire body felt like it was on fire.

Mother came into the room and slipped on the bacon grease and came crashing down next to me. Her eyes were filled with hate as she propped herself up on her elbow and glared at me. "What did you do now, Elizabeth?"

"Nothing!" I yowled.

Father walked into the kitchen and looked at the carnage. "Jordan, please remove your self from the table," he said as he lifted me off of the ground. He put me on the table. "Belinda, please get off of the floor, there is nothing wrong with you. Dial 911. This child's skin is peeling off and she can't breathe. She needs to go to the hospital. Mark, please go outside and wait in case the ambulance gets here in a reasonable time. Katherine, Bradley clean up the mess on the floor. Steve, get Jordan out of here, preferably to bed. NOW."

Father scanned the room. "You are all to finish your homework, then study your Bibles and then pray with all of your dark sinful souls that the rod does not pay you a visit tonight."

Chapter 3

I wound up with a stay in the hospital and a skin graft to my left thigh. Kathy, who neglected to use a hot pad on the cast iron skillet, temporarily burned off most of her fingerprints. With tears in her large baby blue eyes, dear sister claimed I'd threatened her, causing the accident, and of course no adult believed me. Steve and Jordan stayed quiet after threats of death from Mark, Brad and Kathy. After that, all cooking, including use of the microwave, was banned from our home.

While in the hospital recovering from my burns, I was told to pray to God for forgiveness for being such a willful and sinful child. A child psychologist was sent in to talk to me. I lay in my bed quietly, not daring to tell anyone about my fear of what God, Belinda or my siblings might do to me. No eight-year-old had ever given a better performance; spinning lies about a happy home and idyllic childhood.

The child psychologist, a nondescript man with brown hair, asked me a bunch of questions that made no sense to me.

"Are you happy at home?"

I nodded my head yes.

"How about school? Do you like school?"

"Yes, I like school a lot," I said. "I make straight A's." I didn't tell him that school was the only place I was happy.

"Straight A's, you say? I bet you work hard."

I gave him a drug-induced smile. "It's easy. I don't even have to cheat."

"Do you think the accident was your fault?"

"What accident?"

"Your burn. The reason you're here, Elizabeth."

"I don't know," I said, not knowing why I said it.

"Where did the bruises on your legs come from?"

It was time for more lies. "Dodge Ball. I don't feel good." Then I pretended to fall asleep.

Later the minister from our church asked me if I'd ever been abused or mistreated at home. Of course I lied to him too. I'd always liked Reverend Johnson and didn't want him to think badly of me.

"Who do you love Elizabeth?" What a question to ask a child.

I put my hand on Reverend Johnson's hand, just like my brother Mark did when he was about to tell a whopper lie to our mother. "Jesus, my brothers, and my parents."

"What about your sister Kathy?" He chuckled. "I know you love Kathy."

"I hate Kathy," I told him.

"That isn't a nice thing to say. Why do you hate Kathy?"

"Kathy is mean." Our father always told us that we could answer questions from the Bible. God knows the sadistic bastard made us study it for an hour or more a day. I let go of Reverend Johnson's hand. "'Do not be surprised at the fiery ordeal that has come on you to test you, as though something strange were happening to you. But rejoice inasmuch as you participate in the sufferings of Christ, so that you may be overjoyed when his glory is revealed.' That is from Peter. I don't remember the numbers. I don't feel good."

The good Reverend kissed my forehead and left me alone for the night. I wanted to ask him if I could live with him and his nice family but I knew he'd say no.

During the stay in the hospital, I lost the ability to cry. I don't know if it was the ability or just the desire. Why cry at all? It never did me any good. Nobody ever comforted me except Steve, and it only scared Jordan. Maybe it could have been result of being told that I should be feeling both the fear of the fires of Hell and the love of God for saving my skinny little eight-year-old ass from burning to death from a flaming shower of bacon grease.

I'd already learned to hide pain and emotional distress as a means of survival, so it wasn't that big of a deal; at least to me. Over the years, it became creepy and disconcerting to others.

On those few occasions I did feel the need for tears or any other show of emotion or distress it manifested itself into violent stomach cramps and vomiting. I never figured it out and like everything else in my short life; I just accepted things as they were.

Chapter 4

So that was my early childhood. We did our homework, ate a lot of peanut butter, obeyed our parents, told a lot of lies, and learned that if we didn't get good grades we'd be beaten and that we'd go to Hell.

One night when I was fourteen, we were all studying in the basement and Steve announced, "Other people don't live like this."

"What do you mean?" asked Mark, as usual on the defensive.

"Their parents don't hit them. People are actually nice to each other." Steve said back.

I picked up the conversation. "Other families have TVs and actually eat hot meals together."

"Our parents go to church with us," said Kathy, always the decanter.

"Holy shit Kathy, sometimes you're so stupid," said Brad. "They show us off like trained singing monkeys. Belinda sticks out her tits and shows what a fertility goddess she is, while Dad shows what a big dick he has for having so many kids."

Kathy flipped her hair and squinted smugly at the rest of us. "You're disgusting, Brad. Mother said she'd take me out for my sixteenth birthday. Like she'd do that for any of you."

Nobody said anything. We knew our mother would find an excuse not to live up to her end of that deal. We kept doing our homework. Brad leaned over and smacked Steve on the side of the head with a book. Steve lunged at Brad and knocked him off his chair. We all laughed. Until they heard our dad yelling that we'd better be studying. Then it was quiet. My brothers got back into their chairs. We knew the punishment if caught.

Our church and our school were safe havens for us. At church we were admired for our knowledge of scripture (beaten into us by our father), our good behavior and our musical talents. Mark had found a couple of old guitars in our basement and we taught ourselves to play. We were also all blessed with good voices and perfect pitch. By the time Steve and I were in middle school, the six younger Hobbs children were singing once a month at Sunday church services for the general congregation. Mother Belinda and Father Douglas basked in the attention and demanded we practice more and more. They said it was for the "glory of God" but we knew that was a bunch of bull and it was for the glory of Doug and Belinda.

School was our other haven. There we could pretend we had the same normal lives as our friends. My brothers played football. Kathy was involved in cheerleading and student government. Steve and I were in school musicals. We were popular and normal. Life was good during school hours.

Since we were given no allowance or spending money of any kind, we became resourceful at ways to make money. Brad and Mark started a lawn service during the warm months and shoveled snow in the winter. Included was a handyman service. Kathy had a booming babysitting business. Steve and I, being the most musically talented, started to sing at funerals, weddings and parties. We'd be booked solid for months.

Not being kids to throw our hard-earned money away, we discovered thrift stores. Nobody knew the best and most creatively dressed kids in school paid almost nothing for their clothes. Steve started wearing an old black leather bomber jacket and took on a James Dean Rock-a-Billy look. I went for the Victorian lace mixed with a bit of leather. We were the kids to watch: The other Hobbs twins, born ten months apart but still joined at the hip. We were always the most popular kids in our grade.

Steve and I had plans for the future. I was going to be an engineer and build bridges. Steve was going to be a lawyer. Our goal was to get to college, graduate and make enough money to never have to shop at thrift shops again. We'd have a band and a big music studio. We'd live next to each other and raise our happy kids and have smiling spouses who loved us. It was a bright, sunny world we lived in. Jordan would live across the street in a cute little cottage with a fuzzy little dog and a calico cat to keep him company when he wasn't with us.

Chapter 5

We almost survived our childhoods in spite of our parents, but then two incidents changed our world from bad to bad forever.

On the twins' sixteenth birthday, Belinda did indeed tell Kathy that they'd have a mother-daughter day. There were big plans for having hair and nails done, then a day of lunch and shopping in downtown Philadelphia, just the two of them. Mother left early that morning to attend a Bible study meeting. Kathy waited at home on the front porch as the hours passed. Mother was supposed to be home by 11:00 am but she never returned. Brad invited Kathy to go out with him and his friends, but she declined. I offered to go with her to the thrift stores. Around 8:00 pm, our mother returned home from her own shopping spree, with her hair and nails done, as if nothing happened. She never wished her daughter a happy birthday or offered apologies. Mark took Kathy out somewhere and they didn't return until the next morning. Nobody asked where they went, or what they did. We'd find out later.

Kathy was the one who most longed for a perfect life in a perfect world; longed for a perfect family. She became obsessed with historical romance novels she'd hide in her backpack. By then, Mark had gone away to college, but when he returned for visits he'd take her to the bookstores or to sappy movies. She cried when he left and marked the days until his next visits. Unfortunately for Kathy, her twin Brad was lost in his own world of sports, friends and music. He spent as little time around his family as possible. When Kathy was feeling especially frustrated, she'd take it out on Steve or me, telling lies about our misdeeds and watching us back paddle as fast as we could to avoid the fury of our parents.

We'd usually end up with Dad beating the crap out of us, as Kathy watched with an odd, self-satisfied smile on her face. Dad would always say he'd beat me until I cried, but since I never cried he'd give up before he did any permanent physical damage. Despite our family, we almost made it through our teen years. Almost.

David graduated from his expensive and exclusive prep school, then Temple University and medical school, then he left to be a medical missionary on a ship that sailed into dangerous ports of call wherever medical help was needed. Mark went to Drexel University on a football scholarship. Kathy headed off to Drexel on an academic scholarship. Brad landed a place at Penn State, glad to be away from Mark and Kathy.

That left Steve and I at home for our senior year of high school with only our parents to fear, but by then we were all but ignored by our mother and father. I remember when we were a month away from graduating from high school, excited about moving out and moving on. We had both been accepted to Penn. We were so close to our escape that we could hardly contain ourselves.

Chapter 6

On the second weekend of May, Brad, Mark and Kathy all came home from college to visit. There was a big celebration, the opening of a new wing, going on at our church. Brad, Steve, Jordan and I were going to sing together. Our parents had an event with my dad's engineering firm at the opening of a new office building, so we had a blessed night free of Doug and Belinda.

I never noticed when Mark and Kathy left the church. Brad left with the car to give some kids a ride home. Steve, Jordan and I walked home, our guitars slung over our shoulders, happy to go home to a parentless house. We opened the door to noises. Someone was in the house.

Steve put his hand up and motioned for us to be still and quiet. I held onto Jordan. Steve quietly made it up the stairs to the dark hallway, then kicked open the door to Kathy's bedroom.

What happened next was to change our lives forever.

Steve gasped, "Oh my God! Dad is going to hear about this. You're sick. You're totally sick!" He had the camera with him and started to take photos. I could hear Kathy screaming and Mark yelling, "You're dead, Steve!"

I ran up the stairs. In the bedroom, Kathy and Mark were on Kathy's bed. Mark was naked from the waist up. His jeans were unzipped and, well, let's just say he was exposed. Kathy was completely naked, on her hands and knees, her ass up against Mark's crotch. Mark's face was a mask of rage.

Kathy's eyes met mine and she yelled, "Go away! Don't look at me!"

Jordan stared, then froze.

Mark turned to Jordan. "If you say anything Jordan, I will kill you and then I'll kill Liz. Do you understand, idiot boy?" Jordan ran down the stairs.

"You are in so much trouble!" Steve yelled at Mark. "Mom and Dad are so going to fucking hear about this!"

"Give me the camera." said Mark.

"No fucking way, pervert!" Steve yelled back.

Mark lunged at Steve, grabbing for the camera. He grabbed Steve by the hair and slammed him against the wall, over and over. Steve pulled away and then lost his balance at the top of the stairs. He fell. It happened so fast, as everything else at the Hobbs house. Ultimately, someone always got hurt. Someone always had to pay the price.

Brad had just pulled up and came in to find me at the bottom of the stairs with Steve's bloody head cradled in my arms. Jordan sat next to us, wailing in a high-pitched voice like a wounded animal and rocking himself. Brad and I hauled Steve to the car and drove as fast as we could to the hospital. On the way, Steve died in the back seat with his head in my lap, never regaining consciousness. Mark showed up at the hospital with our father. Brad was in shock and said nothing. I was numb in a way I didn't think a human could feel. Our father was visibly shaken. Mark told a convincing story of how Steve had tripped and fallen down the stairs. For the first time, I saw my dad show any emotion other than displeasure toward one of his children. He sat down, put his head in his hands and cried.

A large funeral was held for Steve. News cameras were present and later that night there was footage of us singing at church as well as at weddings. My mother would show that to visitors over and over in the following weeks.

Jordan and I sang Amazing Grace as we averted our gaze at the coffin covered with white flowers and Steve's guitar. Brad and Mark read verses from the Bible. Kathy read a poem. Teachers, the football coach, and friends spoke of what a fine young man my brother was. My father sat in silence. My mother did nothing but smile and praise the lord and tell everyone that Steve was in a better place and how happy she was that Steve was with Jesus. I swear to God I don't know how she explained to Jesus the $500 she spent on a new black dress and shoes for the event.

Chapter 7

I'd never seen anyone so filled with joy to see a child die. Belinda was the center of attention and filled with pride that all of the light of the lord shone directly on her. For weeks our house was filled with casseroles and cakes. Visitors came all day to console my grieving mother. The living room was full of prayers and the celebration of my mother's ability to conceive and give birth to many children. Glory to the blessings of a merciful God. For the remainder of her life, she gloried in being the parent who lost a child.

Jordan more or less stopped speaking after the night Steve died. He rarely said a word unless it was to talk crazy frantic sermons about Steve coming back with the sword of God, or maybe to rattle off a random Bible verse. In school, he made straight A's. At home, he did nothing but sit in his room and read or study. Sometimes he'd go for long walks for hours and hours. He shut off all social contact with anyone. Jordan had found a safe place to go – deep inside the center of his own mind where he couldn't be hurt anymore.

I lay alone in my basement room after Steve's funeral, feeling my life was over, physically and emotionally drained, unable to cry or express my feelings. One day, I would tell the world what really happened. As I lay glued to my thoughts, someone sat on the bed. I opened my eyes. Mark sat there with a slight smile on his face.

"Go away," I rasped out at him.

He came close and growled in my ear, "If you ever say a single word about what you saw, I will kill you. Do you understand?"

"One day, everyone will know what you did."

Mark put both hands on my neck and squeezed, hard. "Nobody will ever believe you. If you tell anyone, I'll kill you. Before I kill you, I will also hurt both you and Jordan in ways you can't imagine. I'll tell everyone you were screwing Steve and they'll believe me. Do you understand?"

"Pervert!" I spat out at him.

Mark fisted his hands like he was going to pound me, but he just glared and said, "Say anything Liz, and I swear I will kill you and make everyone think it was murder suicide with Jordan."

I shook my head and never told a soul about what happened, or at least not for a long, long time. In time I would learn that Mark had taken

Kathy to a hotel the night of her sixteenth birthday and given her the attention and affection she'd always longed for. It was sick and twisted beyond anything any of us Hobbs kids could have ever done until Mark killed Steve. The death certificate said Steve had died due to an accident. I knew better.

The morning after the funeral and Mark's late night visit to my bedroom, I went to the bank to deposit a check from the last wedding Steve and I had sung at. I had been planning to move out and live on my own until college started. I couldn't stay in my parents' house any longer. But when I got to the bank, the account had been cleared out. A little over $6,000 was gone. Mother Belinda had taken it all. When I returned home, I confronted her.

"It was mine. Not yours to take. Steve and I earned that."

My mother gave me her usual smug, self-serving smile. "I opened the account for you."

"Because we were just kids." I said. "You didn't' put a penny into that account. It belonged to Steve and me. What did you do with it?"

"I bought a coffin for Stephen. I needed something to wear to the funeral." My mother said.

"You're a selfish bitch!" I yelled. "Father paid for the funeral. I saw the fucking receipt for it!"

My mother slapped me hard across the face. "You're as good as dead to me Elizabeth. I never wanted another girl. I never wanted you. Just wanted to let you know that before you start on one of your pity parties again," she said, still smiling.

I went to my father. He didn't know about the money and mumbled something about how my mother was in charge. I thought he'd jump up and hit me but he just slowly got up from the desk in his office, took his keys and left. He had been doing that more and more since Steve died. Some nights he'd never come home from work at all. When he was home, he closed the door of his office and didn't come out until we heard his car drive off early in the mornings.

Nothing changed for my mother. It was a whirl of activities with the church and her social clubs, and of course, the spa days for the stressed out mother. Jordan and I were left alone to fend for ourselves.

Occasionally, Father would slip me fifty or a hundred dollars and say, "Don't tell your mother." I never did.

Every night for a month until high school graduation day, I prayed for another life. My childhood was over, but then again, I never really had one to begin with.

Chapter 8

A scholarship for nice smart Christian students helped me get to Penn State. My brother Bradley was also there on both sports and academic scholarships. I did everything in my power to keep from crossing his path. I was living in the dorms and in the Engineering program. Brad was in Sports and majoring in Political Science. We'd inevitably run into each other, so I'd pretend to be a good little sister. The odd thing was, he actually encouraged me and acted like he was proud of me.

Brad and I had been though so much that I thought we were both suffering posttraumatic stress at times. At other times I marveled at how relaxed he was outside of the war zone we'd grown up in, away from the influence of our parents, Mark, and Kathy. He was a new man, happy and confident in ways I'd never imagined.

The newly found freedom was exhilarating but alas, like everything for Liz Hobbs, it was short lived.

On a cool fall day, while meeting new friends for coffee, I was introduced to Marty, a PhD student in Colonial American History. He was tall and muscular and handsome in a different sort of way. An elegant aquiline nose; large warm brown eyes and shaggy chocolate brown hair and pierced ears gave him a romantic European look sort of, but he was from Long Island, New York. We ended up talking for several hours then moved on to his apartment for dinner. He never asked me about my religion or my family. He only wanted to know about where I was now. He was gentle and asked my opinion. It was the first time in my life I never worried about being yelled at or hit. For the first time in my life, I wasn't hiding bruises. I wasn't making excuses.

After a few weeks, Marty and his roommates had a party, but we didn't attend. We went to his room and had our own celebration.

I thought I should have been in love after that night but I didn't feel it. I liked Marty and found him attractive but we had different paths and different futures. I should have felt guilty about losing my virginity to my romantic, candle lighting, scented oil kind of guy but I didn't. He was sweet and gentle. I was urgent and willing. It was fine with me and I was glad it happened, or at least thought I was.

I woke; Marty curled in a spoon around me.

I could hear someone say, "Where's Marty"? I knew the voice.

Someone else yelled, "Getting laid!"

In a panic, I jumped out of bed and started to pull on my clothes. The door opened.

"What are you doing here?" a horribly familiar voice growled.

There was Brad, rage in his eyes, his lips curled into a snarl. I stood there in my jeans and bra staring at my brother. Shit. It was the story of my life. Just for once it would be nice if I had more than three months without being attacked.

"Hi Brad. It isn't what you think."

"Then what the hell is it, Liz?"

"Fuck you. I have a boyfriend. Get over it, asshole."

"We're going. Now. Foul mouthed little whore. I can't believe this."

I grabbed my purse, boots and shirt. Brad put a lock on my wrist. Marty didn't say a word.

"Where are we going?" I asked. I was pissed off. What was Brad thinking?

Bradley said nothing. I'd known him long enough to know he wasn't going to answer me.

We arrived at his house. It was dark. We were alone. As soon as we got through the door, he slapped me full across the face. I went down on the floor.

Then he started to kick me, shouting, "Whore! Whore! Whore!"

He called me a disgrace. He pulled me up by my hair and slammed me into the wall, then he pinned me with his body, his face next to mine.

"Did you know he's a Jew?"

"What?" I tasted blood in my mouth.

He leaned in close, his body smashed into mine, his cheek on mine as he spoke with his lips grazing my ear, "You were sleeping with a Christ-killing Jew."

"We're not Kathy and Mark. Get off of me you perv!" I said, trying to push him off of me.

"You stupid bitch. You were supposed to wait until you got married. You were supposed to save yourself for the right guy. Now you're just another worthless slut." He started to hit me, first in the face then when I turned away he drove his fists into my shoulders and upper back. I tried to get away. Pushing me up against the wall again, Brad kept hitting me. He called me a whore and a cunt and a slut. I kneed him in the groin and he went down. I tried to run but he grabbed my leg. I fell. He was on me, straddling me, slapping me and yelling. I slammed my fist into his face. His nose exploded. I blinked the blood out of my eyes. He howled with pain then came at me with fists again. We rolled on the ground, hitting and pulling at each other. He finally twisted my arm around until I felt my bones snap and my collar bone go and then he slammed my head down over and over until I passed out, thinking I'd be dead like Steve.

When I opened my eyes, just barely, I saw Brad looking at me, on the ground beside me. His nose was a swollen bleeding mess, his eyes almost shut, and a cut was on his forehead. The side of his head was bleeding where I'd apparently almost pulled off his ear. He was breathing hard.

"I thought I'd killed you," he gasped.

"Stupid asshole," I said to him, tasting blood in my mouth.

"Whore," he answered. My brother took a deep breath and closed his eyes for a few seconds. Then with great effort he sat up. "What are we going to do?"

"Do?" I tried to move but bone grinding on bone made me cry out in pain and stay as still as I could.

"I have to get you to a hospital."

I tried to move again but the pain was too much. I wished I could cry.

Brad pushed my shoulder with his fist. "You broke my fucking nose. We need a story."

I was barely maintaining. My lip was cut and open, my nose smashed as badly as Brad's; a broken wrist and my head exploding. Every cell in my body screamed in pain.

"Liz, we have to do something. What do we say?" I was the best liar. My brothers depended on me for that sort of thing.

"Attacked, behind your house," I managed to get out, feeling a loose tooth with my tongue.

"How many. Liz, how many were there?"

"Three, um, no, four."

"Black guys?"

"No, no. What are you stupid or something? White guys." I closed my eyes and tried to get through my pain. "Accents. Russian. Some sort of Eastern European."

"Were we robbed?"

"White slavers. Sex traders. They fucked you in the ass."

He smacked me hard on the side of my head. I yelled out, this time thinking he'd killed me.

"Good idea. We'll go with that, except the last part. Nobody fucked me or you. I protected you. I saved you."

"Okay."

"Four Russians. Big blond guys beat the crap out of us trying to get you in their white van. Full size van, no windows, with a big black scratch on the back. No plates. All were wearing black jeans and black shirts."

"You tell them, Brad. I'll say I don't remember much. You saved me. A car picked them up. They didn't speak English. Just a few words."

He stroked my hair and smiled. "I'll get you fixed up. Don't worry about anything." He leaned over and ripped the front of my shirt open and unhooked my bra. "They wanted you, baby sister."

"I hate you."

"Sure, whatever." He put his hand on his nose and winced. Tears came down his face. "Why'd you do it, Liz?"

"What?"

"Why'd you give away your greatest gift to Marty? You should have saved yourself for your wedding night. After what happened with Kathy and Mark, I expected more from you."

"Fuck you too, Brad."

Chapter 9

Brad suffered a broken nose, two black eyes, and a broken finger. I ended up with four stitches inside of my lip, a broken nose, one black eye and a wrist to shoulder cast put on my left arm with a sling and a couple of butterfly bandages on my face and two broken ribs. Neither Brad nor I had a straight nose, even after we were completely healed.

Marty came the hospital and sat on the edge of my bed for about fifteen minutes. I didn't tell him what happened with Brad. I didn't tell him that I was disappointed that he didn't stand up for me when Brad knocked down the bedroom door. I never saw my kind and handsome Marty again after that. So much for chivalry and romance.

Brad never thanked me for making up a good lie for him. He never forgave me for breaking his nose either.

On Sunday after the attack, the pastor of my church came by to see me at the hospital, along with my parents, the new pastor of my parents' church (Rev. Johnson has since retired and moved to New Mexico), and my brother Brad. Kathy and Mark were there too. I wasn't exactly overjoyed with the party. Nobody brought flowers or candy, so I knew they didn't want to wish me luck.

They came to talk to me about how I'd fallen from grace in the eyes of God. I'd become a common whore who partied and slept around with Jews, Catholics and any other assorted unfavorable men I'd never dated. They'd come to counsel and pray with me about it. Brad put up a protest to defend me.

Earlier that day, Brad told Kathy in confidence that I'd lost my virginity, and in turn she'd told the entire family. Mark had threatened to expose Brad for gambling on games, thus causing the death of his scholarships. Mark had also found girls who would gladly tell how Brad had tempted them with alcohol and date raped them – totally untrue, but Mark had his ways of convincing people to do just about anything for either cash, sex, or blackmail.

I never went back to church again. Nobody came back to visit me except Brad.

Toward the end of the year I was told that my scholarship was not going to be renewed for the next year. Apparently I wasn't the type of young woman they wanted to represent them. I protested because I made almost straight A's. I had B+ in an English class due to the time out for the hospital stay. In my math and engineering courses I had all A's. They didn't care.

I started to research loans and other scholarships. It was overwhelming, as it is with so many students.

The one and only weekend Brad and I went home, he argued and argued with my parents about the decision of my parents to actually write a letter and visit with the scholarship committee, recommending that my scholarship be taken away.

I could hear Brad arguing with our parents. I stood in the doorway, watching. He told them that they were bad parents and how normal Christian people loved their children and would never beat or abuse them the way we were beaten and abused. Doug and Belinda Hobbs were disgusted at their son's accusations. I said nothing as I stared at my brother with both shock and adoration. I said nothing to my parents as we left our childhood home for good. If anyone would break the cycle, it would be Brad and me.

I would never fully thank Brad for telling my parents off for good. Jordan finished high school, made his way to Penn State in the fall, and moved in with Brad.

Mark and Kathy remained loyal to our parents like blood sucking vampires living with the coffin makers.

Chapter 10

Despite my sudden reputation as a bad girl, The Olive Branch Youth Christian Summer Camp hired me right away, due to my impressive resume of musical achievements and youth ministry at my old church.

The Olive Branch had a reputation for being extremely fun and challenging. Challenge courses with trust and wilderness survival during the day. Music and drama in the evenings, was followed by positive message Bible studies for those who wanted it.

I'd never been to summer camp or camping or outside, other than in my backyard when my parents would lock us out of the house. I found myself making friends easily. I was a biblical scholar who could sing and play the guitar like a pro. The campers, ages 8-12, were great. I never knew kids that age could have so much fun. I could feel the joy that I'd never been allowed to experience during my own fear filled childhood.

I also discovered the wonders of alone time. Growing up in a house with 5 other kids never allowed me any privacy. From home it was school or church then home again. I was always with someone else. In college, I'd shared a room with two other girls. It was fun while it lasted, but there again, I was never alone.

In the woods, I could savor the soft sounds of birds and dropping pinecones. Sometime it was so quiet I'd hold my breath and listen to the quiet of the night.

One night, the second week of camp, after the lights were out, I pulled on a sweatshirt and went out to the open field under the stars. I was gazing up at the zillions of stars, wishing Steve were with me, when someone came out of the woods to my clearing. I froze and listened.

A male voice said, "Allison, what you feel for me is a crush. It isn't real love. One day you will have that with a wonderful man but now is not the time."

"Tonight I'll go to bed with you. I'll give myself to you."

The guy spoke again. It was Greg Atkinson.

Twenty-six-year-old Greg Atkinson was in the dreams of all of the female staff and campers at the Olive Branch Youth Christian Summer Camp. Six foot one, muscular ex football star, with a boy-next-door handsome face, a thick head of honey blond hair and a fast smile that could melt the coldest of ice princesses.

He'd just finished a doctorate in Psychology and had a Masters degree in Theology from Harvard. No kidding. The guy was brilliant. As an added bonus, he was also from a wealthy family – a trust fund baby, no less.

I really didn't care. He was the center of attention but I wasn't looking for summer romance. I was still grieving Steve's death, the loss of my college education funding and being beaten to a pulp by my brother Brad. But aside from all that this was a new start for me. It was a new experience that would for once in my life be positive. I'd use the camp to put it all behind me and reinvent myself.

But reinventing or not, I was still a master spy and not below eavesdropping on anyone.

Greg has a serious tone in his voice. "That isn't what either one of us wants. You see me as a leader, as a figurehead."

"I love you," said Allison with pitiful high-pitched, girlish pleading in her voice.

"You love the idea of me, " he said gently, as not to crush her spirit, or at least I imagined that was why he was talking that way. "You don't know the real me, Allison."

"I want to know the real you. I want to know all of you." She threw her arms around him and he pushed her away, ever so gently. It was pathetic, like something out of a bad made-for-TV romance movie.

They babbled on for a few more minutes. I sat, listening. Poor guy. I knew who they were. Pretty, preppy Allison Renee Delaney, who was slightly bossy and thought of herself as the queen of all she cast her eyes upon. Greg, Mr. Dream Date to almost every girl at the camp, but held himself above it all in an unobtainable higher moral standard than all the rest. I would have liked to say they deserved each other, but no man deserved Allison. Well, maybe my brother Mark, but he'd already found himself a pretty trophy doormat to spend his life with.

Allison left in tears. Greg stood under the stars and ran his hands through his hair. I started to play the introduction to Stairway to Heaven.

Then he looked right at me; a halo of blond hair circling his head under the full moon. "That was uncomfortable. You heard everything, didn't you?"

"Mum's the word. My lips are sealed," I said.

He stepped toward me. "Nothing happened between Allison and me. I never even kissed her." His tone was calm and sure, not defensive like most guys would have been.

"I know. But you have to be careful. She's the type of girl who'd accidentally on purpose get pregnant the first time you nail her and you'd have that albatross around your neck for the rest of your life."

"Liz." He looked at me, knowing full well who I was, but saying my name just to make sure.

"Greg." I smiled at him.

"What are you doing out here?"

"You know, watching the stars, playing Kumbaya, eavesdropping on guys with girl problems."

"I don't have girl problems."

"Do too."

He laughed. "You've got an attitude."

"I have five brothers. I come by it honestly."

"Five brothers?"

"And one sister but she's a bitch."

"That isn't a very Christian thing for you to say."

"You shall not hate your brother in your heart. Leviticus 19:17. That doesn't say anything about hating my sister."

"I'll remember that the next time my sister gives me a bad time. Do you hate your brothers as well?"

"Most of them but they deserve it."

"That's a horrible thing to say."

"Hey, you asked and I answered. Crap, if you met them you'd hate them too."

"You seem so sweet at the evening songs."

"I'm like the wind, Greg. I could blow one way or the other."

He didn't respond. I was hoping he'd leave.

I tried another Bible verse. "Proverbs 11:29: He who brings trouble on his family will inherit only wind. Which is fine by me. You don't have to stay here with me you know. I'm sure you have things to do."

"You shouldn't be out here alone." He seemed serious and somewhat confused at the same time. "I'll walk you back."

"Maybe that isn't such a good idea. If you go back now, Allison will be blubbering and begging you to love her forever in the eyes of the Lord. I bet she's crying her eyes out to all her friends right now".

"I never even touched her. You have to believe me Liz, when I say I never led her on."

"You don't have to explain to me."

"Do you want to go for a walk?" he asked.

27

I stood up and hitched my guitar over my shoulder. "Sure, I'll be the slut who stole you away from Allison."

He laughed. We did walk, the first of many after the campfire walks.

Of course, Greg charmed me. From the beginning I was glad to be with a guy who wasn't a worm like Marty. I remember thinking, a guy who takes charge without being an asshole. I made him laugh. He made me think about the possibilities in life.

Chapter 11

I know it sounds like a cliché, but for the first time in my life I was truly happy. I felt as if I was floating. I'd never known that my faith or my ability to love could be so strong. Greg brought me there gently.

As camp was ending, I was frantically trying to get financial aid to college. I didn't want to be stuck with bills. With an Engineering degree, I wasn't too worried about finding a job when I'd graduated, but for a nineteen year old with no family to turn to, the task was frustrating at best.

Greg suggested we go for a drive to help me get my mind off of things and he'd help me after that. We arrived at a lovely house in a wooded area. I asked Greg if this was his parents' house. He smiled. "No, they live in something much larger. This is my place, Liz."

There was hardly any furniture except a couple of wingback chairs in the living room and a large four-poster bed in the master suite. It was like an enchanted cottage with window seats and a view of the woods.

"I'm starting work, two jobs actually, next month." Greg said, taking my hand and leading though the house.

It suddenly reminded me again that camp would be over and I'd be homeless. "Great, tell me about it," I said, hiding my panic, knowing I'd probably never see him again.

He told me about a position he'd been offered with a prestigious marriage counselor. His new boss, Dr. Rich Hudson, was the kind of man who wrote books and appeared on cable TV when expert advice was needed. The second job was as sort of an assistant pastor of a local mega church. His best friend was pastor. Greg's job there was volunteer work but close to his heart.

I suddenly felt very young and inexperienced. "That's awesome, Greg. I'm really happy for you. I know you've worked really hard for this."

"What are you planning after the summer?" he asked me.

"School."

"How are you going to pay for it?"

That was unexpected. He'd never asked me about my finances before. "I have enough saved up for the first semester. I'll find a job and a room and save up for the next. I mean, I can sing at weddings and funerals and maybe get a job on campus or something. I might move in with Brad and Jordan, live on their couch, or sleep on the floor in Jordan's room or something. I don't think their roommates would mind. I'll be in the library most of the time or on campus or working anyway. They're nice guys and it's a big old house so they wouldn't even know I'm there most of the time. Brad would kill them if any of them made a move on me so I'd, you know, be safe." I'd said too much and started to babble, or that was the way I was feeling. Totally lost.

Greg smiled at me and took me in his arms. "I can't let you do that."

"It's okay. I'll be fine. I can find a room with some other girls or a family or something."

"Liz, after camp you're moving in here with me."

"You don't have to do that. I'll be okay. Really." Tempting offer, but I didn't want anyone feeling sorry for me. "The drive to school would be too far."

"Do you love me?" It was more of a demand than a question.

My stomach knotted. "Sure, yes, I guess." I couldn't get out the words. Love wasn't part of my current vocabulary.

"Tell me you love me. I want to hear you say it."

"Greg, I won't take advantage of you. I can take care of myself, okay?"

"Do you love me?"

"I love you," I said, surprised the words came out of my mouth.

He took my hand and slipped a 1.5 ct princess cut diamond ring on my finger. "Marry me, Liz. I want you to move in as my wife."

"Yes. Oh my goodness, yes, I'll marry you." It sounded like someone else was speaking, but it was me, all right.

With that romantic exchange and a beautiful diamond on my young finger, we went upstairs and he made love to me for the first time. It was nothing like my encounter with Marty and I knew Greg wouldn't let anyone beat me up over it.

"How many men have you been with?"

"Just one. One night. It didn't mean anything. I was drunk." I'd hoped this conversation would have never come up, but I answered anyway.

"You don't need to make excuses, Liz. I was no virgin before this afternoon."

"Sure, you're a guy."

"You're number twenty-three. A magical and final number. I don't ever want to be with anyone else, Liz. It's just you and me now, for life, forever."

Chapter 12

We were married at his parents' church with a small reception afterward. My mother made it a point to let everyone know I had no business marrying in white. Yet she seemed proud that I'd managed to get a husband. Let me rephrase that – she was happy to be mother of the bride.

Kathy was incredulous that I was marrying someone like Greg Atkinson. My darling sister was engaged to Mark's best friend Forrest, a nice jock sort of guy, far too nice for anyone in my family, but in no way did he have the high-end pedigree that even came close to Dr. Gregory Atkinson.

We honeymooned in Florida and came back tanned and glowing to glorious fall color that promised a life of happiness. Life settled in for the newly married Atkinsons. I even set up my friend Diana with the pastor of our church and they were also soon married with a baby on the way. Life was a dream.

Genealogy had always been an interest of mine, which was odd, considering how much I hated my family. But I liked the idea of history and finding out where people came from – not my people, but other people's people. I formed a group with our church and soon became the go-to person. From there I started to have classes on Thursday nights for anyone interested. I even had a talk on genealogy of the Bible.

I was the perfect wife in my proper sweater sets and skirts hiding sexy bras and panty sets. Greg thought it was funny that I'd never learned to cook but I soon found help from Diana and some of the other ladies in our church.

Greg was flying high with his job. I decorated our cottage in country blues and yellows with cute crafts and fresh daisies. During the day I played house and volunteered. Of course, nothing was ever out of place. Growing up as a Hobbs child – we were almost all OCD about keeping things in order.

In the evening Greg and I spoke of our work, baby names, made love and were lost in our romance.

My first pregnancy occurred soon after our first anniversary. At twenty-one weeks, I lost my baby. There were condolences and everyone prayed a lot. I'd never had any support like this growing up in the Hobbs household, so it was comforting and encouraging to try again.

I became pregnant again and again over the next six years, totaling in six pregnancies. Three came into the world but none of them made it through their first day. My babies kicked and turned and danced inside of me. They had names and I imagined personalities. Cute little socks and teddy bears, a crib mobile playing Feeling Groovy and parents who would love them waited for their arrival. They came and left before their time.

With the loss of a child through a miscarriage, one can't openly mourn. We are expected to go back to life as if nothing ever happened. Nobody but Greg and I knew these children. They were ours alone.

I held the tiny baby who decided he didn't want to stay. He was so small with almost translucent skin. His tiny hands never held my finger or a crayon or anything. Two days earlier, he'd been kicking inside of me. Now he was gone.

I think of those lost babies often. I'm not sure what to think or speculate on what could have been. What I have is sadness for the babies I loved so much.

Greg used the situation for stories in his bimonthly sermons at the church and for his Christian marriage groups. How God gives us what we can handle. I supposed then God considered me made of steel with all the shit I'd gone through in my now twenty-six years. I started to resent the fact that Greg had made my very private tragedies public.

At the same time, Diana was starting to have her doubts about being a pastor's wife with two active young sons. The children were darling boys, Clayton and Colton, but it wasn't enough for Diana.

She was beautiful and dynamic. Chad was sweet and gentle. But she was getting bored with the life. She often complained that she'd married too young. Then she met the local bazillionaire, Darren Crawford.

Where Chad was comfortable and cute in an average way, Darren was tall with classic Ivy League movie star good looks. He swept beautiful Diana off her feet and they became lovers.

I was torn, because I adored Chad, but I truly liked Darren and had always considered him one of my few close friends. Darren and I both liked history and genealogy. Sometimes we'd get together with a few of the guys at church and play our guitars. He'd profess his love to Diana, as if I would convince her to leave her husband. I was too stupid to do or say anything. I just went along and watched the train wreck in slow motion.

Diana told me in pornographic details of the boring sex with Chad, compared to the erotic and passionate sessions she had with Darren. They didn't do anything Greg and I didn't do almost every night, but for her it was a new world she'd never dreamed of. But with that world came guilt and remorse for the husband she still loved and her young sons.

Diana came to Greg for advice and he told her to leave Darren for her marriage. Greg spoke to her husband about their sex life and gave him some coaching. I think they might have even watched some porn films to give Chad some creative ideas, but I don't know. It all just made me uncomfortable and caught in the middle of somebody else's mess.

In the meantime, it wasn't sex that was boring me. It was just being a wife and nothing else. I'd told Greg that I wanted to go back to school. His response was that I was needed at home. For what? We didn't have any children. One night, I came home from a jam session with Darren and the church music group to find Greg had burned my high school yearbooks and most of my photos. He didn't get to my stash of photos with Steve. But he'd given Steve's guitar away, telling me that it was a piece of junk and some kid could use it.

It was then that I realized how much he controlled me. Who I spent my time with, what I wore, what I did. It was all Greg's suggestion.

His career was blazing. He wrote articles, started to talk on syndicated radio shows, and he even started working on a book.

He used our experiences with love, sex, the inability to have children, our little everyday stories in our lives. But it wasn't exactly our marriage he was talking about in his articles and lectures. Ours was different, so he told me. Ours was something special with almost mystical qualities. We were completely one. I belonged to him. If I did my part, our lives would be perfect. So I did my part. And for the most part things were perfect, whatever that was. How the hell was I supposed to know?

Darren confided in me how heartbroken he was over Diana. He said he'd confronted Greg earlier that day. It ended badly, with Greg calling Darren a home breaker. At that point I decided to back off my friendship with Darren. I couldn't get mixed up in his drama anymore, especially when Greg was involved.

When I got home, Greg had locked up my guitar. He asked if I was going to have an affair with Darren as well. I was shocked. How could he even think I'd cheat on him? We made joyless love that night. Greg was rough and then demanded we pray for our marriage afterward. He said the reason we were childless was because I couldn't be the kind of giving, supportive wife I needed to be. I tried. The more and more I tried, the more controlling and jealous he became.

So every night we'd have sex like porn stars, then get down on our knees naked and pray. And every night I wished I were dead.

Chapter 13

During this period of my life, there was a serial killer in the greater Philadelphia area – The Killer of Virtue. I'd watch the headlines to get my mind off of my own life.

The killer's first victim was a beloved teacher, Sister Ann Timothy. Ann taught Science and was the coach of the girls' soccer team at one of the Catholic high schools. She was a small spitfire with short red hair, cute upturned nose, freckles and a big laugh.

It was September. School had started. The team had won. Sister Ann had celebrated with her girls at a local pizza shop then went to drop some books off at the library. Her car was found the next day at the library. Her wallet and ID were in the car along with the word VIRTUE with a line slashed through it, written in red lipstick across the windshield of the car.

Three days later, Sister Ann was found in a wooded area of a park. She'd been drugged and strangled, but not before she'd been raped. Six deep cuts were carved into her left arm post mortem. A cross was carved into her forehead.

She'd been dressed in a white leather mini skirt with red crotchless panties. On her feet were strappy white patent leather sandals with two-inch platforms and six-inch heels. She wore a red push-up bra and red lace gloves. On her ears were large gold hoops, pierced into her ears, which before now had never been pierced. Her face was made up, complete with gold glitter eye shadow, long false eyelashes and glossy cherry red lipstick. A white-blonde wig of shoulder length curls was put over her own short red hair.

The body was posed on its back with legs spread, white leather skirt hiked up around her waist, and her hands behind her head as if casually relaxing.

It was horrible and enough to make me feel sick just reading about it. I didn't know Sister Ann, but I could imagine the shame and horror she must have gone through.

In October, another car was found with the word VIRTUE crossed out with a single line on the windshield. It belonged to a United Methodist Minister Amy Dorner. Amy was thirty-six, and married with two young sons. She was a popular minister, especially with the youth groups. Amy was tall and thin with long brown hair and a pretty girl-next-door face.

Her husband begged for the killer to return his wife. The congregation put out fliers, held candlelight vigils.

A week later, Amy Dorner was found wearing nothing but a black fake fur stole, thigh high black patent leather boots with 5-inch stiletto heels. Around her neck were twenty strands of fake pearls. On her hands and up her arms were long black gloves accented with pearl bracelets at the wrists. Covering her brown hair was a wild wig of orange hair that cascaded down her shoulders to her waist. Her face was made up with expert accents of black eyeliner, pearly eye shadow and lips of bright pink. It was the same pink lipstick used to write the word virtue on the windshield of her car.

Amy's wrists showed that she had been bound and had struggled to break free. Like Sister Ann, she had been raped, but this time it had been rougher. Bruises covered most of her body. She'd been cut six times on each arm, down to the bone, but unlike the nun, Amy had been alive and struggling when the cuts were made. The killer had also pierced her nipples with 18kt gold hoops.

In November we waited. Diana and I started a fund to send to Amy's family. Her church was large, but every bit helped.

On Thanksgiving Eve, Diana and I had been out shopping together. She dropped me off at my house and then vanished.

Search parties scoured the parks and woods. Darren tearfully joined us, telling me in private that he wished he'd taken her away like she asked, before she'd talked to Greg. It was useless to think about the past. The Killer of Virtue had her.

Diana's body was found two weeks later, about twenty miles away in a wooded park. My beautiful friend had been savagely beaten. Her wrists, ringed with rope burns, were broken. Her perfect cheekbones shattered, her nose smashed. She'd been raped repeatedly with a variety of objects and with brutal violence. Across her chest was a slash of burns caused by a torch, the kind used for welding. Her nipples had been burned off, they said, while she was alive. Knife marks covered her arms, torso and legs. The killer had started to strangle her, and then changed his mind and put a large hunting knife through her heart. The knife was still in her when she was found. Like the others, she had six deep cuts on each arm. Unlike any other the others, her eyes were torn out and the holes covered with dark sunglasses. That, too, was done while she was alive.

Her waist length brown hair had been sprayed red using ordinary spray paint then fanned out around her head in a matted halo. Her broken and bruised face was dusted with white powder. Her lips a deep red slash of lipstick. She had been dressed in a black garter belt with black fishnet stockings and black stiletto pumps with six-inch heels. Around her neck was a black feather boa. On her wrists and ears were large colored rhinestones, vintage Eisenburgh ice. The word "Whore" had been elaborately drawn in an old-fashioned tattoo style on her back with black indelible ink. She'd been dead less than 24 hours when she'd been found. The killer had kept and tortured my friend for thirteen days before he killed her and dumped her body.

The day Diana went missing, I thought I would die. The day she was found, part of me did die.

How could this be God's will? How was she in a better place? What could be a better place than with her two small sons and husband who loved her? Even running away with Darren in shame would have been better than what she'd endured. Darren was shattered with grief unlike anything I'd ever imagined. He looked ten years older the day after Diana was found.

In December, Sharon Stubblefield, the pretty wife of a Baptist minister, was found dead in a snow-covered field wearing a red see-through baby doll pajama set and a red Santa hat. Her black hair had been covered with a blonde pageboy wig. Her face was made up in a thick, doll-like mask. She'd been raped and strangled. Like the others, she also had six deep cuts on each arm but this time the cuts were made after her death. The killer seemed to take a break for the holidays with the violence. Sharon had been gone for three days. Unlike Diana, Sharon had a quick death.

Christmas Eve, Crystal Hall, the wife of a Rabbi was found on the shores of the river, propped up on a park bench as if watching the scenery, wearing a vintage monkey coat from the 1940's, thigh high stockings and stiletto heels, black gloves. A pillbox hat with veil was on her head. She had no wig, but her own hair was curled under the hat. Her pretty face was made up for the period. The coat was open, exposing her naked body. A knife was in her chest and the Star of David carved in her stomach. Six cuts were on each arm. She'd been raped like the others and the wounds were all made while she was alive. One of her eyes had been ruptured but not removed. A cheekbone had been shattered. Bruises could be seen under the makeup that had been expertly applied to her face. Pretty, delicate Crystal Hall had put up a fight but failed to win.

January came and almost went until January 28 when twenty-two-year-old Heather LaMont, a fresh-faced Mormon missionary, vanished. Her companion roommate was in the hospital with food poisoning after attending a church potluck dinner. "Virtue" with a slash was written across the bathroom mirror in red lipstick.

Heather was also raped and strangled. Six deep cuts marked each arm. She was dressed in a slinky gold dress, cut low and off the shoulder, exposing her breasts. Her nipples were gilded with gold paint. She wore a long black wig. On her fingers were long gold artificial fingernails. On her head was a crown with gold glitter words, "Happy New Year". The soles of her feet had been burned off while she was alive; no doubt a punishment for trying to escape.

All of the bodies had been cleaned and perfumed. Their skin had been dusted with shimmering powder. The killer left no trace of his hair, no skin under the cleaned and scrubbed nails. He used a condom when he raped them. No fingerprints were found on the clothes or jewels. There were no witnesses at all, no evidence. The clothing came from many sources so it couldn't be traced to one seller or to any seller for that matter.

Chapter 14

I was lost over Diana's death. She's in a better place people would say, but what about her husband and children? They didn't deserve the sort of nightmarish hell their lives had become.

Greg, in the meantime, was reading numerous articles about serial killers and the nature of evil and forgiveness. We discussed it but couldn't seem to understand how a loving and caring God would test us like this. What sort of evil monster were we dealing with?

Greg read an article to me, written by an expert attorney in Florida. He quoted it back to me in his own words.

"The author, a defense attorney named Goldstein, an expert in sick minds, said the killer did what he did, from an abusive childhood to maybe an evil we couldn't comprehend or try to understand. Goldstein said despite the fact that he has defended cold and calculating murderers in the past, he wouldn't defend the Killer of Virtue. The way he preys on women, and women who have a strong faith in their God appalls him."

So much for popular pop psychology, and the so-called experts. Tell me something I don't know, I thought. All I knew was that my best friend was dead for no apparent reason.

I was devastated by Diana's death. To keep from plunging into depression, I spent time with her boys, giving the grieving Chad a break.

The biggest help with having fundraisers for the children of the women murdered by the Killer of Virtue was Greg unlocked my guitar so I could perform at functions. I almost felt as if I'd found my calling and at the same time doing something for Diana and the others.

Chapter 15

To help with my depression (Greg's word, not mine) Greg insisted we make new friends. Great, that's all I need right now, I thought, but figured he was right, as always.

We started seeing Michelle and Bill, a couple from the church. They were over religious, over friendly and over sugar sweet critical of everything I did. Greg didn't seem to think so. She annoyed the crap out of me.

Of course, Greg liked the way bleached-blonde Michelle, in her tacky tight dresses, laughed out loud at everything. The woman had cute little comments about God and life and crap for everything. She hung on everything Greg said and giggled at his every word in delight like a schoolgirl in heat. Bill smiled the entire time and never talked except about sports, God or how wonderful Michelle was and how blessed he was to have her in his life. It quickly got to the point where I couldn't stand to be around them.

One night after Michelle had spent the evening making suggestions to me about everything from my relationship with my parents (pray and forgive), to my ambitions (she couldn't imagine me being smart enough for college) I'd had it with her.

"I can't imagine what brought the two of you together," she said to me. "I guess God has his plan for all of us. Did you graduate from high school?"

"I was an Engineering major in college."

"Is that why you bombed out?"

It was no use. No matter what I said she had a snotty comment. Greg found it all amusing.

I told Greg I never wanted to see them again. I told him I wanted to go back to school, I wanted to use birth control and stop getting pregnant every six months, I told him I didn't want to just be his wife. I wanted more.

He called me ungrateful and the real nightmare began.

Chapter 16

Fundraisers for the Killer of Virtue victims continued. We called them the Angel Watches. I know it sounds corny but it seemed to fit Diana and the others.

Greg was often asked to speak. He'd been great until the night he decided to bring his own life up as an example of loss. It was loss of our babies and of our friend. Words couldn't describe how angry I was at Greg. When we arrived home, he made his usual move to undress me and then make love before we slept. His hands went to my sweater and he started to pull it up over my head. I stepped away.

"You had no right to violate my right to privacy."

"What are you talking about?" He asked, a flash of anger in his voice.

"My friendship with Diana. You were telling everyone about my feelings and my grief without ever wondering about my feelings. Then you started to talk about my pregnancies and miscarriages. And then everyone started to give me advice and tell me to pray. God's will. You know how I feel about that. You know I don't want to hear it."

"They were just trying to give comfort."

"Bullshit. All I wanted was a nice night without having to deal with death and loss and suddenly the entire night is NOTHING but my losses and failures."

"Oh come on, Liz. You're being unreasonable."

"You never care about my feelings. Ever since we got married it has been always about you and the church and your job and your family. I go along but sometimes I'd like it to be about me."

"I'm going to bed." He walked toward the bedroom. I didn't move. "Are you coming, Liz?"

"No."

He grabbed me by the arm and pushed me down the hall. "Take off your clothes right now or I'll take them off for you."

I got undressed. He did the same. Greg took me in his arms and kissed me then pushed me down on the bed.

"I'm going to give you exactly what you deserve," he said with a smile. Then he was on me, rough and violent, saying, "This is what you need."

Grabbing me by the hair, he pulled me to the floor. "Get on your knees and pray that you'll be a better wife who respects her husband."

I struggled to get away but he slammed me face first to the floor, his knee on my back. I heard a sliding sound and realized he'd taken out his belt. It came down on my back, over and over. The more I struggled, the harder he hit, until I stopped moving. Then he rolled me over. I cried out in pain and he was on me, in me, pounding away again. I wanted to scream as my raw back rubbed against the floor. I tried to push him off of me when the belt came down again on my face, the buckle splitting open the side of my chin. He got off of me and I remember him hitting me with the belt, over and over until I curled into a ball, then he dragged me up by my arm and threw me back on the bed. I couldn't move or think but stayed still in fear of what might happen next. He kept beating me with the belt and hitting me as he told me how he was doing it because he loved me. He lectured me on my duty to love, obey and fulfill his every need. He told me I was a failure and how I needed to be punished. After what seemed like forever (it was about an hour) he stopped.

Unable to sleep or keep warm, I started to shake. Greg came in and out of the room but did nothing but occasionally stroke my hair, sometimes taking a fist full and pull as if he was going to pull me up and hit me again. I closed my eyes and my mind went numb.

Chapter 17

The next day passed, where I could only stumble to the bathroom to pee or for a sip of water or to throw up. I had the chills and the sheets were sticking to my back. Night came again.

I lay in the dark in shock. Greg didn't know what to do. He couldn't send me to a doctor. He didn't have any painkillers strong enough to calm me. There was nothing he could say to me.

It was the shaking that got to him, plus the fact that I wouldn't respond to anything he said. The non-responsiveness was intentional on my part. I could feel him panic. I could see the fear in his eyes as I curled up in a ball under the covers.

I thought about how I'd get out of this situation. I didn't pray. I didn't call anyone. I didn't cry. He'd betrayed me. I'd given him my life, my heart and soul and body. He'd broken all three.

I used to find my joy and peace in his body, being so close to such a beautiful temple of manhood, always there for my safety and there for my complete pleasure. He was strong and large with well-toned muscles, and total control of all of his moves. We'd make love and I'd be totally and completely lost in him. Now I cringed at the thought of him touching me. His masculine perfection had turned repulsive to me.

The first time he'd shown real anger was one Sunday afternoon after I'd just returned home from the hospital after my fourth miscarriage. I'd told him to keep quiet. It was nobody's business. I was tired of advice about birth control and stories of hope from others. I just wanted my privacy. I wasn't ungrateful; I just wanted to handle my own grief in my own way. Greg had brought up the subject at church and said something about it being God's will. He told everyone how blessed we were. He totally ignored my feelings and wishes for privacy. When we got home I asked him what sort of loving God would make it his will to make my child die. I said it was just biology, nothing more or less and to keep God out of it. God was my comfort, not my punisher. I told him I was sick and tired of people invading my privacy.

When I was done, he kissed me then took my hand, led me to the door and slammed it on my hand. When he brought me to the hospital, where I had my crushed and broken fingers set in a cast, we both told the doctors that it was an accident. After that he hurt me where nobody could see. Then it escalated to the bedroom where he used sex and prayers as weapons to make me obey.

One by one I played the past two years over and over and counted the times he'd hurt me. I couldn't keep track.

From my bed, I heard the doorbell. Greg opened it in a happy greeting. Then I heard the devil's own voice in my living room. Anger rose in me. How dare Greg let this demon from Hell into my home? How dare he let the influence of yet more evil come upon us. I was so pissed off that I forgot my pain. I heard the voice.

"What is the problem? Let me see her," Michelle said in a voice as sweet as marshmallows.

No! No! Never again! I silently screamed in my head. I would rather die.

Greg came into the room. "You have a visitor," he said, trying to sound cheerful.

"Let her come in here and I will tell the world what you did to me. Then I will leave you and you will never see me again. Do you understand?" I said quietly, without a hint of emotion.

Greg looked shocked. "She just wanted to pray with you. "

"Go to Hell, Greg."

"What did you say?" Greg said, grabbing my face. If Michelle hadn't been there, I know he would have hit me.

I pushed his hand away. "I'd rather die than see that stupid, self righteous bitch ever again. God, you're so stupid. I hate her. I have always hated every single second I've ever been forced to be with her."

"Liz, don't say things like that."

Michelle poked her ugly head into the room. "Hey, sunshine. Did you lose another one of your angel babies? Don't be so hard on yourself. Take what the lord gives you to make your strong. That is what I feel. Deep in my heart I know…"

"She didn't have a miscarriage," Greg snapped.

"Oh," said Michelle. "What can I get for you? Do you have a nasty cold?"

I sat up in bed and put my feet on the floor, trying not to scream in pain. "You're not welcome in my home."

Michelle looked confused. "I'm your best friend."

"Diana was my best friend. You've never been my friend. You're a stupid, back stabbing cunt who takes every chance you can to belittle me and try to act superior with your sickening sweet condescending remarks. I hate you Michelle, like I hate Satan. I hate you!" I spat out the words, even shocking myself.

Michelle opened her idiot mouth again, "Let's pray about this. Greg, take my hand. Come on, Liz honey, you'll find peace with Jesus. Take my hands sweetie, and we'll pray it away."

"Get out of my house, bitch, or I'll call the police."

The flood of tears started on Michelle's pale face. "Greg, what is going on?"

I spat the words out at her, "Nothing is going on. What part of I hate you Michelle don't you understand?"

"Liz," Greg tried to stop me.

"Get her out of here." I screamed, now in hysterics.

Greg ushered Michelle, who was now in tears, out the door. He came back, furious. "She was only trying to help."

"She is ruining our lives."

"Oh Liz, come on, you can't be serious."

"What is your obsession with her?"

"I don't have an obsession with her."

"She'd screw you silly if you let her."

He slapped me hard across the face. I could feel the cut from the belt buckle split open again under the bandage he'd put on it the night before. I fell back on the bed and lay in shock.

Greg hovered over me. "You know you're the only woman I'll ever be with. I took a vow before God to forsake all others, so don't even think I'd touch or even think of being with another woman."

I lay numb, in pain and shock. It was as if my body was rejecting my soul. The pain in my heart was more than I could stand. As he leaned in closer, I knew he already had an erection.

"Don't touch me again ever."

He stared at me, his face twisted in anger, then left the room, closing the door behind him.

After an hour I stood up. My robe had dried on my bloody back. My life was over. I got into the shower, still in my robe and let the hot water dissolve the mess that held it to me. It was torture and I tried to wash it all away. As blood ran into the drain, I wished I'd bleed to death in the shower. I held my razor but couldn't make the move to cut my own wrists. I could hang myself on the showerhead with my pantyhose that were hanging to dry on the towel rack. I could slip and crack open my head. No matter what I did, it wouldn't make a bit of difference, Greg would find me barely alive and we'd have to start praying again.

I got out of the shower and crawled naked into my bed. I fell into a state half awake and half asleep, unable to move, as if I'd been given a drug to paralyze me.

Greg came in and stroked my damp hair and kissed me. I didn't respond. I never opened my eyes; too afraid he'd want to touch me more.

"Can I get you anything?" he asked.

I thought, a divorce but whispered, "Please don't hit me again."

He wiped a tear off of his cheek. I felt a small spark of sympathy, then hatred took over. The chills started again.

"I'm so cold," I said.

Greg added a comforter to the bed. Then he sat and said nothing. He didn't pray that I knew of. He didn't speak. He just sat. I had no idea what he was thinking but he frightened me. He sat while I lay shaking underneath the piles of blankets. I stayed awake, not daring to fall asleep. Eventually he left, coming back every half hour to check on me.

I could hear him moving around the house. He spoke on the phone. It grew dark outside and he came in, removed his clothing and lay next to me in bed, holding me. His hands went over my breasts. He murmured something about what beautiful a treasure he had. He slid his hand between my legs and caressed me then started to roll me toward him.

"Greg, please..." I said in a whisper, hardly getting the words out, trying to say no but unable to get any sound out of my mouth. Inside, I started to panic but I couldn't move my body. I couldn't get words out to beg him to stay away from me.

"You want me. I love it when you want me, "he said in my ear, "You're my wife and I love you. Now and forever, you are the only woman I'll ever want."

I braced myself and did nothing, letting him roll me on my back and take me. He was gentle at first but became rougher and rougher. Over and over Greg said he loved me as I silently lay underneath him, clenching my teeth in pain, praying for death.

Afterward, he lay holding me, not praying as he'd done for the past year. He kept saying that he loved me as I lay, my entire body on fire, a fever starting to burn.

Chapter 18

It had been two days of torture. I wondered if this was what Diana had gone through with the monster who had tortured and killed her. I thought it would have been better if Greg had been a stranger. Then I could have rationalized it. I wouldn't have taken it so personally. It would have been just physical. Diana hadn't vowed to love, honor and obey her killer.

At 3:30 am, Greg woke in a rage. He said we had to pray and forced me down on the floor. We knelt beside the bed. Then he started to talk of how other men looked at me and desired me. He spoke of how only he would have me. He'd gone absolutely crazy at that point. He got close to me again, naked and erect.

I whispered, "I can't..." and started to crawl away. He said something about duty and love then grabbed me from behind and forced himself on me, biting at my shoulder as he thrust himself into me.

When I begged him to stop, he whispered, "Don't be ashamed to like it."

Then he took me by the arm and hauled me out the back kitchen door and forced me face down on the snow. He held me down with his foot and told me to pray. I stayed still, thinking maybe if he thought I was dead he'd leave me alone.

"You forced me to do this, you ungrateful bitch," he growled at me, then dragged me back into the house, leaving me on the kitchen floor. Walking around me, he lectured on what a willful woman I was and how he was going to break me of my wicked ways. In a haze, I could hear him come and go. He returned with a belt again and hit me all over, then sat down on the floor next to me and started to cry. "I love you so much, Liz. No man has ever loved a woman the way I love you."

I didn't even respond. At 4:30 he stopped and got into bed, leaving me on the floor.

I crawled to the couch in the living room and wrapped myself in a throw blanket. I fell asleep trying to figure out the best way to kill myself.

When I opened my eyes at 8:00 am, I was in my bed again. Greg was already up. I could smell coffee brewing with a touch of cinnamon. I took another shower to wash every bit of him off of me. I was going to get out of this hell, even if it was for just a few hours. I watched blood go down the drain and could feel the life I had left in my body slowly going down with it. I wrapped my body with an entire roll of gauze out of the medical kit then covered that with a cotton cami. Put on a soft pink sweater set with the most delicate of lace collars and a soft flowered skirt with boots. I didn't want anything to rub against my skin.

I curled my dark hair into long almost waist length ringlets, the way Greg liked it, oblivious to the time it took. Next I did my make-up to perfection, covering up the slight bruise on my cheek where he'd hit me the day before. I put on my silver cross and the silver charm bracelet my grandmother had started for me. In my ears were the fresh water pearls Greg had given me on our honeymoon in Florida. I added a silver clip to my hair, sweeping a portion up in the back.

Hiding in the closet, I called my brother Brad. Greg hit me," I said.

There was a pause. "Hit him back."

"I can't. I need help."

"I have my hands full with the baby and Megan bitching and moaning about every little fucking thing. It's a bad time."

"I'm sorry."

"You wanted the stud with the trust fund and you got it. There's a price for everything, Liz."

"I want out, Brad."

"Well so do I but I made a vow when I got married. So did you. You can't run away from everything."

"He hit me with a belt."

"BFD. Kick his ass."

"Brad…he raped me more than once."

"So what, he wants more sex than you do. I don't want to hear about it." I could hear the anger in his voice. "Every time I think I've escaped from my fucking family, one of you morons calls me needing something. I can't help you."

"Okay, sorry, I won't call you again." I was shaking at this point. I don't know why I thought he'd even listen.

"Come by and see the baby. It will get Megan out of my hair," he said, dismissing me.

"Sure, Okay." We said goodbye and I wished I could cry. Of course the asshole wouldn't help me out. He was as bad as Greg.

I put the blood soaked sheets and mattress pad in the washing machine and turned in on hot with enough bleach to almost dissolve the fabric. Greg was writing something, a lecture probably. I didn't ask. He didn't tell me.

"You're up," Greg said with a love-filled smile, as if all was well in the world.

The mantra in my mind said, please don't touch me, please don't touch me, please don't touch me. "I need to do some things, get to the library and stuff. I'm teaching genealogy tonight, remember?"

"How are you feeling?" he asked, as if he didn't know.

"I'm okay," I said automatically and walked slowly to the kitchen, wincing with every move.

"Want me to fix you some breakfast?" he asked, knowing I hadn't eaten in two days.

"No. I'm not hungry," I said in a whisper, trying to eat my pain.

I took my bag, a soft leather satchel sort of deal filled with notes and notebooks and photographs. I put on my heavy winter coat and pulled a pink angora cap over the top of my head.

Greg tried to hug me. I pushed him away. "Don't, it still hurts."

"You okay to drive?" he asked.

"I'll be fine. I took some Aspirin. I'm just waiting for it to kick in."

There was no apology for hurting me. Nothing was ever said about the forced sex, the deep cuts on my back and butt, the bruises and cut on my face.

"Liz, make sure you stay where there are a lot of people," he said, as if he was actually concerned.

"The Killer of Virtue isn't going to go after me," I said, as I pulled my gloves on.

"I worry about you."

I couldn't believe he just said that. I said nothing, wanting to yell and scream at him for hurting me but not daring to say the words that might anger him again.

"See you," I said as I picked up my keys.

He took me in his arms and kissed me. "I love you, Liz," he said. I didn't answer.

"Liz, I love you," he said, louder, letting me know that he expected a response.

I mumbled, "Love you too".

He took my hand and I started to turn cold, thinking he'd drag me back to the bedroom or beat me for showing hesitation. But he just smiled and asked, "When will you be back?"

"In two or three hours. I have a lot of stuff I need to prepare for the genealogy class tonight. See you later."

"Do it for Jesus," he said, expecting me to smile and say in response, "I'm living for the lord!"

"Sure, whatever," I said and walked out the door.

Chapter 19

I drove straight to the library where I looked up names of divorce attorneys and looked up what my rights would be. After taking five pages of notes I realized I couldn't leave Greg. Where would I go? I had no skills, no degree, and no prospects of anything. I couldn't move back in with my family. I was only twenty-six years old but I felt like I was at the end of my life. I didn't want a divorce lawyer, I just wanted to die and get it over with. No more fights or struggles. I'd be someplace where I'd never be hit or kicked or raped or told what to do. No being a failure for having dead babies. No anything. Just cold, then light. God would understand and if not, maybe just cold then nothing. I didn't care. In fact, nothing would have been a nice change from my entire life. If I were lucky I'd see my brother Steve. If I wasn't lucky, I figured anything would be better than my current life.

Down a semi rural road, I drove to the bridge. It was icy cold with snow on the rails. I'd die in minutes like the people on the Titanic, listening to the band. I'd have a song in my head, Nearer My God to Thee, and I'd play it over and over until the cold took me. The swift current would carry me away forever.

It was as if a great weight had been lifted from my soul. I was going to finally be free.

I stopped and got out of the car. I hitched up my skirt and coat then climbed over the railing. The pain of every cut, bruise and whip welt would go away when the ice water engulfed me. I imagined myself sinking in a deep sleep to the bottom and being found like Ophelia in the famous Waterhouse painting, floating, beautiful as if I were asleep. It was weird and peaceful, then I threw up stomach acid into the river.

Just as I was about to let go, a large black SUV drove up next to me. It was Darren Crawford. Crap. What was he doing here?

"Did your car break down?" he called out, holding his jacket closed at the neck.

"I'm fine."

"What are you doing?"

"Nothing. What are you doing here?"

"I followed you."

"Did Greg send you?"

He seemed confused. "Nobody sent me. I wanted to see you."

"I'm not going back."

"Come to me, Liz. Give me your hand."

I thought of all the long nights he'd cried to me over Diana. We'd gone out on the search party together and I'd comforted him. Now I just didn't care anymore. My emotions were as raw and unfeeling as my body would be in a few minutes.

"Go away, Darren. Diana isn't coming back. I can't help you anymore."

"Liz, please don't jump. I can help you."

In the sky above me a flock of tiny black chickadees danced through the sky as if telling me to fly. I thought of the Paul McCartney song Blackbird. I thought of Poe's raven. Nevermore.

I gave Darren a halfhearted smile. "I have to go." Then I took my hands off of the rail and let myself fall.

Chapter 20

I awoke, not finding myself not in a cold icy river but naked and groggy in the most beautiful, comfortable bed I'd ever been in. Darren Crawford was sitting on top of the covers next to me.

Was I dead? Was this the morgue?

Darren smiled at me. "Finally awake. I thought you'd never come around," he said. "What happened to you? Who hurt you?"

"Greg did," I whispered, barely able to function, thinking he was going to help me. "Punishment for not being a better wife. Where are we?"

"My bedroom. That sick bastard husband of yours got you before I even had a chance. I never would have guessed that of Greg. Not in a million years."

His tone of voice changed. He became more relaxed, almost a different man. "I had a feeling Greg didn't appreciate you. I've always thought you were cute in a girl-next-door sort of way. Who'd have known you had the body of a centerfold under all those frumpy flowered skirts and old lady blouses you wear." He kissed me on the forehead and said, "I didn't think I'd ever get you pulled out of the river. How are you feeling now?"

"Okay, I guess." I still couldn't get a grasp on where I was or whom I was with.

"I'm still angry at Greg for telling Diana to stay with her husband. But I know you liked the idea of your friend having a passionate affair under the nose of all of her pious friends."

"I didn't know what... what to think. Darren... it wasn't my choice to make." I was too tired to make any sense. I wanted to close my eyes and sleep forever.

"Greg ruined my life. Looks like he ruined yours too."

He stood up and tucked the blankets around my chin. "You need your rest now. You need to heal."

I slept. He went out and came back. He brought me a soft shirt and a robe to wear that wouldn't hurt my back.

We talked about Diana. On his dresser was a photo of both of them smiling and happy.

"Does Greg know I'm here?" I had to ask.

"No. Actually, I was with Greg while you were asleep. Don't worry he doesn't know you're here."

"Oh no. What did he say?"

"He's worried about you."

I wasn't even sure what to think or feel.

Darren turned on the TV. "They're looking for you. After I'm done here I'm going out to join the search party. I convinced Greg that I'd be a big help."

Greg was on the screen. I started to cry out to him. "Shut up Liz, he can't hear you," Darren snapped and pulled my arms up to the headboard. Plastic restraints were around my wrists. "The more you fight, the worse it will hurt. I suggest you lie back and enjoy the ride." Darren smiled and pulled his shirt over his head then dropped his pants. "Lights, camera, action. You'll be a great little porn star, Liz."

I won't go into all of the details of the following week. It was in the news and documentaries. People searched for me. Greg tried to move heaven and earth to find me. Darren tortured me and filmed it. He filmed everything he did to me. Willing myself to die wasn't working.

Darren Crawford was the Killer of Virtue. "It was all Diana's fault," he told me after he'd raped me. "But it was Greg's fault too. Greg told her to leave me. Since I can't have Diana anymore, Greg can't have you."

"You killed the others. Were you having affairs with them too?" I asked, almost in shock.

"Of course not. I killed them to cover up the death of my pious little whore, Diana. Come on Liz, I'm not stupid."

"I'm your friend."

"Sure, I know you are. In fact, this is the most fun we've ever had. I can't believe I never seduced you before now. I was quick with the others but I'm going to keep you. You're mine Liz, all mine for however long I want you."

No, this wasn't going to happen, not to me, not after what I'd been through. By then, he'd undone the restraints on my wrists. I tried to get off of the bed. He grabbed my hair and pulled me back. I clawed at his face. My finger went into an eye socket. He screamed and started to stab at me. The knife cut through my hands and arms as I struggled to get him away. Then my shoulder exploded in pain. He'd stabbed me, and then he was on top of me. I made one last effort and pushed him off of me. He rolled off of the bed, then after the crash of the large lamp on the nightstand, all was silent. I lay still for what seemed like forever then I looked down. He was dead; his dark eyes closed, his mouth open. Blood pooled around the back of his head. Darren Crawford was now as dead as Diana. I took a breath and said a prayer, then hoped I wouldn't bleed to death.

Chapter 21

Crawling out of bed and stepping over Darren, I scanned the room. My clothes were neatly folded on the dresser: Cotton candy pink sweater with lace trim, brown a-line skirt, brown tights, brown low-heeled boots. The pretty pink lace bra and panties were folded on top. The contents of my purse were laid out. My notes from the library were neatly arranged in a pile. My earrings, small gold roses, were set next to my plain gold wedding band and my diamond engagement ring. The gold tone clip that held my waist length hair up sat next to everything else, plain and unremarkable. My necklace with the plain gold cross was laid next to the clip.

A dresser drawer was open. There were more clothes: Jeans and a purple tee shirt with small pink hearts on it. The description of what Susan Jackson, the minister of the Hillside New Christian Church, had worn to the grocery store the day she was abducted. They'd find her body soon, that's how he worked. He dumped the body in the morning and abducted his next woman that afternoon. He kept them for about a week for slow torture, then dressed them in whore clothes and laid them out. He'd abducted Susan a few days ago. I'd heard her screams for two nights, then nothing. I thought he'd already dumped her, but Darren wouldn't tell me anything.

"Susan!" I called out. No answer. It was completely silent except for my own heart and lungs.

I was bleeding what seemed like gallons. I went to the bathroom and wrapped my arms in towels then looked for a first aid kit. There was a box of small bandages, the kind that go on paper cuts and small skinned knees.

I went down the hall and down the stairs. The house was huge. I'd been to a party in the house. I knew where the kitchen was.

There was nothing. Then I thought of something I'd seen on one of those shows about survival called Survivor Guy or something like that, where someone is dropped in the woods with only five items: A knife, a rope, a jacket, a water bottle and DUCT TAPE. Duct tape closed wounds better than anything. I went out to the garage. It was freezing, but I didn't care. I'd dealt with worse the night before with Greg. My head was starting to spin from pain and blood loss. Maybe the cold meant I would die.

"Dear God," I said aloud, "Where is the duct tape?"

On a top shelf of an open cabinet, about eight feet up, were three silver gray rolls of the magical tape I was seeking. About a dozen cardboard boxes were stacked in front of the cabinets. I climbed up three boxes. The top box contained books. I closed the flaps and stood on it. The box held. I thanked God again for giving me solid books instead of crystal goblets. I grabbed the tape and covered my deep cuts. I wiped and covered. It held over the slippery mess. Hair and blood was in my eyes. I was shaking but I was done. I stepped back to get down and fell on my back. My ankle twisted. For the first time in as long as I could remember, I almost started to cry.

A noise made me turn.

"Stupid bitch." There stood Darren, naked, blood on his shoulder. "You're fucking dead."

I was in shock to the point where I couldn't even scream. Nothing came out of my mouth except a hoarse hiss. Then it happened.

Darren had a look of pain on his face, like someone gets when they're carsick, then he turned back toward the door and fell down flat on his face. I lay still for what seemed like forever. Then I called his name.

"Darren?" No answer. I called again but he didn't respond.

When I tried to stand, my ankle screamed with pain. It was yet another insult to an already bad situation. I picked up a book and threw it at him. No movement. I threw another book. Nothing.

I crawled over to Darren. His eyes were open. He was dead, or at least I thought he was. I found a screwdriver and held it to his neck as I checked his pulse. No pulse.

He was dead.

Eight cars occupied the garage. I'd never seen so many cars in a garage before: Two Porsches, a Mercedes, a Ford Explorer, a Cadillac Escalade, a BMW convertible, a brand new full-sized Ford truck and a Prius.

I was going to get the tape, just in case I needed it again, and noticed the boxes. The books were scattered around, but what got my attention was that the box underneath it was filled with money. Yes, money. A box filled with cash. Bundles of $50 and $100 bills. I just stared. My mind went blank. Money. Lots and lots of money.

I should have been wondering where it came from. I should have been thinking of good works but I just sat on my naked butt in front of the box, and then started to open the other boxes. One box of books, fourteen boxes of cash.

I was cold and ready to pass out. For some unknown reason, maybe because I wanted order in so much disorder, I picked up the books I'd thrown at Darren. One was about New England birds. I tossed it at Darren. No movement. He was still dead.

When I saw the title of the other book, a light bulb went off in my head, like a shot of adrenaline straight to my brain. It was as if the sky had opened up and the angels had handed me the holy text.

The book was Huckleberry Finn by Mark Twain. My brother Mark said it was racist and immoral because of the drinking and violence and that he'd never let his children read it. I, on the other hand, loved the book. I loved Huck Finn. I had wished I was Huck Finn, traveling down the river with Jim. Huck was smart. Huck was resourceful. Huck faked his own death and got away with it.

The police were already searching for my body miles away, near where the others were found. I was already dead. Now I had money. I didn't have to go back to Greg or my family. I could go down the river with Huck and Jim or whomever I wanted to be with.

I usually thought, WWJD when I was in a bind. What would Jesus do? Over the past week, I had no idea what Jesus would do if he was raped and beaten by the person he loved the most, then raped and tortured by another friend, but then again, that DID happen to Jesus more or less and I didn't know what to do. I had prayed for mercy and hope and forgiveness. And I received hope as I looked at the books and the money and the dead body of Darren Crawford. Then my thoughts changed to WWHD. What would Huck do?

First, before I did anything else, I had to rest. I had to figure it out.

Chapter 22

I went back inside and put on a soft robe I'd found in the bathroom. I sat in the warm living room, thinking out my plan. I turned on the TV, just in time for the nighttime news. There was Greg, pleading for my return. His voice cracked. He had tears in his eyes. He spoke of how much he loved me. It frightened me to see that handsome young man with the amazing gentle and mesmerizing voice. He was as bad as Darren, except Darren had shown mercy and killed his victims. Greg kept me in Hell forever. I looked into the handsome face of the Devil, then turned off the TV and staggered off to find something for my pain.

Darren apparently had a doctor who was quite liberal with his prescription pad. I found more than the usual stash of prescription painkillers in the medicine cabinet. I took some strong narcotics. I curled up in Darren's beautiful bedroom, cocooned in comforters and his clean silk pajamas and slept for twelve hours. It didn't matter if anyone found traces of my blood or hair or other DNA in his bed. I was dead. He had filmed himself raping me and cutting me. Anything could have happened in that house and after I was gone it wouldn't matter.

His phones would ring and go unanswered. Sooner later someone would start to worry about him and show up. I guessed the cold, heavy rain and snow kept anyone from stopping by. I maybe had two or three days, four at the most.

Now what? I had to go. The best bet was in a medium sized city with a fairly transient population. I figured I'd just drive down I-95 until I reached Key West then jump in the ocean. Okay, it wasn't like that. I didn't even think of Florida. I just wanted to get as far away as possible.

I dressed in a pair of jeans that were a couple of sizes too large but I used one of Darren's belts to keep them on. I didn't know which woman they belonged to and didn't care. I matched those with one of Darren's black tees and a black cashmere sweater. The man was evil but he had some nice clothes. Over that I pulled one of those button up Irish fisherman type cardigans. I found another woman's boots in my size. I took my own underwear back.

My bag was there. I would never leave my bag. Photos of Steve and my life before Greg were hidden in an inside pocket I'd cut into the lining. Next to the photos was a journal documenting everything Greg had done to me. I put the photos and notebooks, along with my

Grandmother's charm bracelet in new leather satchel I found in Darren's closet. I left my laptop, my wallet, my favorite pink lip-gloss and my prized pink cashmere gloves. With Greg it was all about pink and girlish charm.

Luckily for me, there was a lot of my blood leading out to the garage from Darren's torture chamber. Blood saved Huck Finn and it would save me. In case you don't remember, Huck had killed a pig, put it in a bag and dragged it across the floor, making it look like a murder, his murder, had taken place. I sort of did the same thing.

Chapter 23

My blood was already in the bedroom, bathroom, down the hall and into the garage. I put the bloody towels in the back seat of the Cadillac Escalade. Next, I ran my hands through my hair and dropped a dozen long brown strands in the back of the car. I put my hands all over the back seat to make whoever found the car think I'd struggled. I even got in a few bare footprints on the glass. I took off my pants and planted my naked butt on the leather seat, just in case they were looking for imprints. I didn't know anything about evidence except what I saw on TV, where the police used the ACME DNA finder to get all of the facts within 20 minutes. Then I clenched my teeth and ripped off one of the pieces of duct tape on my arm. I bled all over the nice leather seat and spotless carpet.

Back in the bedroom, I found the stash of whore clothes he'd used to dress his virtuous women. I took a blonde pageboy cut wig and a long black wig with a shag cut. From his closet I took an assortment of sweaters, tees and oxford type shirts. I didn't risk taking anything that might be recognized. Next I raided his well-stocked gourmet pantry and filled up a cooler. I found some Vicodin, Codeine, Valium, Aspirin, and ibuprofen in the bathroom and took them as well. I packed the cooler, my bag of clothes and wigs, the boxes of money, the paperback copy of Huck Finn, a blanket, and a plain black umbrella into the older Ford Explorer and drove out to the end of the driveway.

By 3:00 a.m. I was on the road. It started to snow and a gentle white powder covered up my tire tracks. My first stop was an open 24/7 big box store about seventy-five miles down the road. On went a wig and a lot of slut makeup.

If anyone saw me, they'd have seen a blonde with too much blue eye shadow pushing a full cart. I filled my basket with clothes, underwear, pants that might fit, sweats, hair stuff, food, tools and shoes, plus a few girls' size six clothes and some baby formula, just to keep them off my track. I paid with four $100 bills and received $66 in change.

I drove south all day, only stopping for the bathroom and drive through fast food. At 6:00 pm, I came to a small town and stopped at a ratty hotel for the night. Across the street I got orange juice and a bottle of vodka at a liquor store then went to a deli and got a sandwich. While I ate, I watched the news on a fuzzy TV. The police had gone to Darren's house after his tax attorney had stopped by with some paperwork and found the front door wide open. They'd found blood, pictures of all of the victims, clothes, and the bloody towels in the back of the car. They'd also found Darren. It was assumed that I was dead too. A few hours later they'd found Susan Jackson's body. I'd find out later that Darren had dressed her in nothing but an unbuttoned white man's dress shirt, with pearls around her neck, dangling pearl earrings and a blonde wig. If they'd come twelve hours earlier they would have found me. I sat, numb. There was no going back.

It suddenly seemed more scary and weird to be sitting in a strange hotel room five hundred miles from home. After throwing up for what seemed like forever, I ate my panic and got busy planning.

Chapter 24

The only reason I grew my hair so long was because of Greg. I was glad to cut it off to right below my shoulders. I colored the light brown to a deep, dark brown. I changed my middle part to the side and brushed my bangs back off of my forehead. I cut the hair up in tiny pieces and flushed it down the toilet, one bit at a time.

By then it was 9:00. I turned on the TV, but put it on the travel channel. Then I put on my new socks, new underwear and new pajamas and slept for ten hours.

After an early morning shower, I swiped the Maryland license plate off of a car parked on the street and put it on the Explorer. The car looked too good and made me think of Darren and a fun idea. After packing up, I made another stop at a large chain hardware store for supplies. After driving about an hour, I turned down a dirt road into a wooded area, where I trashed the car. There was a satisfaction in taking sandpaper to the shiny surface of the car, splattering it with house paint then finishing off with mud. I scratched the surface with keys and hammer claws then beat the crap out of the fenders. On the bumper I put an I BREAK FOR UNICORNS bumper sticker. In the back windows went soccer ball decals and a large flying duck decal. To top it all off, I added a final bumper sticker with the words I love my husband.

So how much money did I have? I had to find out. I sat in the back of the Explorer and started to count, then estimated after two boxes. Twenty million dollars. I went numb and sat for about an hour, then I threw up and continued my drive.

In an effort to remove myself from the snow, I traveled along the Atlantic coast. Nobody gave me a second look in the blonde wig, red stocking cap and blue eye shadow. Nobody questioned me in the small gross hotels I stayed in. Anyway, I had a gun. I didn't know how to use it, but just having it made me feel sort of safe.

I was running a fever, throwing up, sleeping when I could. This wasn't going to work. The turn off for Charleston was in a mile, so I turned.

Chapter 25

Charleston seemed like a good place to rest (hide) for a while. I'll skip my tale of aimless wandering around until I found the exit to the college. On a bulletin board in a local coffee house I saw a cottage for rent. An hour later, I paid three months' rent in cash up front. Calling the place a cottage was generous. It was more like a big storage shed shaped like a barn with a small wooden front porch. Inside was one large room with a kitchen area, a two burner stove, a bathroom just large enough for a shower and toilet, and a small loft that I used as a bedroom. It was a cute part of town near the university. I'd fit right in. I called myself Lisa O'Reiley and hoped nobody would ask me for an I.D.

It was time for a new style for Lisa. She liked cargo pants and plaid shirts and fleece vests. I topped off the outfit with a black knit hat. I hated the clothes, but that was why I wore them. Nobody would have guessed I'd pick anything like that. Greg would have told me I looked like a lesbian.

The hair continued to evolve. I went into a "walk ins welcome" hair place in a strip mall and came out with a plain chin length bob. Back at the cottage, I colored it black.

The next day I purchased a refurbished laptop computer at the same mall from a couple of cute geeky guys. They gave me a rundown on cafes and other businesses with free Internet service. One, named Kyle, invited me to meet them for a beer after work. Cheerfully I said yes, but I never showed up. I couldn't get them involved with my mess.

The following weeks I kept to myself and hibernated. On TV, the unfolding news about The Killer of Virtue was fading away. Appearances from my brother Mark and my sainted mother had trickled down to almost nothing. More often than not Greg's name would come up. My husband was charismatic in ways I couldn't have imagined. He took control of the screen and caused all who saw him to think about love, loss and feel compassion. Watching him gave me stomach cramps. I wanted him to be a mean spirited fool but he came off as a hero; even worse, as a man who loved a woman with the kind of passion and devotion that is rarely seen outside of fiction. I'd escaped from that wonderful man and now sat in a dump of a cottage with ugly clothes, a bad haircut and millions of dollars in cash. Liz belonged to Greg. I didn't know if I'd ever belong to anyone or anywhere again.

My landlady Jennifer would come by every other evening with a beer and yack about her dysfunctional life. Everybody was doing something wrong or in rehab or sleeping with somebody they shouldn't have. That said, I'd always hear them laughing from inside the big house. Once, she said her family put the fun in dysfunction. I'd have that kind of dysfunction any day over what my life had been. Jennifer and her family thought I was from New York, a graduate student doing a research project. They didn't know the difference between a New York and Philadelphia accent. Why should they?

We'd sit on the porch more or less doing nothing. It was so weird being nobody and anybody I wanted to be. I told Jennifer that I was divorced from a real son of a bitch who'd hit me and cheated on me. The lie came easily. She didn't ask for details because she told me she'd known a lot of women in that same situation.

Charleston was a beautiful city full of interesting things. Any girl with money would have loved it there but I didn't go out. I was sick. The cuts on my arms never seemed to heal. I had a high fever and the ongoing cramps that never went away turned into horrible pain that kept me doubled over in bed. My side ached. I suspected Greg or Darren had cracked a few ribs but it should have been healed by now.

Jennifer drove me to the hospital against my protests, but I knew I had to go. The doctor, a guy named Charles Larson was all straight angles and perfect lines, like he'd just come out of central casting for a daytime soap. When he walked into the room I tried to sit up, but the pain in my ribs stabbed at me. Looking down at my feet, I saw blood dripping on the floor.

A few hours later, after I'd been cleaned out and cleaned up, Dr. Larson came to my room.

"Tell me what's going on with you," he said, all concerned and serious.

I've just come from hell. Satan says hello, I wanted to say. I shrugged.

"I haven't been feeling well."

"Are you in a relationship?"

"No."

"Did you know you were pregnant before you miscarried?"

I shrugged again and turned away. I was like Jordan. I had no need to speak to anyone anymore. I had no need to tell the truth or have pleasant conversations.

"I figure you were about four months along. Did you know?"

I didn't answer.

He took my hand. "Who did this to you? Lisa? Your back and buttocks are covered with cuts. You have bite marks on your shoulder. Was he your husband? It looks like you've been wearing a wedding ring for a while. The indentation is still on your finger."

I'd said too much. I wasn't about to tell them that one beat me out of a religious frenzy and the other out of revenge.

"Listen, I'd rather just forget it ever happened. I've moved on, Dr. Larson," I said, giving him a leave me alone before I dance over your cold bare grave stare.

"There are people who can help you."

"I've already helped myself by leaving."

"What if the man who hurt you does this to someone else?"

"Then she deserves it for being stupid enough to be with him."

"Do you think you deserved it?"

"Why should you care? Oh right, you're a doctor." As Elizabeth, I would have never said that, but as Lisa it came flowing out of me. I didn't like Lisa, but right now she was my best friend.

Doctor Larson took out one of his business cards and wrote something on the back of it. "I'm going to give you the name of someone who can help you, an old friend of mine. He'll help you with a restraining order and a divorce if you're married. He can even help get you a new name. It's all legal."

"I've done fine on my own," I lied.

"You haven't done fine. You could have died."

"But I didn't die, did I?"

"I'll give you the information anyway. You might change your mind."

I put the card in my purse without looking at it. Back at the cottage, I self medicated with codeine and some pot brownies Jennifer had made for me. After day three, I strangely started to feel human again.

Chapter 26

On day four of my recuperation, Dr. Larson came calling. He made a few small talk comments about how pretty and neat the cottage was. Of course it was neat and pretty. I'm compulsive that way. It will always be neat and pretty. Always.

I poured us iced tea I'd made that morning and we sat on the worn flowered couch. I'd put a small vase of white daisies Jennifer had brought me on a scarred up old coffee table covered with a dozen crocheted lace doilies I'd found at an antique store.

"I've thought about this a while. You're that girl, the missing young wife, Elizabeth Atkinson," he said.

Busted. I said nothing.

"I won't tell anyone," he continued, "How did you get away from Darren Crawford? Why didn't you go home?"

I could just imagine Dr. Larson making the talk show and news circuit, telling of how he discovered Liz Atkinson. He was savvy enough to become his own traveling road show. He'd be asked back. He'd become an expert in abused women and their savior. He'd start a foundation. I closed my eyes and rested my head against the back of the couch.

"You're barking up the wrong tree," I said, opening my eyes.

"Call the number I gave you in the hospital. Do you still have it?"

I gently pulled my hand away. "That friend of yours, can I trust him?"

"Yes, of course you can trust him. He's the best there is," the good doctor said gently.

I pulled the card out of my purse and glanced at the name scrawled on the back. The area code was unfamiliar.

"He deals with cases all over the country. You can call him anytime. 24/7," said Dr. Larson.

I looked down at the card again. I didn't know what to do but no matter what I did, it would be on my own terms.

"Elizabeth?" he asked. "Liz?"

"Thanks for your help. I'll send you a postcard when I get to Shangri-La."

"Where is Shangri-La for you?"

"Wisconsin. I have friends in Lake Oswego. They said I could stay with them. They even have a job lined up for me. If that doesn't work out

65

I'll move to Italy and become a nun. I hear Florence is nice." I gave him an insincere smile.

The good doctor may as well have signed my death warrant again, as far as I was concerned. I sat at the kitchen table feeling so alone, listening to the rain come down. I couldn't go through life running and hiding.

Handsome and kind Dr. Larson told me to keep in touch with him. I said I would. I thanked him and almost gave him a hug, but decided not to. Dr. Larson left me alone with a name scrawled on the back of a business card. Yes, I could say this was my one-way ticket out of Hell but that would be well, stupid. But, I had to find out. I needed someone who could help me and I knew it wasn't Dr. Larson.

Chapter 27

An hour after Dr. Larson left, I went to a payphone at a nearby mini mart with a bag full of change and called the number on the card. A woman answered the phone.

"The law offices of Alexander and Goldstein. How may I help you?"

"My husband tried to kill me but nobody will believe me. Can you help?" I attempted to use a Southern accent but it didn't come out very well.

"Are you in a safe place?" the woman on the other end asked.

"Not really. Where are you?"

She gave me a street address and a city. Miami.

"Miami, Florida?" I asked, wondering why in the world Dr. Larson had given me a Miami number.

"Yes, Miami, Florida."

"I'll call you back later." I hung up.

That evening, I opened a bottle of expensive wine, poured a glass, and curled up in front of the TV. A show about nature was on, but I wasn't really following it. I was thinking; planning my future.

Florida would be good. Palm trees, warm breezes, transient population; all worked for me. Nobody knew me; nobody cared. There were plastic surgeons in Florida. Loads of them. I could change my face, get a tan, live on the beach, open a vintage clothing store and learn to scuba dive. When I turned 80 I'd write my life story, all leathery tanned and still wearing a bikini. I could play my guitar and sing soulful love songs at a local bar. Miami had great architecture. And it was warm. Then again, I was covered with scars. Oh well. I could tell everyone I'd been attacked by a shark while snorkeling in Australia. If I did an English accent over my Philadelphia accent it could pass or Australian, or maybe South African. I finally had a future and maybe even a past. Life was good.

The next three days were spent in a cleaning frenzy. Most of my clothes and personal items went into a dumpster across town. I couldn't leave so much as a single hair or fingerprint behind.

On Jennifer's door, I left a thank you note along with the silver plated Victorian bridal basket she had admired in an antique shop window, all fingerprints expertly polished off of it. I also left two hundred dollars in cash, making sure none of the bills were from my original stash. I couldn't risk being tracked down through Darren's cash.

I drove to Miami in a single sixteen-hour stretch, only stopping for food, a few catnaps, and shopping for my new identity.

I did a lot of thinking on my trip. At consignment shop I purchased a plain gold engagement ring with a single quarter carat diamond for my left hand. I figured it was safer to travel as a married woman.

The remaining baggy kakis and plaid shirts went into dumpsters along the way. I'd replaced them with jeans and a wardrobe of gauzed embroidered hippie shirts and Indian scarves from an import store. I went into the drug store next door and found a pair of glasses that matched the driver's license I'd taken from the purse of a young woman in the library in Charleston.

I'd lost around twenty pounds; I was too skinny but still had a shape. With my new heavy on the black eye liner makeup, red nails and lips and bobbed black hair, I was nothing like me, whoever me was.

I checked into a small, nondescript Miami hotel that didn't ask for an I.D. and spent an hour showering off the road. The balcony had a crappy view of another crappy hotel that probably rented rooms by the hour. I took a deep breath and called the number Dr. Larson had given me.

"Law offices of Alexander and Goldstein," the woman on the other end said.

I looked at the card again, trying to make out the name. If I squinted, it looked like Allen Gilmore or Alec Colman, but it could have been Goldstein.

"I'd like to make an appointment with Mr. Goldstein." My voice went up as a question, like a teenage girl would say it. I wanted to hang up then and there. I felt like a fool.

"Is this a new appointment or are you an existing client?"

"New."

"What's your name, dear?"

"Shannon," I hesitated and glanced at the local map. I saw Coral Gables. "Shannon Gables."

"What is the reason for your visit?"

"I need advice. It's urgent. My husband tried to kill me. I'm scared and alone."

"You called last week, didn't you, dear?"

"I'm sorry I hung up on you. I just need to talk to an experienced attorney about some things."

"I can set you up with Greg Holloway, our expert in domestic cases."

I couldn't see anyone named Greg. "I'd like to see Mr. Goldstein. He was the one I was told to call."

"Hold on and I'll see what I can do." The wait seemed to take forever. "Alexander Goldstein can see you at 4:00 tomorrow afternoon. Will that work for you?"

"Perfect. Thank you so much."

"Are you safe where you are right now?" she asked. She'd obviously received calls like this before.

"I'm okay. I'll, um… see you tomorrow." I hung up fast, feeling like a bad child who was going to get hit again for lying.

Chapter 28

I didn't know what to wear. I figured I'd be taken seriously if I wore something conservative. After a morning of shopping I came back that afternoon with a tan silk linen blend suit, with a solid jacket and a coordinating flower print skirt. I had matching low-heeled tan pumps. The outfit was set off with a string of faux pearls and matching earrings. Underneath the suit jacket was a pale pink silk knit sleeveless lace blouse. I thought I appeared respectable. I kept my makeup simple, just mascara and a little pink lip-gloss. I'd get sympathy from the kindly Mr. Goldstein.

That night as usual, I brought fast food back to my room. I watched a program about beavers building their dams for the winter. I wished I were a beaver, safe with my happy beaver family. Then I fell asleep. The next morning I drove to the beach and tried to clear my brain but it didn't work.

As I was getting ready my appointment, carefully applying lotion to my wounds, as if anything would help, listening to the noon news, I heard my name and Greg's voice. There was Greg, in front of the cameras looking stoic, but with a sadness in his voice that broke every heart in America. Elizabeth Atkinson had been more or less declared dead.

I didn't know how to process that information. I was dead, but I was alive. I'd gotten exactly want I wanted, but I didn't feel good at all. I was in trouble, big time. I should have gone back. I should have gone home. I should have been the good wife.

Why was I dead so soon? I didn't have a will. No life insurance. Was there another woman? I thought I was going to get sick. Since I don't cry and have an inability to express my grief or frustration, everything upsetting makes me want to throw up.

There was no going back now. Greg would be happy to see me, praise the Lord, then it would all start over again.

On the way, my heart pounded. More than a few stitches in my skirt popped as I climbed into the Explorer. I didn't even care at that point. I'm dead. I'm dead. I'm dead. I am dead. The thought went through my head over and over again like a mantra. My head spun. I felt like I was going to pass out. I looked sideways at my reflection in the side mirror of the car. My over processed hair had started to turn frizzy and looked plastic in the humidity. I tried to smooth it down my wrinkled skirt with no luck. To make matters worse, much worse, I was wearing panty hose. My legs felt like they were encased in molten plastic.

As I drove to the Law Office of Alexander and Goldstein, I imagined Mr. Goldstein would be a sensitive man with either a New York accent or maybe a slight southern drawl. I hoped for the drawl. He'd be wearing a rumpled suit and maybe a funky tie, or in this weather he'd have a white shirt with his sleeves rolled up, a plain gold band on his left hand, photos of his wife and kids on his utilitarian desk. He'd be average looking, but on the round comfortable side of fifty-something and maybe even cute in a puppy dog sort of way. But looks aside, He'd have a sparkle in his eye and a kind voice with an underlying "vengeance is mine" tone as he listened to my story. The office would be full of other women, maybe some with children, waiting for help. The doctor said he'd helped other women. He'd help me, maybe. I still wasn't sold on the idea. Or he'd be young and aggressive, like a pit bull of a man, sharp spoken, fast moving and moved to feel emotions he'd never imagined. He'd be wearing jeans and a Metallica tee shirt, with a suit hanging on the back of the door. He'd have a ponytail and ride a motorcycle. Bright young assistants would be there, helping him in the cause of the downtrodden and oppressed.

Maybe Alexander Goldstein would step out of the office as soon as he saw me and call the police. Maybe he'd blackmail me. Maybe he'd take me to Disney World. My mind was spinning, then for the last three or four blocks, it went blank and numb like the back of my legs, sweating in their imprisonment in touch-of-tan slinky silk finish panty hose. I swore I'd never let anything that didn't naturally occur in nature touch my skin again.

The offices of Alexander and Goldstein were in an expensive building with landscaping that could rival any botanical garden anywhere. Too bad I couldn't stop and smell the flowers.

I was smoothing out my skirt by my car when I overheard a well-dressed man on his phone in the black Mercedes parked next to me.

"He'll win. Oh hands down. Juries love Goldstein. Jesus, everybody loves him. Hell, I love him. Goldstein is good. Scary good. Sure, but the guy is a fucking freak. Look at him. Nobody human looks like that. No. It's enough to scare anyone. God yes, I've never seen anyone put down the booze like him. No it doesn't do a thing to him. Like I said, the guy is a freak. Yeah, maybe an olive. Sure, I know who his partner is. Some guys are born lucky. Pisser, isn't it." He changed subjects about the location of a softball game then hung up. I stayed behind my car until he drove off.

Was I getting involved with a brilliant drunk who looked like Lon Chaney playing the Quasimodo? I tried to get my heart and stomach back in place and went into the office. But everyone loves him, right?

The large office was equipped with real tropical flowers. The receptionist was a well-dressed, well-tanned and well coifed middle-aged woman. Attractive in a cool flawless efficient way that only women with ice cold blood can pull off.

The reception area was empty, aside from modern and obviously expensive but comfortable chairs. No hordes of tired looking women with their hordes of dirty, snot nosed children waiting for help. My jacket was hot and scratchy. Perspiration ran down my back. I wanted to take it off, but couldn't show my ugly arms. My head grew light again and my stomach turned to knots. I thought of the old movie called Skyscraper with the art deco interior. I half expected the receptionist to speak in that high-pitched smart type of movie voice of the 1930's.

I approached the desk. "I have a 4:00 appointment with Mr. Goldstein. I'm Shannon Gables." I barely got the name out of my mouth. I wanted to say, I'm Liz Atkinson, and I'm dead. I couldn't get it out of my mind. I was dead. The reality was too weird to understand.

She said something about waiting a minute in a seat but I hardly heard her. I sat down, unable to flip through a magazine or get my mind around what I was doing.

I'd had my story planned out but now, since I was now dead, it had all changed. It must be against the law to be dead and alive at the same time. If I was thought to be dead, but lived, it was a lie. Or did I have protection? What I really wanted to do was stay dead, and that was why I was in the offices of Alexander and Goldstein, waiting for Mr. Goldstein, the freak. Maybe he had snakeskin tattooed all over his arms or an extra set of legs. It was a stupid thought. Staring blankly out the window in revelry of confusion, I didn't see Mr. Goldstein enter the room.

"Ms. Gables?" I heard a name, Ms. Gables, but couldn't respond. "Shannon?"

I looked up. He offered a hand. "I'm Alex Goldstein".

Chapter 29

There before me like a vision of something too unbelievable to imagine, was Alexander Goldstein. He was the most perfect, beautiful, handsome living being I'd ever seen in my life. He was what angels must look like. He was every woman's dream and desire. He was perfection personified.

Glossy black hair and flawless light olive skin, expressive chocolate brown eyes surrounded by long dark lashes, strong perfect lines, lips that were proportioned perfectly for a passionate kiss of a lover or words of a saint. He had broad shoulders and a perfect build under the beautiful gray suit. A slight dimple in his left cheek was the final touch to this magnificent creature. Was I dead and in Heaven after all?

It wasn't that he was a good-looking guy; it was the fact that he was perfect. Absolutely physical perfection.

He took my hand in a firm shake. His hands looked like he'd never used them. These were hand model hands.

But somehow, in the sheltered world of Liz Atkinson, the name and the person didn't match up. He looked kind of Latin, which made sense being in Miami, but he could have passed for an Italian Renaissance heartthrob or any fairy tale prince or a dark Viking lord of romantic tales ready to sweep me off my feet and onto his longboat or on the cover of any bodice ripper romance. He was Valentino's much better-looking brother. He took my breath away.

His voice was smooth without an accent; a perfect radio voice. The perfect bedroom voice.

I almost choked out a response, "Yes, Mr. Goldstein, I'm here. Thank you for seeing me."

"Let's go to my office," he said, holding out his hand and helping me out of my seat. I stood and followed without a word.

We got to his large, beautifully decorated office and he motioned for me to sit. An attractive, well-dressed young woman appeared out of nowhere, carrying a tray with a crystal carafe of water with lemon slices and two matching glasses.

Alex Goldstein smiled at her and said, "Thank you, Rachael." She smiled back then left, closing the door behind her.

He sat, not behind his desk, but in chair next to me. "What can I do for you, Miss Gables?"

I handed him the card. "Dr. Larson gave me your name. He said you could help me."

He looked the card over and with a slight smile, handed it back with his left hand. I noticed a shining platinum wedding band set with three glittering diamonds.

"What did Dr. Larson say I could help you with?"

"Can you help me get a new identity?"

"Did Dr. Larson tell you I could get you a new identity?"

"Yes. He said you helped women in trouble. I need a new identity more than anything."

"Did you discuss the details of a new identity with Dr. Larson?"

"No, I didn't say much of anything to him. He did most of the talking. He said you could help, but no, he didn't exactly say new identity. Well, he did say you might be able to help me change my name. I didn't give him any details so, no, we didn't discuss it. I didn't trust Dr. Larson. I was afraid he'd turn me over to the authorities, so I told him I was going to Wisconsin to stay with friends. Nobody knows I'm here." I was rambling, so I stopped.

"Did you plan on going to Wisconsin?"

"No, I lied. I don't know anyone in Wisconsin. I told him that to get him off my back."

Alexander Goldstein smiled slightly, as if amused. "I see. Shannon, have you broken any laws?"

"I don't know. I can't go back to where I came from. I can't go back, ever." My skin was starting to crawl. I could feel sweat on the back of my neck starting to run down my back.

"Why can't you go back?"

"Will everything I tell you be completely confidential?"

"Yes, it will be."

"So, if I tell you anything, you are legally bound to keep it confidential. Right?" I asked, feeling the panic rise in me.

"Correct." Goldstein didn't flinch.

"Even if I broke the law."

"Yes."

"You can't tell anyone what I'm going to tell you."

He gave me a wee bit of a comforting smile. "Not a soul, unless you say otherwise. What you say to me is protected by the law."

"Okay. Can I trust you?"

"Absolutely."

I looked down at my scarred hands. They were shaking.

"You're scared." The concern in his voice sounded genuine.

"You're the first person I haven't lied to in three months."

"Why is that?"

"I need a new identity. A new social security number. I need an offshore bank account or somewhere safe I can put a large amount of cash."

Then he gave me a look that surprised me. It was almost as it he was mocking me. "Why does a young attractive woman like you need this sort of service? What did you do?"

"You won't believe anything I say." More panic on my part, but I didn't show it.

"Try me."

I sat next to Alexander Goldstein. unable to get any words out. He reached over and gently touched my arm. "You're wearing long, thick sleeves. You look hot and uncomfortable."

"You're wearing a suit." I glanced at his lapels then to his handsome face, to his hand on my arm.

"Good point, Ms. Gables, but I'm not uncomfortable. Are you a drug user?"

"No, never. Absolutely not."

"I'm sure it isn't organized crime. Certainly not prostitution, but I could be wrong. What is it that has you so frightened?"

I hesitated.

"You're hiding from someone who hurt you," he said, ever so gently.

"My husband." I took a deep breath. "My husband..." I couldn't get the words out. "I went to the library to research divorce lawyers, but realized that I could never leave him. I know this sounds stupid, but he would never have let me go."

I couldn't bring myself to admit I'd tried to kill myself. I paused again. Alex Goldstein waited like a saint. I took a drink of water.

"So I parked by a bridge and I jumped. There was ice on the water. I should have died, but I was rescued by a friend. Then instead of helping me, he, my friend, turned out not to be my friend." The words stuck in my mouth. "He made me..." There again the words stuck. I couldn't say what Darren did out loud but I had to make myself. I took a deep breath and a sip of water. "He brought me back to his house then he raped me and hurt me. He kept me for almost two weeks." I had to stop and catch a breath. I sipped more water. Alexander Goldstein waited patiently, without judgment. I looked up at him and continued, speaking quickly so I could get all of the words out and get it over with. "He filmed us, and played it back to me over and over. He threatened me with an acetylene torch if I didn't do exactly what he wanted me to do. He said I was just like a porn star. Then he prepared me for death. He cut me with a knife, just like he'd cut all the other women he'd hurt. He laid out clothing he was going to dress me in after I was dead." I took a breath and sat back. I looked at Alex Goldstein, who looked like an angel in an expensive suit and silk tie. His brown eyes showed nothing but compassion and understanding.

I steadied the glass in shaking hands and took another drink of water. I thought I was going to pass out, but I kept talking. "He was forty-two years old and in good shape, really good shape. I kicked him and he hit his head on a table by the bed. I thought he was dead, but he came after me again. Then he just fell down dead, right in front of me."

I paused. "I'm not making any sense."

"You're making sense. We'll go back later for details."

"You don't believe me."

"I'm listening, Shannon. Tell me what happened next."

"It was divine intervention, as far as I'm concerned." I put my head in my hands, trying not to pass out.

Alexander Goldstein waited, and then asked, "After he died, what did you do?"

"I pulled a Huck Finn and faked my own death." I wasn't making any sense. "Did you read Huckleberry Finn?"

"Huck fabricated his own death to escape his abusive father." Alexander Goldstein smiled, this time an amused smile.

"I should be happy, because I want everyone to think I'm dead, but I feel like I'm going to throw up."

"Do you need to take a break?"

"I'm okay, really." I took a sip of water and wiped sweat from my face with my sleeve.

"Did anyone help you escape?"

"No."

"Does your husband or any of your family or friends know where you are?"

"You don't understand. I wanted everyone to think I was dead and now I am dead for real." my voice cracked, like I was going to start to cry. Alexander Goldstein handed me a box of tissues (the really soft expensive kind). I put the tissues back on the desk. "I don't cry."

He didn't comment. "Who helped you?" he asked.

"Nobody."

"Did the man who rescued you from the river hurt anyone else while you were with him?"

"Yes, he hurt another woman while he had me but I never saw her. She screamed and yelled at him. She was only there a day or two. He killed my best friend back in November."

Alexander Goldstein took my hand. His hauntingly beautiful brown eyes looked straight into my soul.

"You're Liz Atkinson."

I froze. Alex Goldstein continued, "I knew who you were the second you opened your mouth. It was the face, and then your voice gave you away. Then you told me your story. Am I right?"

"You're right."

"As of today, you're legally dead. A memorial service has been planned."

"They never found my body."

"Obviously," said Alex Goldstein. "You must have had a compelling reason to not go back to your loving husband."

"I'll show you." I stood up in front of Alex Goldstein. He was so handsome. I was transfixed for a moment. He said nothing, but waited in support.

I peeled the bandage off of the side of my face. Alex Goldstein's beautiful face visibly changed from calm to that of mild shock. Then I took off my jacket and held out my arms.

The knife wounds were thick and puckered from the infections. The wound on my face was ugly and red where it had attempted to heal.

"There's more," I said. I turned around and pulled my shirt over my head, leaving me standing there in my skirt and bra. "It isn't just my back. The marks go down to my butt and all over my hips."

"Good God," he said under his breath.

"Darren Crawford cut up my arms. He stabbed me in the shoulder too. The cuts on my hands are from Darren too.

Alex Goldstein's eyes went to my shoulder. "Who made the bite marks?"

"My husband. The belt and whip marks on my back are from Greg, too. "

"How long were you in Charleston?"

"Almost two months. I was really sick. I had a miscarriage."

"How far along was your pregnancy?"

"Three months, I think. I don't know if it was Greg's or Darren's, but it was probably Greg's. It doesn't matter because it would have been mine, not..." I paused, feeling so tired. "The baby would have been all mine."

"We can take a break if you like."

"No, I'm fine." I took a sip of water.

"Put your blouse back on. I've seen enough. Did anyone in Charleston know who you are?"

"Nobody. Nobody knows but you. Dr. Larson in Charleston, he said he was going to call you."

"Did he now?" He picked up the business card again. "Darren Crawford stabbed you and cut your arms."

"Yes. Greg did the rest. More damage from Greg will show up on x-rays, but a lot of the older stuff was from my brother Brad."

"Brad?" Alex Goldstein asked. I could tell I'd thrown him off on that one. Nobody knew about what went on in the Hobbs happy household.

I backtracked my story. "That was a long time ago, before I married Greg. It doesn't have anything to do with what happened with Greg and Darren."

"I see. Your husband, Dr. Gregory Atkinson, made the welts on your back and the bite marks?"

"Yes."

"Before or after your encounter with Darren Crawford?"

"Before."

"Why do you think your husband did that to you?"

"I was an obedient wife, but I wasn't obedient enough..." I trailed off. "He kept saying he did it because he loved me." I looked out the window, which faced a courtyard garden. My eyes glassed over on some red flowers. I didn't know what else to say. I looked back at Alexander Goldstein. He looked concerned, but I didn't know, it could have been an act.

"I know this is difficult for you." His voice was so oddly comforting. It made me want to both stay and run.

I wanted him to know everything. "Sex with Greg was always exciting but then it got violent. The punishment always came with sex. He got rougher with me, but there was nothing I could do. Then when he was done with me, he'd make me pray. I'd have to ask for forgiveness. I'd ask God to help me become a good wife. I'd be forced to pray for my willful nature to go away and enjoy the virtues of being an obedient wife. Only then could I have true spiritual and sexual fulfillment as a married woman. It was sick, what he made me do. He got off on my pain."

I realized I was almost spitting the words out at him. I paused. Alexander Goldstein said nothing. It was a cue for me to continue. I took another sip of water.

"I lost five babies. Three were later term births. I think it put him over the edge."

"Did your husband mistreat you while you were pregnant?"

"No. I was angry with Greg for making my loss and private grief public. He shared our private life in his classes and Sunday sermons. I told him to stop. I spoke out and paid the price for not appreciating the lessons God had given me. He said I was selfish for not sharing my lessons with others. He tried to erase anything in my life outside of our marriage."

"Was he always so controlling?"

"The control was there from the start. He did it with guilt. I wasn't a good Christian. I wasn't a good wife. I wasn't a good person if I didn't do exactly what he said. He said I was weak and needed to be guided by a strong husband. He kept saying he was trying to be a strong Christian husband and my rebellious behaviors were keeping him from keeping his commitment to God and his wife. He'd refer to me as "his" wife, as if I was somebody else or property. After Diana was murdered, it got worse."

"Diana was your best friend."

"I miss her so much." Again, my stomach cramped. "When she died, I felt like my flame went out."

"You said you jumped off a bridge, to escape your husband."

"It was my only option at the time. Greg beat me so badly the last time that I should have been hospitalized. He was on a rampage for three days. He forced me outside naked, and pushed me down in the snow. He told me to pray. He held me down with his foot on my back until he was satisfied that I showed enough faith. Then he forced me to have sex with him over and over. He hurt me really bad. I don't know how he kept it up, honestly. When it was normal he could go a few times a night, but this was crazed. He wanted to hurt me.

I had a fever. I couldn't stop shaking and he wouldn't stop. He beat my soul out of me, so I figured I might as well die, that's why I jumped off the bridge." I took a deep breath. "So anyway, I'm here now, so I can start a new life and put it all behind me. Right?"

Chapter 30

"Do you mind if I call someone else in? Tasha Alexander, my partner and my wife. I want her to see what your husband and Darren Crawford did to you. I want you to tell both of us everything. Can you do that?" Alex Goldstein stood, went to his desk and put his hand on the office phone.

"Sure, Okay. Will she be able to tell anyone?"

"She can't tell a soul unless she wants to be disbarred."

"Okay."

He picked up the phone. His voice was the same gentle tone he'd used with me.

"Tasha, I need you to come to my office... I know, I know. This is important... I'm with Liz Atkinson... Yes, the dead girl. I know. I swear it's her. She's here, in my office... Yes, I'm sure.

"I'm glad you came in.," Alexander Goldstein said, taking my hand for a moment in his, then letting it go.

"I need to tell you something else too," I said, "I can't go back to my family. My parents are worse than Greg. I just want it to stop. I don't want anyone to hit me or hurt me again. Do you understand?" Feeling dizzy, I fell forward and grabbed for the couch. My hand landed on Goldstein's leg, slipping up his thigh. I quickly pulled my hand away.

"I'm sorry." I wanted to crawl into a hole.

"Liz, are you all right?"

"No. Don't call me that. Liz is dead," I whispered. I started to shake.

Alexander Goldstein put his arms around me. Nobody had held me for so long. It had been months since I'd felt safe. I put my head on his shoulder and closed my eyes for what seemed like forever. "You'll be all right." He was my avenging angel.

Chapter 31

Just as Alexander Goldstein had silently appeared like an apparition, so did his wife Tasha Alexander.

She said nothing as she watched her husband comfort me. She never rushed us. Tasha Alexander wasn't one to needlessly rush anything.

She was almost as perfect has her husband. Tall and blonde, with a figure that would be the envy of any swimsuit model or Barbie doll, she was a perfect compliment to her husband. She looked like an angel in a pale yellow suit.

Their eyes met. They communicated without words, the language of long married couples.

She said softly to me, "I'm Tasha Alexander."

"Do you feel like telling both of us your story from the beginning?" asked Alexander Goldstein.

I told them everything without sparing a detail. I showed them the contents of my satchel and my diary. They asked a few detailed questions, but let me talk. A small recorder sat on the table.

Alexander handed Tasha the card. She gave him an all knowing look and raised an eyebrow. Then Alexander spoke.

"I recognized you, and apparently so did Dr. Larson."

"I've thought about that a lot. I need to change my identity. I have to change my face. Not drastically but... this is Miami, you have to know someone you can recommend who will be discreet. "

"We know someone who can fix the wounds on your arms as well as any other medical issues that need to be taken care of," said Tasha.

"Before we do anything or make any decisions," said Alexander, "We need you to tell us everything. We need to know your background, the relationship you had with your husband. I understand you knew Darren Crawford. We need to know what that relationship was as well. Take your time. Where are your siblings or Greg's family? You couldn't have turned to them?"

"Nobody would have helped me. I tried to get my brother to help, but he refused. He said he had his own problems. Greg's family wouldn't have helped me. They worship the ground he walks on. They hate me," I said.

"You could have said no to Greg," said Tasha.

"Greg was always ready for me. He'd planned the first real beating, the first time with a belt, then with a whip. I tried to get away after he raped me and hit me. He had those plastic ties, the kind used to tie up fencing and trees. He used them on my wrists, around the slats on the headboard. They were the same kind of ties that Darren Crawford used to tie me down."

Tasha's eyes grew wide. Despite the fact that both Tasha and Alexander were trained not to respond to evil, they were noticeably disturbed by my story. I don't know if it was what happened to me or that I accepted the abuse for so long. That said, they sat and politely listened to the entire story from when I first met Greg up through the time when I arrived in Miami.

"I didn't have any close friends after Diana died. There was nobody who would have believed Greg was capable of doing what he did to me. I told you, I can't go back. I need your help. Can you help me?"

"We'll help," said Alexander.

"What about the money?" I asked, "I'll pay you well, but it's all cash."

Tasha spoke up. "We'll do what we can." She looked at Alexander. "You know who might be able to help." It was a statement, not a question.

"Maybe." Alexander said, for the first time seeming unsure of himself.

"Who?" I asked.

They didn't answer, but just smiled.

Chapter 32

Alexander Goldstein and Tasha Alexander decided that it would be best if I went home with them. Suddenly, I did believe in miracles. This wasn't a different world; it was a different universe. They were rich, beautiful, and nonjudgmental. It was totally and completely unreal.

On a weirder note, I kept thinking of Brad. Brad and I broke each other's noses. Brad spent years tormenting me, but in the end he'd stood up for me. He didn't rescue me from Greg and that made me so angry, but I knew if he knew I was going to jump he would have saved me. The night Steve died, he was the one who had turned against Mark and Kathy. He'd turned against our parents and finally become my brother. That logic might not make sense to some, but I wanted to call him in the worst way. He was talking care of Jordan and had married a nice girl who put up with my insane family. Then I thought, screw it, I'm dead. I'll call him in twenty years.

I followed the directions to the home of Alexander and Alexander home. It was a house of glass and palm trees, beautiful and modern. I'd never been in a house like this. Tile floors. Interesting art. Clean lines.

The pool house was right out of a luxury home magazine. Alex said they'd based it on the guesthouses at Hearst's Castle in California. At the time that meant nothing to me, but I imagined it was opulence and comfort.

Dinner with Alex and Tasha was a casual affair in their large, ultra modern kitchen. Tasha casually mentioned that their personal chef had left dinner for three.

When I arrived, Alexander Goldstein was already drinking more martinis than I could count. It was true. He could drink all night and it was never apparent. Tasha opened a bottle of California Chardonnay and offered me a glass.

The food was wonderful. Pork stuffed with fruit, a salad of every shade of green with candied nuts and fresh mangos and pineapple. A far cry from anything I'd ever cooked or eaten.

I'd changed out of the suit into a plain longish blue cotton skirt with a white cotton tee.

"You look comfortable," said Tasha, "But that's not a great style for you. However, it is so much better than that horrible suit you were wearing."

I'd thought it was nice; the sort of thing respectable women wore, but she was right. The suit was horrible. Greg would have approved of it.

"I used to shop at thrift stores and had this sort of Victorian Rock-a-Billy thing going on. Greg didn't think it was grown up enough," I said in my defense.

"I take it your husband liked having a wife who dressed like a frumpy senior citizen," she said as she twirled the wine in her glass.

"Greg picked out most of my clothes," I said flatly. "He liked conservative on the outside because it was so different from what I wore underneath. I think that excited him."

"I see. Most men like nice under things. If they don't, there's something wrong with them." Alex gave a slight acknowledging smile. Tasha continued. "You'll need a new signature style. You've got the build for anything you want. Just depends on who you want to be."

"Who do you want to be?" asked Alexander Goldstein.

"I want to be the woman who never gets hit. I'm sorry. That wasn't the answer you were looking for."

Tasha put her arm around my shoulders. "It's as good of an answer as any."

They laughed in unison, as pretty as could be. I asked them about their lives a bit. I didn't want to talk about myself. It had been months since I'd had a real dinner with another person. These two were fascinating, odd animals.

Alexander was from Miami. His father was a Florida native and his mother, a refugee from Cuba. He was the youngest of three successful brothers.

Tasha had grown up in St Petersburg. She had a brother who'd been in law enforcement and now had his own consulting business. I didn't ask what he consulted on, but according to Tasha, he mostly lived like a pirate, sailing all around the islands off the coast of Florida with assorted friends. Tasha did pro-bono work for various charitable organizations and traveled all over the country, but her heart was in always in Miami.

They'd met in law school at the University of Florida Gainesville. Upon graduation they'd worked for other law firms, but after a couple of years on the fast track, they decided to open up their own firm with astonishing success. Now, the Law Firm of Alexander and Goldstein had eighteen employees and owned their own building.

After dinner, Tasha set me up in the pool house for the night. The gates were all locked and the outside lights were on. I was told there was also an alarm set on the outside gate. Sinking into the soft bed, I marveled at the dream world I seemed to have fallen into. Beauty and calm encircled me as I drifted off into deep sleep. It was the first time in months I'd gone to bed feeling safe.

Chapter 33

I woke with the full weight of someone on top of me. The halo of blond hair, a slash of light showed one angry blue eye. A hand held my throat. I tried to move and a gun went to my temple. It was over. I was back in Hell. Greg had found me.

"I'll go back. I'll be the perfect wife. I'll do whatever you want," I rasped out under his weight. Lie, lie, lie. I wished Darren had killed me. I wished I were dead. Wait, I was dead. Greg was on the news, saying I was dead.

The hand tightened on my neck. I gagged. "Greg, please don't hurt me. I love you."

"Now that's a stupid thing to say." A slow buttery voice drawled into my ear.

It wasn't Greg. The blond stranger reached over and opened the curtains to let more of the pool light in.

"Shit, I thought you were that skeevy Misty Ann." He looked at my face, then my bare arms. "Looks like you've taken the slow bus to Hell. Whose bitch are you anyway? One of Bee Bee's girls?" He yanked the covers off of me then scanned my body. "Nice tits. A little skinny, but I'd do you if I was desperate."

The hair was much paler than Greg's, and longer in a shaggy cut around his face, almost long enough to fall on his shoulders. The face was thin and rangy like a cowboy loner out of central casting. That said, the white-blond hair and tan made him pure Florida beach bum. His slid a smooth hand under my cami top to my bare stomach.

"Don't touch me!" I yelled at him. Nobody was going to ever touch me or force me into anything against my will ever again. Then I did the unthinkable and yanked the gun out of his hand and hit him square across the jaw as hard as I could. He reeled back in pain. I scrambled out of bed. I'd ended up in a corner and couldn't run.

"Son of a bitch in heat," he said, putting his hand to his head. Then he laughed. "Fuck. I'm bleeding. Who are you?"

"Who are you?" I demanded.

"I asked you first," he said, just like a fifth-grade boy.

"I'm not telling you anything," I said back.

"For the love of Pete, you're almost naked. You aren't exactly in a position to negotiate. Put the gun down."

"You crawled into my bed with this thing."

He gave a slight laugh under his breath. "You got me there. A good looking man in your bed with a big gun can be a little disconcerting."

"Who's Misty Ann?" I asked, still not lightening up on him.

"Some slut Tasha gets information from. You have the same hair color, same cut, sort of. Are you a friend?"

"Go away."

"Did Greg make those marks on your arms?"

I still didn't answer. I didn't know what to say.

He stepped closer. His voice got quiet. "You called me Greg. Is Greg your boyfriend? Husband? Your pimp? It's okay. A lot of pretty young ladies get pimped out by their husbands or boyfriends. Sometimes it isn't a choice."

"I'm not a prostitute. I'm just a normal girl," I told him. How dare he think I was a whore?

"I hate to break this to you, but darlin', you're no girl. And if you're hanging out in Tasha's guest house you sure aren't normal."

I held the gun steady before me. "Go away, or I will shoot you."

"Do you even know how to use that thing?"

I said nothing and stood my ground. He took another step toward me. I backed into the wall.

"All right, I give. Jerry Alexander." He pulled out his wallet and held out some sort of official looking identification I didn't recognize. "Look that's me." I could barely read it but I could make out enough.

"You're law enforcement? How do I know that's real?"

"It's real enough. Who are you?"

"Alexander Goldstein is my attorney. I can't talk to you."

"He's my brother-in-law. I'm Tasha Alexander's brother. You wanna call her?"

I didn't let go of the gun.

"Where are you from? New York? Boston?" He squinted up his eyes at me like he was trying to figure it all out.

"I'm not telling you anything."

"Philadelphia. Right? It's Philadelphia? I know by the way your eyes flickered when I said it. Great place. Very historic. Very musical. Very museumey, Great cheese steaks." He was slowly moving toward me. "Who hurt you? Was it Greg? You didn't sound like you really love him. In my book, any man who hurts a helpless woman, especially one who claims to love him is a piece of..." Jerry moved to the wall and flicked on the light. "Shit. Jesus, Mary and Joseph. Holy crap. You're that dead chick."

"I'm not dead. Okay, I am, but don't call me 'that dead chick'."

He looked at me more in the light. "Liz, Liz, Liz, Liz Elizabeth Atkinson. Killer of Virtue. Gregory Atkinson's missing wife. What the hell are you doing here?" He ran his hand through his hair. "Oh man, I can't fucking believe this."

"You can go away now!" I snapped at him.

"Hey, I was asked here by Tasha to help a client, who I assume now is you. Since I'm working for Tasha and Alex, I'm working for you."

"You're law enforcement. "

"Well, yeah, I am, not technically anymore, but sort of, but not officially. I work with a lot of people, including my sister and Alex."

"Please don't turn me in."

"I can't arrest a dead girl. What are you afraid of?"

"My husband. I'd rather be dead than go back to my husband."

"You're more afraid of Greg than you are of Darren Crawford," he said quietly.

I held the gun in front of me. I wasn't about to answer him or talk to him about my situation.

"Did Darren Crawford kidnap you?"

"Yes, but he died while he was trying to kill me."

"But you didn't go home to your husband Greg?"

"No. Don't you get it? I can't go back. He'll hurt me again."

"Again? What did he do to you?"

I turned around and showed him my back. "The strap marks are from Greg. So is the cut on my face. He pushed me down naked in the snow and held me down with his foot on my back and told me to pray. Then he raped me and beat me until I passed out. It wasn't the first time but I made sure it would be the last. I can't go back."

"Didn't Darren Crawford kidnap you? Your blood was all over his house."

"He did. I knew Darren. I thought he was my friend. But he lied. It's complicated." I paused, sick of repeating my story. "Darren did horrible things to me, just like he did to those other women. Okay, you can go away and leave me alone now."

"What about your family? Do they know you're alive?"

"I'm more valuable to them dead."

"Life insurance?"

"Who the heck would take life insurance out on a twenty-six-year-old? They get off on the publicity and being the center of attention. They get to go on TV and pretend they're normal."

"You have an interesting passive aggressive side to your personality."

I just pointed the gun, too angry to say anything.

"Tell me what the fuck you're thinking, Mrs. Atkinson."

"You're one of the most foul mouthed, offensive human beings I've ever met," I spat out at him. I'm the best liar I've ever met, but my hands started to shake. I couldn't catch my breath.

He gently took the gun away from and put his hand on my arm. "Trust me. Shhhh. Poor baby. If I have my way, nobody will hurt you ever again. Come on honey, just let it out."

"Thanks for the chivalry, but I don't cry. Okay? Don't touch me please, don't."

Jerry took a step back, finally respecting my space. "How the hell did you find Tasha and Alex?"

"Just a sec." I crossed the room and dug in my purse and handed him the card.

He studied it for a minute then laughed. "Jesus Christ darlin', you were supposed to call Allen Gilmore."

"Who?" I asked, wondering what the crap he was talking about.

"Allen Gilmore. He deals with battered women, divorce, and child custody cases all over the US. He runs a national network of shelters, support groups; you know to help at risk women. He's good people. An expert on the subject. Gets a lot of cable news and radio gigs whenever some chick disappears and her husband or boyfriend is a suspect." Jerry turned over the card in his hand again. "Oh man, I can't fucking believe this. I went to college with Allen. Jeeze, this is weird." He sat down on the couch and motioned for me to do the same. "Who the hell wrote this?"

I sat on the edge of a chair near him. "Dr. Ronald Larson in Charleston. He didn't know who I am. What?"

He pointed to the numbers on the card. "That isn't three, it's an eight. 805 is Ventura, California. You called 305 in Miami."

"I didn't dial the right number?"

"No baby, you didn't dial the right number, but it's a good thing you didn't. Allen would have called his publicists and had you on every news station in the United States. You would have been his own personal poster girl for the cause. He'd be in hog fat heaven and you'd be toast. Rich toast with all of the book deals and appearances. Did you think of that?"

"I don't need the money."

"Lucky you."

"I guess God was watching out for me when I dialed the wrong number."

"I guess so. Thank God and all the saints that you have Jerry Alexander on your side."

"I have Alex and Tasha on my side."

"Shit, Liz." Jerry laughed under his breath. "Ahhh, Alexander and Goldstein, the friends of the rich and famous, glamorous and fabulous. And I mean the really insanely rich too. They also have an impressive line up of big time drug lords and organized crime folks on retainer. Tasha and Alex are about as slick and Teflon coated as they come, but all within the letter of the law. They can hide people. They've done it before. Secret deals. New identities. They're good. Really good. How much did you offer to pay them?"

"Enough."

"Tell me."

The man was like a snake, ready to wrap me up and strangle me. "I'm sure you'll get your cut." I stood up, looking for a blanket or shirt to cover myself.

Chapter 34

Jerry got up and took a step toward me. "Sweet Jesus, the prim and proper pictures on the news don't do you justice." He looked me up and down again. I backed away, crossing my arms over my chest.

A silhouette stood in the door as if right on cue. Alex Goldstein stood in the doorway in nothing but white cotton drawstring pants. He looked better out of his expensive suit than I could have ever imagined. If I hadn't been so pissed off a Jerry I might have gasped.

"Touch her and I swear I'll kill you, Jerry." Alex Goldstein looked as if he could freeze lava with his look.

"Don't threaten me, asshole." Said Jerry.

"What are you doing here?"

"You called. Said you needed help. Remember? I thought I'd make myself at home until morning until I found someone sleeping in my bed."

Alex turned to me. "I'm sorry. This is inexcusable. Did he hurt you in any way?"

"I didn't hurt her," said Jerry, obviously annoyed.

"Jerry didn't hurt me," I said, having second thoughts about coming to his defense.

"She is my guest and under my protection," said Alex.

Jerry snapped back at his brother-in-law. "Since when have you protected clients in your home? Alex, do you realize..."

"This is different," said Alex.

"No shit, but why'd you have to bring her here? The risk of anyone finding out is huge. Everyone in the country knows that face and voice," answered Jerry.

"She needs our help. The utmost discretion and privacy is required. We'll talk more in the morning."

"Do you realize how big this is? She's fucking Elizabeth Atkinson."

"I couldn't risk leaving her alone."

"Alex, if this gets out..."

"It won't get out. And Jerry, if you tell anyone about this your body will never be found."

"Got it." Jerry looked my way, "Who would believe me anyway? Right?"

"I need to speak to her alone."

"What about?"

"Client confidential. Go away."

"She's my client too."

"Do you want Tasha to find out about your affair with Judge Sorono?"

"Shit, Alex. That's low."

"8 by 10 glossy photos Jerry."

"I'll um, stay in the other room to make sure Shannon is safe."

"Good idea. Goodnight Jerry."

"Goodnight Alex. Goodnight darlin'. If you need anything, I'm right on the other side there." Jerry winked and blew me a kiss.

I was alone with Alexander Goldstein.

"Did he do anything? Hurt you? Make a pass at you?" Alex asked.

"We had a little scuffle, but I'll be okay."

"Are you sure? Do you need anything? Pain medication? Sedative?"

"No. I'm fine, really." I looked away, trying not to look at him. I didn't want to show him anything I was feeling.

Then I almost started cry for the first time since I was a kid, when my sister burned me with hot bacon grease. I started to shake and felt like I was going to throw up. Alexander wrapped his arms around me and I didn't push him away. I held tight, my arms around him and my head on his bare chest and tried to catch my breath. I could feel the warmth of his skin, the softness of his hair, and hear the beat of his heart. I shut my eyes, savoring the warmth of another and attempting to feel safe. For the second time in months I let someone touch me, and again it was Alexander Goldstein. To feel another human close to me, stroking my back, feeling his breath on the top of my head as he kissed my hair, did more healing than any drug or hospital stay. It wasn't a lover's touch or that of someone wanting something. It was the touch of comfort and caring. But my mind was always racing. I opened my eyes.

"I thought Jerry was Greg and I said I loved him. I said it so he wouldn't hit me."

"You're safe. Shannon," he gently called me by my new name, "Promise me that you won't run."

"I promise." I dropped my arms away. He took both of my hands and held them.

"Do you want to stay in the main house? There's a guest room right next to the master suite. Tasha will be right there."

"It's okay. I'll be okay here."

"Listen, we won't betray you. Do you understand?"

"What about Jerry?"

"He's a good man. You can trust him with your life."

"Okay."

"Yes, it is okay, Shannon. Get some sleep. You have a big day tomorrow." Alex gave me another quick hug and left.

I lay awake in bed for the rest of the night until the sky started to lighten up then I fell into a deep sleep.

Chapter 35

I woke to the smell of coffee. Was I at home? No. I didn't have a home. I pulled on my jeans and a shirt and wandered out to the kitchen.

"Your old diet will make you fat and kill you," Jerry said, "When you turn thirty, it will all go directly to your waist and your ass and you'll never know what hit you. Your butt will turn into a pumpkin and your tits will be down to your belly button. Right now, you're underweight. You don't need fat. You don't need burgers and fries, you need good lean protein and fruits and vegetables to build muscle. You need the right oils to get your skin and hair back into shape." He put something in front of me.

"What is this?"

"Egg white omelet full of vegetables topped with mango salsa."

"Is it spicy?"

"You gotta learn to eat spicy food. It keeps your metabolism in shape. The mango helps with digestion."

"I'm not picky, I just haven't tried a lot of ethnic food."

"This isn't ethnic. I bet there's a lot of things you don't like because you've never had it fixed right." He went on a tirade about nutrition while I picked through the omelet. "Eat the green bell pepper, not just the red."

"It's gross."

"It's good for you. Learn to love it."

I gagged it down.

It was the first morning in three months I'd felt like myself. I was having coffee with someone I'd never have had coffee with at home, but I felt at home, like I'd known this strange man for years. He had tattoos on his arms of horses running across waves and tropical flowers. His hair was streaked all shades of blond, tipped in white. Crow's feet made by years of playing in the sun and water were like sunrays coming out from the corners of his eyes.

Jerry used bad language that would have made him fit right in with the Hobbs kids. Unlike the Hobbs family, he was a walking encyclopedia of facts on health and nutrition.

I told him all of what I'd told Alex and Tasha the day before, but this time it was like telling a friend.

Alex came by, wearing black suit pants and a pale lavender shirt, his sleeves rolled up. He was taking off his tie.

"How'd it go this morning?" asked Jerry

"Five years probation and sixty hours of community service."

"Scumbag should have done time."

"You have the right to your own opinions."

"Come on, Alex..."

"You know I won't discuss any of my ongoing cases with you."

"You should have worn a white shirt."

"You should have your tattoos removed." Alex turned to me. "On Saturday, there will be a memorial service for Elizabeth Hobbs Atkinson. Hundreds, if not thousands of people are expected to express their grief and give support to your husband."

This was a surprise. "There shouldn't be that many people there. I didn't know that many people."

"As a dead woman, your life is no longer yours. You're a public figure now. Your life and picture have been in the public eye since you vanished. There have been search parties and prayer vigils. There have been countless interviews of your husband, family and friends on network and cable news. A foundation has been set up in your name to help families who have been touched by murder. Web sites have been devoted to you. Articles have been written. The next thing you know, your local state representative will be wanting to pass a bill called 'Elizabeth's Law'".

"I wasn't that important."

"Your family has publicly told the world how much they love and miss you. Your husband is reported to still be in deep shock and mourning. By the size of the search parties and the public outpouring on this, you're a very important young woman and well loved in their eyes. Thousands of hours have been spent by law enforcement and volunteers searching for your body."

"Do you want me to go back?"

"That's up to you. The service starts in three hours. We could stop it if you wanted to."

Reports of my death are greatly exaggerated. - Mark Twain.

They were mourning. I looked out the window and let the guilt roll over me and wrap me like a big scratchy burlap bag. As always, my family sucked the life out of everything I did, even my death. Even a thousand miles away, they could make me feel bad and make me feel like everything was my fault. I sat for a few minutes, staring out the window. Alex waited. Jerry waited without a word.

"It's too late, guys. I'm dead. I'm sorry. I didn't know it would be so much trouble for everyone, but... nobody would help me when I was alive. Nobody listened."

"I'm sorry," said Alex.

"After Diana died, I was alone. I couldn't count the times I reached out for help and was treated like a delusional child."

"I'm going to still assume you don't want me to call and let someone know you're alive and safe."

"I'm dead. Let's just leave it at that. Okay?" I drank down more coffee and looked at the two men waiting on me hand and foot. "Why are you helping me hide?"

"The burning question," said Jerry.

"I'm more valuable to you alive," I said to Alex.

"Why do you think that? Either way, I'm getting paid," said Alex.

"You could have a field day with the press. This could be the biggest event of your professional career. You'd be famous if you publicly represented me."

Alex sat down at the table next to me and took my hand. "My mother was in an abusive marriage before she met my father. She lived in Cuba, with her first husband. She tried to leave several times but her husband always tracked her down and punished her, much in the same manner your husband did to you. The first time she ran away, he beat her and as a consequence she lost hearing in her left ear. The next time she ran away, he beat her until she lost the child she was carrying. After that, she lost count of the injuries she received. Forget the ideology of equality; she belonged to her husband, body and soul. She escaped Cuba on a boat when she was only twenty years old and started a new life. Her former husband tried to find her, but she vanished off the face of the earth and was reborn as another woman with a different name, a new accent and a new country.

Like you, my mother has scars left on her from that first marriage. Her former husband is still alive. After forty-two years, she believes he still has his spies looking for her. I didn't even know her real name until a few years ago. I understand why you ran. I understand why you don't want to be found.

I also guarantee you that when your transformation is complete, nobody will be able to find anything out of order in the history of a sweet Florida girl named Shannon Gables.

If you choose to go back, I will stand by you 100%, but you will have to face the public and tell the world about the abuse at the hands of your husband, as well as your ordeal with Darren Crawford.

If you choose to start a new life with a new identity, you will never be able to go back to your old life or acknowledge that life. Either way, it won't be easy."

Jerry sat down on my other side. "Don't go back."

I got up and went to a mirror and looked at the scar on my face. I rolled my shoulders and could feel the skin on my back tighten where the whip had dug into my skin and left tight scars.

"If I decide to become Shannon Gables, what are the chances of my being found out?"

"Slim, but there is always a chance," said Alex. "However, that is up to you. Can you completely abandon your old self?"

"I've done fine for the past three months. What about the money? I can't carry around boxes of cash forever."

"No problem. I'll get it into an offshore account for you," said Jerry.

"I don't even know you guys."

Jerry came close and spoke softly, "Where's your faith? Come on Shannon, you didn't get here by accident. Fate, hand of God, karma, whatever led you here did it for a purpose." Alex sat back and let Jerry continue to convince me I was doing the right thing. "Do you know how many people would give their right hand for a chance like this – to start over completely from scratch?"

"What's in it for you, aside from the money?" I asked, not even thinking I didn't care what the answer was.

"The satisfaction of doing the right thing."

"Is it the right thing, Jerry? Alex?"

"This isn't a right or wrong thing. It is your choice," said Alex. "Either way, I'll stand by you and do everything I can to make sure you come out of this safely."

"Okay then, I'm staying."

"Are you absolutely sure?"

"I truly believe God brought me to you. It was no accident I dialed the wrong number."

"We won't betray you."

I took a deep breath and sat. "Now what?"

"We're going to Disney World," said Jerry.

"Shut up, Jerry," said Alex, and they both started to laugh.

We had a lot of serious work to do.

Chapter 36

That evening, Alexander came to the guesthouse. I expected him to be in his office but he was home alone. He put his laptop on the table and sat down.

"Arrangements have been made for your surgery. The scars on your arms and back will be softened and your face will be slightly altered."

"That was fast," I said. It was fast. The past forty-eight hours had been the fastest in my entire life.

"After tomorrow, there's no going back for you. When you look in the mirror, you'll see a different face."

"I'm okay with it. It's what I want." Actually, I was scared to death. Your face is who you are. I was going to change and though I had a vague idea of what I'd look like, I had no idea who was going to look back at me in the mirror.

"I want you to see something first, to make absolutely sure."

He opened up the laptop and showed me a news special that had been on earlier that night. It was all about my wonderful happy life with Greg and my fate with Darren Crawford. I closed the laptop.

"I saw it already," I said, frowning at him, hoping he'd get the idea that I'd left it all behind.

"It was a touching tribute. Greg was clearly heartbroken," said Alex.

"As well he should be," I said, holding back the anger that was boiling up inside of me. "Alex, you need to understand that my life is not going to be defined by Darren Crawford. I don't want to be known as the woman who escaped from the Killer of Virtue. My life is definitely not going to be defined by Gregory Atkinson."

He answered just as I expected him to. "Whether you decide to keep the face you were born with or become someone else, your life is how you define it."

"That's easy for you to say." It was easy for Alexander Goldstein to say. He had a wife who loved him, a thriving business, what seemed like a halfway sane family and as far as I could tell, not a scar on his perfect body. "Imagine living a life where you have no control over what you say or do or even think. When I was with Greg, I had no secrets, no privacy except for the abuse. Everything about my life was an open book for him to use in his sermons and lectures. Oh yeah, magazine articles too. Miscarriages, fertility issues, or my grocery shopping, what I read, what I watched on TV, our sex life, or at least the normal part of our sex life, were all public record. Now the whole world knows everything about me. Except the fact that I'm still alive."

"You can go back and expose Greg for what he is."

"Liz is dead. Let her rest in peace," I said, in hopes that he'd drop the subject once and for all.

"I understand. I just wanted you to be sure. You might not feel the same in a year or two." Alex was still calm to the point of annoying.

"I'm sure. Stop asking me about it."

His face changed from the lawyer to a concerned friend. "I saw the other video this morning."

"What other video?" I imagined some other piece of crap media about my family.

"The one Darren Crawford made of you and him."

My head went light. "What did you see?"

"Everything," he said, showing more concern. That scared me.

"What everything?" I asked.

"What he did to you."

"He did a lot of things to me. What did you see?"

"The video showed a little over six hours of unedited sexual abuse and an hour of other types of torture. Obviously, I didn't watch all of it. A few minutes were enough to make me ill."

"Is this public? The video?"

"No."

"Then how did you see it?"

"Some see me as an authority on serial killers. My opinion was asked."

"You, an authority on serial killers? Isn't that too much of a coincidence, Alex?" I snapped at him, really snapped for the first time.

He hesitated. It was the first time he wasn't ready to jump on an answer with supreme confidence. "I've written articles about being on the defense team of serial killers. I've lectured on the subject."

"Don't make me a case study."

"Don't worry, I'd already added my two cents worth to the speculation before you showed up at my office."

He'd always seemed so calm about everything. I wondered how shocked or surprised he'd been to see me. That comment hit me hard and he knew it. We sat staring at each other. I looked away.

"I'm a criminal defense attorney. It's my job to be an expert on criminal behavior. I know people who know people. I was given access."

"Who else is looking at it?"

"The tapes aren't public but someone, a crime writer, is already writing a book about Darren Crawford. She's a well-known author, Mandy White. I know you've heard of her, maybe even read her books."

I was at a loss for words and so angry that I didn't even respond.

"The fact that you're alive is amazing..." he stalled and took a breath. "I've seen a lot of horrible things, but what he did to you was pure evil."

"Why did you want to see it? Didn't you think I was telling the truth?"

"I've never doubted you."

"I didn't want you to see me like that." The idea of Alexander Goldstein seeing me naked, bound, with Darren Crawford touching me, forcing me to have sex with him, cutting me with a knife, and worst of all, hearing me beg – it made me sick. It was like being raped all over again.

He took my hands in his. I pulled away, curled up alone in an armchair on the other side of the room. We sat for a minute that seemed like an hour of deathly uncomfortable silence. "You violated me by looking at that video. You might have well raped me again." I said it just to hurt him; I was so pissed off.

His response was annoyingly calm and compassionate. "I heard your screams. You called out your husband's name."

"I would have called out to the devil if I thought it would have helped. Ever had a client who was the charming man who got away with everything and never spent a day in jail in spite of his crimes? Well, that's Greg. No matter what I say, he'll twist and turn it to make me look bad and make himself look like the good husband. I'm done with it. Done. I will not go public, ever."

"Understood. No food or anything but water for the next twelve hours. Alex kissed me on the cheek. "You aren't alone, Shannon. Good night."

Chapter 37

The next morning I looked at the face of Liz Atkinson for the last time and Tasha drove me down the coast to the resort-like villa where I was remade.

So this is where people come be reborn, I thought as I walked through the double front doors into the structure that looked more like something out of a Maxfield Parrish mural than a medical facility.

We were greeted by a woman Tasha introduced as Serenity. No kidding, that was her name. They exchanged air kisses and both seemed cool and calm. Honestly, I felt like a troll next to these two. Tasha looked like a fairy tale princess, all milk white in a yellow sheath dress with her magnificent bone structure and cascading blonde hair. Movie star gorgeous Serenity wore a spotless simple white dress that contrasted with her flawless coffee colored skin. Her hair was swept up and clipped on top of her head with white fresh daisies. Serenity's large emerald green eyes had to be contacts, but they could have been real. My perception of reality had changed so much over the past few months, that I might have well been on another planet.

Maybe I'd be beautiful in a few hours too. The feeling of calm and beauty was almost overwhelming, even for a jaded skeptic like me. At that moment I could feel the scar tissue pulling on my hands, arms and back. How could I not be happy to become someone else?

Serenity led Tasha and me to a large deck overlooking the Atlantic Ocean. A man stood facing the water, and then he turned as we entered. If I thought Alexander Goldstein was gorgeous, this man was beyond perfection.

He smiled and stepped my way. The man didn't look real.

Tasha was the first to make a move. She took his hand and kissed him lightly on the cheek. He smiled then turned back to me. "You must be Shannon. I'm Rob Goldstein. Alex is my baby brother."

It was then I found out the clinic belonged to Alex's brother Rob. He was the eldest of the Goldstein brothers, slightly taller than Alex, with brushed back black hair graying at the temples. His features were sharper, more chiseled and elegant. It was only fitting that he spent his days transforming people like me into beautiful and perfect creations.

My transformation had begun. I was now Shannon Amelia Gables, girl with a future.

In a comfortable examination room, Rob took my hands and held out my arms, gently touching the scars.

"Does that hurt?"

"It's sort of numb and weird feeling, kind of tingly and uncomfortable in some spots."

"Do you mind if I look at your back? Alex said you had scars there as well."

I showed him my back, the burn scar on my leg, my arms. He didn't ask about my situation, only gently about my physical appearance.

"What is your full name?"

"Elizabeth Ann Hobbs Atkinson."

"Your new name."

"Shannon Amelia Gables."

"Tell me in your own words why you want to change your face and become another woman."

Again, I told my story. Rob Goldstein listened quietly with an intense interest.

"Do you believe changing your face will help?"

"Other people recognize my face."

"Is that the only reason? How attached are you to your past?"

"Rob," Tasha spoke up, "Have you heard a word she said? You're talking to someone who has been through both physical and emotional trauma since the day she was born. She has overcome most of it due to the fact that she is an extraordinarily grounded and strong individual. I guarantee you that her choice is well thought out and grounded in reason."

"Tasha, this isn't your choice."

"We need to talk. In private." Tasha went to the door and motioned to her brother-in-law.

I was left alone looking at a before and after album of trauma victims made normal. There was also a good sampling of average looking people made beautiful and old people made to look younger. Rob Goldstein's work was extraordinary. Normally when you see plastic surgery, everyone has that weird stretched look like they've been in a fire or been hit in the mouth with a baseball bat. These people looked amazing and natural.

I thought about Brad and wondered if he'd ever get his nose straightened and if he thought of me when he looked at how crooked I'd made it when I busted it. Women were always asking him about it and coming on to him when he told them about the attack. Then he got tired of it all and married the first girl he ever got serious about. I liked her well enough but we never got close. Hobbs siblings never got close to anyone. I thought of how lonely she must be, living with Brad.

Brad's wife Sophie was pretty, like her name. But she'd never have her skirts blowing in the wind on a romantic desolate moor in some Gothic novel. She was a cheerleader and a Math major who taught high school math and was mother to Brad's spawn. The woman was a saint. I always wondered what she saw in my brother Bradley.

My brother Jordan could also use plastic surgery to refine his doughy face. I swear to God the boy was born without bones; just soft rubbery skin, spread over a weak frame like thick cream cheese icing. No muscles for definition, just pinkish-white butter and hardened lard. I was lost in deep thoughts of my family when Rob and Tasha returned.

Earlier, I'd told Rob point blank that I never thought of my family. I thought about them all the time but it didn't mean I was going to be Liz again, so it was none of Dr. Goldstein's business.

Rob sat down and asked me about how I would like to look and if I had any ideas. He had a lot of suggestions and at that point I really didn't care. I was numb with the exotic drugs called Alexander and Tasha. I was also frightened out of my mind and excited at the same time. Based on Rob's portfolio, I had nothing to worry about as long as he made me beautiful.

He led me to a monitor and showed me images of what I might look like after my surgery, depending on what he did. Right now, I wasn't beautiful but I wasn't ugly. I guess I could have been called cute and pretty if I dressed up and put on the right makeup. Okay, I'll admit I was kind of pretty, otherwise Greg would have never noticed me.

My eyes were my best feature, bright, almost glacier blue with a nice shape. My eyes would remain the same windows into my soul. The term made me uncomfortable but sounded so peaceful and perfect when Rob said it in his beautiful, masculine voice.

"Make me into a goddess, Dr. Goldstein." I wanted to say that, but I didn't. What I told him was, "As long as it looks natural. I don't want to be some stretched out looking freak."

He assured me the results would be completely natural.

Chapter 38

When I came out of the fog three days later, my face was still swollen. It would be at least a month until I'd know exactly how I would look. My hair was now layered, collar length and a highlighted ash blonde. My brows had been expertly shaped and colored to match my hair. My arms were bandaged where the scars had been made thinner and less noticeable.

Fat had been sucked from my cheeks and subtle implants made my cheekbones higher. My chin now was a little more defined with a small but obvious cleft in it. My nose was bandaged, but I'd soon find it was slightly smaller and straight and ever so perfect. A small brown mole on my left cheek had been removed. My teeth had real looking veneers. The slightly crooked top teeth were now as straight as if I'd had three years of braces. With my dry tongue, I felt a permanent retainer behind my teeth. My lips and blue eyes were the same, but it wasn't Liz who looked back. It was Quasimodo, or a bruised and beaten and bandaged woman called Shannon.

When the bandages came off of my arms, the angry, heavy scars were thinner. Soon they fade with age and only three were easily noticeable after a year. Nothing had been done to the scars on my hands, and as I'd requested, the scar remained on the edge of my jaw line where Greg had hit me with the belt buckle.

As the swelling went down and the creature I'd become emerged, I couldn't stop looking at myself in every mirror, window or other reflective surface.

Over the next few weeks I recovered in the clinic, reading, relaxing and thinking about what I'd do now. Each afternoon Rob would spend extra time with me. This lovely man was obviously nothing like my own pasty faced, bug-eyed, mean spirited, emotionally deranged brother David. The two men were doctors and carbon based life forms, but that was where the similarities ended.

I learned later that Rob Goldstein's wife had died in a car accident three years earlier, leaving him with a baby and a toddler. He had never remarried or had serious relationships with women. He built his clinic and with the help of family and friends, took care of his two small sons.

"When Ava died, I had to go on for my boys," he told me.

I thought he was going to mention Greg and what Greg might be going through with my loss, but he didn't.

"My little guys, August and Chase, miss having a mom, but they have a large support system. Alex and Tasha are like second parents to them."

"Do you think Alex and Tasha will ever have children?"

"Alex wants kids but Tasha," he paused, "I don't know if Tasha would ever want to share Alex with anyone."

I didn't want to pry too much or seem obvious, but over the next few weeks I learned quite a lot about Tasha Alexander and even more about Alexander Goldstein.

For example, I asked Rob about their mother. Yes, she was from Cuba. She'd come to Florida in 1959 and lived with a cousin. She met their father in the college library. She was in medical school. He was getting his graduate degree in education. He asked her to a jazz club. They were married six months later. It was her only marriage. She didn't have an abusive ex-husband. Nobody was searching for her. She never changed her name. She became a doctor. Their father was a teacher, then high school principal. Everything Alexander Goldstein had told me about his mother was a lie.

"Alex wanted to be a journalist since he was a kid. Every school newspaper from elementary school to college featured his work. His undergraduate major is in writing. Alex was going to go out into the world and document conflict and social injustice."

"What happened?"

"Tasha. He didn't want to be away from her. She was the best thing that ever happened to him. I can't imagine him traveling the unwashed world, finding the truth in dust and all of that." Rob shrugged his shoulders. "He still writes quite a bit, you know, about the law and crime."

"Do you think he'll write about me?"

Rob smiled and did a slight shake of his perfect head. "No, my brother would never write about you. You're personal now and he never shares anything personal."

That was a blessing indeed.

Chapter 39

Do not be anxious about tomorrow, for tomorrow will be anxious for itself. Let the day's own trouble be sufficient for the day. Matthew 6:34

When you decide you want to become another person, it is serious business. A good and discreet surgeon is required to take care of any scars or facial reconstruction. In my case, a vocal coach was needed for my regional accent and what I was told was a high, girlish tone. Something I'd never considered was my cultural knowledge base.

As Liz, I'd lived in a small world. I'd become a junior biblical scholar, an accomplished musician and knew little of the outside world other than what interested Greg. Most of what I'd learned from late night college talks in the dorms had long been forgotten.

Tasha gave me a pile of books to read during my recovery. Literature, popular fiction, history, social issues and politics, travel and science.

"Read one fiction and one non-fiction at a time. You're a smart cookie, so you'll get around to three or four a week. Some will take longer of course, you can skim some of the drier books," she told me. Along with the books were movies and magazines, and web sites to check out.

And then there was the food. I'd grown up on an exclusive diet of potluck fare, peanut butter sandwiches and institutional school lunches and dorm food. When I met Greg, my horizons expanded to include classics such as mixed greens salads, pot roast, regular roasts, ham and cheese omelets, and other basic cooked foods. The exotic went so far as the occasional baked Brie with fancy crackers. But other than that, I was a food ignoramus.

Losing my regional accent wasn't that hard, especially after I heard recordings of myself. It was losing my culture; the habits and patterns of my closed little world that I never even thought of.

At a high school, teens will speak their own language and slang. Certain professionals, computer geeks, government employees, people who work for certain unions or large corporations have their own talk. Some speak in strings of acronyms. Teens use the word "like" like every other word. Apparently it was my words not my accent that gave me away, at least according to Alex.

Alexander took me to lunch at a place overlooking the ocean. We sat at his usual semi private table and looked at the menu over cocktails.

I was feeling a bit odd, like Cinderella pretending to be a princess. The only problem was, I had no idea what time it was or if Alex would turn into a mouse at midnight.

"You're a beautiful woman, Ms. Gables," Alex said. "I noticed you can't pass a window without looking at your reflection."

"I bet you do that all the time."

He smiled. I'd caught him off guard. "Keep that our secret. I wouldn't want anyone thinking I'm vain. You feel healed then, at least physically?"

"Yes, praise the Lord."

He leaned toward me, grabbing my wrist. "Don't do that anymore."

"What?"

"Stop the church talk. No praise the lords, references to God's mercy, no Jesus talk. Your speech is to be purely secular."

"But..." I'd never even thought about how I spoke, aside from the regional accent.

"Shannon, I'm serious. If you're serious about your new life, you must stop making faith based references to anything."

"That goes against everything..."

"It goes against nothing. Your faith is in your heart."

"You're not a Christian, you don't..."

"I do know. My mother is Roman Catholic. Little Alexander Goldstein went to Mass every single Sunday and Wednesday. Don't tell me what I am or am not as far as my own faith is concerned. I'd tell you to stop making the sign of the cross if you were Catholic."

"I thought you were Jewish."

"I am."

"You just said you're Catholic..."

"If you want to be Shannon Gables, you'll have to grow up and face the fact that there are many different ways people feel about religion and their spiritual well being. It is a personal choice, no matter how unconventional that may sound to your narrow point of view. You must respect that personal choice and keep your opinions to yourself."

"I agree with what you just said, but I also believe that..."

"Believe what you will, but keep it to yourself."

"I can't."

"Then go back to Greg."

I didn't even know what to say. So I just looked at him I'm sure with a shocked expression on my face.

"Go back to your loving husband and your old life. Ah, but your old life isn't there anymore. You'll have to explain how a good Christian wife stole millions of dollars, and faked her own death. Tell that to the caring people who were involved in the massive hunt for you. Tell that to the people who spent their nights holding endless candlelight walks and prayer sessions because they loved you. They won't know the ungrateful little bitch ran off to Miami where she changed herself into a sexy blonde and she is now living the good life and spending her afternoons drinking cocktails and holding hands with her slick, expensive, good-looking married lawyer. One false word and you could end up in prison for a long, long time. You have to make some changes."

I suddenly felt flushed. "Okay, I get it." I thought about the last time I'd seen Greg. He'd said living for the lord and I said nothing.

"It isn't a matter of expressing yourself. It is how your express yourself as Liz versus how you express yourself as Shannon. Beware of practicing your faith in front of others in order to be noticed by them, because your public piety will give you no reward from your father in Heaven.

And when you pray, don't be like the hypocrite who loves to stand and pray in the churches, synagogues and in other public places so that they'll be seen by others. When you pray, Shannon Amelia Gables, go into your room and shut the door and pray to your Father who is in secret and your Father who sees you praying and by keeping your faith in solitude, you will be rewarded."

"Matthew 6:1 and Matthew 6:5," I said, "Interesting interpretation, Alex. I didn't know you were a biblical scholar. Matthew 7:15: *Beware of false prophets, who come to you in sheep's clothing but inwardly are ravenous wolves.*"

He let go of my wrist. I'd hurt him, maybe. I took a deep breath. I was ready to say I was sorry, but he spoke first.

"Greg was the wolf. Don't ever forget that, my darling little lamb."

He was right. I looked out toward the ocean. Now, I'd swear, but back then I didn't know how. He was right. I didn't want to admit it, but everything he said was right.

"Shannon, I'm not asking you to lose your faith. It isn't your faith. It is the cultural way you speak, as if you must bring God into everything. Your faith will show in the way you live your life. It will show what you do, not what you say. You lost your accent, now lose those cultural speech patterns.

Nobody will question the ugly scars on your arms or those beautiful blue eyes. What they will question first and foremost is your words. That will give you away faster than anything."

"So what do you believe?"

He didn't get a chance to answer me. Two men approached, both wearing expensive suits.

"Congratulations, Alex," one said, and they all shook hands. Alex had won a case that morning. He introduced me without a title. Nobody flinched that he was out in the afternoon with a young woman. He had won a big case. I was introduced as a family friend. Nothing more. Nothing was suspected.

"Why didn't you tell me about your win?" I asked, after the men left.

He gave a quick smile as if it was no big deal. "I'll be on the local news at eleven. Network news and cable, if my publicist does her job."

His client had killed his wife's lover in self-defense. They were a wealthy power couple – like Tasha and Alex. He'd convinced a jury that the husband was completely innocent; acting in defense of his wife, whom he thought was being attacked. But nonetheless, the public assumed the wife was a whore and not just an innocent victim of a slick and twisted Romeo. Funny how the husband had assumed Romeo was "just friends" with his wife before the day of the murder.

"Just like people will assume things about you if you speak like you used to. One day, something will slip out and your cover will be blown," Alex told me.

Then I thought about "just friends". Darren Crawford was just friends with me. He didn't speak like me. Neither did Diana. Neither did Greg when he was with his old college buddies or his family. But my mother's words were always full of references to God and Jesus and blessings. My siblings and I tended to do the same through the frequent swear words.

My words were the only things left of my past life and they could kill me if I used them. I started to feel sick and like a fool. I hated my mother, but I hated the snobbery of Greg's family. At the same time I wanted to be like his mother and sisters. I wanted to be refined and elegant. I wanted to be accepted, but as long as I was Liz Hobbs, in her Victorian inspired dresses, regional accent, lack of education and down home sharing of my faith, they would never accept me.

I hated Darren Crawford. I missed and hated Diana more than I'd ever missed or hated anyone or anything in my entire life, because if she'd said no to Darren Crawford none of this would have ever happened. And more than anything I hated myself for my living such a stupid life. I was twenty-six and I had no identity outside of my marriage and my childhood. Now I had no identity period, except... well, I didn't know what that "except" was. Except was mainly regrets. I had nothing but regrets. I wished I could cry. I downed half of the drink in front of me and looked back at the ocean.

"What's on your mind?" asked Alex.
I glanced back his way. "Nothing."

Chapter 40

"I have paperwork for you. Alex opened his briefcase and handed me a large envelope. "In here is your new birth certificate, passport, driver's license, credit cards, checking account, library card and even a Public Radio membership card. I've changed your age slightly but you still have the same birthday."

"How old am I now?"

"Twenty-four." He'd taken off two years. "It will be easier to cover up for the lack of a resume and education history. You're in a tourist state. It's easy for a pretty girl to have a blank resume. You could have been living with a rich boyfriend off the grid."

"Okay, so you made me into a slut."

"You could have been taking care of an elderly relative or doing seasonal work as well." Then he paused and just stared at me for a second. "Why is it, Shannon, that people like you take every little thing and throw it in the gutter?"

"What do you mean by, 'people like me'?"

He looked disgusted. I knew what he meant. "You could be a Jew or Muslim or one of any Christian denominations but a certain population is always prepared to take every little snippet of information and twist and turn it into something vile. What is that obsession with sex and religion? Pray tell, enlighten me, won't you Shannon?" He folded his hands on the table and waited for me to think up a response.

"It's just that... you made it sound like you wanted me to tell everyone I'd been some man's mistress for my entire adult life."

"No I did not. God, you're defensive."

"I'm sorry. I didn't come from the same world as you. My mother gave away my wedding dress a week before my wedding because she said I couldn't get married in white because I wasn't a virgin. It was my dream dress. I worked a second job to pay for it. After I had my miscarriages she told everyone it was because I was promiscuous before I met Greg. I slept with one guy, a total of two times. A guy I dated for a few months in college. I wasn't a whore."

"Luckily for you, Shannon, she's not your mother anymore. What she said was a lie then, and it is a lie now. Don't forget it."

"Good or bad, I had a life."

"Now, by your own choice, that life is over."

"But..."

"It is over, dear." He raised his glass. "Here's to your new life."

"How long will you be around, I mean for me, with me, in all of this?"

"Forever, if you want."

"You mean that?"

"Always." Alex kissed my hand. My head went a little light. Every time he touched me, something fluttered and made me feel like I was sixteen again.

"Why would you do that for me?"

"That's what friends do. That, and the fact that you paid me two million dollars to help you."

I studied the man sitting across from me. I'd gotten over the looks thing and tried to really see the man himself. With the suit, the office, the trappings of power, he exuded youth and vitality; he was either young, or he'd had work done. His hands, too, looked young and of course perfect like a hand model. There were no scars, no excessive hair, no moles or freckles, not a single flaw to give away any life experience.

"May I ask you a personal question?"

"Sure," he answered with a sunshine smile.

"How old are you?" I asked.

"Thirty-two. Six years older than you."

He was young. It didn't seem so young to me then but looking back now we were both young.

Jerry arrived and joined us. "Hey, beautiful," he said to me. "Alex."

"Jerry is thirty-six," said Alex, with a wink at me. "An old man by all standards."

We made small talk about the weather. The waiter came along and we ordered appetizers. Tasha showed up in a stunning form fitting yellow dress and matching sandals. Her blonde hair was loose and falling down her back.

She ordered a glass of wine then took control of the conversation.

"Jerry will be taking you to a location where you can set up an offshore bank account. He'll teach you how to manage your money and keep it safe. While you're at it, you might as well take a few weeks off for a vacation. We have a proposition for the two of you."

"It's just an idea," said Alex, "You can take it or leave it."

Tasha smiled and leaned toward her brother. "Shannon needs a history, so we think the two of you should get married."

"Whoa." Jerry pulled his hand away. "I'm not getting married."

"Just in name. Go on a trip. Have fun. Show Shannon a good time. You can learn to scuba dive and sight see, take a lot of pictures. I've already got you a house right on the beach with two bedrooms. When the training, I mean honeymoon, is over, the two of you come home. Shannon's mail comes to your house and she gets on the map. Then, after a few months, get a friendly divorce. Shannon gets a tax record, a credit history and a personal history. You get a nice trip out of it, all expenses paid, with a cash bonus when the divorce is finalized. Mind you, that is a six figure cash bonus."

"You guys," Jerry said, "This is a really stupid idea."

"Brilliantly stupid," said Tasha, "Congratulations on your engagement. Your flight for St. Kitts leaves tomorrow morning."

Chapter 41

Two days later Jerry and I were married at a small resort on St. Kits. It was at one of the resorts where we had lunch after a brief wedding overlooking the ocean. Then we drove to a beach house that was like something out of a movie set.

I took my guitar to St. Kits. I figured that was a good thing, since Jerry started drinking the moment we got to the house. He avoided me as he unpacked and played house with a bottle of rum and a blender.

"When are we going to get down to work? This isn't a vacation," I told him.

"It's our wedding night, sweetheart. I'm not working on anything." He looked at the guitar. "You going to play Kumbaya, or House on Pooh Corner?"

"Are you going to be a jerk for the rest of the month?" I smelled the fruit and rum concoction he'd made in the blender. There was only about a thimble full left.

Jerry grinned at me. "The good little girl wants a drink?

"You've seen me drink alcohol, Jerry."

"Sweet Jesus, I never thought I'd be married to a holy roller. Alex told me that he was worried about you, so he married you off to the Devil."

"Give it a break, will you?"

"Come to Jesus and praise the lord."

"Shut up, Jerry."

"Our first fight. How about some make up sex?"

"I'll never in a million years have sex with you. You're such an asshole, you know that, Jerry?"

"I didn't know you used four letter words."

"Asshole has seven letters."

"Wait. You're not going to have sex with me? It's our honeymoon, baby."

I poured a large glass of vodka, only half filled with ice, with about half a lime squeezed into it. Then I left Jerry and went out to the beach, glass in one hand, guitar over my shoulder.

I planted my drink in the sand and waited for the sunset. Jerry sat down next to me, took my glass and took a slug of my drink.

"How can you drink this? It's solid vodka."

I took my glass back and didn't say anything.

"I'm sorry I was a jerk. Can you forgive me?"

"I bet when you're out with your usual bimbos and sluts, you couldn't care less what they think about as long as it's about your dick."

"Sure, but since you're no bimbo or slut, I do care about what you think."

"Screw you."

"I don't like this anymore than you do. It was a stupid idea."

"It wasn't mine."

"Wasn't mine either."

I played some music.

Jerry took off his shirt and lay down in the sand next to me.

"You're good," he said when I was done.

"Alex and Tasha fight a lot," I said, waiting to see if he would give me any insights.

"They make up."

"Has Alex ever hit her?"

Jerry looked at me in sort of a strange way like I'd just told him I'd killed somebody. "No, he never hit her. What the fuck kind of question is that?"

"Did your dad ever hit you or your mom?"

"No. Real men don't hit women and kids. For your information, Ms. Holier-than-Thou, Alex Goldstein worships the ground my sister walks on. He'd die before he ever hurt her. What the hell is wrong with you?"

I started to get up. "Nothing is wrong with me. A lot was wrong with my family and my husband. I've never experienced what you call right."

"Normal people don't act like that."

"I've never been around normal people. I'd like to think that they aren't supposed to hurt each other but I've yet to see otherwise."

"I'd never hurt you. Sit down, Shannon. I'm sorry if I was a jerk. I'm nervous. I've never been in a fake marriage before." He patted the sand. "Sit down. None of us, my sister, Alex, me, will ever hurt you. We're on your side."

I sat back down but I refused to tell him it was okay or that I cared about him even one small bit. He'd done a lot for me, but I was so angry I wasn't about to give in.

Jerry put his arm around my shoulder. "Listen, darlin', the people who hurt you, they were wrong. They were evil. You didn't do anything wrong."

I wished I could cry. The pain came in a wave that made me want to throw up. I downed the vodka and hugged my knees up close to my body.

I looked at Jerry, wondering what he was thinking but I wasn't going to ask. He changed the subject and started to talk about the island and boats and sea birds. Jerry told me tales of the islands and the romance of pirates and musicians and deep-sea treasure hunts. He told me about how he and Tasha would run up and down the sandy Florida beaches as children, with amber colored tans and hair bleached white from the sun. He told me about how she'd fallen in love with Alex and swore it was a fairy tale come true. They were married on a yacht covered with flowers with both a priest and a rabbi and a string quartet playing Vivaldi. Tasha was the most beautiful bride ever to walk the face of the earth. Jerry was a natural storyteller.

Then he gave me his best charming, dimpled smile. "In your book, how long is a million years?"

"What?" I asked.

"You said you wouldn't have sex with me in a million years. Can I talk you down to maybe a hundred?"

"Maybe a thousand."

He smiled and leaned over and kissed me.

"How about now?"

"Now is good," I said, and kissed him back. "It's a fake marriage so it will be fake sex."

He tipped his head back and laughed.

We went back to the house. His skin was smooth, over a hard lean body. He went slowly, saying sweet things, always waiting until I would make a move. It surprised me, considering he was almost crazily active most of the time.

He was so different from Greg. There was no urgency or meeting of souls or violence. It was just two people in the warm ocean air, sharing kisses and small talk. We made love slowly and silently to the sound of the waves and our own breathing. It was so quiet and weird almost, being with this man covered with beautiful pictures, who talked of birds and drug busts and the constellations of the stars between kissing every inch of my body.

Jerry lay next to me sleeping, sweat still covering his chest and face. I dozed next to him, savoring what had just happened. I honestly hadn't thought I'd ever touch a man again as long as I lived.

He opened one eye and smiled at me looking at him. "Don't fall in love with me, Mrs. Alexander."

"Don't worry, I won't," I said as I reached out for him again and he laughed with a quiet Southern lilt.

The following week was a crash course in the art of hiding large amounts of money around without being picked up by the IRS or other enforcement agencies. We went over banks, creating and hiding accounts, moving funds around, laundering money and setting up corporations. We went over precious metal. I never knew how important having several safety deposit boxes could be just in case. We set up non-profit agencies so I could contribute money to my favorite causes, including the one I'd set up after Diana died.

Jerry also made sure I'd have several passports and documentation in other names in case I had to flee.

I thought he was going to jump on my back because the money was "stolen" but he never said a word, never passed judgment.

He was impressed that I was a mathematical genius (according to him) and could do all of the figures in my head, figure out the formulas and remember it all. Numbers were never an issue with me. I just had problems in the gray areas, which covered just about everything in my life.

The house next door is for sale. You should buy it. You can come here on your British passport if things get hot.

We went out and pretended like we were silly in love, then went back to the house and worked on the serious issues of getting my new life in order. In between, we made love with the windows open with only the sound of the waves.

Chapter 42

Back from the honeymoon, Jerry and I purchased a condo with an ocean view, set up local bank accounts and then filed for legal separation. Marriage had been fun but we were both glad it was over.

My coming out as Shannon Gables was a high-end charity event. I'd been to charity events before. Greg had picked out my one evening outfit, a white silk blouse with a long blue silk skirt. Even Greg's mother approved. If they'd found my body, I'm sure I would have been buried in it. My mother I'm sure would have protested had I been buried in my virginal white wedding dress. I wonder what Greg did with all of my clothes and belongings. I only hoped that my small collection of treasured vintage jewelry went to someone who appreciated it.

I wore a pale pink colored low cut dress with long, sheer sleeves. No backless or sleeveless dresses for me. It was form fitting and incredibly sexy. I was covered from head to toe except the front, where I was exceptionally naked, and the sheer sides that held it together. I know the description sounds tacky, but the dress was unquestionably classy and beautiful.

Jerry was in a suit, looking handsome and unlike himself. Apparently he had a closet full of suits for another life I knew nothing about.

He pointed out a tall blond man with broad shoulders. He was handsome, with those all-American good looks that reminded me of Greg. I felt a little sick.

In fact, I said to Jerry, "He looks a lot like Greg."

"Tom Mather. Worked his way through law school doing hits for rich husbands and wives who didn't want to deal with a messy divorce."

"Hits, like in killing people?"

"Yeah, just like that. Three or four a year paid for school, plus some left over for a comfortable lifestyle. Tasha didn't like him. She said Tom was the biggest asshole she'd ever met."

"You're joking, right?"

"I kid you not." Jerry's eyes stayed on Tom Mather. "He's a divorce lawyer now. He doesn't kill people anymore but he's still an asshole."

"Makes sense to me." I thought of how I should have maybe talked to someone like Tom Mather before I ran away. My problems with Greg could have gone away permanently.

"My sister had an affair with him. I told Tom I'd hunt him down and cut his balls off if Alex ever found out," said Jerry, as calm as could be.

"Tasha?"

"She's the only sister I've got. It was a long time ago, a few months after she married Alex."

"Does Alex know?"

"Not about this one."

"This one? There were others?"

"Tom wasn't the first or the last."

I said nothing, but watched as Tom Mather made charming small talk with Tasha and Alex.

"Are you shocked?" asked Jerry.

"Come on Jerry, why should I be shocked about anything anybody does? My best friend, Diana was tortured to death by her former lover, Darren, who hid his crime by becoming a serial killer. Then Darren raped me and tried to kill me as well, for the simple fact that my husband had advised Diana to go back to her husband. My husband, the guy who both physically and mentally tortured me on a regular basis and treated me like I was his personal property, was a Christian marriage counselor. I am a born again Christian, but I faked my own death, stole twenty-four million dollars and had my face completely rebuilt so nobody would find out. Then just for a fleeting second, when I saw tall and handsome, blond Tom Mather, I wondered if maybe I did still love Greg and wondered if this lie I'm living is a horrible mistake. But then I remembered that I'm sitting next to my new husband, an immature surfer dude who launders money to offshore accounts for a hobby. Jerry darling, I don't even like you, and I paid you to marry me. If that doesn't take the cake of weirdness, I don't know what does."

"I would have married you for free," said Jerry.

"You could have said no."

"You have a hot body and a bad attitude. I couldn't resist," he said with a wide grin. "Do you still love your husband?"

"Which one?"

"Atkinson."

"No."

We stood in silence for a while, watching the party below. "I love my second husband and he is now a dear friend to me, but if I had to live with the man I'd probably hire Tom Mather to kill him."

"You said you don't like me."

"I don't like you. Not one bit."

"I'll miss you when the divorce is final."

"No you won't. I'm so disappointed and sad about Tasha."

"She's not a bad person."

"Does she still cheat on Alex?"

Jerry shrugged and pretended to be interested in the ice cubes in his glass.

I'd never think the same about Tasha again. I was still torn about Diana. Her infidelities had caused her own death and the death of six other women. Sure, you could argue that it wasn't her fault, but how could I separate it?

"Tasha broke her vows to Alex."

Jerry nudged me with his elbow. "You're always so holy-rollerish about everything."

"I'm not a holy-roller."

"Are too," he said with a wide grin.

"Don't ever make fun of me or what I believe in again."

"Aren't you touchy tonight."

"Screw yourself, Jerry."

"I should wash your mouth out with soap!"

"I take marriage seriously."

"Does that mean I get to sleep with my wife tonight?"

"Fuck you, Jerry."

Alex came up and gave me a kiss and embrace. He still took my breath away. My face felt hot, feeling guilty about the attraction, especially after I'd snapped about Tasha. At the same time I was so sorry for him.

He held me at arm's length. "Shannon, you look amazing."

"Can you tell it's really me?"

"Only because you're standing next to this fool." Someone called Alex's name and he excused himself.

Jerry watched Alex move away. "You're in love with Alexander Goldstein."

"I'm not in love with him."

"He's like, the best looking man who ever lived. How can you not be in love with him?"

"He's married to your sister."

"Come on, she cheats on him all the time."

"Does he cheat back?"

"No. Never. I don't think so. But you could be the first if you really wanted to. Alex is obsessed with you."

I walked away from Jerry. I couldn't believe him, after I'd spent weeks with the man. After I'd slept with him. I felt dirty.

Jerry followed me. "Come on Shannon, I was just kidding."

"Marriage means something to me. You make it seem like a joke that Tasha cheats on Alex."

"It isn't a joke. It hurts me a lot. Jesus Shannon, do you think I like it? It kills me. It kills me to think my sister is a cheating slut. It kills me to think how much it hurts Alex. I love Alex. He's the best guy I ever met. He doesn't deserve this, but there's nothing I can do about it so I joke about it. This is my way of dealing with it."

"You could talk to her."

"I have and it didn't make any difference."

"It should have."

"Well it didn't. Not all women can be as fucking perfect at you are. You're so God damned judgmental."

Jerry left me alone to feel bad about myself. He'd hurt my feelings, something I wasn't going to show to him.

I walked around, making smiles at people, filling up my drink over and over. I didn't see Alex or Tasha anywhere. Jerry had hooked up with a couple of women who seemed fascinated by every word he said.

I stood by an open window and looked over the crowd, wondering why I was there. My eye caught the eyes of Tom Mather. Without so much as a smile, he walked my way.

I spoke first. "Sorry I was staring. You look a lot like Greg Atkinson, the guy with the murdered wife."

He took my arm. "We need to talk."

I'd had too much to drink and unfortunately started to talk. "I know what this means. You want to break up with me don't you? All kidding aside, what do you want?" I thought my heart was going to jump out of my chest. He'd found me out.

We went out the door onto a balcony. "What's your game?" he asked, so coolly and calmly I thought I'd die of embarrassment.

"Excuse me?" I answered with all the innocence and ignorance I could muster.

"What is going on?"

"I'm a little drunk. I'm pissed off at Jerry."

He cracked a smile. "Get in line. Everyone is pissed off at Jerry."

"What do you mean by my game? I don't have a game."

He pushed up my long sleeves. I could see the reaction in his eyes when he saw the scars. "Sorry, I was looking for track marks."

I jerked my arms back. "Track marks? I've never used drugs in my life. What do you want?"

"Listen, Alex means a lot to me. I don't know who you are or where you came from…"

121

"Oh, that's funny. Still screwing Tasha behind Alex's back?"

He stopped in his tracks. Apparently this wasn't public knowledge outside of Tasha and Jerry.

I was on a roll. "Do you make it a habit to sleep with other man's wives?"

"An unfortunate mistake on my part."

"Alex is my attorney. I met Jerry and Tasha through him. We enjoy each other's company. End of story."

"Jerry's a lucky man."

"Too bad I filed for divorce last week."

He handed me his card. "Call me if you ever need anything."

"Anything?"

"Anything and more."

"I'm Shannon Gables, formerly Mrs. Jerry Alexander."

"So I heard." He was a little shorter than Greg, but the resemblance was frightening. "If you fuck with Alex, I swear I'll come back and kill you myself. I don't have a good feeling about you, Ms. Gables; I don't care if you were married to Jerry or to the President of the United States. You're bad news."

"I'm sorry you feel that way."

"So am I. Don't lose my card."

Tom Mather turned and left through the crowd. I saw him leave alone in a white convertible. So that was Alexander Goldstein's best friend. What an odd and protective man. It was still scary and weird how he resembled Greg. Then again, I guess anyone could resemble anything. Before my surgery I looked sort of like a pretty young Dolly Madison. Now I look like a cross between a Waterhouse painting and a 1960's Nordic sex bomb. No matter how I looked, I just felt stupid and wanted to go home.

Chapter 43

At one point we all dream of starting over. We dream of leaving a bad marriage, or job we hate, or a place we hate. We believe the possibilities would be endless if only we could start fresh. For some, those with a plan, and those with relentless determination, it works.

I had a new life. I had money. I had no idea what to do with myself as Shannon Gables. Endless shopping sprees and crazy nightlife wasn't my idea of fun. Sure, I took cooking classes, read a lot of books I'd never imagined reading and tried to keep busy. Then I found my new passions were really my old passions.

The first was genealogy. It didn't matter that I despised my own biological family because I'd created a new family.

In antique stores I'd find old photos from the nineteenth century. Once home, these anonymous people of the past would be given new names and added to my family tree. With a little bit of imagination and editing of old documents one can really screw up the ancestry sites. The branches of my tree were carefully manicured and clipped so that lines of ancestors died off before possible modern descendants would find them.

If you looked me up, you'd find my past. I even made a branch that reached out and attached to Alex Goldstein's family. He found it amusing that our seventeenth century ancestors crossed paths.

In, what I thought was a brilliant move, I started to link Gregory Atkinson's family to men who'd murdered their wives. With any luck, someone would make a connection.

"Oh Shannon," Alex would say, and then laugh. "You have to do something to make yourself useful."

He stopped by one afternoon while I was busy making up alternative histories for people I didn't like.

"Shannon, dear, I want you to come with me. I want you to meet some of my friends," he told me. He wouldn't tell me anything else.

This wasn't cocktails on the beach. Alex took me to a part of town I would never have gone to on my own. I was the only white girl for miles.

Hand painted shop signs were in English and Spanish, yelling out in bright colors, alternating with boarded up buildings and garbage-strewn lots. As we turned into a residential neighborhood I saw small houses, some in bright colors; most were shabby but kept clean. It reminded me of neighborhoods where I grew up, where every house had a car on blocks, and a couch on the front porch. Eventually we stopped at a school.

Alex got out of the car and took off his tie, then rolled up his sleeves. "I come here once a week to work with the kids. I help them with whatever they need. They mostly just need someone to talk to," he told me.

My purse always contained a book so I figured I could read, or pretend to read while he was doing his thing. I felt so out of place and so shallow.

I could hear Alex speaking Cuban accented Spanish to the parents and grandparents, English to the kids. He'd hold the hand of a mother or grandmother while he told of progress then in turn listened intently to each word the woman said back to him. Their words were important to Alex.

A lot of the kids didn't like the idea of being here, but Alex was an effective tutor and had a way of convincing teens that the "way out" was through education and training, be it college or vocational training.

He worked with other kids who'd run away to the dream of Miami from up north, just like kids run away to Hollywood, thinking they'll get a modeling job or the good life and end up on the streets. Reality was never the same as it was in the movies. Now they needed to go back to school, graduate and get on with their lives in the real world – not as victims but as strong adults.

The runaways were the kids I could relate to. Most of them came from homes where they were abused and neglected. I knew what it was like to feel unwanted. I knew what it was like to make excuses for bruises and cuts. Funny that none of the Hobbs kids even considered running away an option.

"I'm helping them now so I won't have them as clients later." Alex told me. He looked at me with those deep brown eyes under the insanely thick lashes and my knees wanted to buckle. I was standing in front of a saint. A tall, sexy saint.

Alexander Goldstein didn't need a church to tell him to be a good person. He just was. He told me he went to "church" with his parents (each to their own house of worship) because the ritual calmed him and made him feel like he belonged to something larger that he couldn't and wouldn't explain.

I could have become a volunteer full time and helped kids and battered women, but I didn't. If I had, this story would be over and I'd be living comfortably in a bungalow in Miami, sipping tea with my neighbors and doing good deeds. But like all good cockroaches, my only concern was my own survival. I would have liked to have been pure of heart, maybe I was, but my soul had been beaten black by my family then finally ripped out of my body by Greg. More than likely, I was just born that way.

I'm not a good person. I made everyone think I was a good person, but there was little human kindness or charity in my soul until I met my friends in Charleston, then Alex, Tasha and Jerry.

I did charitable acts and acted kind and sweet and nice because it was expected of me. Sure, nobody could quote scripture as I could. Nobody feared God as I did. But Alex, the tormented soul that he was, the shrewd attorney and slick charmer, was a good person. He was pure of heart. Okay, at least it seemed like he was pure of heart.

As we drove back to my condo I said a quick prayer (the hypocrite I was) in hopes that I was right and that Alex was indeed pure of heart and a good person.

Chapter 44

I fell into a nice life of leisure in Florida, unlike anything I'd ever imagined. I moved out of the pool house into the condo I'd purchased with Jerry. It was complete with a beach view and no Jerry.

The lawyers didn't want me to move out of the pool house, but it was time. On most nights Tasha arrived home late. Alex would sit by the pool with a bucket of ice, a bottle of vodka, a few cut up limes and me. We'd drink and talk about everything under the sun and moon. I swear sometimes I'd feel like it was the best time of my life. Why wouldn't it be? There I was with a smart, insanely handsome, intelligent, entertaining man who didn't ask anything of me or expect anything of me.

I'd get tired from the booze and go to bed. Then Alex would sit alone, drinking by the pool until around midnight. Next I'd hear him fighting with Tasha after she came in. Then through the upstairs bedroom window I could see them, clothes coming off, entangling in each other's arms, naked, perfect and passionate. It was more than I wanted to see.

After I moved I still saw Alex and Tasha almost every day. When Jerry was in Miami he'd sometimes stay with me to show off his new ink and try to get sex. After a while I told him to stay with Alex and Tasha. After Jerry invited himself in one night and found Tom there, he never came back without calling first.

Tasha took me under her wing as her little pet. Don't get me wrong; I enjoyed the mantic sort of friendship and all of the superficial trappings. Even with her lead, I'd never had more fun or more freedom in my life. Not to mention, I'd never had control of so much money.

Tasha was always there for me in her calm and condescending way.

She'd tell me I looked "cute, like a stay at home mom trying to be fashionable." Or, "You know you'll never have a successful relationship with a man."

I think my turning point with her was the day we went to a day spa with two of her girlfriends. They were both successful professionals like Tasha. I thought it would be fun.

During pedicures Tasha mentioned the only reason I married her brother Jerry was because the sex was fantastic. I was caught so off guard with the statement and the resulting laughter that I said nothing. Then it got ugly.

Tasha picked up a magazine, one of those tabloid sort of celebrity rags that everyone finds in the grocery isle or in waiting rooms. Inside was a story about Greg Atkinson and his search for answers. Tasha showed her friends the page with a photo of Greg and me taken two years ago.

"She must have been remarkable because I have no idea how a man that good looking could love a woman so utterly frumpy," Tasha told her friends with such sincerity.

"Maybe he liked the way she looked," I said.

"Some men like fat girls," said one of the friends. Considering I am five foot five inches tall and weighed a hundred and twenty pounds when the photo was taken, I didn't consider myself fat.

"Her nose is lopsided," said friend number two. "Damn, she was one ugly housewife. I guess love is blind."

Then the subject changed. I went from being average in a cute sort of way to being ugly. I felt flushed and wanted to flee. Instead, I stayed and pretended that Shannon was the only person I ever was.

I thought about the time Tasha and I were talking to Rob Goldstein over cocktails one night out by the pool. It was a lovely evening until Rob said, "Alex told me you sing."

"Yes," I said.

Then Tasha broke in, "Shannon has a unique sound. Sort of like a cross between Billy Holiday and a frightened kitten. Very sweet, in a gritty little girl sort of way. Um, Shannon, could you excuse Rob and me for a minute? I have to talk to him about something." Tasha took her brother-in-law's arm and led him away to an undisclosed location. I had no idea where she came up with that description of my voice. Oh right, unjustified spite and malice.

Private conversations with Tasha always led back to Greg. She wanted to know everything about him – all of the intimate details that were never published in the press. The woman seemed obsessed in a weird calm, cool way that was almost creepy.

Like the good little Hobbs girl I was, I lied. I made up stories I knew Tasha would want to hear about kinky sex. It was all she seemed to be interested in. She'd always ask in such a concerned way, as she put her hand on mine and looked into my eyes like my own fairy princess girlfriend. I knew better. If Tasha thought she could tell me lies, I could tell them a hundred times better.

With a straight face, I told her that Greg would have me dress up like a clown and force me to give him blowjobs. I'd tell her about the strange places he'd want to have sex, like on the pulpit of our church, or on top of a row of hot dryers in a laundromat. I told her that Greg could have an erection that lasted three hours. I gave her the sick and twisted fantasy rape stories she wanted to hear.

I wanted to ask her if she liked to tie Alex up and beat him but I kept my questions to myself. I didn't want to know the answer.

So why did I stay friends with Tasha? The reason was simple. She knew who I was. She could easily ruin my life with one call to Greg or the press or even the police.

Alex assured me that Tasha adored me. I let him believe her lies. After all, he'd believed her for years.

In the meantime, I'd become better acquainted with Tom Mather, Alex's best friend, Tasha's ex-lover and now my source for information about the partnership of Alexander and Goldstein.

From Tom, I learned that Tasha was a serial cheater from the day she married Alexander Goldstein. In turn, she considered Alex hers and hers alone. He was her property and she'd made an investment in him that had paid off a hundred times over. Alex, on the other hand, tried to ignore the fact that he was sharing his wife. He was devoted to her and to their practice. He had wanted children but she ignored him. As for his fidelity, he'd cheated once or twice in the beginning but had stopped. It was too much of an emotional toll for him. Theirs was an unusual relationship and in my view it was repugnant, but then again nobody was tortured or abused. Well, that wasn't completely true; Tom told me he thought Alex was in an abusive relationship.

"How so?" I asked him.

"He won't leave her. Nobody with a normal healthy self worth would stay with Tasha."

"He loves her. They have a good partnership."

"Business. It is all business."

"What if he met someone else?"

"He has met someone else, more than once. He would never act on it."

"That makes him a better person."

"That makes him a fool. What kind of rock have you been living under, Shannon?"

Like with Tasha, I acted naive around Tom. Despite my suspicions, I didn't want to believe Alex would allow Tasha to torture him the way Greg had tortured me. He was successful, whereas I was a failure. Alex was someone I admired. How could he be abused? Sure, she might have cheated on him, but I'd never seen her with another man. Plus, it appeared they had sex all the time, at least that was what it looked like from the pool house.

They were like a finely tuned machine at Alexander & Goldstein. The media ate them up on the occasions they had spotlight cases. Their PR people were working full force to get the young, attractive couple out front and center.

When Tom asked about my past, I produced a couple of snapshots I'd found in a junk store. One was of a small blond boy and girl. The other showed the same children with two other girls. I told him what would now be my story, of a life on a boat in South Florida with a hippie drug abusing mother and occasional father of Irish origin. There were rumors that dear old dad might have belonged to the IRA and run to America to hide, but I never knew if it was true or not. We never went to school and quickly scattered after our mother died when I was sixteen. I earned my keep with music. I hadn't seen my brother or sisters for years and had completely lost track of all of them.

To back it all up, I had a complete profile of it all on every ancestry and genealogy website I could think of. I linked my family to dead family trees with no modern ancestors. It wasn't like I didn't have anything else to do except create family trees. Of course, Tom did a background check and let me know in a smug, self-serving way that he was watching me anyway.

Through his extensive research, and my meticulous foolery, Tom found out that I had a mother named Karen and a father named Michael. My siblings were Sean, Erin and Kathleen. My mother was dead. The location of my father and siblings was unknown. I didn't really care where they were, or at least Shannon didn't care where they were.

On the other hand, Liz kept close watch of her five living siblings and what they were doing. I followed the news. I made fake profiles online to keep tabs on bulletin boards and social networking sites. God forbid any of them went looking for me. They'd never find me, but I wasn't going to take any chances. But the real reason I kept watch was because I wanted to hear bad news about them. Aside from Jordan, I wanted them to fail.

Tom Mather asked me a lot of questions about my family. I remembered my lies in case he asked again. I had the entire story in my head as if I'd lived it my entire life.

Tom was such an asshole but I was impressed by his loyalty to Alex.

Chapter 45

My relationship with Alex was simple, natural and complicated. We became friends, like old friends who'd known each other all of their lives. We'd talk for hours, with Alex often taking my hand in an unromantic way. We talked twice a day. I was still his responsibility as far as he was concerned. When Greg surfaced in the press with stories of missing women, talks on love and marriage or other bullshit, Alex would call to let me know that it I was in the right and that someday karma would take Greg down. I didn't believe in karma but it was sweet of him to share the thought.

That was the simple and natural part. The complicated part was that I was finding myself feeling smothered by Alex. The more I wanted to pull away, the more I wanted to stay. While it angered me how Tasha treated him, at the same time I was glad she was there, controlling his heart so I wouldn't have to "go there".

While I rarely saw Alex noticeably intoxicated, from 6:00 pm to midnight he had a drink in his hand or a bottle of vodka nearby. Business and social lunches all included cocktails or a glass of wine. I knew he kept a well-stocked liquor cabinet at his office. The booze was never a problem but it was always there.

Late at night I'd watch him sitting by his pool, alone with a bottle and a glass of ice. I'd wonder what he thought about. I wondered whom he thought about. Tasha had a thousand girlfriends, or so it seemed. I knew Alex had friends, but when he wasn't working he chose to be alone.

Fast forward to the wonderful new world of Shannon Gables...

It had been seven months since I'd arrived in Miami. Thanksgiving was right around the corner and I'd been invited to spend it with the Goldsteins.

Chapter 46

In Miami I took a few cooking classes in order to become the new and improved Shannon Gables and learned to make a wonderful orange cranberry sauce. I put it in a bright red glass bowl and garnished it with a flower made of shaved lime and orange peel. Over the river and through the woods, to the Goldsteins' house I went.

The Goldsteins lived in a sprawling one-story house about an hour out of Miami along the coast. The grounds were covered with lush everything. This, I thought, was what the Garden of Eden must have looked like and Alex's parents were Adam and Eve.

Rob, the same Rob who'd rebuilt my face and fixed my scars, greeted me at the door. He was, as always, kind, and seemed genuinely happy to see me. He took a look at the red bowl and told me he couldn't wait to try it. I almost looked behind me to see if he was talking to somebody else.

With a gentle hand on my back, he took me aside for a minute and inspected my new face.

"How are you, Shannon?" he asked, taking my hand the same way Alex always did.

"Great. I still like my face. It looks real. Feels good."

"How about emotionally, with the holiday and all?"

"I'm great. Holidays don't mean much to me. But people do, so I'm very glad to be here."

He took my breath away even more than Alex did. He was an angel as far as I was concerned. "I'm so glad you made it," he said, then kissed me on the cheek.

Tasha appeared out of nowhere with a smile, casually dressed in a patterned brown skirt and cream colored lightweight sweater set and bronze colored flats. Sounds frumpy, but she made it look like the sexiest outfit on earth.

"You think he's attractive?" she asked me.

"I'm alive, of course I do. But not in that way. God no. He's like a brother."

"Good to know. Rob is damaged goods. Even more than you are. Don't get involved with him."

A few weeks earlier, the comment would have been like a slap in the face, but I'd come to terms with Tasha's toxic remarks. She was constantly implying I'd do something stupid. No man could love me. No person could find me attractive, even with all of my surgery. I had no worth outside of her and Alex. It would be her burden to make me into someone worthy to be in her company. Part of me, the sick and twisted damaged part, wanted to believe she was doing me a favor. The other part of me knew better.

Arthur and Isabella Goldstein, Alex's parents, greeted me with hugs and kisses. They knew who I'd been and the entire story. Alex had brought me over months before to meet his mother. She'd taken me to church with her on several occasions. I'd brought my guitar over and played her favorite songs to her, and I'd brought it with me today by her request.

Isabella and Arthur were physically stunning like their three sons. Philip, the youngest of the three, was as handsome as his brothers. Arthur was tall, with steel gray hair, sharp features and smiling hazel green eyes. Isabella was small, with large dark brown doe eyes with thick lashes, like a princess out of a fairy tale who had grown up to be the wise and beautiful queen. She was always smiling and touching and hugging. I swear, a day with the Goldstein family was like a day in a monkey farm. They couldn't keep their hands to themselves – but it was nice.

The children were a joy. Phil and his wife... other friends... perfect day...

"You've been a good project for Alex, "Arthur told me. "Shhhh – I won't tell anyone. You mean too much to us. The children love you. You're like a little sister to my boys."

"Well then, how do you see yourself? Henry Higgins or maybe Dr. Frankenstein?" Of course, as soon as the words left my mouth I felt like a fool and wished I could take them back.

"Dear God Shannon, how do you come up with this stuff?" Alex said. "Shannon has always been there inside of you waiting to come out. I just gave you permission."

How different Alex was from Tasha or anyone else I'd ever met.

Chapter 47

Through Alexander's encouragement, I began to rediscover my music. I also discovered an up and coming guitar maker named Royal Knight. He lived in California, the land of milk and honey and movie stars, and soon I had an order in for a custom guitar.

Royal Knight was laid back about life and passionate about music and his craft. He was also about to be kicked out of the building he'd been in since he opened three years earlier. The building was going to be sold and all six businesses on the block were to be evacuated. Royal needed help, so I bought the building.

It was a turn of the twentieth century two-story structure in Sacramento, California. Not exactly the land of movie stars but it was the land of music and art and year round good weather.

I flew out to Sacramento to see my purchase. The building was unremarkable but it was in a busy area of friendly businesses and quaint houses.

I walked through the door of Royal Knight Guitars. Standing in a showroom full of beautifully crafted guitars was Winter Knight, Royal's younger sister. I'd seen her picture, but in person she was even more glorious in her own weird way.

She was tall with the shape of a Barbie doll, a long lean face with a nose and mouth that were just a little too big and a little crooked. This was set off by masses of dark crazy curls, intense robin egg blue eyes, skinny jeans, black boots and a military/steampunk style jacket complete with a full set of Victorian military medals, and gunmetal gray nail polish. Her eyes were lined in Cleopatra black with fake lashes. Sounds awful, but it worked in a weird sort of highly successful way that most women would envy.

Royal Knight had the same intense blue eyes and black curls. He was quick to smile and totally down to earth and comfortable. I'd only heard about people like the Knights. There was always an agenda with my Miami folks, and before them with my family, but I never felt that way with the Knight family.

There was a third Knight sibling, Chaste Knight. He went by Chase and was anything but Chaste, according to Winter. While Royal and Winter worked the day to day operations of the company, Chase was the man behind the publicity machine, getting a Royal Knight guitar in the hands of every up and coming musician and every old guitar player of any consequence.

I soon discovered Chase's idea of a perfect date was a six pack of beer and a girl who liked to do it leaning over the hood of a car – any car – any girl. Believe me, there were plenty of girls willing to accommodate him.

I asked the Royals why they didn't have their own building. The all shrugged and said it worked out where they were. They had plans for later, but for now they were happy in their location. I'd never met three more content, laid back, happy people in my life.

And it wasn't for the love of Jesus or money or a romantic crush that made them happy. They were just happy for the sheer sake of life itself.

I settled into an unoccupied comfortably shabby chic apartment in the building for the night. There was a knock along with the front door opening. Chase Knight came in wearing a concert tee shirt from a band with a lot of zombies and tropical flowers on it. He had a six-pack of microbrew and a couple of burgers and fries.

"I thought you'd be hungry." He smiled and made himself at home.

We ate and talked about the neighborhood, the guitar business, beer, and the weather. It was all good. Then he leaned back in his chair and asked, "Want to fuck?"

"No." I said flatly. What an idiot.

"I can appreciate that," he said, without a hint of surprise in his voice.

The door burst open again. Winter came into the room with a couple bottles of wine and a large pink box. "I brought a cake. Hope you like cake. It's chocolate."

"Everybody likes cake. They'd be insane not to," I said. I made a mental note about door locks, bells and the fact that the Knight siblings had no sense of personal space.

Chase raised a beer. "To cake." We then all toasted cake.

Over the next twenty minutes the entire neighborhood came by. There was charming Jeff and his puppy from the coin and antiques shop, next came Sage-Marie and Karma from the frame shop, Big Josh and Katie the accountants, and Ben, the owner of the bar two buildings down. Everyone brought food and drink. An hour passed with the warmest and most down to earth people I'd ever met. I was getting a slight buzz and on my second piece of cake when Royal Knight came in with a small child under each arm and a plump pretty blonde woman wearing a black leather skirt and fishnet stockings. Like Winter, she somehow made her mashed up style work. She was Jillian, Royal's wife, along with Zoe, age two and Mason, age four.

The next morning, Winter took me to the local coffee spot, filled with hipsters, artist looking folks, landscapers, well-dressed men in suits and people wearing scrubs. We sat on the patio; actually it was the sidewalk and watched the morning rush. There was something about this smaller, slightly artsy city with a sense of community that I liked.

Winter gave me an intense look and said, "You should move here. I mean, you don't seem to fit into the Miami scene, at least from what you've told me."

I shrugged.

She didn't take shrugs for an answer. "You'd fit in here. And we're close to everything. San Francisco, Tahoe, Napa, Yosemite, Mt. Lassen."

"Mt. Lassen?" I asked.

"Mt. Lassen Volcanic National Park. Just north. When I was a kid you could see it on a clear day. Amazing place."

"I'd like to see it," I said. I'd never even imagined seeing a volcano.

Winter took a sip of her coffee and a bite of scone. "This summer, I'll take you. But you gotta move here."

Royal expressed the same sentiments with a twist. "That whole thing with Boris and Natasha is just creepy," he said about my relationship with Alex and Tasha.

I had to defend my saviors. "Alex and Tasha, and they aren't creepy. Where did you get that idea?"

"You can't wipe your ass without talking to him." Royal was never subtle with his words.

"Just say what you really feel, Royal."

He gave me a look of brotherly concern. "You're in love with Alex. It's all over you. You gotta get away from him, Shannon."

"I'm not in love with him."

"I'd be in love with him if I lived in Miami. But Shannon, we're all in love with you, so you have to move out here. You can double date with my sister. But not with Chase. Has he asked you to, you know?"

I told him about Chase's proposition the night before over beer and burgers.

"Yeah, that sounds like my brother. He's such a horn dog. Next time just hose him down and hit him with a broom."

135

Chapter 48

Deciding to give Sacramento a go wasn't hard. Telling Alex and Tasha was another matter. They were my creators and the only people aside from Jerry who knew who I was. They were my family. Despite Tasha's cool bitchiness, Jerry's crazy manic personality, and Alex's overprotective smothering, I loved them. I honestly believed they loved me. But it was time. I'd found them because of fear. I found Royal and Winter out of passion for my music. Then I found a friendship that wasn't based on anything except common interests and enjoying each other's company.

It had been a little over a year since I'd thrown myself off of a bridge and vanished off the face of the earth. I continued to see articles written about Greg, as well as articles written by Greg, in major magazines and on websites and blogs. There were also interviews on TV and radio from the tragic and brave man who could love a woman like no other. It made me sick but I followed it like the sick and twisted girl I was.

Packing wasn't difficult. There were a few clothes, most of which I'd leave at the condo. I took my satchel and laptop with my few precious photos and journals. I could get clothing when I arrived. I shipped my guitars directly to Royal's shop.

Alex came by, obviously just from work, still in dress shirt and tie. His sleeves were rolled up, something that makes men look sexy as hell. Don't ask me to explain. It just is.

"What is the real reason you are leaving?" He sounded so formal, as if I were under an oath of law. "Did we harm you or make you want to leave?"

"You've been amazing. I just need to be on my own…"

"With a new group of strangers."

"No. It just feels more like home or where I want to be right now." There was a long uncomfortable pause.

"I'll be back every few months".

He took my hand and gently pulled me into a hug. "I will miss you."

I put my head on his chest and could hear his heartbeat. I could hear Darren's voice: "I will cut out your heart and send it to Greg." I involuntarily gasped and backed away. "I have to go someplace where nobody knows about me. I need my own life."

"You have a life here."

"You have a life with your own busy law office and your wife and your family and friends."

"You're part of that."

Then the bomb dropped out of the sky. I didn't even know I'd pressed the release switch. "You're married."

He looked confused then it hit him – hard. "What does that have to do with anything?"

"Okay, nothing I guess."

"Have we done something to offend you?"

"No. Of course not." Yes, I lied a little bit but that was okay. "I'm keeping my condo here. I'll be back to visit every few months. We'll still talk everyday. Like, every single day Alex. I'm not going away forever."

Alex stepped away from me and walked over the sliding glass doors and went out on the balcony. I followed. He turned to me, of course for dramatic effect.

"Shannon, before you go I have a favor to ask."

"What?"

"I know a woman who needs help, like we helped you. I need a woman to help me with this project."

"I'm not going into the business of rescuing people. Tasha can do it."

"No, Tasha can't."

"Why not?"

"Tasha and I are known to the people she is escaping. You're a stranger. You're a woman. I need a woman."

We discussed the situation for another half hour and I agreed to help. Our damsel in distress was another woman with an abusive husband, in a no win situation. Divorce wasn't an option. Death was the only solution – or at least a faked death and new identity.

"So what happens to her after she dies?"

"She can't stay in Florida. I figured she could eventually move out to California. She could be like a sister."

"I had a sister. I didn't like her."

Alex gave me a sly smile. "You won't like this one either. It will make it more real."

A week later, Jerry and I headed to California in a rented motor home. I left most of my clothes in the condo in Miami. The only other things I brought were my car, a box of books and old photos I'd picked up at antique shops, and my four guitars.

I watched Jerry hook up the car. He looked up at me when he was done and grinned at me.

"What?" I asked.

"Hey Shannon, what's the difference between a Porsche and a porcupine?"

"I don't know Jerry, you tell me."

"The prick is on the outside of the porcupine."

"Funny, Jerry."

"That is a ridiculous car."

"I like it. We gotta go."

Unknown to Jerry, Alex and Tasha was the bit of Liz I'd kept with me. In my satchel were two diaries. One was from my teen years. The other was from the few months before my untimely death. In a brown envelope were photos of my brother Steve and me. Along with the photos, in a scratched up plastic jewel case was a CD marked family. Those were the photos Jordan had saved from Steve's camera the night he died. Mark thought he'd destroyed the images when he crushed the camera. He was too stupid to think that Jordan had removed the memory card. I also had my charm bracelet, a small reminder of one family member who'd seen me as something other than flawed.

Jerry and I ate our way across the country. We stopped at every barbecue joint, local ice cream shop, and fruit stand. We gorged on burgers and fries, tacos, coffee, and milkshakes in every flavor imaginable. At night we'd camp in luxury. During the day we'd drive, only stopping for food. The two exceptions were the Grand Canyon and Las Vegas.

In the Grand Canyon, we hiked for a day and took a lot of photos. I swear I couldn't open my eyes wide enough to take it all in. In Las Vegas, we opted out of camping and stayed in a five star honeymoon suite at one of the luxury hotels. It was the only night we fooled around. It was kind of weird and sad in a way. The last stop before Sacramento was Lake Tahoe. As we started the drive down through the mountains to Sacramento, I knew I was home.

Chapter 49

I spent my fifth anniversary as Shannon in Miami.

Life had been good. Really, it had. I had a home, business interests, a band, and a wide circle of friends in Sacramento. I even went back to college. Every other month I flew out to Miami. When Tasha had meetings in San Francisco I'd meet her there for the weekend. Best of all was that Alex and I talked every single day.

My anniversary week was low-key, just like any other visit. On the final night, Alex came to my condo carrying a small coconut cake and a bottle of vodka. We sat on the balcony enjoying the cake and vodka, like friends who'd known each other for decades.

In the soft light his profile was a perfect outline. How could someone live like that and not be conceited? Alex looked over and smiled.

"Stop staring at me, Shannon."

"You're so perfect." It was said as a humorous joke but it was true.

"Are you seeing anyone?"

"Not really," I answered. "You know, just when I feel like it."

"Friends with benefits usually just benefit the man. Remember that."

"You're so sexist. I can't get attached, Alex."

"Can't? I doubt that." He lifted his glass. "To love. Love that is and love that is to come."

I lifted my glass. "To love. If such a thing exists."

I didn't ask. He didn't say anything else about it.

That was the way it was for Alex and me. We could sit for hours and more or less talk about nothing, or we could solve all the problems of the world. It really didn't matter which one.

So five years had passed. I was still Shannon. I still talked to Alex at least five days a week. I kept in touch with Tasha and Jerry.

Over the course of five years I'd managed to get a college degree with a BA in Art. I opened a vintage photography studio and gallery next to the guitar shop and learned how to make tintypes and daguerreotypes. Three of my former college classmates also used the studio for their own portrait work. Royal invited me to join his band. Life was good and fairly normal. I guess.

I'd purchased a beautiful two-story house that was way too large for one person, but I couldn't live in a little apartment over a guitar factory forever. What the house gave me was privacy, something I never had until I became Shannon.

Next I found a beach house on the Central Coast of California. I let my bandmates and friends stay there when they wanted to. Life was good.

So why did I feel so restless and out of sorts when I arrived home from Miami? It was good to be home, but nobody greeted me at the door. I didn't have anyone I even needed to call. Not even a dog or cat was home to greet me. I ordered a pizza and opened a bottle of Zinfandel. It was okay. I guess.

The next morning I turned on the radio while I was fixing coffee, just like I always did. A familiar voice came on. No, it wasn't Scott Simon. It was Greg Atkinson, being interviewed by Scott Simon. He had a new book out. Then he said the title. *To Elizabeth With Love.* I stepped over to the sink as my stomach cramped.

As I bent over the sink expecting to lose whatever was left in my stomach from last night's lemon chicken, I heard Scott Simon's voice, drenched in emotion. Then I listened to Greg's voice, likewise drenched in emotion.

Then everything hit the fan.

"Scott, I want to believe that somewhere, somehow, Liz is still alive," said Greg.

I gasped; a high-pitched noise came from my throat. He was looking for me. I knew he was still looking. My head felt light. I had to get out of the house. I had to get to the bookstore.

I had known this might happen but I had no idea how upset I'd be. Catching my reflection in the window, I almost panicked.

As I crossed the parking lot and looked up at the store window I thought my legs would go out from under me. There was Greg's handsome smiling face beaming from a large poster, and I was, with long ringlets, in a pale yellow sweater set, standing right next to him. Large red script spelled out, *To Elizabeth With Love.*

Inside of the store the display for *To Elizabeth With Love* was huge. I looked into my smiling eyes and felt my stomach cramp. Aside from my thinner face, a dimple in my chin and a straight nose I really didn't look that different. I took one of the books and held it to my chest.

Next I grabbed a few other books, mysteries I'd planned on getting anyway. The woman who checked me out mentioned how much she loved Greg's books. I just gave a weak polite smile.

"You look a little bit like her."

"What?"

"Elizabeth Atkinson. You have the same eyes."

Oh, she had no idea what a stomach cramp she'd just given me.

After checking out, I drove to my studio. Nobody was scheduled in so I figured I'd do busy work to keep my mind off of Greg.

It wasn't enough that he'd exploited my death for five years already. He'd published nearly a dozen books about building a good marriage. Now he'd put out front a new version of my life with every detail he could either remember or make up that he could jam into four hundred pages. Along with his outpouring of love and attempt to make me into a saint, and more so make himself into a saint, were dozens of photographs of our life together.

I kept telling myself that I'd left it behind.

I barely made it to the studio without getting sick again and called Alex.

"Goldstein," he answered.

I kicked the table and dumped over my favorite coffee cup, it broke on the floor. I snapped up the art books on the table.

"Crap." A broken piece of cup with kitten face design looked up at me.

"Shannon? Are you all right?"

"No, I'm not. I am so pissed off right now."

There was a silence again. Alex and I could do that.

"Did you see the book? Did you know about *To Elizabeth With Love*?" I almost hissed out the words, I was so angry.

"Greg had no respect for your privacy when you were alive, so this shouldn't surprise you."

I didn't know what to say. There was more silence.

"You're not Liz anymore. I thought you were happy with your life."

"I am happy with my life when I'm not being stabbed in the back by my best friend. You knew that book was coming out today. I know you knew."

"Stop going into hysterics every time Gregory Atkinson writes a book and mentions Liz. We just celebrated your new life. It is time to bury Liz once and for all."

"Okay Alex, I get it. Thanks for your support."

"Don't be mad at me. You spend too much time thinking about him. If he is on television, you see it. If he is being interviewed on the radio, you listen to it. If he is in print or on the Internet, you read it. You own every single one of his books. I wouldn't be surprised if you've secretly seen him in person at one of his lectures."

"This one is personal."

"It is all personal for you. Every single time he is mentioned in the media you act like this. And forget the media, the way you stalk him and your family I'm surprised you didn't know about the book in advance."

"I don't stalk them."

"You're on your sister's Facebook page. You're in her online reading group. You're friends with your brothers in their online sports groups. You follow them on Twitter. How many fake profiles do you have now? Ten, twenty? You need to stop."

"Fine, Alex. You always know best."

"Your sarcasm is not appreciated."

"Greg is a bad person. Why do people love him?"

"You know the answer to that question."

"I have to go."

I hung up. And then added asshole.

By then I was angry and hurt. He'd never brushed me off like that before. Okay, he had, but not when I was upset like that. He called back. I didn't answer. I didn't check the message he left.

I put a be right back sign on the gallery door and headed down the street for coffee. I didn't need it, but the nearest coffee place where I could get coffee to go with minimal interaction with another human was five blocks away and I needed to walk off the steam.

Sure, I'd made up a bunch of fake names and stalked my family members online. Everyone does stuff like that. How dare Alex scold me for being curious? I knew what all of the Hobbs spawn were up to. I looked up their profiles on every social media site I could find. That included Greg's family. There was nothing wrong with that.

I stopped midstep and closed my eyes. Alex was right. I had to stop. I had to forget about Liz and Greg. I had to forget I was ever part of the Hobbs family. I opened my eyes to the empty street and started to walk again.

I heard a "Hey, excuse me."

I had stopped in front of an Italianate style Victorian house. There on a scaffold between the first and second floor was a man. "Good morning. Would you mind handing me that brush? In the flower bed by the rose bush."

A man wearing wire rim glasses speckled with paint and worn out Metallica tee shirt and ripped up jeans looked down at me. He was so bright and happy. It was almost as good as seeing a puppy.

"Thanks." He took the brush and swung his legs around on the scaffolding and faced me.

"You're doing a great job," I said.

"Your face says one thing and your voice another."

I was puzzled.

"You look like you're mad. Don't like the color?"

"No, I'm sorry. I really like the color. I just had a bad morning."

He climbed down and held his hand out to me. "Laurence Yantz."

Giving his hand a slight squeeze, I said my name, "Shannon Gables."

Laurence said it was great to meet me. I smiled. He smiled. We chatted a bit about the building. He was restoring it for his law office and for now was living upstairs. He went back to painting and I went on my way.

On the way back I brought him coffee and cranberry scones. I guessed that he liked it with half and half but no sugar. I was right. From there we decided to meet for dinner.

The evening was casual with dinner at local brewpub. I wore jeans and a black wrap around sweater. He wore jeans and a gray button down shirt that went well with his hazel gray eyes.

He said he was an attorney. He was a defense attorney. Go figure.

Conversation was easy and fun. I kept it light, until after we'd finished our meal and were working on cheesecake with fresh blueberries.

"So Laurence," I asked, "Have you ever defended a serial killer?"

"No. That's pretty rare."

"Would you have defended Darren Crawford?"

"The Killer of Virtue. It would have paid well. No, I wouldn't have worked with him."

"Nine women in nine months. Seven were to cover up a revenge killing of his mistress and her best girlfriend. Think they'll ever find the body of Elizabeth Atkinson?"

"I don't know. One of these days some hiker or dog walker will find a skull or some other fragment of her."

"Her husband has made quite the cottage industry out of her death. I'm sure her disappearance was the best thing that ever happened to him."

"You're going to go straight to Hell for saying that, Miss Gables."

"Surely you jest."

"No, I'm not jesting. He gives most of the money to helping family members of murder victims, so you have to give the guy a break."

"I guess. He just seems so phony to me."

"Most women think he's hot."

I laughed and took his hand. "Most women haven't met you, Counselor." And with that, I got my silent and very private revenge on Greg.

Laurence blushed and we finished our cheesecake and ordered coffee. We were done with serial killers and Greg and all things horrible.

He asked me about my past. I told him I'd been married to a wild and crazy guy in Florida and we were still friends. I told him that except for Jerry I had no family. They'd scattered and died and I was fine with that because I'd lived for so long on my own.

I told him that I was twenty-nine when in fact I was thirty-one.

Laurence was thirty-eight, divorced with two daughters named Bekka and Brynn, who spent half of their time with him and half with their mom. He had nothing bad to say about his ex-wife and she had nothing bad to say about him. She had cheated on him, but the marriage was so broken that he was almost relieved and gave her the opportunity to break free of him. They divorced for the girls, who were now doing well in school and liked the new stepdad. He admitted that he liked the new stepdad too.

He walked me to my car and kissed me goodnight. Then I drove home, thinking maybe I'd finally had my revenge on Greg. I could be happy.

Chapter 50

At home, I poured a glass of wine and sat down with *To Elizabeth With Love*.

I read the first chapter then threw the book across the room. Then I picked it up and read until it was almost time for the sun to come up.

For obvious reasons, trust is a big issue with me. It doesn't matter that nobody in their right mind should trust me, but you know, my circumstances aren't exactly normal.

There always comes that time fairly early into a potentially serious relationship where you have to have one of those "we need to talk" talks.

This one was a Laurence's house. We'd been together for about four months. I'd met his girls, his ex-wife, his best friends, and his parents. He'd met Jerry, Tasha, and Alex, plus Royal, Winter and everyone in my circle. It was good. Everything was pretty normal, especially since he had no idea who I used to be.

I walked in the door already pissed off.

He'd texted me, "We need to talk."

It was just another Friday night at home with his girlfriend with a movie and pizza. I'd brought a bottle of wine and brought it to the kitchen. I didn't pour any, just in case I decided to leave.

I started the conversation. "My ex-husband Jerry Alexander told me you'd done a background check on me."

Caught. Laurence actually looked surprised.

I continued, "My friend and attorney Alexander Goldstein also informed me you'd been asking about me. Do you have a background check done on every woman you think might suit your needs?"

"It isn't what you think," my boyfriend said, with only a slight tinge of annoyance.

"It's okay if you're curious, but you could have just asked me."

He paced around the island in the middle of the kitchen and looked at me.

"What did you find out about me, Laurence?"

"Not much." He shrugged his shoulders.

"Don't lie to me. I bet you found all sorts of interesting information."

"You're right. I found out a lot."

"Like what?"

"You made the highest score in math on your SAT and GMAT. Almost a perfect score on everything else."

"I'm a smart cookie."

"It just surprised me."

"Did you think I was just some dingy blonde?"

"Well, no. I just expected you'd be doing something else with scores like that."

"Like what? Engineering?"

"You own an art gallery."

"Right, nobody told me that only slackers own art. By the way, I run a daguerreotype studio and antique photograph emporium, but I guess you could call it an art gallery in your ignorance."

"You had a 3.9 GPA. You finished your degree program in three years. But Art? You could have…"

"I could have done a lot of things, but I followed my passion. What else did you discover that you don't already know?"

"You're a wealthy woman."

"You already suspected that."

"I knew you owned a building and your home. I didn't know you owned an entire block of buildings, houses in Tahoe and Moro Bay, plus half a dozen properties in Florida. You also have an impressive investment portfolio. You don't have any outstanding debt. No house payment. No car payments. Where did the money come from?"

"I'm good at math."

"Obviously. Looks like you and Jerry put together quite a portfolio in your short marriage."

"I've had to take care of myself for a long time. I saved everything I ever made. I've had to learn to be resourceful."

"Any off shore accounts?"

"Did you see off shore accounts in your reports about me?"

"No. But you have associations with off shore corporations."

"I've diversified. What is the deal with you? Every 401k has foreign investments. Listen Laurence, I'm not looking for a man to take care of me and I'll never go after your assets, if that's what you're worried about."

"No past history before you were an adult. I couldn't find anything about your family."

"There is an entire subculture of people who live off the grid outside of the normal system. I didn't even have a birth certificate or a driver's license until I was in my twenties."

I stood there watching him. He just stared at me. Then he took off his glasses and cleaned him on his shirt.

"If you aren't going to wear your contacts you shouldn't be cleaning your glasses with your shirt."

Laurence put his glasses back on. "Thank you for the sage advice."

"Sure, anytime."

"Your life is a bit unconventional."

"My past is unconventional. My present life is about as dull and conventional and middle class as it gets. Live with it."

"Where'd you learn how to play the guitar?"

"I picked it up when I was a kid. I've been taking lessons from Royal Knight for the past five or six years. It is perfectly normal for someone who plays a musical instrument to want to do better. What is your problem?"

"I love you."

"Excuse me?"

"I love you. I want to build a life with you."

"You sure?"

"I'm sure."

I could almost believe my own lies. "Oh Laurence, I think I'm going to fall in love with you too," I told him. That wasn't a lie.

Chapter 51

Laurence asked about my family. I'd already made up that story as soon as I'd found a photograph in a thrift store of three small children playing on the Florida beach. It was oh, so easy and natural for my revised history to slide out of my mouth. To make it really real I had documented all of it in obscure corners of the big online genealogy web sites. I made sure that everyone I was related to was dead.

I told him my canned story. "I grew up on a boat with my mom, and my brother Sean, and sister Erin. Mom was an earthy hippie sort of boat girl. Erin, Sean and I were born on the boat, the Manatee Princess. We never saw our dad much. He was from Ireland. I'm sure he has another family over there. We were just by products of a six-year fling he had with my mom.

I'm not sure what my mom did to support us. I think a little odds and ends work, a little drug running, maybe a little family money. I know she sold pot.

We never went to school because we never stayed in one place. Mom was always moving from one port or dock to another. Sometimes we'd go off to an island. Mostly stayed in Florida.

When I was sixteen we went on a trip to St. Thomas. Sean stayed behind in Florida for a job. Erin went off with some guy to New York, or maybe New Mexico. I don't remember. Mom got sick in St. Thomas and died in the hospital. I didn't want to end up in child protective services or be slammed for hospital bills, so I left. When I got back to the Manatee Princess she was gone. Someone had taken the boat."

"Shannon, I'm so sorry. What did you do? Did you have any family to go to?" I could see the concern in Laurence's eyes.

"There was nobody and I didn't know where Erin and Sean were. Anyway, I met two guys on the dock. Rich guys in their early twenties, just out of college with lot of family money. I'd just lost my mom and didn't have anything except my purse and the clothes I was wearing. They took me in. We sailed around for a couple of months and they dropped me off in Key West."

"They just took you in?"

"Sure. They were nice guys. I didn't do anything I was uncomfortable with and they treated me with respect. They were there for me when I missed my mom. When we got to Florida they gave me $1,000."

"Who were they?"

"Beau and Don. I never got a last name. Never asked."

"Did you have sex with them?"

"What? No. Does it matter? I was sixteen and alone. My mom had just died. Don't judge me."

"When I met my ex-husband Jerry, he was able to get me the documents I needed to be legal, through Alex and Tasha. That's how I met them. I was a natural at doing research, so they hired me. Jerry and I got serious fast and married. That worked out all of four months. We're still friends."

"So you're alone now?"

"Of course not. One is only alone if one feels alone. Are you done asking questions? Because I'm done answering them."

Chapter 52

"Danny Jackson Dewitt is a sensitive young man caught in a web of violence and mistrust, trapped by his ex-wife, her brothers and their attorneys into a living hell." That was what Alex told me about my next potential sibling.

"Aren't you being a little melodramatic?" I asked. Danny Dewitt was the last person on earth I would have expected to be risking my life and comfort for.

I had become famous after I died, but this guy was exceptionally famous alive. He was the most famous person I'd ever thought I'd meet and once he vanished he'd be even more famous. I wondered if he'd be as famous as Elizabeth Atkinson, considering the franchise Greg had created in my loving memory.

No, DeWitt will fade away out of the public collective memory, I thought, but I could only selfishly hope he'd settle into big time missing person lore along with Amelia Earhart, D.B. Cooper and me.

Danny Dewitt was the thirty-four-year-old soon to be ex-husband of an heiress pop star diva, Kayla Rutledge. He'd married her because she was beautiful, exciting and she said she needed him. He was smart, sweet, and sexy. At the time he seemed a perfect compliment to her public image. We all knew her public persona had always been the sweet, flirty, candy pink pop idol.

Anyway, Danny had given her life a slightly normal tone and in return he got to sleep with her for the rest of her life. When he couldn't take the insanity of her fairy tale life anymore, he left.

That was an almost fatal mistake. Kayla's manager, her brothers, her attorneys and other members of her entourage came after Danny. Nobody hurt Princess Kayla. Nobody would tarnish her image and their bank accounts.

In order to get Danny to change his mind about his soon to be ex-wife, they chased Danny down in their fast cars and ran him off the road. They sent thugs to beat him up and humiliated him, especially when he spent time with other women. They convinced the press and paparazzi to invade his privacy. Danny was subjected to hidden cameras in his bedroom and hacking on his computer, not to mention his garbage cans and mail box being robbed. The cyber attacks in social media were relentless.

To make the transition to his new single life, he asked people to stop calling him Danny, and asked to be called Dan. After his bank accounts were drained by unknown sources, he changed his social security number. He started to be summoned to court for traffic violations he never committed, so he changed his driver's license number. He moved, time and again, but they always found him. They found his new bank accounts, they stole his identity, they vandalized his house and beat him up.

Distant cousins, old classmates and past coworkers were harassed – nobody he'd ever had contact with was safe. He called the police but there was nothing he could do. There was never proof that tied anything to his wife. Or at least nothing that he'd report to the police.

Kayla refused to sign the divorce papers and held up the finalization with any legal means she could. Dan's attorney mysteriously quit. He found another attorney who had the balls to take on his case. He too was threatened but this one didn't wince. It got ugly. Kayla went public with false accusations of mistreatment and a broken heart. Women came up to Dan in public and slapped his face, calling him a monster. His half sister he'd only met half a dozen times left a phone message saying she was ashamed to be related to him.

About eighteen months after he was legally separated, bad things started to happen to women Dan dated. One was driven from her job and moved out of town due to excessive phone calls and stalking. Another was slapped around and sexually threatened by a couple of men, who told her they'd cut off her nose if she ever saw Danny again. A year later, a young woman he'd dated for a few months was killed in a hit and run accident. At this point Dan thought he was going to have a nervous breakdown.

By chance, or maybe in my jaded opinion, "an act of God", a well meaning acquaintance he'd met at a high priced charity event, who happened to be Tasha Alexander, had asked Danny to come to a charity golf tournament in Florida. It was for a good cause (prosthetic limbs) and Danny could partner with her husband, Alexander Goldstein. The event would be in public, so nobody could hurt Danny and he'd look good in the press. He agreed to go.

Alexander Goldstein just happened to mention to Dan that he occasionally helped people who wanted to start over. The attorney and his firm had a flawless reputation. Everything was in perfect legal order, well respected, successful and most of all, confidential in every sense of the word.

In the meantime, aside from Greg's annual book publications, which all had at least one chapter about me, I never thought much about my former life as Liz Atkinson. At least not for the past year or when I checked his web site about once a month or when I was feeling pissed off about his success at my expense.

Laurence and I had built a relationship upon love and trust and my lies. His girls and I became close. It turned out he had known Tasha for years. They'd met while working on one of their justice programs for former foster children. To make it all perfect, Tasha approved of Laurence and my relationship with him. Life was finally good.

I was in love with Laurence. We'd just returned from London with Alex and Tasha on what was the most magical, romantic trip I'd ever imagined. Laurence had asked me to marry him. I told him I needed time, but I was floating on air in love, with hints of anger trying to figure out if I was going to say yes, and how he'd react when I told him I was not who he thought I was.

Of course, Tasha was excited and already planning our wedding. Visions of fluffy white dresses and orchids filled our conversations. Well, at least filled her side of the conversations. Alex was a different matter. He made it clear that marrying Laurence would be a mistake. I wondered if marrying anyone would be a mistake according to Alex.

The following day Alex and I spent a lot of time exploring in the cold rain while Laurence and Tasha kept their activities to pub hopping and shopping. While standing at a window at the Victoria and Albert museum, watching the storm outside, Alex and I talked of art and what it must have been like to have lived in Victorian times.

"Structure was important. God only knows if we would have met. Do you think you could have escaped from Jack the Ripper?"

"I would have escaped and killed him," I said. 'Then again, I wasn't a sad, bottom of the gutter prostitute so he wouldn't have gone after me."

"You're just a runaway wife captured by a slick Miami attorney. We would have been star crossed no matter what time in history we would have met," said Alex.

"Star crossed?" That was an odd expression.

We looked at each other, close; our eyes locked. I put my hand on his chest. His lips brushed the corner of my eye, then the top of my head. He held me close in his arms.

"If Laurence ever hurts you, I will kill him," Alex whispered.

No one else was in the gallery, or even in the universe at that moment. I didn't pull back or stop. Voices came into the adjoining hall and we stopped, stepped back from each other, then continued to explore the museum's lesser-known galleries. Nothing else was said about the moment. That night I made love to Laurence, but my mind was still in the museum. To this day, I can still see the small painting of a dog, whose eyes seemed to watch Alex and me, and an angel in a stairwell who guarded our path.

Three days after we returned from Europe, I got the call from Alex. He said he was going to help Danny Dewitt in a few months' time. I told him good luck, then made a few snide remarks about Danny's bad reputation as tabloid fodder and forgot about it. I had other things on my mind, like figuring out if I was ever going to tell Laurence about my real past and trying to imagine how he would react to such bizarre news.

Alex and Tasha made me promise that if I ever told Laurence about Liz Hobbs Atkinson that they would be there. They'd make sure it would go smoothly and safely.

Life went on. We started planning for our next trip with Alex and Tasha. Laurence's practice was thriving. I was completely content with my life. The band was playing every other weekend and I was getting ready for a full schedule of photography shows at my gallery. Alex and I still spoke every day. Tasha dropped by on her monthly west coast spa and shop till we drop weekends. I had my friends. All was well in the world. Well, at least until Alex called much too early one Wednesday morning.

It was 4 am. "I need your help," Alex said, in a serious business voice.
"Are you okay?" I asked
"Never been better."
"Are you sober?"
"Yes, Shannon."
"Do you know what time it is here?"
"I imagine it's still dark. Are you alone?"
"I'm alone. What is it?"
He filled me in on Danny. I was supposed to meet him in San Francisco at 3:30 pm. It was a two-hour drive from my house, that was, if there was absolutely no traffic or road construction. Unfortunately there was always traffic and road construction so it would take forever. Damn.
"You know, Alex, I wasn't supposed to meet with him until next month."
"Danny wants to do it now."
"Why now?"
"He feels he is in danger. You, of all people, know how that feels."
"Okay fine. I'll rearrange my entire life..."

"What do you do besides play around and pretend you have a business?"

"Screw you, Goldstein. I have a real business."

"A hobby that someone else manages for you."

"I have my own life. I'm in a real relationship."

"What you have with Laurence is a lie."

"He loves me."

"He loves the abundant sex and the fact that you bring excitement to his otherwise ordinary, mundane life. He is so God damned smug and self serving, it makes me sick to see you fawning all over him like a sixteen-year-old girl."

"Why are you being such a jerk?"

"He's using you."

I stopped cold. "I guess you'd know what it's like to be used by someone," I said.

"Let's not go there, Shannon," said Alex, the anger starting to edge on his voice.

"One of these days you are going to have to go there. You're such a hypocrite."

"Are you planning on ever telling Laurence who you are?"

"Sure, about the same time you tell Tasha to keep her panties on and stop screwing other men behind your back."

There was silence. Things had been tense between Alex and me since our return and Laurence's proposal, but never this bad. I wondered if he was still on the line.

"Alex?"

"I'm here."

"We've been over all of this before."

"Yes, we have, Shannon."

"I'm sorry."

"Another lie."

"I said I'm sorry."

"I seriously doubt that. Are you going to help me with Dan or not?"

"Okay, I told you I'd help. Fill me in."

He then filled me I on the new information. I guess it was time to rescue this one.

Chapter 53

Considering Danny DeWitt was famous and being stalked by a bunch of violent lunatics, I told Alex I didn't want to go into the city, and that I'd meet Danny at Point Reyes National Seashore. It wasn't that far from San Francisco, and on an October weekday hardly anyone would be there, especially anyone looking for a runaway celebrity.

After I got off the phone, I still felt flushed from the conversation with Alex. I knew I shouldn't have made the remark about Tasha and her wayward panties, but it made me angry so many levels.

At a decent hour, 8:00 am, I got on the line with a property manager I knew and booked a house near Tamales Bay. It was a two-bedroom cottage with a view of the water, a marsh, a bunch of dairy cows and a lot of privacy.

I put on jeans, a white tee, some silver bangles, and threw a purple sweater in the back of the car. Alex told me to wear purple and my sweater was a nice eggplant color.

The drive to the coast was easy. I blasted my music all the way there until I came within a few miles of the coast. Then I rolled down the windows and took in the glorious coastal air.

Only one other car was in the gravel parking lot at the beach. A couple with gray hair was getting out and heading for a walk. I watched them laughing and acting like a couple of college kids. How unlike they were from my own parents. From out of the backseat they pulled two small children, then headed down to the beach. I watched and smiled, thinking of Laurence and me. One day, that could possibly be us.

It was a cool and beautifully clear day without a lot of wind. I walked up the path to the beach and stopped to look at the marsh. It was one of the most beautiful views in the entire universe.

I was going to have to evaluate this man who'd been so much tabloid trash. I'd seen photos of him at the beach with his six-pack abs and his zillion-watt smile. I looked him up online when Alex told me he'd taken on the project. There were blogs and fan sites. The man was still popular.

After about twenty minutes sitting on a bench by the trailhead, I saw Danny drive up in a nondescript silver rental sedan. He got out and spotted the blonde in the purple sweater he was supposed to contact. Looking better in person and larger than I thought he'd be, he froze like a deer in the headlights. I made the first move.

"Danny," I said gently as I approached him. He looked to be recovering from a black eye. A butterfly bandage was on his left cheek. Bruises were fading on the side of his face and forehead as well. "I'm Shannon. Alex sent me." I didn't use last names until I knew he was for real.

"Dan, call me Dan."

"Okay. Dan."

"Nobody called me Danny until I met Kayla."

I held out my hand. "It's good to meet you. I know this is an odd situation, but I will do my best to help you."

He looked skeptical. "Thanks. How do I know you're the right person?"

"You don't."

"He, um, Alex, said to look at the tops of your hands."

I put my hands up. He saw the scars.

Dan nodded and tried to smile, but was either too nervous or too polite to make a comment about my old injuries.

"Um, are, ah, you alone?" he asked me, sounding a little paranoid.

"I'm alone. How about you?" I answered gently.

"I'm alone. Alex said this was short notice for you."

That was an understatement, but I just smiled. My job was to see how strong he was. If he embraced being a victim, we couldn't help him. We needed someone who wouldn't miss the old life. He needed to prove that this was a positive and permanent move.

Danny DeWitt hadn't done anything to change his appearance. Dressed in fashionably well-worn jeans, a black tee shirt and a heavyweight gray hoodie, he would have fit in anywhere had it not been for his famous face. He had a Dodgers ball cap on his almost shaved head. I hate caps almost worse than I hated guys with buzz cuts who weren't in the Military or naturally going bald. Right after his marriage to Kayla, Danny had shaved off his pretty brown locks at her request. Bad move, in my opinion. He also had something akin to a small brown hamster growing on his chin. That would be the first thing to go.

How attached was he to his face, I wondered. That was a no brainer. Most of us are extremely attached to our faces just as they are, despite the gazillions of articles about plastic surgery. But back to HIS face. All would be easy to change. Straighten and lift nose up a bit, give a slight brow lift, a little work on the chin and presto, he'd be a different man. It was too bad because he did have a really nice face and it was a shame to have to change it. And of course, he had an extremely famous, extremely obscene tattoo of his ex-wife that would have to be removed.

"You know, you might be risking your life meeting me here," he said. "As soon as they find out I've left town, they'll be here." Home right now was Los Angeles. I didn't ask who "they" were.

"You flew into San Francisco, right?"

"Sure. I checked into my hotel and drove here."

"Anybody recognize you?" I asked.

"A few people. A couple of girls came up to me in the lobby told me the bitch didn't deserve me. I gave them an autograph and gave them hugs and kisses. Made their day." I could tell he appreciated the girls but he didn't smile. Danny started to shift his weight from foot to foot. He was nervous. "It's beautiful here. No people. I saw a couple of elk on the way in. The big ones with the white butts are elk, right?"

"Yeah, those are elk. Pretty magnificent creatures," I said. He was right, they were magnificent but we weren't here to watch nature.

"That's the first time I've ever seen one in the wild." He was still trying to make polite conversation.

"What happened to your face?" I asked. Now was not the time to stand back and be coy.

"A friend of my ex-wife was waiting for me at home a few days ago."

"What happened?"

"I went out to a club to meet with friends. It's just a neighborhood bar. There was a local band. Flirted and danced with some girls I always see at the neighborhood coffee place. You know, they were regular women. One is in advertising; the other is a film editor or something like that. Normal, not like my ex. At 10:25 I arrived home alone, like I always do. As soon as I get through the door I get the crap beat out of me."

"How many were there?"

"Three. Can you believe it? Two held me down and the other…" He looked out at the water. I waited a few seconds while he composed himself.

"Did you call the police?" I asked.

"No. The press would have been all over me."

"Did you get any medical help?"

"No. They would have called in the cops. I have ice. I have pain killers." He paused and looked me straight in the eye. "You don't think very highly of me, do you?"

"I don't know you well enough to form an opinion." I put the back of my hand gently on his cheek, as a mother would do. "I know what you're going through. I will make sure no one will ever hurt you again."

He looked away, eyes watering up.

"Let's talk. Come on," I said, walking down the sandy hill toward the surf. Only the silver haired couple with the two small children was in the distance, on the long stretch of beach. Nobody would take a second look at us. I threw a towel down on the sand and motioned for him to sit down next to me. I pulled a thermos of coffee out of my bag along with some chocolate chip cookies I'd baked that morning as soon as I got off the phone with Alex. "I have cream and sugar as well." I fixed my coffee the usual way, half coffee, half milk, and a lot of sugar. He had his black.

"Great coffee," he said.

I offered him a cookie.

He took a bite. "Oh my God. I haven't had cookies this good in years."

"Thanks," I said, taking a cookie for myself. "I made them this morning." Cookies equal trust; especially if they are made by the person you're eating them with.

"Tell me why you're here. Tell me your story, in your own words," I said.

At the time Danny Dewitt met his ex-wife, he was working for a manufacturing company that made high-end custom roller skates and boots, speed, artistic, street skates. He was going to make the old sport of roller skating the new hot sport. His dream was to get the sport into the Olympics. He had an MBA from UCLA and a big future ahead of him. Daniel ran the marketing department. Business was booming.

He'd seen Kayla Rutledge from a distance at clubs and events he'd managed to get into but they'd never met. A few times their eyes met and she'd blown him a kiss or two. Then he found out that she loved to roller skate, not roller blades but good old fashioned quad skates. Four wheels, skimpy outfits, good times. Everything that could be done on ice could be done on wheels but a lot more exciting.

Dan contacted Kayla's agent and sent her a pair of skates. In her next video she was skating, flashing her booty under a short skirt and wearing the skates he'd sent her. Sales skyrocketed. He invited her for a tour of the factory.

She'd expected a middle-aged family man. What she saw was the exceptionally cute jock and well-built boy next door, all grown up in an expensive suit at her beck and call. She didn't remember blowing him kisses, but she asked him to dinner. He gave her another pair of skates in bright pink along with two dozen matching hot pink roses.

As a thank you she took him home, screwed him silly and told him that she was falling in love with him.

From then on out they were always together. He proposed on the beach with a humongous diamond and a bottle of champagne. They had the million-dollar wedding with 500 of her closest friends, 50 of his friends, his father, stepmother and his three siblings, whom he barely knew.

Dan's parents were divorced when he was eight. His father remarried, started a new family, moved out of state and lost interest in him. His mom died when Dan was a senior in college. His older brother, a Marine, had died in Iraq the year after he married Kayla.

Dan had a few relatives in Ohio. They were close enough for Christmas cards, but not close enough to invite him for Thanksgiving.

After they got married, Kayla insisted Dan quit his job. She cut him off from his friends and former business associates. Kayla became enraged when he talked to other women, any women. Their life was no longer their own but a circus sideshow complete with her freakish friends. They were all so pretty, but like vampires ready to suck the life out of him and leave him drained and lifeless at any moment.

While Dan talked, he would look around to see if he'd been followed.

"I was tired of the clubs, parties and the constant media attention. Kayla would do anything for attention. She'd take her top off at parties and let guys lick her tits or go out in short skirts without underwear flashing her crotch and daring guys to feel her up. Parties, clubs, anywhere she'd be out there... doing whatever she felt like, with whomever she felt like. I'd always end up going home early or not going at all.

Then there was the religion. Every bearded guru, new age freak, born again whatever, atheist zealot, you name it, she'd be all over it for a few weeks then move on to the next thing. She was always hooked on whatever self-help book was on the bestseller list. I hate those people, you know, the ones who write the books."

He poured more coffee and held it in his hands. I think the warm cup was a comfort. He took a sip and continued. "She even called Gregory Atkinson, you know, the marriage relationship guy."

I kept my composure and poker face. "I know who Gregory Atkinson is. She actually called him to help you? Did you meet him?"

"Sure, I met him. Kayla begged him to come help save our joke of a marriage. She wanted to have it filmed like some freaks on reality TV."

My stomach flipped but I didn't show it "What did Dr. Atkinson say to that?"

"He'd only agree to private counseling. No cameras. No media."

"Did you do it, I mean private counseling?"

"Of course not. I wanted it private and she threw a fit. She wouldn't do anything unless she could have a press release out about it. You have to understand, there was no privacy in our life. Kayla called Dr. Atkinson again, wanting to do some sort of reality show out of our personal problems. Atkinson said he'd had enough media attention from his wife's murder. He gave me a list of marriage counselors who'd be willing to go by her terms, but there was no way I'd take my problems that public."

"So that was it for Dr. Atkinson," I said, fishing for more information.

"I met with him a few times alone. He gave me tools to work through things, you know, like evaluating my life and figuring out what sort of emotional toll this was taking on me. We talked a lot about how Kayla and I had different goals and dreams, or the fact that I had dreams and she was just riding the wave and not caring if and when she was going to crash or who was along with her. He was the first person I'd talked to since I hooked up with her who made any sense."

"What did you think of him?" I asked, only out of morbid curiosity.

"Oh, man. He was like the only person in the world who understood and didn't rush to judge me. I owe him my life in a lot of ways."

"Gregory Atkinson's wife was murdered by the Killer of Virtue," I said out loud. I wanted to see his reaction.

"Yeah, the guy raped Atkinson's wife and cut her to ribbons. How many women did he kill? Six, seven?"

"Eight, including Elizabeth Atkinson."

"Sick bastard. I know it sounds bad but I envy Gregory Atkinson, what he had with his wife Elizabeth. I can't imagine ever having that kind of love."

I smiled to cover up my desire to scream. "Do you think your marriage could have been saved?"

"What marriage? She was either high or drunk or into some health or spiritual craze. If she could have been into our marriage as much as she was into…" he paused. "She was into everything but me. Even quiet trips, you know, trips so we could get away from it all turned into media events. We couldn't go anywhere without her friends and her brothers and the rest of the entourage. She couldn't even put on her own make-up or brush her hair without a group of people hovering over her."

"When did you decide it was all over? What broke the deal?"

"One of her producers, Beck Aaronson, died in a car accident. He was actually a pretty decent guy. Anyway, I was pretty shook up about it. It brought back, you know, everything with my mom dying in a car accident and my brother dying in the war.

On the morning of the funeral, I couldn't find Kayla so I went alone. She never showed. I came home later that afternoon and she's by the pool topless with her current spiritual guru and her faggot personal assistant and some bone skinny naked chick with a bad boob. It was like a freak show right in my own back yard.

I just stared at them before I said anything. I asked her about the funeral and she just sat there and started to cry and look all confused. Then she made some lame excuse about forgetting. I told her it was over.

I walked out and she started to scream like she was in a horror movie, but she didn't follow me. The guru guy called me an insensitive jerk and started to hug her. She was topless and the guy was all over her, practically fondling her right in front of me. I packed up some clothes and was out of there.

Despite the fact that I'd hired a lawyer, the weird stuff started to happen. My bank accounts were frozen. I got my old job back but that didn't last long. I'd get so many calls at work. Every day Kayla or one of her brothers would call me, once an hour. At least once a week she'd show up crying, yeah and her whole publicity team would be there, filming it all. It was insane. Then after about three weeks of Kayla's drama I get a call from my boss. I'm VP of Marketing. He's the CEO. He asks me to roll up my sleeves and checked my arms for tracks. For God's sake, he was my college roommate. We'd been friends for years. I was in his wedding. But he didn't believe me and fired me three days later. I wasn't welcome anywhere because of her.

Kayla keeps going in front of cameras and interviews, telling everyone how much she loves me and that she'd do anything to get me back. She comes off sounding so sweet and innocent. Everyone thinks I'm some selfish prick who broke her heart. They don't know her. They don't know what she was like."

I knew all too well what she was like. I said nothing and let him talk. Dan was beaten down, but not so much that he'd lost confidence. This was a man who took small joys in things like kittens and small talk. He commented on the wild flowers and the surf and the way the marsh held so much beauty. For Dan Dewitt, the world still held wonder and joy. His new life would work. I hoped.

Chapter 54

"What's it worth to you? A new life?" I asked Dan. I was pretty sure he wanted this but I had to make sure.

"As in money?"

"Not money. Would you be willing to give up everything from your past?"

He paused then composed himself. "Everyone who really cared about me is either dead or have turned their backs on me. I don't have anything else to give up."

I let Dan compose himself. He brushed back a tear.

His long time friends had abandoned him long before that for lies Kayla had told about him. The final straw was when his new girlfriend found blurry sex tapes of herself and Dan online. A few months after that, while at a charity event, Danny DeWitt met Tasha Alexander and Alexander Goldstein.

Alex instinctively knew something wasn't right. In a way, Alex said, Dan had reminded him of me. Dan was lost and in a no-win situation.

Tasha and Alex talked to Daniel and listened to his story in a calm, reserved manner that gave no indication that they'd do anything one way or the other. They asked Dan if he was serious about making a new start.

Next, they told Dan to go back home and call his ex-wife. He was to give her the impression he wanted to get back with her. The next day he visited her in person for a session of make-up sex and too much to drink.

He had no intention of going back to Kayla. It was a trick to keep her minions off of his back. But he tripped up and didn't return Kayla's calls. She sent her friends to visit him but by then he'd taken the flight to San Francisco.

We walked down the beach in silence for a while. Then he said, "I brought someone with me."

All right, it's over, I thought. Unless it is his blind ninety-year-old grandmother, this guy is on his own.

"Who?" I asked, trying to hold back my temper.

"Daisy, my cat. She's a two-year-old calico I got from the county shelter a few months ago. I can't just leave her."

I had to smile. "I think we can handle a cat."

"Good," he said, "She's in my car."

Helping people build new lives is always interesting. I never thought I'd be doing it. The risks are huge. First of all, I risk my own discovery by exposing what I know about starting over with a new identity. I'm breaking the law by helping others fake their own deaths, or making it look like they might be dead. I'm going to sources to forge documents about births, education and citizenship. I'm risking the professions of doctors and speech coaches, not to mention a couple of slick, good-looking attorneys in Miami.

We left Dan's rental car on a side street in San Francisco, not far from the Golden Gate Bridge. The car would eventually be towed, but by that time Danny Dewitt would be long gone.

After that, we backtracked and drove to the small house on the coast I'd rented for the week. Dan, looking like he'd lost his last friend, brought in the cat.

"What's wrong?" I asked.

"Kayla left a message on my phone. She knows I was in San Francisco. She sent someone up to get me. They'll check the hotels."

"Did anyone follow you? Think, Dan. Did you see anyone who looked like they might have been watching you?"

"No. I don't think so."

"Did you make any stops between there and Point Reyes?"

"I just stopped for coffee and um, to stretch my legs. I paid cash for coffee. I don't know how she and her goons get the information. It can't be legal. You know, I told her to get a life and she said I was her life. She said I'd have to kill her before she'd stop trying to get me back. She said she'd rather see me dead than see me with another woman."

"Hold that thought," I said. I got my gun out of the trunk. I have a permit to carry. It's all legal. I would have noticed if someone had followed us but just in case, I checked the car for any added on GPS devices. Actually, I had no idea what I was looking for but I didn't find anything.

I put the gun on the table so he'd see it.

"Give me your phone." I took it with a gloved hand, turned it off and put it in a plastic bag. "This is it, Dan. If you want to turn back, this is your last chance. Are you ready for a new life?"

"I'm ready". He took in a deep breath and let it out slowly. "If I vanish, it will make headline news.

"Don't worry, nobody will ever find you, of course, unless you talk. If you talk, you'll endanger the lives of others. You have to be committed to changing. Are you committed, Dan? Are you willing to leave everything behind and start with a clean slate, a new name, a new life?"

"Sure, but you don't what it's like to see your own face on grocery store tabloids. Everyone will be looking for me."

I looked him straight in the eye. "I was front page tabloid news for years. I know what it's like."

It suddenly clicked with him that I wasn't born Shannon Gables. "Who are you?"

"Right now, I'm whoever I want to be. Okay, let's do this. Are you in? Do you want a new life?"

"Yes, I want a new life more than anything." He gave me a sly smile. "You're that senator's wife. The one who vanished in Florida."

"I'm not Heather Ann Cole." He was so off course. Heather Ann was in a loveless abusive marriage to a powerful abusive husband with no way out. She tried to leave, but like Dan, she was stalked and threatened, so she returned to the horror show that was her life. She was childless, with family she hardly knew or cared about so vanishing was easy with a little help from some newfound friends.

I'd had some good experience, being the wife and assistant to a marriage counselor. I'd learned how to listen. If you listen, people talk. And given the opportunity with a safe but complete stranger they'll spill all of their problems, no matter how personal.

Heather Ann Cole and I had met before at charity events, briefly, over cocktails and meaningless small talk.

She'd met her husband in college. She married him at twenty-four after getting her masters degree and he finished law school. He was perfect and now he owned her. I knew the story. It was my story but even more sick and twisted, in my opinion.

She was now a powerful United States Senator's wife. As the perfect political wife, she stood by her husband in her fashionable suits and dazzled all who met her with charm, brains and a good dash of blatant patriotism. Her interviews were brilliant and charming. Invitations to her parties were coveted, as well as the way she looked in an evening gown.

But life was less than perfect and there wasn't a thing she could do about it. If she divorced her husband she'd be shunned and damming photos would be published.

He'd made her do things for him, things with other people, men and women. He'd watch and direct and tell her what to do as she performed for him with whomever he brought home. He wasn't in them. She didn't want to do those things but felt she had no choice at the time. It was what he wanted. He always got what he wanted. "No" wasn't an option.

Everything she did, everyone she knew, and everything she wore, was controlled by her husband. On the outside she looked happy. Inside, she'd died years ago.

He rarely hit her, but the mental abuse was what finally took her down. Day after day she heard how she needed to be perfect, she couldn't let him down, she was a horrible person, her friends were wrong, everything about her was wrong. For years she heard it. For years, she watched his power grow and she finally gave up.

Heather Ann was always the perfect political wife. Everyone loved her. Everyone shared the grief when she miscarried her child. She wanted to try again but her husband told her to "get over it."

I never asked her why she agreed to do what she did. If you ever have had your soul taken, you'll agree to a lot of things you don't want to. You'll use bad judgment and hate yourself for the rest of your life. You'll smile and pretend everything is okay because that's what is expected of you. You soon forget that you have a choice, until that choice is forced upon you, just like the choice was forced upon me when I found the money at Darren Crawford's house.

Chapter 55

Heather Ann made it a point to see me at a big dollar charity event we'd both attended in Miami. I knew she was bothered by something and asked if she wanted to talk. We'd clicked the first time we'd met. I was willing to listen and she badly wanted to talk.

We'd walked to the end of the pier making small talk, drinks in hand, arm in arm like old childhood friends; two women in slinky, expensive evening dresses. She wore red; I wore a shimmering pale blue. By the time we got to the end of the pier, our $600 heels now in our hands, walking barefoot, Heather Ann was on edge.

After everything she told me, she was still under his control. It's really not that bad, she said. Life is never dull.

Stroking my bare arm with her soft warm hand, she looked me in the eyes. "You look like the ice queen tonight in that dress. You look good." She ran her tongue over the bottom of her teeth and smiled a pretty smile. "I'd like you to join Tom and me in a more intimate and personal way. He usually just likes to watch me with others, but this time," she put her hand on my chest, her finger hooked inside of my neckline. "He wants to be with you too. Tom is extremely talented at pleasing a woman. So am I." She leaned in close and brushed a kiss on my neck.

"Heather Ann, I'm not so sure this is a good idea," I said, ready to crawl out of my skin while I gently pulled her hand off of my chest and tried to step back.

Her hand ran down my arm and she took my hand. "Nobody will know but us. I promise there won't be any photos. Everything will be for your pleasure. I'll make it a night you'll never forget." She stepped closer, her breasts against mine so close I could feel her hard nipples, and hand now slowly moving on my hip and sliding to my butt, pulling my front close to hers.

Heather Ann was extremely seductive, like a seasoned politician going in for the kill on election eve. The sudden change in personality was scary.

"I want to taste your sweetness, Shannon." Her eyes locked on mine. I hadn't been around anyone so predatory since I left Pennsylvania.

As she leaned in to kiss me, I took a step back just as her mouth and tongue touched my lips.

"Heather Ann, you just told me your husband treats you like his personal porn star and now you're soliciting for him too," I said calmly.

She turned away. Then she hugged herself and started to cry.

"A friend told me you had come to him for help. He said you wanted a new start with a new identity."

"Alex?"

"I'm an expert on this sort of thing."

"He'll help me?"

"I'll help you. He'll be on the sidelines and to pick up the stray pieces."

Alex had told me that Heather Ann's husband was looking for another woman at the party for the two of them to get "hot and nasty" with. Fortunately, he'd suggested she get to know the attractive, mysterious blonde named Shannon. They'd make it a threesome, Tom, Heather and Shannon. Oh boy.

Heather Ann and I sat on the end of the dock as she poured out her heart to me, our feet hanging over above the water. She said she wanted to die. Despite the fact that she gave me the creeps, I told her I'd help her.

When she rejoined her husband at the party, she told him I was too much of a prude. To make it up to him, she willingly did whatever her husband told her to with one of his top staff members. It was no big deal for her. The guy, a good-looking man in his thirties, had "performed" with her before. He was skilled, creative, enthusiastic and bisexual. She did what was expected and went to sleep with a smile on her face.

The next morning, Heather Ann told her husband she wanted to go shopping. After that she was meeting with friends for lunch, other political wives in his circle. She made a joke to him about eating something healthy and grilled and then they'd all drink too much white wine. She told her husband that she'd bring back some good gossip and maybe seduce one of her lunch companions into their bed later that afternoon.

But Heather Ann never showed up for lunch. Two days later, her car was found at the end of a road that led out to an abandoned pier. Her purse and keys were in the trunk; along with the clothes she was wearing that day. Also found in the trunk were pieces of balled up wide gray duct tape that had been pulled off her wrists and mouth, with bits of hair and traces of skin still attached. The $500 in cash her husband had given her the previous night and her credit cards were still in her purse. Her cell phone was found still plugged into the car charger. Her favorite trademark necklace, a delicate gold butterfly was found by the car in the puddle of a large boot print. Her body was never found. Any telltale footprints had been washed away by the afternoon storm.

An envelope containing explicit photos of Heather Ann, her husband and others in comprising sexual situations was found in her purse. The senator had to pay a fortune to have them kept out of the public eye. He hired the firm of Alexander and Goldstein to do the task and keep it quiet.

It was easy for Heather Ann to vanish. She had no family she cared about and no children. She wasn't allowed close friends so there was nobody she'd miss.

Jerry and I met her with a small fishing boat at the end of the abandoned pier and Heather Ann Cole was gone to the world forever.

I remember her looking at Jerry up and down.

"You know," she said, "My husband got jealous if I ever even looked at another man. He'd have other men fuck me in every hole in my body while he watched but if I ever saw ANY man in a romantic way, even just flirting, he'd go ballistic. Jesus Mary and Joseph, you're cute."

"Thank you dear. I'll keep you in mind next time I'm in need of a little womanly company."

I rolled my eyes.

Then she looked at me, straight, hard and long. "So, who were you before you turned into Shannon Gables?"

"Elizabeth Atkinson."

"The Killer of Virtue Elizabeth Atkinson?"

"That's me."

She put back her stylish head and laughed out loud. "Holy shit. Well, I'm in good company then. Why'd you leave your husband?"

"He was a controlling asshole who beat me."

"What about the Killer of Virtue?"

"Rotting in Hell as we speak."

"Damn, Shannon Gables. You're good."

I hadn't felt so good in years.

She turned to Jerry. "What's your story, lover boy?"

"I'm the ex-husband who didn't beat her."

"You're really Jerry Alexander, Tasha's brother."

"Sure as the twinkle in my eye, darlin'."

And with that, Heather Ann Cole became Erin Gables, my long lost sister.

Now Heather Ann, as Erin, turned her blonde hair back to the glossy dark brown it had been when she was a child. She had a cute new nose, new chin and a generously enhanced bust line, plus laser treatments to remove sun damage and scars. Her eyes, with new tucked lids, were no longer covered by green contacts and now were the color of light milk chocolate.

Erin, with the help of her sister Shannon, purchased a lovely Queen Ann Victorian in the Napa Valley and made it into a bed and breakfast inn. She settled down quickly and quietly in her new life as successful hostess to the hottest romantic get-a-way in Northern California.

Heather Ann, excuse me, Erin, needed some training. She tried to "thank" Jerry for his help, with sex. That was how her husband had her thank people who'd done him favors. Jerry and I had to explain that it was not exactly appropriate behavior in any circle. Other than that, she adjusted better than I expected. In fact, she thrived.

Chapter 56

"Do you know what happened to Heather Ann Cole?" Dan asked me.

"Same thing that is going to happen to you," I told him.

"She's alive? Where is she?"

"If I knew, do you think I'd tell you?"

"Come on, tell me."

"Later."

"She's alive, holy cow."

"I didn't say that. She's dead, just like you'll be."

I'd brought a few bottles of wine. I told Dan to make himself as comfortable as he could in the small rented cottage. I had planned to make dinner, but decided I didn't want the mess. He flipped on the TV, cat in lap, a glass of wine in hand.

"Let's go into town. We can get sandwiches or something, you know, whatever looks good to bring back here. There was a market a few miles down the road at Point Reyes Station. I doubt anyone would give us a second look."

Then I heard my name. Elizabeth Atkinson. I stood, transfixed to the TV.

My old satchel, the bag I carried everywhere with me until I threw it into the woods thirty miles from Darren's house. It had been found. Inside was my wallet, complete with credit cards, driver's license, twenty-six dollars, my genealogy notebook and a half written suicide note that ended up looking like a love letter.

Dear Greg,
You are the only man I have ever loved. You are the only man I ever wanted to be with. No woman has ever loved a man as I love you. We are

I'd also left a dozen photos in the bag of Diana, and Greg, and one of Darren before I knew what he was. My favorite was of Darren, Greg and me, taken at a Christmas party. Everyone knew I always carried photos with me. I never left home without a pocket of my bag full of them.

That was it. I had decided not to finish the note and pushed it back in my bag before I climbed over the bridge rail. Nothing more. I had no hidden agenda. It was just words that at the time were true.

I was transfixed by the news report. Experts talked about me. Photos of my life with Greg popped up. Greg released a statement thanking the police for their support but declined a personal appearance, being too distraught to speak in public. My brother Mark was interviewed, smugly saying he was happy knowing I was with Jesus but no matter what was in God's plan, that justice had been served with Darren Crawford's death.

"God rest the soul of Liz Hobbs," I said, under my breath.

Dan looked at me with a confused look on his face.

I turned off the TV and turned to Dan. "Nobody deserves what she went through. You don't deserve what you went through, Dan."

"Poor Gregory Atkinson. If I had a wife like Liz... it just isn't right. They were so happy. They had such a perfect marriage," said Dan, his voice almost sounding like he was ready to choke up on me.

I resisted my urge to smack him on the head. "There will be stories like this about you. Can you handle it?"

"Sure, I mean, who's going to care about me? My life is nothing but a lot of shallow bullshit and tabloid fodder. I've alienated all of my friends. I don't even know my family. Anyone who is close to me gets hurt."

"A lot of people are going to care. More than you can imagine right now. Can you handle it? Can you go on with your life and never tell a soul who you were? Will you be able to handle it when your estranged wife goes before the cameras with tears in her eyes telling the world how much she loved you?"

The phone rang. It was Alex. "Shannon, they found your bag. Did you see it?"

"We just watched it on the news. Did you see that son of a bitch comment on it?"

"Forget him, Shannon."

"Mark Hobbs will burn in Hell."

"I'm sure he will."

"He fucked his own sister."

"Shannon, stop it. Let it go."

"It's sort of weird, considering Dan and all," I said.

"How's it going with Dan?"

"I think we're okay. Kayla found out he went into San Francisco."

"I figured as much."

"That's all. Nobody followed us here. Did he tell you he'd be bringing a cat?"

"A cat? No, he didn't say anything about a cat."

"Her name is Daisy. She's really cute."

171

"A live cat?"

"A calico. Beautiful animal."

"Does Dan know about you and Liz?"

"Not yet. Did you know he'd met Greg about marriage counseling?"

"Yes. It slipped my mind."

"Liar."

"I love you too."

"You should have told me."

"I guess I should have. I'm sorry. So how is Danny Dewitt in the mental health department?"

"Perfect. He's excited but scared to death."

"Well, keep up the good work."

"You should have told me Dan knows Greg."

"It doesn't matter. As far as I'm concerned, Dan is dead already."

I said goodnight and sat down in front of the TV next to Dan.

Dan looked at me in a panic. "What's going on, Shannon?"

"You're okay. You're safe. Life is good, huh? You've done a good job of not going to the press or police about the terror in your life. Dan, can you honestly tell me that you'll be able to handle the fallout of your disappearance and not flip out or tell someone?"

Dan looked down at his hands then up at me. I knew he was trying to figure it all out. "I can handle it. You were talking to Goldstein about Atkinson's wife. Why?"

"We're interested in everyone who vanishes. We learn from it so that you'll be a success. Come on, let's get something to eat." I didn't feel right leaving the cat there alone so we took her with us.

Chapter 57

Nobody looked twice at us at the market. We got sandwiches at the deli, a few snacks and left. A couple of young guys were looking at my old Porsche. I smiled. We talked for about two minutes about what a great car I had. Once they knew it was my car, they didn't even notice Dan.

Driving back to the house, a light flashed behind me. The SUV behind me tried to either pass me or eat my bumper.

"Asshole," I swore under my breath as I floored the gas.

Dan was in a panic. "It's them."

"Did you see a face?"

"No. But they've done this before." He started to panic. "Oh my God. Oh God."

I floored it and sped around the corner. I knew this road. I went around two corners, losing the SUV, and pulled over.

"Get out!" I yelled. "Get in the woods and no matter what don't come out until I tell you to."

He looked in shock. "Are you dumping me?"

"NOW! GO HIDE! You want to die tonight? Get into the woods NOW! Take the cat."

Dan ran into a wooded ravine with the cat carrier. I got out and stood by my car. I hoped to God they wouldn't find his bag in the trunk. Screw that, I hoped they wouldn't stop and that Dan and I would have a great laugh about it. The SUV came to a dusty stop, almost wiping out in the turnout.

Out of the oversized car came a well-dressed man in a leather jacket and tie. He was in his late thirties, maybe early forties, with longish brown hair. He outweighed me but I could outrun him. Okay, maybe not. Bad idea.

Two other men got out and came out to my car. I had my hand on the gun in my coat pocket. One was wearing a black tee shirt without a jacket. His face and body screamed generic bouncer. The other had some sort of windbreaker on. I noticed windbreaker guy because of his crazy curly red hair.

I looked them over. I could be a helpless girl or I could be something else.

"What do you think you're doing?" I yelled at them. "You could have killed all of us! What the crap is wrong with you?"

They were caught off guard.

"We're looking for Danny Dewitt," said the main guy. I'll call him Leather Jacket Guy.

"Danny Dewitt? Are you crazy or what?" I said.

"We have reason to believe Danny Dewitt is in your car."

"Are you police officers?"

"Concerned friends of Danny."

"Take a look asshole, nobody is in my car."

The other two guys didn't move or react in any way. Leather Jacket Guy just sort of smirked with one of those shit eating grins assholes like him love to display.

I rummaged through my purse and found a pen and paper. I wrote down the plate number of the car. Then pulled out my phone.

"I don't know Danny Dewitt, so leave me alone. Stop following me or I'll call 911."

"I'm concerned about Danny," said Leather Jacket Guy.

"Good for you. Like I said, I don't know Danny."

Bouncer guy came close and looked in the car.

"Empty," he said.

"Pop the trunk," barked Leather Jacket Guy.

Bouncer guy opened my door and opened the trunk. He didn't seem too concerned about the two small overnight bags stashed behind the groceries and a case of wine.

"Hey, get away from my car!" I yelled.

Leather Jacket Guy came closer to me.

"We heard Danny was with a blonde in an older Porsche."

"Good for him. I'm not the blonde. This is not the car."

Red Head Guy pulled a gun. I could feel something horrible coming up out of my stomach into my throat. Bad idea.

Leather Jacket Guy took my arm like a vise and leaned me up against the car. "In an hour I'll know who you are." He was smooth. Not a thug type. It was dark, but I could tell he was handsome, well dressed, over groomed. I didn't recognize him.

Bouncer Guy had gotten to the registration in my glove box. "Her name is Shannon Gables. She's from Sacramento."

"Shannon Gables from Sacramento," Leather Jacket Guy said, his body leaned into mine. I thought in a fraction of a second of my brothers, of Greg, of Darren. Not again. Never again. But if I hurt him, he could smash my face or rape me. He could do a multitude of evil things to hurt me, things that had already happened to me that I didn't want to happen again.

So I did the only thing I could do: I begged. "Please don't hurt me."

He put his face close to mine. "Sorry for the inconvenience, Shannon Gables. If I find out you're involved with Danny, I'll be the last guy you'll ever be involved with."

"What bad movie did you get your lines from?" I almost added the word asshole but thought better of it.

He drew his hand back as if he was going to hit me, I braced myself for the impact, and then he smiled.

"You've been hit before. I can tell by the way you handle yourself. Watch yourself, Blondie."

"Fuck you, asshole," I said back, with a sarcastic smile.

He laughed and motioned for his men to drive away. As he got into his car he blew me a kiss. "I'll fuck you first, sweetheart," he said, "And you'll like it."

I got in my car, shaking, my heart pounding a thousand beats per minute and drove off, leaving Danny Dewitt and his cat in the woods. The SUV followed me for about ten minutes then turned around and went the other direction. About five more miles down the road, I turned around and drove back to get Dan. I pulled over then called out into the woods. He was still there, frozen with fear.

"You owe me big time," I snarled, "Get in the car." I started to lecture, "I didn't want to do this, but you're going to have to die faster than I'd planned."

Dan went for the door.

"Don't go anywhere," I snapped at him. "You have die so they'll stop looking for you. You know, I hate doing this. I'll be breaking the law and risking my own life for you, again."

"Please…" Dan tried to say something.

"Shut up, Dan. Who were those guys?"

He stammered. I couldn't understand what he said and I couldn't have cared less at the time.

"You know who they are. Tell me."

"Kayla's brother Kyle Rutledge and his friends Brandon and Jet."

"Kyle was the one in the leather jacket? The one who pushed me up against the car?"

"Yes, that was Kyle. I'm sorry, Shannon. If I had any idea…"

I cut Dan off and continued my tirade. "I'm not spending the rest of MY life being chased by your ex-wife's brother."

He leaned back and closed his eyes. "I'm sorry, Shannon. I am so sorry. I didn't know I'd been followed."

"Did you tell anyone where you were going?"

"No."

"I don't believe you. Who did you tell?"

"My agent. I told my public relations gal, Jackie. It's a habit, so at least someone will know where I am in case I don't come back."

"I can't help you anymore."

"Come on, Shannon. Alexander Goldstein said it was a done deal."

"Fine. I'll put you on the first plane to Miami."

"Jackie wouldn't have told anyone where I am. It wasn't her."

"Did you tell her you're planning on vanishing?"

"No, I said I just needed to get away for a few days."

"Call her."

"Jackie? Why?"

"Ask her if anyone contacted her. Ask if she had dinner with a friend and happened to mention that you went to San Francisco. Ask if anyone threatened to hurt her if she didn't tell them where Danny Dewitt had gone."

I was getting tired of Danny. I am usually a compassionate person but I'd lost all patience with him.

"Call her."

He called. I could tell the answering machine had kicked in. "Hey, this is Danny. Just checking in. I'll call..." someone answered, "Hi is Jackie around?" Long pause as he listened. His hands started to shake. "Yeah, it's Dan. How?" Another pause. "Oh, my God." Tears.

I knew she was dead.

"What can I do? Anything. Just let me know." He wiped his eyes. "I'll call you tomorrow. And I mean it. If you need anything, call me."

Dan turned to me. "She's dead. They killed her."

I pulled over on a turn out and got out of the car. I needed air. I was still shaken by the men in the SUV. Now I felt like I was falling back into the world of Darren Crawford.

I told Dan to get out of the car and tell me what was going on. He told me Jackie's sister had answered the phone. Her boyfriend had found her beaten to death, curled in a corner of her bedroom. The house was ransacked. It looked like a robbery. She might have been raped.

"Shannon, just drop me off someplace. If they see you with me, they'll kill you. I've tried getting the police involved. My attorneys have tried. They're too good at getting away with this." Then he started to sob.

I put my arms around him and whispered a prayer, "Dear Lord, please protect us."

I was too tired and shook up to drive San Francisco to drop Danny off. I went back to the cottage. We didn't say a word the entire time.

A large SUV, the same one that had pulled us over before was parked in front of the cottage. The only things we'd left inside were a couple of wine glasses in the sink and an empty bottle. We left, knowing we couldn't' call the police. I drove way too fast for about five miles under the full moon with my lights off. Danny gripped his seat in fear of both speed and the death, by either my driving or by the threats.

I felt sick. This was my punishment for not being able to cry or show open grief.

Pulling over, I threw up on the side of the highway.

"Dear God, help me. Show me the wisdom to do what is right. Please forgive me for the death and destruction I feel I've caused. These people are worse than Darren. How in your mercy can something like this happen? Oh God, forgive me. Please," I gasped. "Please tell me where to go."

Danny got out of the car. "Who are you talking to?"

My phone rang. Danny picked it up from between the car seats.

"It's someone named Erin."

My prayers were answered.

Chapter 58

Erin waited like one of Dracula's brides at the front door of her Napa Victorian while I unloaded Dan and the cat out of the car. She smiled at us as we walked up and gave me an all-knowing, almost seductive nod. I was ready to hiss at her as she looked at Dan as if she wanted to eat him.

We needed to make this quick and final. After the run-in with Kyle Rutledge, Dan had to make the total commitment and come into our fold or we had to cut him loose upon threat of death if he ever told a soul about meeting with us.

I made brief introductions. Erin, Dan, Dan, Erin. Into a comfortable living room we went, to find candles and wine waiting for us.

Erin was the product of a wealthy father and social climbing mother. It wasn't that they were bad people. They just didn't know how to be good parents. Okay, they were bad people in a lot of ways, but not evil people like my parents.

Her father had been married before to his college sweetheart and produced two sons, who at age fifteen were sent off to a prestigious boarding school. Just about that time, he had an affair with a stunning young marketing manager that produced Heather Ann. He left his old wife, who was a nag anyway, for a new Mrs. Cole. They lived happily for five years with their little daughter then parted ways. Both parents remarried and produced additional offspring; her father another son and a daughter; her mother two girls. Her father divorced again and another son was born with wife number four. Her mother moved on to husband number three with no more children.

Heather Ann was raised by a series of well-educated and high-strung nannies. She rarely saw either of her parents. When she did, on the assorted holidays, she mingled at meals and shared space with her various siblings; strangers who looked slightly like her parents. Vacations were fun but there again, it was like going with nice friends she wasn't all that close with. She never felt connected but wasn't altogether unhappy. At age six, she was shipped off to the same affluent boarding school to which her elder brothers had been sent. She excelled in academics.

On the summer of her sixteenth birthday, she spent a few weeks on the family yacht and had an affair with a handsome thirty-six-year-old business associate of her father's. From there, she found she could get the attentions of good looking older men and in turn, she learned how to fulfill their every sexual fantasy and get exactly what she wanted out of them (travel, excitement, attention).

Her parents knew what was going on but neither seemed concerned as long as she didn't publicly get involved with any married men, didn't get pregnant and got into a good university. After graduating with honors from boarding school, she went on to Yale University and met her husband, a good-looking boy with political ambitions. And yes, he was the one who turned into her psycho husband from Hell.

"Take off your sweat shirt, sweetie," Erin told Dan, after the extremely brief small talk. "We need to poke you with a needle."

"A needle?" Dan looked surprised.

Erin patted his arm. "It will be found in your suitcase, on your clothing. Do you see where we're going with this? I need you to dump your bag. Just put everything on the couch for now. Now, take your hoodie off. Come on."

Erin and I put on latex gloves and started to assemble the suitcase.

"I need your shirt in the morning. The one you're wearing. A clean one won't have your smell or any trace of you."

Erin brushed her hands over the purring Daisy and got a hand full of fur.

Erin and I stared at the tattoo on Dan's arm.

"The crazy bitch made me get it," said Dan. "I didn't want it, but whatever she wanted she got." It was her name in script with the word forever in a ribbon after it. A naked pinup picture of his ex-wife was laying face up, a come hither pout on a beautiful face, with giant breasts with bright magenta nipples pointing up to the heavens, her legs were spread as well as her, well, um, let's say all of her lips were rosy red and ready for action. "The anorexic bitch didn't look anything like that, except her face and the tits. She vomited up her own breasts so she had to buy replacements."

"Excuse me?" I was even taken aback by that one.

Dan sighed out loud in disgust. "My wife lost so much weight making herself puke and starving herself that her curves went away so she went out and had a couple of bowling balls implanted into her bony chest." He rubbed the tattoo. "I want it off. She wanted me to get one of her bending over and looking over her shoulder."

"Lovely," said Erin.

"She wanted it on my belly button," said Dan.

Erin and I both groaned in disgust, then started to laugh.

"I kid you not, ladies," said Dan, then just shrugged.

"We'll get it off or cover it up. Would you object to having something go over it? There will be sort of a scar. Tattoos are so common that nobody will notice that much," I said.

I sat Dan down and gave him a small syringe with a needle. "We know you've done needles before. Stick that in your arm then pull it out. It will have your DNA on it. The stuff inside is heroin so don't inject it. Just stick the needle in and pull it out."

Erin put in her sage advice. "You can't do this without a little pain and discomfort. In fact you might as well sit back and enjoy the ride. I certainly did."

I pulled three yellow roses out of a vase and wrapped them in the shirt along with a well-worn paperback book Erin had grabbed off of the shelf.

"It's a French translation of War and Peace. You don't speak French, do you Dan?" Erin asked.

"A little. I took it in high school," said Dan.

"Do you know enough to read War and Peace in French?"

"No. I don't know any language well enough to read War and Peace. I read Anna Karenna."

"What did you think of it?" I asked him.

"Depressing. I can relate to Anna right now. No home. No place I can fit in."

I just smiled. He felt the same way about Anna as I felt about Jane Eyre. The sad thing was that Anna Karenna never had a second chance. Jane did, kind of sort of, in a weird falling in love with a dashing soon to be blind guy with a crazy wife sort of thing. I guess we were both hoping for that sort of mind numbing, crazy in love without the weirdness.

Dan poked around at our little package of weirdness. "What are the roses and book for?"

"Nothing," I told him, "Just another sick and twisted way to send whoever finds this on a wild goose chase. I'm going to drop you back off at your car in the morning. It should still be there. Empty the bag into the trunk of your rental car. Then take all of the cash out of your wallet. Leave the rest of the contents, including photos, credit cards, your driver's license and anything else in the car.

Drive around a while. Stop by a fast food place, any will do. Get a bunch of burgers or tacos. Throw them out, leave the wrappers in the back seat of the car. Kind of crumple them up and get food on them so it will look like someone was eating. Since you're a vegetarian that will add more mystery to the puzzle. Then call me with this phone." I handed him a throwaway burner phone. "Drop your personal phone on the back seat floor. Then lock the car and walk away. I'll meet you. From there I'll put you on a private plane to Miami. You'll meet Tasha Alexander on the plane. She'll take you to a wonderful place where you'll start your new life. Do you agree to do everything I say?"

"Yes," said Dan.

"You realize that you can't go back," I said.

I gave him a small photo, a CDV from 1865 of a dark haired man in a long jacket.

"Welcome to the family. This is your great great great grandfather. His name was Daniel. Your name is now Sean Gables."

"This photo, the guy looks sort of like me. Why are you doing this? You don't even know me."

"I know you. You're my brother, Sean Gables," I said.

"And I'm your sister, Erin. I'm the oldest. You're the middle child," said Erin.

Chapter 59

Later that night, we stood on the deck listening to the birds in their marsh. I had a glass of wine. Daniel had sparkling water with a twist of lime. Erin was inside.

He gave me a hug. "I don't know how to thank you enough." He stepped back and smiled. "It's been so long since I've even dared to touch a woman, even to give a hug to a friend without wondering if she'd get hurt because of me."

"You are going to have to be cautious about who you kiss and who you have sex with. Old habits are hard to break, but you're going to have to change parts of your personality. You are going to have to keep your most deep-seated beliefs; those things that make other people think of you as Daniel, you'll have to shelve them. Keep them inside."

"I know," he said, taking my hands. "I'm glad you're here."

"I'm glad you're here too," I said, "My boyfriend thinks I'm at an art show in Los Angeles."

"He doesn't know you help people like me?"

"He doesn't have a clue."

That would have been the end of the perfect evening if we'd been in a movie or a TV show. But Dan had to open his mouth and express his ignorance out loud.

"I know I'm doing the right thing but I was thinking…"

"Don't think. Not anymore tonight."

"Seriously, I was thinking of calling Greg Atkinson. When my marriage was falling apart, he had a lot of good things to say."

"He has no idea. If you want to do this, you cannot call Greg Atkinson or anyone else. Do you understand?"

"It isn't just my marriage. Jackie is gone because of me. I don't know what to do."

"There is nothing you can do. Greg is a bad person."

"Based on what?" Dan snapped at me.

"I can't talk about it. Trust me."

"I don't even know you. I know Atkinson."

"No you don't. The man is evil."

"You're crazy. Greg Atkinson told me that he knows what it feels like to take on loss and betrayal. He knows what I'm going through."

"Sure, he might, but he isn't what he seems to be."

"Everything you say is a riddle. Smoke and mirrors, Shannon, if that is your real name. I've had enough games. I need to talk to someone who cares. You know, after today I believe Greg Atkinson is someone who can help me."

"Dan, listen to me…"

Then he came at me like a pit bull. "I don't know you. What do Goldstein and his wife have on you? At least Greg Atkinson is living in the real world. I know he cares."

"I care," I said, like some high school girl trying to get a boy to like her. Dan turned and went back inside. "Where are you going?"

"To bed, then I'm not sure."

Chapter 60

At 7:00 a.m. I scratched my nails on the door of Dan's room and waited. I could hear him in there moving around. I knocked quietly and picked up the coffee mugs from the floor.

Dan opened the door, fresh out of the shower in just jeans. His torso was bare with the just-dried, dewy look. He'd stopped waxing his finely sculpted chest (as so many media photos showed him bare chested) but that wasn't what surprised me. His left side was dark blackish purple, yellow and red ran across his stomach, more dark purple and a greenish hue covered his left shoulder. The vulgar tattoo of his ex-wife's image looked me in the eye.

He motioned for me to come in. I put the cups down on the windowsill. He looked me up and down, like guys do, but in a way I couldn't read. It wasn't sexual. It was more like the way one looks at something they find both beautiful and disgusting at the same time, like his ex-wife.

"You should have told me last night it was this bad." I could hardly get the words out.

"You don't like or respect me. Why should I have expected you to care?"

"I'm sorry if I came off that way. I know what you're going through."

"I doubt it. You ran off last night as soon as I mentioned getting real help."

"What are you talking about? I risked my life for you last night."

"You flipped as soon as I mentioned Dr. Greg."

Time for a deep breath and a plunge into the dark abyss.

"Greg is not going to help you. On the surface maybe, but..."

"I'm calling him this morning as soon as I can get a phone."

"Hear me out first."

"Why should I?" He glared at me.

I pulled my shirt over my head and stood in front of him in my bra and jeans.

"Impressive, but I'm not in the mood."

"Just shut the fuck up and listen to me. I'm Elizabeth Atkinson. Greg Atkinson was my husband."

I turned around, just like I had with Alex and Tasha years before. The look on Dan's face was shock and disbelief.

"The scars on my back are from where Greg whipped me for not being a good Christian wife. They go half way down my ass."

I turned back to face him. "The scar on my face is from where he hit me with a belt buckle. If we had an x-ray machine, I'd show you the bones he broke. See the way my fingers are crooked," I held out my right hand. "He slammed my hand in the door the day I came home from the hospital after having a stillborn son. All I did was ask him not to talk about my health or my baby in public. He knew the one thing I loved the most was playing my guitar, so to punish me for disagreeing with him, he broke my fingers so I couldn't play."

"You don't look anything like Elizabeth Hobbs."

"My eyes haven't changed. And the bite mark on my shoulder matches Greg's perfect teeth."

"I don't get it. If you're Elizabeth Hobbs... you were never kidnapped by the Killer of Virtue?"

"I was kidnapped by Darren Crawford after he saved me from a suicide attempt."

"Wait, I thought... you tried to kill yourself? Why?"

"I couldn't live with the abuse from Greg anymore. I thought I was too broken to live, so I jumped off of a bridge. Darren pulled me out of the water."

"Darren Crawford helped you escape Greg?"

"No, Darren did not help me escape. Darren held me for two weeks. During the day he was in the search party looking for me. He showed me the news stories. I watched Greg saying how much he loved me and begging for my return. Everyone was praying for me. Then Darren would stop praying with his friends and go to his home, where he would rape and torture me. The scars on my arms and hands are from Darren Crawford. He filmed it all, the rapes, the cutting, everything. He might have impregnated me, or it could have been Greg, I don't know. Darren died by natural causes. I thought he was going to kill me and he dropped dead of a brain aneurysm. I couldn't go back to Greg, so I ran like a common criminal.

I miscarried a baby a few months later. It almost killed me, but I survived. The prayers were answered when I found Alex and Tasha. They're my angels. Now I'm going to be your angel. I'm going to help you survive. Okay?"

Dan wiped a tear from his face. "I'm sorry. I didn't know."

"How would you? Your coffee is getting cold." I put my shirt back on and motioned for him to sit down.

I told him the entire story. He listened with only the occasional question. His eyes glistened. He was so sweet.

In the end I took his hand, just as Alex always took my hand. "So yes, I do know what you're going through. I'm going to help you, but you have to trust me. You have to listen to me."

He gave me a hug, like the brother I should have had.

Then he asked, "If you're Elizabeth Hobbs, then who is Erin?"

I smiled. "Heather Ann Cole."

Chapter 61

"So do not worry about tomorrow, for tomorrow will bring worries of its own. Today's trouble is enough for today." Matthew 6:34 (NRSV)
"Ask, and it will be given to you; seek, and you will find; knock, and it will be opened to you." Matthew 7:7

I walked to the gallery door, thinking it was UPS but hoping it was someone with coffee.

No such luck. It was Kyle Rutledge, the guy who ran me off the road and threatened me the night I met Danny Dewitt. I pretended I didn't recognize him.

"I'm sorry we're only open for appointments today," I told him.

"Hello Shannon," he said, not smiling. "Seen Danny lately?" He put his hand on the door and pushed himself halfway through.

"I don't know anyone named Danny. Get off of my property."

"I just want to talk."

"We don't have anything to talk to you about."

"I know you probably don't know where Danny is, but you fascinate me, Shannon Gables. I want to get to know you better."

"Who are you?" I knew who he was, but I had to pretend I didn't know.

"Kyle Rutledge. My sister is Kayla Rutledge. You might have heard of her."

"The most popular singer in America. She's playing in town tonight. Sold out. Not exactly my style," I said.

He smiled.

I glared at him. "Okay, Kyle, I'm impressed that you have such a famous sister. You can go now."

"I'm sorry Shannon, that I frightened you."

"Yeah, so am I."

As I started to close the door, he blocked it and forced himself through.

"You're a friend of Alexander Goldstein. I saw his portrait here yesterday when you were out. Nice work. You're a talented photographer. Your little gallery manager told me you and Goldstein are close friends. If you had to choose between lovers, who would you pick, Shannon? Goldstein or Dewitt?"

What is it with guys thinking just because a woman knows a guy it means she's slept with him? "You're disgusting."

He continued to smile. "Goldstein is an attorney in Miami. High dollars. I hear he is brilliant in the courtroom."

"Alex Goldstein is brilliant at criminal law. You might want to hire him," I said sarcastically.

"Goldstein is an exceptionally handsome man. Almost too handsome. It would be tragic if something happened to his perfect face. How would you feel if that handsome face was splashed with acid or had a close call with a belt sander?"

"Go away, Mr. Rutledge."

"I like Miami. Great city. I might take a trip there soon."

"I'm calling 911."

I turned to get my phone and he grabbed my arm. I froze like a deer in the headlights. The music next door was turned up so loud that nobody would hear me if I screamed.

"No need to be unfriendly, Shannon. Tell me why you were with Danny and I'll go." He pushed me against the wall, his chest pressing against mine, his hands locked on my arms.

"I don't know Danny."

"Of course you don't, Shannon. Have you spoken to Laurence Yantz today? He's your boyfriend, isn't he? Another defense attorney. I'm sure Laurence would be heartbroken if anything happened to you, or even more so if something happened to one of his daughters."

"Leave him out of this."

"Out of what, Shannon? I'm just making conversation."

"Leave Laurence and his kids alone, or so help me God, I'll kill you."

"Sure you will." He pressed closer to me, holding me against the wall with a shit-eating grin I wanted to just slap off of his face. "I like you. I think we could be friends."

It took everything I had inside of me not to hurt him really, really bad. Still smiling, he moved forward, putting his mouth close to mine like he was going to kiss me, then he stepped back and let go of my arms.

"Here's my card. Call me if you remember anything." I could smell an expensive cologne and cinnamon mixed with cigarette smoke. "I won't forget you, Shannon Gables," Kyle Rutledge whispered in my ear, then left with a laugh.

I wanted to throw up. I could still feel him holding me to the wall, his breath against my face.

I called Alex and left a generic, "Hi, call me tonight, it's important. I need to talk to you about Sean," message. He had a big trial going on and would be in court or at the office. No time to chat about having his face sanded off.

Next, I called Jerry. He told everyone that he was on a sailboat with Tasha and a few friends in the middle of nowhere for another three days. That was the story.

Jerry and Tasha were with Danny. Danny was in God-knows-where, some island St. Somewhere recovering from major plastic surgery, thanks to Rob Goldstein. I was scheduled to meet him at that undisclosed location in three months, but I didn't have three months to see what Kyle was going to do to my friends or me. I wondered why nobody had found Dan's bag or why it wasn't reported in the news if they had. I looked it up online and found nothing.

I couldn't call Laurence or tell him anything. "Hey Honey. I'm helping a famous guy fake his own death, and a famous crazy guy is out to kill or disfigure everyone I care for including your children and by the way, I used to be Liz Atkinson. How was your day?"

Erin was en route to Florida to see Danny, aka Sean. She was the only one who'd truly understand other than Alex.

If I called the police I'd have to explain why I didn't call them the first time and why I was protecting Danny Dewitt. It was another no win situation.

I opened my Bible that I kept on the shelf with all of my photography books.

"A friend owes kindness to one in despair..." Job 6:14

What did that mean? Anybody I could ask for help or even a shoulder to lean on was unavailable. I decided to send a message to the top.

Please dear Lord, give me guidance. Kyle Rutledge is a murderer. He has threatened to hurt Alex. Please. I don't care about myself. I've made a mess of things. Sean has made a mess of things but he isn't a bad guy. His heart is in the right place. You have to give him a chance at being Sean. Please just show me what to do. If you have an avenging angel or want to send a rock out of the sky to kill Kyle please, just for me, I promise I won't do anything else foolish. I know I've been a pain in the ass but I don't know where else to turn.

I sat waiting for lightning to hit me. Nothing happened.

I fixed a pot of coffee and checked my voicemail. The milk in the fridge had gone bad.

"God Damn it," I said out loud, wanting to kick something but didn't because I was wearing sandals.

First message was from Tom Mather.

"I'm in Sacramento. Let me take you to dinner tonight."

A friend who owed me kindness. Tom Mather, divorce and family law lawyer, former hit man and with any luck, my hero.

Chapter 62

Tom and I had run into each other frequently in Miami and almost a year into my new life as Shannon, unbeknownst to Alex and Tasha, Tom and I had gone on a two week vacation together to the Bahamas. After a week of too much sun and sex, we went on with our lives. Forever or a lasting romantic relationship would never happen with us. He was emotionally distant and talked too much about politics. He called me a small-minded bitch more than once. I called him an asshole at least twice a day. But all in all we had a great time and remained friends. He got married to a nice girl who kept him in line and had two small children, a boy and a girl, and became the model husband and father.

I always felt a little guilty about my time with him in the Bahamas. It was wrong in so many ways. But in so many ways it was right. It was wrong because of too much sun and sex with a man I hardly knew. It was right because it got me on the road to living my own life, out from under the protection of Alex and Tasha. Of course they never knew about the trip. I'd lied and told them I'd been in Key West with Jerry.

We went to my favorite downtown restaurant and got a prime seat by the window. It was one of those rare, elegant places where I could wear a little black dress and not feel like it was overkill. After we'd ordered cocktails we got down to catching up.

After making a toast to each other with gin and tonics, Tom gave me a rare smile.

"You need to settle down, get married to that guy Laurence, have a few babies."

"I'm already settled."

"Marriage is good for women."

It was time to change the subject. "Tell me about your kids, Tom."

His face lit up. He showed me pictures on his smart phone. They were amazingly cute and cuddly. A blond boy with a tiny brunette sister. I cooed over the images.

Now that Tom's children, dogs, cats and his lovely wife were out of the way, it was time for business.

"Um, Tom."

"Um, Shannon."

"I need to hire you."

The waiter, a charming young man named Garrett, brought us curried butternut squash soup. I smiled. So did Tom, but not about the soup.

"Shannon, you need prenuptial advice. Are congratulations in order after all for you and Laurence?"

I leaned toward him. "I need you to kill someone for me."

"Shhhh. Jesus, Shannon. No." He actually looked shocked.

"Listen to me, Tom. The man has killed at least three people already that I know of. He's looking for my friend and will kill me too if I don't get rid of him."

"Take it to the police."

"I can't."

"If the guy is a threat and did what you said he did, then turn him in."

"I'd risk my life and that of my friend."

"Are you dealing drugs, or what?"

Our entrees came along with a nice bottle of wine. Tom had the quail with figs. I had crusted with Macadamia nuts with a fresh herb sauce that had come straight from Heaven. We paired it all with a nice bottle of Coastal Zinfandel. As soon as Garrett the waiter left, I continued to explain my situation to Tom.

"My friend is extremely famous and has found it necessary to change his identity and drop off the face of the earth."

"What did he do?"

"Married the wrong woman."

"I'll get him a divorce and a restraining order."

"He's already divorced."

"Who is your client?"

"If I pay for dinner, will we have attorney-client confidentiality?"

"Sure."

I pulled out a paper and Mont Blanc pen from my purse. "Sign this."

"Always prepared, aren't you?" He signed the paper and handed it back.

I finished up my wine and took a bite of fish. After putting down my fork, I told him the truth.

"My client is Danny Dewitt."

Tom gave me his typical don't-shit-me look. "The guy who was married to Kayla Rutledge? The guy who is missing and presumed dead?"

"Dan is alive. Long story, short version. I helped him fake his death and get a new identity."

"You've got to be kidding."

"Danny was terrorized for two years. His bank accounts were drained. His phones tapped. No matter where he went, they found him. Restraining orders don't work. Rutledge killed Danny's manager. Danny was a good guy. Really he was. He deserves a second chance."

"How much is he paying you, Shannon? Don't tell me you're doing this for free. I'm sorry, but you're one of the most selfish people I've ever met."

"I'm getting paid a lot."

"So what about Rutledge?"

"He ran me off the road and threatened me last month. This morning he showed up at my gallery, asking about Danny. He threatened to take a belt sander to Alex's face."

Tom's voice took on an angry, urgent tone. "How does he know Alex?"

"Rutledge saw Alex's portrait in my gallery and looked him up. I thought he was going to beat me up or rape me. Tom, I was scared. This guy won't back down."

"Fuck, Shannon. How did you get mixed up with Danny Dewitt?"

"I live in California. I meet all sorts of famous people."

"You live in Sacramento. Come on, tell me what's going on."

"I was asked to help Danny. He is okay now, like underground forever, but…" I wasn't sure how much to tell him. "We, Dan and I, were followed by Kyle Rutledge. I told you. He forced himself into my store and threatened me. It was a real threat. He is the type to follow through. I'm scared, Tom."

"You met DeWitt through Tasha. I know it's her. She met Danny Dewitt after Alex partnered with him at a golf tournament. She had sex with him after the cocktail reception in the back of a limo."

"Tom, I didn't want to hear that." Really, I did not want to hear that.

"Me neither, but it happened. I keep telling Alex to dump Tasha." Tom almost snarled out that last statement.

"It would be too expensive for him in too many ways. Back to my problem. Rutledge threatened to take a belt sander to Alex's face. He also threatened to hurt Laurence's daughters if I didn't tell him where Danny is."

"A belt sander? On Alex? That would be unfortunate."

"Kyle Rutledge knows where my business is. He knows who my friends are."

In a rare gesture, Tom took both of my hands in his. "Shannon, I love you, but I can't help you. I'm not that guy anymore. You, of all people, should understand."

"Tom, I'm over my head on this one. I've looked the Devil in the eye and walked away, but I've got some guy after me who could destroy my life for good."

Tom leaned over the table. "Who are you?"

"Excuse me?"

"You heard what I said."

"Nobody. I'm nobody."

"I could tell the first time I met you. Oh come on, it was obvious. You appeared out of nowhere like Eliza Doolittle and Alex was your Henry Higgins, showing you off at the ball, pretending you were happily married to Jerry. You danced with Alex like you were Fred Astaire and Ginger Rogers. You'd practiced. He was on that night like he is in court. Smooth and sober. God, you looked good together, like it was meant to be."

"I left an abusive marriage and hired Alex to help me. I already told you that."

"You've had work done on your face, too. Don't get me wrong, Shannon, you look totally natural. I just know what to look for."

"Okay, this isn't exactly the face I was born with. A lot of people get cosmetic work done."

"What happened to you? Did someone beat you until you looked like Quasimodo then dump you at Goldstein's door?"

"Something like that. Can we get back to Danny?"

"Your marriage to Jerry was weird. I can't imagine you ever having a natural attraction to the man."

"He isn't that bad."

"The guy is freaking Peter Pan. And you're no Wendy."

"I'll be the first to admit, marrying Jerry was a mistake but it seemed like a good idea at the time. We all make mistakes."

"You've been married before. Come on Shannon, I've been dealing with married women for years. You are the kind of woman who needs to be married to have the perfect life, and it isn't like you haven't had ample opportunity to meet that man of your dreams. I'm not belittling you. It's just a fact. You're the wife type."

"I don't want to talk about it."

"Fine, I'll be more than happy to identify your body, considering the fact that you have no family and I've had the good fortune to have seen you naked and therefore know your interesting and extensive identifying marks. Your back looks like a photo of a former slave."

"I told you, I had an abusive husband, hence the scars. I started a new life. That's all. It's over and done with. I told you I don't want to talk about it anymore."

We ordered dessert and coffee.

Tom continued our conversation as soon as the waiter left. "You want me take care of your ex-husband for you?"

"No." I wanted to tell him to blow Kyle Rutledge's brains out and Greg Atkinson's while he was at it, but I said nothing. I then excused myself and went to the ladies' room and threw up my dinner, but saved myself by splashing cold water on my face and touching up my makeup. I returned looking as fresh as a spring morning. Coffee and something amazing made of chocolate and berries were on our table.

"I wasn't sure you were coming back," Tom said to me with a nice sweet smile that made me want to slap him silly.

"I was thinking of that girl in Los Angeles that Danny dated. I read about her but I didn't ask Dan about it. They beat her up and raped her, then killed her by strangling her with one of Dan's ties. Rutledge had an alibi. Loads of witnesses, including his sister."

I fixed my coffee. Lots of cream. Lots of sugar. Tom put in a small shot of cream, no sugar.

"Come back to Miami with me for a month or two," he said. "You still have your condo, don't you?"

"I guess. I hadn't planned on it. What about Rutledge?"

"He's the least of your worries."

We spent the rest of the evening talking about Tom's kids and my music.

The next day, there was a story about Danny Dewitt's bag, containing bloodstained clothing, his wallet, tablet and phone. Someone found it in on the UC Berkeley campus hidden under some bushes. Nobody had seen Danny or his cat for over a month.

Two days later, Rutledge and his buddies were found in the bottom of the Sacramento River, still strapped into the seats of their rented Lexus. They'd run off the road for no apparent reason. It was called a tragic accident. I didn't ask Tom about it. He didn't say anything about it.

As a footnote in the news, it was mentioned that Kayla Rutledge was seeking grief counseling from Greg Atkinson for the loss of both her husband and brother. I was sure both of them would make money off the events.

Chapter 63

Three months after the death of Kyle Rutledge, I flew out to Miami to meet my new brother, Sean.

The man I met was a tall, good-looking guy with short ash blond hair, a cleft in his chin and a slightly thinner face. He looked good. He looked nervous. He looked like he could be my brother.

Sean's voice was a little lower than Danny's, with a slight hint of a sexy Southern drawl. A smile formed on his face when he saw me, his teeth now movie star perfect. And yes, people do remember teeth, so we have to change them as well and it might as well be for the better.

Rob greeted me with a hug and a kiss, and then preceded to tell me everything he'd done to create Sean. For the first time in three years, he seemed truly comfortable around me. By that I don't mean professional comfortable, but personal comfortable.

With a big, perfect grin, Sean showed me his arm. The vulgar Kayla tattoo had been expertly covered up with an angel of singular beauty, holding a Celtic cross and a goblet of wine. She was my design. I'd spent a week drawing her over and over to get it right. Then an expert tattoo artist had done his magic and refined the design and covered up Sean's old life forever.

I ran my hand over his arm and couldn't help but laugh. Sean gave me a big bear hug, lifting me off of my feet.

"Thank you Sis," he said.

Alex and Tasha were also there, beaming at Rob's results. They had plans for Sean. He'd live in Miami with some sort of business. Maybe something with imports. Danny had the business and manufacturing background for a variety of ventures.

I listened to their plans, which even included a 1920's Art Deco cottage that I'd purchased before I moved to California. Tasha even mentioned women she'd like him to meet. They were all beautiful professional women, hand picked just for him. Alex mentioned golf in an offhanded way. Tasha continued with her description of a perfect life for a successful single man in Miami. Life would be good for Sean Gables.

I glanced at Sean and he caught my eyes. We let Tasha talk, both knowing full well that Sean would be coming back to California with me.

The three Gables kids had become like a family of adult children, in touch but out of touch, with an unbreakable bond of secrets between us. It was normal for me, this family bound by lies, just like the Hobbs kids. Only I could trust these two.

Sean bought an aging roller rink and started to date Winter Knight. Erin continued to live in Napa, quietly away from me and everyone who had anything to do with Alex and Tasha. I continued to play in the band with Royal. Laurence and I became like any other long-term couple. Life was good, at least for a while.

Chapter 64

A man in a plain white shirt and khaki pants sat on the bench, reading under the trees. As I approached he looked up and smiled. How unlike him to smile, but it was still Jordan, with his round face and small blue eyes and round button nose. He was still cute in a childlike way, his hair still light brown, the same color mine had been, but now thin at the temples, just like our dad's and pulled back in a ponytail.

"Pastor Hobbs," I said, giving him my hand.

"Call me Jordan. I can't tell you how much joy your donations have brought our kids."

"Thanks for the pictures and letters."

"When I was a kid, I had a sister who protected me. You remind me of her."

"How so?"

"Liz had the voice of an angel when she sang. She could play anything on her guitar. I'd go down into the basement where she lived with our brother Steve, and they'd sing and play to me for hours. It was my Heaven on earth. It was my escape from the Hell our lives had become."

I sat up in bed.

In reality, Jordan wasn't a pastor. I knew that because I followed all of my siblings on social media sites.

Jordan had a job as a night-shift technician in a drug lab. He'd moved in with his weird, pink-haired pug-faced girlfriend. In her defense, she was sweet; at least she seemed sweet on her social media sites. Her name was Trinity. She fostered abandoned dogs and raised chickens in their backyard. Trinity believed that all people were good deep down inside, but she also believed in conspiracy theories, aliens on Mars, and patiently waited for the second coming of Christ, and believed the theory that Jordan's brother Liz was still alive and living in Spain.

I didn't care about her beliefs. I just cared that she loved my brother. Jordan was a happy introvert. At least I hoped he was happy. The only family members on Trinity's social media pages were Brad and his family. Go figure.

I'd had dreams about all of them. At night, my brother David would start working for terrorists in the Middle East. Kathy would murder her husband and children. Mark would find me and do things to me that would make Darren Crawford look like a saint.

Laurence rolled over and opened his eyes. "What's wrong now?"

"Nightmare. Sorry."

"You need to see someone about your dreams. Get some drugs or therapy."

"I don't need drugs."

"Herbal tea with Winter Knight, and hours on the phone with Alex isn't doing you any good."

I slid my arms around his waist and kissed him. "I know what will help me sleep."

He rolled away from me. "Shannon, you can't keep waking me up like this. I have to be up early. Didn't you remember I have to be in San Francisco by 9:00 tomorrow morning?"

"I'm sorry. Next time I'll go home."

"That might be a good idea. Goodnight, Shannon."

I was up at 4:00 am with Laurence. While he was in the shower I made coffee. He was in a better mood than he'd been the night before. I turned on the radio, just in time to hear that Gregory Atkinson had finally remarried.

Laurence's phone vibrated on the counter. Before I grew completely numb, I tapped his phone and saw the message:

Don't worry about Shannon's nightmares. Two words: narcissistic & delusional. See you soon.

The number was Tasha's. Of course it was. She was going to be a keynote speaker at the conference Laurence was attending that morning.

I was narcissistic and delusional. Good to know. Bitch. Greg had a new wife. Another bitch.

Laurence came into the kitchen impeccably dressed, wearing a red paisley patterned tie I'd given him. His arm went around my waist and he kissed me.

"Good morning, beautiful. I love you so much," he told me.

"I love you, Laurence," I said, but my mind was on Greg and Tasha.

Chapter 65

Greg's second wife was nothing like the young Elizabeth Hobbs.

Dr. Candice Turner was a psychiatrist. She had an MBA and a degree in theology along with her medical degree. Physically she couldn't have been more different than me. She was tall and graceful with few curves but definitely feminine. I guess she'd be described as willowy.

She wore her hair in sleek black pageboy, not a severe kind that plastered to her head, but a swinging glossy head of hair right out of a shampoo commercial. She had large brown eyes and a large, sensuous mouth, which she expertly applied perfect shades of deep red lipstick. She wore exquisite suits. She was rich and it was her own money from books and her private clinic. She did a lot of volunteer work, starting foundations and clinics for the underprivileged. Unlike Liz, Dr. Candice Turner was perfect.

Greg had met her at a seminar on Christian family and marriage. She was a young widow; her husband had died of a heart attack five years before she met Greg. Greg took solace with this beautiful woman with a history so much like his own. She was attracted to the sensitive man with the kind voice who had inspired thousands, even millions with his story and his books on happy equality in a Christian marriage.

She was everything I was never allowed to be.

I'd gone underground, broken the law, lived in fear, and for what? So the man who left scars on my flesh and my soul would live a perfect life with his perfect new wife? After I died it was as if everything in the world had been handed to him on a golden plate.

Maybe this was my punishment for not facing my enemy, for being a coward and a fool. Then again, I kept telling myself, I would have been a fool to stay.

I couldn't hate her. She was a lovely woman who did so much for so many people.

I wondered if Greg made her pray after they made love. I wondered if he'd ever hit her or forced her naked out into the snow. I wondered if he ever raped her over and over until she bled. Did he burn her old photos and break her fingers? I doubted it. She was perfection. I was damaged goods, to be treated accordingly. I clenched my teeth and my fists. I could feel my blood pressure rising.

I wondered what sort of pact with the Devil Greg had made. Or had he been so overcome with guilt about what he'd done to me that he vowed to God never to hurt another living thing as long as he lived? No, he'd find someone to hurt and control.

I drove down to my studio to meet Winter Knight. Once there, I walked down to the corner coffee place to get my brew and stew alone in the gallery and play my guitar until Winter showed up.

I looked at the case of pastries and got Winter's favorite, a huge apple cinnamon roll. I got coffee for myself, and a dozen donuts, plus half dozen sweet rolls for whomever stopped by. I knew it was too much sugar but I was beyond caring. I just liked the happy pink box, despite the fact that I was ready to scream. I made small talk with Charles and Will, the married owners of the café. My mother would have been appalled and then spoken to them about how Jesus could heal them of their affliction.

Sean showed up first, unexpected. He shared my coffee and helped himself to donuts.

I told him about Greg's new wife.

"I hope she makes him miserable," he said. Sean was the only one who could have understood.

"I shouldn't be so upset."

"Every time I hear anything about Kayla, or she comes out with a new song, I get pissed off. It isn't fair that the people who hurt us the most are doing great. But think about it. They think we're dead. Imagine the guilt they feel."

"Not them. People like Greg and Kayla don't feel guilt. It isn't part of their universe. Do you think I'm narcissistic and delusional?"

"No. Why?"

"Tasha thinks I am." I told him about the text.

"Screw Tasha. I don't know why Alex stays with her."

I shrugged and handed him the pink donut box. I didn't know why he stayed with her either.

"Erin hates Tasha," I said, grabbing a chocolate cake donut.

"No shit," said Sean, "Tasha treats Erin like a second class citizen. I think Tasha sees Erin as a threat too, you know, with Alex. She's always making comments about how Erin is such a slut and telling her to keep her hands off of Alex and Jerry."

"Really?" That was new to me.

"Erin isn't interested in Alex. You know she's gay, don't you?"

I laughed out loud. I'd had no idea, but it made sense. "The joke is on Tasha."

"Screw Tasha."

We both laughed again.

"So do you think I should send Greg a wedding gift?" I had to ask.

We laughed again. There was nothing else to do. We had our own lives. Success is the best revenge, even if nobody else knows about it.

Tasha was at a conference in San Francisco. Laurence said he'd meet her there. I admired them for their work to help children. As a child from an abusive home, I couldn't say enough about their work.

Alex had come out with Tasha and spent a few days at my house. Of course, he thought he knew everything before I did.

"I have news. Greg Atkinson remarried in a small private ceremony at the home of his sister."

"Alex, I know. I've been dead for years, so it isn't as if I had any legal right to the man."

I grabbed my laptop while we talked and I looked up everything I could find on the new Mrs. Atkinson.

"She used to live in Sacramento. Jackson Turner, her husband, died. They had lived a couple of blocks from Laurence's house. Son of a bitch," I said, "It looks like poor Candice came home after an out of town visit with her sister, only to find her husband dead. There was a murder investigation but the final conclusion was natural causes."

Unlike Liz, Candice was a woman of the world. Photos showed a smiling Greg with his arm around a woman who had never spilled anything on her shirt in her entire life. Her face was that of a classic beauty of good breeding. Her pale pink silk blouse and pearls made her look even more classic and beautiful. The woman was an inspiration to so many. It made me want to barf.

"Do you think he'll keep writing about me?"

"Maybe," said Alex, "But in the context of closure and moving on."

I kept browsing the Internet for stories about Greg and Candice.

It seemed they'd kept the marriage secret. Candice had become pregnant and had a miscarriage. I thought it was time for Greg to give up on the fatherhood deal. Maybe it had been him and not me. Maybe she'd become pregnant to trap him into marriage.

"Greg refused genetic testing. I bet he knew something he wasn't telling me. He said it was in the hands of God. Hey Alex," I said, "I bet if you got me pregnant, it would work out. Think about it."

"That is, if Tasha didn't kill both of us first," he said to me. I didn't even comment.

That night Tasha arrived with Laurence. Sean and Winter joined us. It was one of the last nights of the season we could have dinner on the deck before it became too cold. After we'd cleared up the plates, I stood alone with Laurence under the stars.

"Do you think you'd ever want any more kids?" I asked him.

"My girls are in high school. They'll be grown soon. I can't imagine starting over. It wouldn't be fair to them. Do you want kids?"

"No, I can't. You know that. I was just wondering. Just making sure."

He kissed me and said, "You'll make a wonderful grandmother one of these days."

As I hugged Laurence, I looked over his shoulder into the house. Tasha stood with her hands on Alex's waist. He casually had his arms over her shoulders. Despite their issues there was something magical about the two of them together.

Chapter 66

After Tasha and Laurence went back to Miami I felt like I had finally made a life of my own. Liz was gone. There was only Shannon.

I had friends. I had a new family with Sean and Erin. I was in a band. I had a man who loved me. Life was great. It was my normal. I was even thinking about going to the shelter and adopting a dog or cat. Maybe even one of each.

Then about three weeks later, life was not normal. Greg Atkinson was in the news again. I was listening to the radio, as usual, and heard the news. Then Alex called.

"Shannon, did you hear the latest about Greg Atkinson?"

"Greg's wife has been accused of killing her first husband, Jackson Turner. With any luck, she'll kill Greg, too."

"The trial will be in Sacramento," said Alex. "This is big, Shannon."

"So I heard. I'll turn off the radio and TV. I'll go to the beach house. You can meet me there. I'll open a nice bottle of wine. We can walk on the beach and grill fish. Alex, I don't care anymore."

"Greg is still looking for you."

"Who told you that?"

"Tasha."

"Where'd she get her information?"

"I don't know."

"Ask her. Why don't you ever ask her anything?"

There was a pause. Something was wrong. For someone so brilliant, when he was off the clock, the man couldn't say two words if I put him on the spot.

"She's out of town this week. She was on her way to a meeting. Don't question me on everything, Shannon."

"I'm going to marry Laurence."

"Since when?"

"Since this morning. I'm headed out right now to meet him for coffee, just like every Saturday when he doesn't spend the night at my house."

"Shannon, think about it. He doesn't love you."

"We'll talk later. I have to go. And yes, he does love me."

Laurence usually spent Sunday mornings in the office alone. He'd leave a side door open for me. I'd bring coffee and read while he worked for an hour or two. Then we'd go to lunch, then back to his house to make love for a few hours. Then we'd go to a movie, or out shopping. Then we'd go back to his house for dinner and end up in bed again.

This Sunday morning, I had a special treat for him. I put on the diamond ring he'd given me, along with a new black lace bra with matching panties. Over that I'd put on a short black sweater dress, black lace tights and royal blue knee high boots. I looked good. I couldn't stop smiling.

I started up the stairs to Laurence's second floor office, then paused when I heard voices. He was talking to another man but I couldn't place the voice.

It was familiar. Another friend, maybe?

Sometimes even Sean was known to stop by if he was in the neighborhood.

Laurence smiled and stood up when I arrived. Another man sat in the chair across from Laurence. He turned around.

It was Greg Atkinson.

Laurence smiled and stood up. "Greg, this is my coffee pal, Shannon Gables."

An older version of my husband smiled, stood and held out a hand. Gregory Atkinson shouldn't have looked so good but damn it, he did. I forced myself to smile with straightened and veneered teeth he'd never seen.

My mind raced to take inventory. The hands could give me away. My nail polish was dark silver gray. Liz only wore pale pink or clear polish. My hair was in front of my ears. I made note of the fact that I had five earrings in each ear. Liz would never have more than one pair of earrings. My shoulder length hair was a pale streaked ash blonde with no dark roots. Liz didn't have the high cheekbones or a dimple in her chin. Liz would have never worn black. Liz didn't wear eyeliner or bronzer. Liz was dead.

Greg took a quick glance at my engagement ring. Laurence didn't even notice.

Laurence smiled, having no idea what was going on.

"Shannon is in a band. They're playing this week. Greg, you should come with me to see them play."

"I'd love to," said Greg, looking at me, not at Laurence.

Laurence kept talking, "Shannon plays the guitar. She also has one of the best singing voices I've ever heard."

I tried to get Laurence to stop. "It will be kind of loud. You don't need to come if you don't want to. Laurence is just being nice. Will you be in Sacramento long?"

Greg's eyes kept on mine. "Laurence is representing my wife, Candice. I'm sure you've heard about it."

"Yes, I'm sorry. What a nightmare," I said, feeling sweat at back of my neck.

"Laurence will take care of her," said Greg. I bet Laurence would if Greg didn't take care of her first.

Laurence put his hand on my back and nudged me toward the door, "I hate to send you off, Shannon, but I'm booked all day. I'll give you a call in a few days."

A few days? "Okay, I guess. I have to go too," I mumbled, trying not to go into complete shock.

"Good to meet you Shannon," Greg took both of my hands and gave them a gentle squeeze.

"Um, you too, Greg," I said, without another look at Laurence.

I left without coffee and threw up in the bushes behind Laurence's office.

Chapter 67

I didn't tell Laurence I'd marry him or even meet with him later. I'd talk to him and tell him the truth about me. He'd understand. Okay, maybe he'd understand.

Arriving home to a cold house, I tried to play the guitar but ended up flipping through the gazillion channels on my TV as I sat and thought about Greg. I turned off the TV. It started to rain. I sat at the window and tried to will myself to stop shaking. I thought about Greg some more.

Laurence called three times but I didn't answer. Around 5:00 another call came in from Jerry. I'd never been so happy to hear from anyone in my entire life. I'd have company for the night.

After a quick check of the liquor cabinet, I ordered Chinese from a place that delivered. Made sure I had extra cash for the tip.

I fixed a strong gin and tonic and called Alex. He listened quietly as I poured out my nightmare experience.

"When is Jerry getting there?" he asked.

"Anytime," I answered.

"Jerry called me a few hours ago. He told me you saw Greg."

"I'm about to have a nervous breakdown. Alex, he was right there in Laurence's office. Laurence is going to represent Greg's wife in her murder trial."

"Forget about Greg and Laurence. Come to Miami. Book it tonight and get on a plane in the morning. You haven't been out here for a while."

"I'm playing tomorrow at the Metro."

"Cancel."

"I can't. We've been planning this forever. We're debuting Royal's new songs. Sean is going to sing, too."

There was a long pause as there so often was in our conversations.

Alex was the first to speak up. "Do you want me to come out there?"

"You're busy."

"I can be there Wednesday. I'm not booked for court again for a couple of weeks."

"If I could cry, I'd be crying right now."

I asked Alex over and over what I should do if Greg recognized me.

Alex told me, "He won't recognize you."

"Should I tell Laurence who I am?"

"He already knows who you are. You're Shannon Gables, formerly of Miami, Florida."

"Should I tell him about Liz? You know I'm going to have to."

"Absolutely not. At least wait until I'm there or at least Tasha, like we've discussed. Shannon, don't get angry, but," he paused. Alex never paused unless it was for dramatic effect.

"What?" I snapped.

"Laurence isn't the love of your life. Break it off with him."

"Excuse me? Where did that come from?"

"I don't trust him."

"Because?"

"Gut feeling."

"Gut feeling? Okay, Alex, when do you do anything on a gut feeling?"

"I do this for a living. I know when there is something wrong."

"I love him, Alex. I'm going to marry him."

"You can't marry him, Shannon. For God's sake, he called you his 'coffee pal'."

"You're drinking, aren't you? I can see you sitting outside with your bottle and bucket of ice solving everyone's problems."

"What if I told you that he won't marry you?"

"That is a conversation for later. What do I do if Greg recognizes me?"

"He won't. Is Jerry there yet?"

"I'll have him call you when he gets in."

"Shannon."

"What?"

"Be careful."

"I'll try."

"Remember that I love you."

"Love you too. I gotta go. Goodnight, Alex." I hung up, steaming and still in a panic.

Chapter 68

The next morning I was still feeling sick, not due to alcohol, but wondering if this was the end with Laurence.

I thought Laurence would understand, being a defense attorney and all, but I wouldn't understand. No sane and rational person would understand why someone would go underground and completely change their identity. I never spoke of my first twenty-six years. I never spoke of my parents, who called me an "angry willful child" and beat me until I couldn't breathe. I could explain that I was like Jane Eyre in the fact that I wasn't willful, I just didn't want to conform to something that I felt was wrong in every cell of my body and every part of my soul. I thought of the line from the book that I clung to as my own.

I looked at the quote in my own handwriting taped to the wall about my computer monitor:

"If all the world hated you, and believed you wicked, while your own conscience approved you, and absolved you from guilt, you would not be without friends."
- Charlotte Bronte, Jane Eyre

I had friends and I wasn't wicked or willful or horrible. I followed my own conscience. That was my religion now.

So, Shannon Amelia Gables. what are you going to do now?

Laurence called again and I answered.

"Where have you been?" he asked, sounding both worried and annoyed.

"Jerry is in town. We had Chinese. He showed me some cute pictures of his girls. Oh my, they are cute. I designed a new tattoo for him."

"Is Jerry there now?"

"He's still in bed. Not my bed, he slept in the guest room."

"We need to talk."

"Yes, we do."

"Shannon, tell me what's the matter. Is it Jerry?"

"It's Greg Atkinson. Don't take him on as a client. The man is evil."

"Based on what?"

"I can't talk about it on the phone. I'll call you later. Okay?"

"I have meetings all day. Shannon, I don't need this, not from you."

"When I stopped by, like I always do, you introduced me to Greg Atkinson as your friend. The friend you have coffee with."

"Is that what this is about?"

"Your 'little coffee pal'? Is that what you think of me?"

"Don't be ridiculous. I was in a professional situation. Right now, you aren't the center of my universe."

His comment stung. "Laurence, this isn't about you or your lack of respect for me. This is about Gregory Atkinson. Don't work with him."

"Shannon..."

"It will end badly for all of us. Trust me on this."

"I don't have time for this." He said a curt, "Goodbye, Shannon," and hung up. I made coffee, took a long shower and got dressed.

Chapter 69

I rehearsed in my mind what I'd tell Laurence. I thought I'd just tell him that I considered Greg Atkinson morally repugnant. But that wouldn't be an excuse because I thought most of Laurence's clients were morally repugnant, even the ones like me with secrets and off shore bank accounts holding millions of stolen dollars.

Then again, I had earned every single penny of that money.

In the midst of my reverie, the sound of the doorbell startled me. It was 8:00. Too early for Fed-X or UPS or my mail carrier, Jack. The Jehovah witnesses had come the day before. The young Mormons on their bikes were here last week.

I looked out the window. Unfamiliar American made silver sedan. My heart almost stopped.

Greg was standing at my front door.

Ignoring him wasn't an option because he saw me through the glass and waved, a hopeful smile on his still boyishly handsome face.

The cold weather and memories made my hands ache where Greg had broken my fingers in the door jamb years ago. I unconsciously touched my chin, the chin with the little cleft in it that I didn't have when I was married to Greg. Then the thought occurred that I was still married to the man at my door. The scar on my jaw line was an open wound the last time he saw me.

I opened the door trying not to snarl.

"Dr. Atkinson," I stammered, without a trace of a Philadelphia accent, trying to sound surprised, but showing the absolute heart-stopping fear and anger that almost paralyzed me.

"Shannon, I know this is a surprise visit. I hope I haven't come at an inconvenient time."

"No, not at all." The wind blew rain onto the porch. It was bad out. I could rudely let him stay outside in the cold or let America's most beloved man of God and marriage into my humble home. "Come in," I heard myself saying, in a voice that sounded alien. I took his wet raincoat and umbrella. "Um, do you drink coffee? I just made a new pot." I stammered, then wished I'd told him that I was on my way out.

As I led him into the kitchen, I saw him glancing around, checking it out. It was nothing like anything Liz would have picked out. There were no happy country florals or summertime colors. No counted cross-stitch works with warm and fuzzy sayings about Jesus or ever-loving angels. I always kept fresh flowers in modern vases, mixed with antique teapots. The mirrors were modern. The furniture was modern. The artwork a mix of modern and my own originals. He fixed his eye on a pastel of a portrait I'd done of Jerry.

"I like that one, Shannon. Is that one of yours?"

"Yes."

"I like it. You're very good."

"Thanks."

"Who is he?"

"Just a friend. Um, Jerry. His name is Jerry. He lives in Florida."

His eyes went to the two guitars on the stands in the living room. "Laurence said you played with a band at local clubs. Royal Hunt? Fun name for a band. He said you're an incredibly talented musician."

My heart almost stopped. "I have to give most of the credit to Royal Knight. He heads up the band. You know, the guitar maker."

"My first wife Liz played beautifully. Maybe you could play something for me later."

"Mr. Atkinson...or is it Dr. Atkinson?"

"Call me Greg. Shannon, I can tell you're wondering why I'm here."

"Why are you here?" I said, taking out a couple of plain black mugs. Mugs Liz would have never picked out.

"I want you to help me convince Laurence into taking my wife's case. He wasn't sold on it yesterday. I need your help."

"Why don't you ask God for help?" I couldn't believe the words came out like that.

"You don't believe, do you?"

"What? In God, or in you?"

"Both."

"I am a Christian, I just don't buy your brand of religion."

"I'm not here to convert you, Shannon," he said quietly in a voice that could calm a rabid wolverine. "I need your help. This isn't just for me but for my wife."

"You don't even know me."

I poured the coffee and only added half and half, skipping the sugar, wishing I'd put in whiskey. I fixed his without even thinking.

"I'm sorry, I just automatically fixed it. I'll pour you another cup."

"This is perfect," he said, taking the mug from me and setting it on the counter.

I could feel his eyes on me. I was wearing something Liz would have never worn – a skin tight black tee shirt with a deep V neck, dangly jet black crystal earrings, well worn jeans, black work shoes. Everything showed off my figure to my best, or right now worst, advantage. No Liz Atkinson lace-trimmed tops or flowing skirts here.

My shoulder from where Darren had stabbed me began to ache. It always ached when I was cold or under extreme stress, and I was both now.

Greg looked into my face, searching for Liz. My cheeks, my chin, then he set on my eyes, underneath the rectangular olive green frames I wore today. Liz didn't wear glasses, she didn't look like me. Even my teeth were different, the chips gone, the slight crooked bottom teeth straightened. They were perfect. There was nothing I could do about my mouth, but it was covered with a glossy rose that Liz would have never worn. Liz only wore simple clear gloss and a hint of mascara and a little blush. Shannon had smoky gray eyeliner and lids, light foundation, thick dark lashes, overly pierced ears, high cheekbones, dimpled chin, and blonde hair.

I knew he was wondering what sort of bra I was wearing. That part of me was original equipment. I backed up against the counter.

"You're quite beautiful. I don't think you realize that," Greg said to me quietly. He used to tell me that all the time.

I could feel my heart trying to jump out of my chest. I thought of screaming down the hall for Jerry to come shoot Greg right between the eyes. I looked down into my coffee cup, then back up to Greg. If he touched me I was ready to throw hot coffee in his face, only the amount of milk I'd put in it had made it barely warm. I grabbed my oversized sweatshirt off of a kitchen chair, put it on and zipped it half way up.

"Listen, Dr. Atkinson, Greg, I can't tell Laurence what to do. If he takes you on as a client it will have to be because he believes in the merits of your wife's case." I paused and took a few sips of coffee. "I don't interfere with Laurence's business. I'm sorry, it's just a rule I have to separate that part of our lives."

"Laurence said you're into genealogy."

"A little."

"He said you were obsessed with it."

I almost rolled my eyes. "I don't know where he came up with that. I am a photographer who uses antique cameras and techniques. Genealogy is a tool in my research, just like any other tool."

"Liz, my first wife, was obsessed with genealogy."

"A lot of people are. I just dabble in it for my photography research."

I poured more coffee in silence. The rain came down in torrents. I glanced out the window to see it splashing in the pool.

"You and Liz have a lot in common."

"I doubt it," I said, wanting to run out the door.

"Liz was heavily into genealogy and music, as are you. But it's more than that. I suppose it is the way you stand, the way you hold your coffee mug, that reminds me of her."

"You could make those comparisons about anyone."

I took a swig off of my coffee and tried to think of words to get him out of my house.

Greg spoke first. "Laurence told me a lot about you."

"Why would he do that? I'm just his coffee pal."

"I was curious about the skittish blonde who'd all but bounced into his office this morning. We were discussing murder and there you were like sunshine personified. Then he said something to piss you off. I don't know exactly what it was, but I could see it in your eyes."

"I didn't expect him to have company."

"I know you're involved with him, romantically, maybe even in love with him. I saw the ring on your finger."

"We're engaged, sort of."

"I can't imagine Laurence not being in love with you. He'd be an idiot not to be."

"Why are you really here?" I asked, with just a hint of anger in my voice.

"I'm desperate to help my wife. I need Laurence Yantz on my team."

"I can't help you."

"Please, Shannon." He took my hand, "You're my only hope."

I gently pulled my hand away. "Like I said before, tell God about it. I'm not the one you need to be talking to."

He stepped closer, leaning next to me over the counter, his shoulder touching mine. "I think we'll be spending a lot of time talking in the near future," he said, "My marriage with Candice is a lie. It is all but over. I'm a free man, Shannon."

I wanted to crawl out of my skin, when behind me a voice sounding like the angel of hope spoke up in a slight southern drawl.

Chapter 70

"Whoa, Dude, I can't believe it. Holy Moly. Dr. Gregory Atkinson is here in the flesh."

And from the hallway came Jerry Anderson, in all his glory. Shirtless, drawstring red pajama bottoms hanging low on his narrow hips, shaggy white-blond hair brushing his shoulders, six-pack abs tanned to perfection, and on his perfectly sculpted arms, full sleeves of finely wrought tattoos.

Greg looked noticeably surprised but remained calm in his most perfect pastoral way. Not the kind of guy Greg would like to see in my house, much less know I'd been married to the man.

Jerry held out his hand, "Jerry Alexander. Shannon's ex-husband. Just passing through."

Greg looked confused but quickly hid it with a bright smile and shook Jerry's hand.

"Jerry is just passing through on business," I added.

"Hey, don't get the wrong idea. Laurence is the love of her life, her passion of passions, her man. I'm just the lowly ex. Slept in the guest room."

"Check this out, Greg." Jerry turned around and showed a large, finely done and extremely realistic tattoo on his back of a beautiful woman and two small children. "This is my wife, Heather and our beautiful daughters, Lilly and Jasmine. Shannon drew them for me and I had them put on me permanently. You know why?" he asked Greg, quietly and mysteriously.

"Why?"

"So that they'll always be watching my back. They're always with me in here," Jerry touched his heart, "And here," he pointed to his back.

"Can I ask why you two got divorced? You seem pretty comfortable with each other."

Jerry had a quick answer, "Aside from the unbelievably fantastic sex, we didn't have anything in common. Goals, dreams, lifestyle, you know, the usual."

"Did you go to counseling?" Of course, Greg asked about counseling.

I spoke up, "We didn't need it. Why blow a good friendship over a bad marriage?"

"Plus, I'm an asshole," said Jerry. "So Greg, Shannon tells me you've been meeting with Laurence over your wife's murder case."

At that point I was about to deck Jerry. "Jerry, honey, anything between Laurence and Dr. Atkinson is confidential. He can't go into details."

Jerry looked at Greg with a sarcastic smile. "Do you love your current wife, Greg?"

"Yes, of course I do," said Greg.

Jerry shot back again. "You'd do anything for her, wouldn't you?"

"That is why I'm here," said Greg, still calm as ever.

"Do you think she killed her first husband?" Jerry asked.

"The accusations are ridiculous. Candice didn't do it," said Greg.

Jerry squinted his eyes at Greg. "Did you love your first wife? You know, Liz, the one who died."

Greg glanced at me. I stood, poker faced, wanting to run out of the room.

"You don't have to answer that," I said to Greg. "Jerry, don't be rude," I hissed at my former husband and soon to be former friend.

"I still love Liz with all my soul. Not a day goes by when I don't think of her," Greg said quietly.

Jerry continued his thoughts, "Liz was murdered. Man, I don't know how you lived through that."

"My love for Liz and my faith helped me get through it," said Greg.

Jerry leaned against the kitchen counter and squinted his eyes again. "A serial killer. The Killer of Virtue. Did you ever wonder how a man could do such horrible things to a woman? Could you imagine beating and sexually violating a woman until she begs you to stop? That is pure evil."

"Liz is in a better place now," said Greg.

Jerry turned to me. "What do you think Shannon? Do you think Liz is in a better place?"

"Yes, Jerry, I know in my heart Liz is in a better place," I said, trying not to grit my teeth and ball my fists.

Jerry turned back to Greg. "So Greg, let me ask you this, did you love Elizabeth Atkinson when you gave away her brother Steve's guitar and burned her photo albums? Did you love her when you refused to let her go back to engineering?"

Finally Greg looked surprised. "What are you talking about?"

Jerry was on a roll now. "Did you love her when you told her the reason she had all of those miscarriages was because God was punishing her for being a bad wife? Did you love her when you publicly humiliated her by calling her barren? Did you love her when you let her family and yours belittle her and treat her like their dog?"

"What a minute…" But Greg was cut off.

At this point Jerry was yelling like a crazed rattlesnake-waving hellfire and damnation preacher. I knew at this point I couldn't do anything to stop him. Nobody could.

"Tell me Greg, did you love Liz the nights alone in your bedroom when you degraded her in every way a man could degrade a woman? Did you love her when you raped and sodomized her, then dragged her naked out to the snow and forced her to lie flat on her belly and confess her sins as she cried and begged you to let her go inside? And when you returned inside you raped her again and again, until she was bruised and bleeding and begging you to stop, so you got out your belt and beat her until she stopped begging and confessed her sins to you and your God. Then a few hours later, with blood flowing from her back and from between her legs like an evil river of shame, you did it all over again and then realized what you'd done and forced her, down on her knees again to pray to God once again for forgiveness and obedience."

I stood in shock, listening and trying not to scream.

"That's ridiculous. You're crazy. Shannon, you can't believe that."

"Greg, please, you need to go now," I whispered, almost ready to tell him who I really was when another voice interrupted.

Chapter 71

"Jerry Alexander, what the hell are you doing?" I turned. There was Laurence in the dining room, coming toward the kitchen, raincoat and umbrella in hand.

Jerry's eyes narrowed. Gone was the Florida beach bum. Behind those eyes lay something cold and hard.

"Elizabeth Atkinson was habitually tortured and degraded by the Reverend Dr. Gregory Atkinson. The day she was abducted by the Killer of Virtue she wrote in her journal about what he'd done to her in the days before. It was as bad as anything that monster did to her, or worse because it was done to her by her husband. By the man she loved. By the man joined to her in the name of Christ."

"Where did you get this information, Jerry?" Laurence asked cautiously, not giving away much.

"He used to be a narcotics detective in Florida. He did a lot of undercover work," I said.

Jerry started yelling at Greg. "Elizabeth kept a diary! I've read it. I know what you did to her before she was murdered. I know what you did to her night after night! I know the shame…"

"Shut up, Jerry," said Laurence. "Greg, is that true?"

"I loved my wife," said Greg.

"That isn't what I asked," said Laurence.

"Of course it isn't true. Whatever he read, if he did read anything, was a lie."

"Women usually don't lie about things like that," I said in a low voice.

Greg looked at me in shock, with a hint of recognition. But it couldn't have been me because I was dead. I looked at Laurence and almost died again, seeing the shock on his usually calm face. "Jerry is obviously mentally ill."

'You shouldn't be here," Laurence took Greg by the arm and led him to the living room.

Jerry turned to me, "I had to confront the evil bastard. I had to protect Elizabeth's honor."

"Liz is dead, you asshole. You never knew her. Now my life is over. Thanks a fucking million, Jerry."

"Come on Shannon, you're glad I told the bastard off."

"Judas. You just signed my death warrant."

"Greg isn't coming back."

"I'm dead. Again."

We stood in silence and waited. I heard the door open and shut. A car started. Laurence came back into the room.

"Both of you'd better have a good story," he said to us. I'd never seen him so angry.

"Or what?" asked Jerry.

"Let me take care of this," I said. "Don't say anything else, Jerry."

I went to my office and brought back two identical documents that I'd prepared a while back. I always knew one day I'd have to do this. I grabbed my checkbook out of my purse. I started to write out a check out to Laurence for $30,000.

"What are you doing?" asked Laurence.

"I'm hiring you. $15,000 is for me, and $15,000 for Jerry. That should be a sufficient retainer."

"Shannon, I don't understand. Why would I need a retainer?"

I put the paper in front of him and slammed a pen on the counter. "Just sign the papers. It states that you are our attorney. As our attorney, anything we say to you is confidential and you can not repeat it unless you want to be disbarred and lose everything."

"Shannon, what is going on?"

I gave Laurence the check. "I'm not saying anything until you sign the contracts."

"What have the two of you done?"

"Just sign." I looked at my second ex-husband. "Jerry, just shut up. Don't say anything until I tell you to."

Laurence signed the contracts. "All right. Tell me what is going on."

I looked at Jerry. He glared at me and ran his hands through his hair.

Laurence glared at me. "Shannon, what is going on?"

I glared back. "Don't you have meetings this morning?"

"I've cancelled."

"Go back to your work. I'm sure you have business with Greg Atkinson to take care of."

"4:45 this afternoon. Meet me in my office."

"Fine. I'll be there."

Chapter 72

Today I would lose Laurence. My new family tree would end on my short broken branch. I might go into hiding again. I might go to jail. I might have to leave the country. My fate was in the hands of a man who I knew loved me, or maybe didn't love me.

I had to admit, it had been an interesting morning. That afternoon, Laurence was still seething in a calm rage. He motioned for me to sit.

I spoke carefully, "Greg Atkinson showed up at my house to ask me to plead his case to you."

"What sort of game are you and Jerry playing?"

"We're not playing a game. I didn't know Greg Atkinson was going to show up and I sure as hell didn't know Jerry would spout his idiot mouth off. "Laurence, don't blame..."

"Where's Jerry?"

"On his way back to Florida."

"Tell me about this diary Jerry claimed he'd read."

"The diary was written by Elizabeth Atkinson. As with many who write diaries, it was a way for her to write down her innermost feelings and most private experiences without exposing herself to others. I've come across many such documents in my research. Most diaries are just chronicles of the weather and common events, but in rare cases the writer's most intimate experiences, thoughts and ideas are expressed."

Laurence slammed his fist on his desk. "Cut the crap, Shannon."

"What do you want me to say?" My stomach started to cramp.

"I want you to say that Jerry is fucking crazy and there is no diary."

"Jerry is crazy, but he was telling the truth about what happened to Elizabeth Atkinson."

"Jerry's accusations, if true, will turn Greg Atkinson's life upside down."

Greg Atkinson's life? He had no idea it would ruin my life as well. "Nobody has to know about it."

"You're damned right nobody will know about it. When Greg came to me I did a little research, read his books, I called old friends. He loved Elizabeth. I talked to him about her. The man is still deeply in love with her. Jerry's accusations are insane."

I put my hand to my jaw line and felt the scar. "What Jerry said is true."

"Maybe Jerry mistook him for Darren Crawford."

"Jerry didn't mistake Greg Atkinson for Darren Crawford."

"Have you read To Elizabeth With Love?"

"Sure. Everyone cried when they read it." I knew I sounded sarcastic. I was being sarcastic but it was true, unfortunately.

"Well?"

"It was a piece of schlocky sentimental drivel, written so Greg Atkinson could make himself look like a saint. Handsome ex-foot ball player, intellectual theologian, Dr. Gregory Atkinson, the man with the halo and a heart of gold. Blah, blah, blah. Marries a college dropout and whips her into shape, making her the perfect wife, and mother, that is, if she could ever have enough faith to carry a pregnancy to full term."

"I don't need the attitude, Shannon."

"He profited from his wife's death. He didn't love her, so much as he owned her."

"That's not what he said in the book, or what he said to me."

"I don't care what Greg Atkinson told you."

"Do you honestly think he could have raped and beaten his wife?"

"I know for a fact that he raped and beat his wife. He physically and psychologically tortured Liz for years before Darren Crawford got to her."

We sat across from each other, staring. I broke off his gaze. I wasn't going to play stare down with him.

Laurence spoke first. "Where is the diary? Do you know?"

"I'm not telling you anything until you agree to be my attorney."

"Why the secrecy? What's the deal, Shannon? Did Jerry steal crime scene evidence, or what? Tell me."

"Are you going to cash the check?"

He looked at me blankly. I asked again, "The check for $30,000 I gave you this morning. Are you going to cash it?"

"No. Of course not."

"You signed the contract. Are you my lawyer?"

"I'm your lover."

"No, you're a guy I have casual coffee with."

"Shannon, come on."

"Are you my lawyer?"

"Shannon, what do you have against Greg Atkinson?"

"Don't change the subject. Are you my lawyer?"

"Yes."

"So whatever we speak about is confidential."

"Yes."

"I have Elizabeth's diary."

"Jesus Christ, Shannon. What are you doing with it?"

I paused, trying to decide if I'd tell him the whole truth and nothing but the truth or just leave and never see him again.

He glared at me. "Have you ever considered it might be a fake? Have you?"

"Her body was never found," I said quietly, trying to calm him down.

"Are you telling me you and Jerry know where her body is?"

"Well, yes, I suppose."

"What do you mean, you suppose? Shannon, what do you and Jerry know about Elizabeth Atkinson? What is your connection with Elizabeth Hobbs? Did you know her? Shannon, I am running out of patience with you."

I'd run out of words. My stomach cramped again. I hugged myself, trying not to get sick.

Laurence kept on his lecture at me. "Greg has done nothing wrong. Your story is sheer fantasy."

"You'll defend the Devil himself, but you have no faith me." I got up to leave.

Laurence got up. "Stay where you are."

I said nothing and put on my coat.

"I am bound by law as your attorney to keep anything you say to me confidential. Please, Shannon, tell me what is going on." He blocked the door and then put his hands on my shoulders. I thought of Greg and Darren. I could hardly catch my breath.

"Let me go!" I snapped, pushing his hands off of me.

My reaction actually frightened him. He backed off and looked shocked, hurt, concerned. I really couldn't tell. Then the trial lawyer, just like something out of a movie kicked in, and he was on the attack. "What do you know about the whereabouts of Elizabeth Atkinson's body?"

"I'll show you exactly what happened to her body." I pulled my coat off and threw it to the floor, then pushed up the sleeves of my sweater and held up my arms in front of his face. "Darren Crawford made these cuts on Elizabeth's arms. The scars on Elizabeth's backside, the raised welts you've touched when we make love, are from when Greg beat her with a belt, then a whip because she wasn't an obedient wife. The dark scar on her knee is from when she was forced by her husband to kneel naked in the snow and gravel and pray for forgiveness. The scar on her jaw happened when Elizabeth turned her head so she wouldn't have to see the anger in her husband's face and Greg hit her with the belt buckle." I took a deep breath and touched the scar. "I didn't have the plastic surgeon completely remove it when he rebuilt my face, so I'd never forget what that man had done to me."

My voice remained steady but my hands were shaking at that point. I'd never been so angry in my life. And it was my life, not something controlled by my family or husband, serial killer or church, and sure as hell not by my current boyfriend. I had a voice and so did Liz.

"Shannon..."

I pulled the pink hardbound notebook out of my purse and pushed it into his hands.

"I am Liz Atkinson. This is my diary. Everything I wrote in this book is true. Every single word. If you tell a soul about this, you will never see me again. I will go someplace where you will never find me. I will vanish off the face of the earth. But before I go, I will expose Gregory Atkinson for the sick bastard he is."

Chapter 73

People have several reactions when they hear something that is so bizarre they can't believe it. I hate to use a cliché, but Laurence actually did look like he'd seen a ghost.

"You need more proof, Laurence? In To Elizabeth With Love, Greg wrote that the inscription in our wedding rings read, True Love E&G. The real inscription is, True Love L&G. I never went by Elizabeth. I was always Liz. Tell Greg you want to see the ring. He'll be happy to show it to you.

Fingerprints, DNA, dental records - it will all match. Look at my eyes. They're still the same. You want the voice? I can still do the voice. Look at the writing. Get samples from Greg. It will all match up."

Laurence opened the diary and started to read my handwriting. He flipped through the pages, his face expressionless. Then he closed his eyes and took a deep breath. He got up and locked his office door, then called his admin and told her that he didn't want to be disturbed by anyone except an emergency with his daughters.

We talked for two straight hours. Laurence learned about my dysfunctional, loveless family. I told him about the night Steve died and the night Brad and I almost killed each other. I told him everything about my life with Greg. After that, he listened to the entire story about my two weeks in captivity with Darren Crawford and my escape. I told him everything except about finding the money and the real reason I married Jerry. I wasn't about to tell him about that. I didn't go into details about my friendship with Alex Goldstein.

He asked questions but gave me no strong reactions.

"Who else knows about this besides Jerry?"

"Just Alex and Tasha," I lied again.

"What about Sean and Erin? They aren't your siblings."

"They're just friends. We call ourselves family because..." I didn't want to go into it. "They started over too, in their own way. We made our own family. I don't want to get them involved in my problems. Okay?"

"Are you and Jerry still involved?"

"Excuse me? Don't be stupid. I divorced him years ago. The marriage was a sham to give me a history. You're the only man I've loved since Greg. Laurence, there is nobody else."

"What about Goldstein?"

"No. Where did that come from?"

"You lied to me about everything else. The lies come so easy to you, don't they?"

Of course lies came easy to me. I was a natural liar, but I wasn't going to tell Laurence that.

"Shannon." He said my name deliberately, as if making a statement just by saying it. "Give me some time to figure out what I'm going to do about your situation. I'll call you."

"There is nothing to figure out," I said. "Tell Greg to go home. If it's the money you're worried about, I can compensate you for whatever you would have made from Greg."

Laurence gave me a look of disgust. "You need to go now."

"This shouldn't make a difference."

"You lied to me. I gave you my heart and in return you gave me a lie."

My entire body went numb. "Laurence, how I feel about you, about us, has never been a lie. I'd never lie to you what we have and who I am right now."

"Tell me, Shannon, did you date me because I'm a defense attorney? Am I just a convenient safety net just in case you got caught?" He handed me my coat and purse. "You need to go now."

I looked into his eyes. There was nothing there.

"I don't get it. You stand by the man who abused me and drove me to suicide, then profited from my death," I said, trying to convince him one more time that I was right.

"Do you know how pathetic you sound right now?"

"Screw you, Laurence or Larry or whatever the fuck your name is! You're just as fake as I am, or maybe even more so."

In my usual way, I threw up by my car, which was parked next to Laurence's car. He would have to step over it. It was a small triumph. I took a deep breath and wished I could cry. I checked my dinging phone. There were five messages from Royal and Sean. We had a concert to get ready for. I couldn't be late.

Chapter 74

A few years back, on my way out to California with Jerry, I picked out a Gibson Les Paul custom 1958 Black Beauty at a vintage guitar shop in Las Vegas. Despite the fact that I had two custom guitars from Royal, this was, well, this was my 1958 Black Beauty. Of course, it was the perfect accessory for my red wiggle dress with the sweetheart neckline and open back. I wore my old silver charm bracelet that had belonged to my grandmother. Good luck charms, I thought to myself.

For a few hours, I'd be able to forget Laurence and Greg, and everything except the band and our fans.

We had a good crowd of about two hundred. Royal and I sang lead vocals plus guitar. Sean sang back up and played keyboards, Chase was on the bass and our drummer, Winter, in a white halter dress, sang back-up. Two families – one band. It was magic, at least to me.

Our style was kind of Punk Pop with a bit of Rock-a-Billy thrown in. We had our fixed set but we'd do whatever people shouted out to us, too. Since I owned the building, we could play all night if we wanted to.

Someone shouted Sleep Walk! and then everyone started to chant. It was the 1959 song by The Farina brothers, Santo and Johnny. Royal and I did a guitar duo. Then I sang some original lyrics, and then we were back to an extended guitar version.

All of the stress of my life was gone. Royal and I were one, together, in a moment of pure musical perfection. Sometimes during practice, I'd imagine my brother Steve was there with us as a guitar trio.

We finished. The crowd went crazy cheering and clapping. Royal and I gave each other a sweaty hug. Then I looked at the back of the club and almost stopped breathing. Laurence and Greg stood at the bar, smiling at me.

Sean saw them too, and stepped over to me for support. He put his arm around my waist and whispered, "Don't panic. I'm here. No matter what. Shit. Why tonight?"

"We're screwed," I said. Sean kissed my cheek and went back to his place behind the keyboard.

Royal made the signal for the next song, a new one we'd just started to practice on. Something crazy that got my mind somewhere else again, sort of, but not really.

After that Royal said we were going to take a fifteen minute break. The crowd cheered. I watched Greg Atkinson come toward the stage where I was standing, pretending to fool around with my guitar.

Greg approached and smiled up at me. "Black Beauty. Is it original or a reissue?"

"Original. Don't touch it."

"Shannon, I'll be in town for a few more days. Come to dinner with me tomorrow."

"You're married."

"Separated. I filed for divorce last Wednesday."

"I'm busy."

"Saturday, then."

"I'm sorry, Greg. You're a nice guy and all but this isn't going to happen. Okay?"

"Hey, Shan." Sean stepped in between us. "My sister's pretty talented isn't she?" he said to Greg.

"Greg Atkinson, this is my brother Sean. Sean, this is Greg." It was a lie of a lifetime. I was off the hook.

Greg was charming. "The family resemblance is uncanny. Good to meet you, Sean."

Greg took my hand and looked into my eyes. "Say yes to tomorrow. Just think about it."

Feeling like I wanted to chew my arm off, I pulled it away.

An hour later we finished the show. Sean and I were both ready to run, but not before I had a talk with Laurence.

Laurence was at the bar talking to Royal and a few friends. I grabbed his arm and dragged him away.

"What the hell are you doing here with Greg? Do you hate me that much? Do you?"

"You've been rehearsing this show for a month. You think I'd miss it?"

"You brought Greg." I almost added some profanity but thought the better of it.

"He doesn't know who you are."

"Laurence, you shouldn't have brought him here. Greg is hitting on me. Did you tell him who I am? Does he know?"

"No, of course not. Cut the hostile crap."

"If anything bad happens, it will be your fault." I just blurted it out. I didn't even know why.

"What will happen? Greg thinks you're attractive. So what? Get over yourself."

I balled my hand into a fist, about to slam him the same way I used to hit my brothers, but I stopped myself. "I hate you."

"Shannon, you don't mean that."

227

I didn't answer or turn around. I was shaking. I put my guitar in its case, grabbed my purse and coat and left out the back door for my apartment that I still kept next door.

I hauled my guitar down the sidewalk and almost twisted my ankle in my heels. I took off my shoes and continued barefoot to the door. After dropping the keys, I finally got the door open. Then I heard the voice behind me.

"Shannon." It was Greg. "May I come in?"

"Please, leave me alone. I don't feel well. Just leave me alone." I tried to stay calm but the panic was starting to set in.

"I need to talk to you."

"Shannon, wait up." It was Sean at the bottom of the stairs. "Sorry, am I interrupting something?"

"No, come on up. I was just going to call you to help me with something."

"Sure no problem," said Sean, coming to my rescue. "Are you staying, Greg?"

"He has to leave," I said quickly, "He just wanted to tell me he enjoyed the show. Goodnight, Greg."

Greg smiled and kissed me on the cheek. "Dream of me," he whispered in my ear.

I took Sean's arm and pulled him into the apartment then slammed and locked the door.

Sean just stood with a look of shock on his face. "Does Greg know who you are?"

"I don't know."

"What about Laurence?"

"He knows. He broke up with me when I told him." I told him what had happened with Jerry.

"I never liked Laurence. He treated you like a child. Hey, do you want me to stay at your house tonight? Or I can stay here with you."

"I'm okay. Go be with Winter."

"Hey, Sean?"

"Hey, Shannon?"

"Could you switch cars with me? I'll bring yours back this weekend."

He smiled. "No problem, sis. What do I tell Greg when he follows me home?"

For the first time in the past 48 hours, I laughed.

Chapter 75

After arriving home and changing into old sweat pants and my favorite old worn out hoodie, I couldn't even think straight. Sleep wasn't an option. All I could think of was Greg. I thought about Sean and what might happen to him if he was exposed. I needed to cry so badly so I poured myself a glass of vodka over ice with a chunk of lime and tried to figure out what I'd do now.

If I had to leave I'd lose the people I loved. Royal, Winter, Chase and maybe even Sean and Erin would be gone. Alex and Tasha would be gone. Jerry would be gone.

I'd learned to survive, to be without, and to stay distant. I lived in my own self-made world of lies, so who was I to mourn the loss of anything? What right did I have to let people in my life care about me? What right did I have to love anyone or have friends or family?

I got on the computer, looking at travel sites. Maybe I could go to Europe and bring Sean with me. We'd take the grand tour. I could go up to Yellowstone and spend my days watching steam rise out of the snow while drinking whiskey-laced hot chocolate. I had to stop thinking about drinking.

Laurence knew who I was. Excuse me, who I am now.

Greg. I couldn't get Greg out of my head. The way he swept in trying to seduce me, to lure me into his clutches. If he knew who I was... I had no idea what he'd do. I'd imagined it over and over but it was nothing like this.

My mind shot to Alex. I closed my eyes and my head filled with his voice, the touch of his hand...

"Shannon? Hi."

I came out of my pity party and whipped around. Greg was standing behind me, hair damp from the rain, his coat obviously somewhere else in the house.

"The door was open. I knocked but you didn't answer."

"What are you doing here?" I didn't know what else to say.

"I wanted to spend some time with you, alone," he said quietly.

"That isn't going to happen," I told him.

"You have a connection to Liz."

"Could be, but it doesn't really matter, Dr. Atkinson. I'm not going to talk to you anymore and I'd like you to leave."

"Liz had problems. She came from an extremely abusive home. The diary was an exaggeration of her fears of abuse going back to her childhood."

"You're so full of crap. Get out of my house."

"You're scared, because you know I'm telling the truth. All of those things you told Jerry about Liz were just the signs of possible mental illness brought on by the perverse torture Darren Crawford inflicted on her, compounded by the abuse at the hands of her own family."

"Get out, before I call the police."

"You can't call the police. They'll discover your real name. Can't let that happen, can you, Liz?"

I didn't know what to say. I was frozen.

He stepped closer. "I knew I'd find you, one day, alive."

I had to get away. If I could get out of the house I'd be out of the country in a matter of hours. I moved past him, trying to get to the stairs. He grabbed the back of my sweatshirt. I pulled out of it.

The charms on my bracelet made a musical noise and for a moment snagged on the sleeve. He grabbed my wrist in a viselike grip. I'd forgotten how fast he was, but not how strong.

"If you'd left that bracelet at Darren's house, I would have believed you were dead. I knew you'd never leave that behind," he said.

The bracelet that my grandmother had given me that I wore almost every single day I was married to him. Yes, I had a grandma until I was ten. She didn't like my parents or me for that matter, but she gave me her bracelet. It made me feel normal. I was wearing it the day I saw him in Laurence's office.

Years of working out and taking various classes at the gym paid off. I stomped on Greg's foot and twisted myself out of his grip. I ran down the hall. Then the unexpected happened. The forty-four-year-old ex-jock football player tackled me to the ground. As I hit the carpet, my lungs seemed to collapse underneath his weight. I felt the sting of the rug burn on my elbows and knees.

I tried to get up. He kept his hold on me and started to work at my pants. I fought him with nails and elbows, trying to get away. As Greg roughly yanked my sweat pants off like an expert, I swore to God he was going to rape me right there between the linen closet and the spare bathroom. But he just looked down, his eyes on the scar from the skin graft on my leg where Kathy had burned me with hot bacon grease. He flipped me over to my back and held me down.

"Not a day has gone by, not an hour has gone by, in twelve years, when I haven't thought of you," he said, his voice almost a whisper.

We were both breathing hard. His full weight was on me, his face close to mine, lying between my legs, my bare thighs around his hips. There was nothing between Greg and me except my small lace panties and a thin cotton tank top. I'd never been so scared in my life.

"Get off of me, Greg."

"I saw him cut your arms. I saw the video." His voice was calm but so sad, so anguished. "He made twelve cuts, six on each arm, each time asking you to denounce your faith. He cut slow to make you suffer. You screamed and begged him to stop but he kept cutting deeper and deeper, once down to the bone. With each cut and each scream part of me died."

"Please," I whispered, "Let me go." I could hear myself saying the same thing over and over to Darren Crawford.

Greg kept talking, "They told me not to watch it but I had to see what he did to you. I watched him touch you with his hands and his mouth. I watched him grind himself in and out of you like an animal. I heard you begging him to stop. Over and over you called my name, asking for me to save you."

This couldn't be happening. There was rage in his eyes but also a profound sadness. His voice actually cracked before he composed himself.

"You called my name. I couldn't help you." He put his forehead against mine and closed his eyes.

I called for help? I might have. I probably did. Alex said I did. After spending years blocking whatever I could about my experience with Darren Crawford out of my brain, I honestly didn't want to relive it again.

I tried to roll over and push him off. Greg held me down tight. He kept talking.

"I went to Darren's house after his body had been found, after they'd found his torture chamber. I was told you'd lost too much blood to survive, but I couldn't give up hope that I'd find you alive."

I closed my eyes then opened wide. He was still there. We stared at each other, neither blinking nor speaking. I tried to figure out what was behind his eyes.

Finally I spoke. "Yes, I am alive, now get off of me."

He didn't get off of me. In fact, he ignored anything I said about it. He just kept talking. "When I saw you in Laurence's office, it was a strain to recognize you. But your eyes haven't changed. Your mouth is the same. The same lips I kissed so many times." He kissed me gently. "Yes, it is you."

I said nothing. I'd frozen, like when I was a kid. It was better to say nothing than to risk being hit, again.

"Why didn't you come home?" he asked, with more anger in his voice.

I couldn't say anything. I had thousands of words in my head to answer him but I couldn't get anything out.

"Why?" he demanded again.

My voice jump-started, "I was afraid."

His expression became gentler. "Darren is dead. He can't hurt you. What he did to you will never change the way I love you. Nothing can change that." His mouth met mine in a soft, sweet kiss. I felt my chest grow tight. Soft and sweet turned more urgent. I turned my head.

"You killed my soul," I said, barely a whisper.

"What did you say?" he asked, looking shocked and indignant.

"You killed my soul!" I yelled, trying to push him away. His grip loosened but he held me down tight.

"Liz..."

"Liz is dead. You killed her the night you dragged me out into the snow and beat the crap out of me and broke my ribs and forced me to have sex with you until I was ill. I went to the bridge and I jumped because I wanted to die rather than go back to you. I was already dead when Darren pulled me out of the river. You killed me."

"Dear God," he gasped, "Liz, dear sweet Liz."

"Let go of me, or so help me God, I'll kill you."

He hit me full across the face. I thought my eye was going to explode. I gasped, but no words came out.

"Still can't cry, can you?" he snarled, with the sadistic smile I'd seen too many times before, always right after he'd hurt me.

I couldn't move; the pain was so intense. I could feel myself going into some sort of shock.

"You're my wife. You made a vow to love, honor and obey until death."

I focused myself for an answer. "For heaven's sake Greg, get off of me and get the hell out of whatever delusional world you're living in."

His face changed to that of a man in charge. He put his face close to mine. Nose to nose, lips to lips. His voice grew unemotional and serious. I'd heard it before. Greg was in control again.

"Excuse me, Shannon? You've broken how many laws? False identity, stolen money, offshore accounts, lying to law enforcement, to start. I'm your lord and savior as far as you're concerned. You're going down, little girl, and you want me on your side as your loving husband, not your adversary."

I was speechless. How did he know? Did Laurence tell him? Son of a bitch.

"If you say anything to contradict me, nobody will believe you." He was right. Nobody would believe me. How could Greg, a man who loved me still after all these years be the monster I claimed he was? I was screwed any way I looked at it.

He could have known about changing identity, but nobody knew about the money except Alex, Tasha and Jerry. I know he didn't get the information from Jerry. I tried to think quickly but my brain fogged over.

"I never believed you were dead," Greg said, still holding me down. "A few months after Darren died, I got a call from a doctor in South Carolina. He said he'd seen a girl with deep, infected cuts on her arms. She'd been raped and was suffering with extreme pelvic infections. She'd had a miscarriage. She had an east coast accent and a burn mark on her thigh. It was you, Liz."

I was feeling really stupid and scared out of my mind.

"Who was the father of the child?"

"I don't know. It could have been you. It could have been Darren. I'm sure it was yours, but I don't know. It doesn't matter."

"Dear God."

"Greg, I can't breathe. Please get off of me."

"You ruined my life. You're going to make up for lost time."

"I ruined your life? My death made you a star. It was the best thing that ever happened to you."

He seemed surprised I'd even think that.

I kept talking. "Listen to me, Greg. If I came back, everything would be gone. You've made a career of me. To Elizabeth with Love is still on every bestseller list. You've got the marriage and grief recovery books. All are best sellers. You have zillions of interviews, the speaking engagements. How many times have you told people that you knew I'd gone to heaven? For Pete's sake, how many times have you told the story about seeing a vision of me with an angel, beckoning me no less, to come to heaven with him. Nobody would believe you anymore. If I came back, your faith would be a lie and everything you ever said, and ever felt would be a lie."

He rolled off of me and sat up looking up at the ceiling. I could have run or hit him with a blunt object but I just stared at him. I moved to sit up and he grabbed my arm in a death grip. So much for running.

I kept talking, saying everything I'd been wanting to say for years. "I'll tell the world what you did to me, Greg. I'll tell them how you humiliated me over and over until I was willing to gladly die at the hands of a serial killer than go back to you."

Greg took both my hands in his and squeezed so hard I thought he'd break bones again. "My dear wife, I'd have you put away in a mental institution, and then I'd have you cured of your delusional thinking. Then you'll come home and my love and prayers will keep you healed. I'll even write a book about our experience and your full recovery as the lone survivor of a brutal serial killer."

"I will never…"

He bent the fingers back on my right hand until I almost screamed. "I will make sure you never play the guitar again."

I tried to pull away but he held me tight. He gave me a smug smile. "Next, I'll expose Sean Gables if you say a word against me, or should I say, Danny Dewitt. After that dyke, Heather Ann Cole."

The home phone rang. Greg let go of my crushed hands and I held them to my chest. We sat on the floor in silence as the answering machine clicked on.

The message was short. "Shannon, call me. It's important. It can't wait."

"Who was that?" Greg demanded.

"Alexander Goldstein. My attorney."

"You're the one who donated the funds through Alexander Goldstein and his wife Tasha Alexander to the Liz Atkinson foundation every year."

"Yes, that was me."

"I know. Tasha told me everything about you. She told me about Sean and Erin too."

"That is privileged information. She's our attorney."

"Tasha Alexander is a predator. She told me she'd hand over the ultimate gift if I hired Laurence Yantz as my attorney after Candice was arrested. Tasha told me you were Laurence's girlfriend. He never loved you."

I stopped him. "Laurence asked me to marry him. He gave me a ring."

"Yantz is having an affair with Tasha Alexander. The engagement was a trick to throw Goldstein off track."

My life was over but I thought of Sean and the others who were in hiding. I was a cockroach; I could survive anything, but this stung like a hard slap… "No, Laurence wouldn't do that, not with Tasha," I said.

"Believe what you want. It doesn't matter now that we're together again." Greg smiled. "A few weeks ago, Tasha showed me photos of you and your new face. I can't even describe what I felt when I saw what you look like now. The photo she gave me was of you on a beach, the wind in your hair in a string bikini. Who were you smiling at, Liz, as you stood there almost naked? Was it Alexander Goldstein?"

"Stop, why were you talking to Tasha?"

"I met her eight years ago, she'd flown into Philadelphia to drop off a check from an anonymous donor to the foundation… I didn't know she was married."

"Jesus Christ Greg, you didn't sleep with her did you?"

"I didn't know she was married. Year after year, she dropped of the checks in person. Year after year we had our annual weekend together. Sometimes she'd see me more than once a year, maybe two, three, four times. Now it makes sense why she seemed to know so much about Liz."

"You slept with Tasha. You asshole."

"I was still heartbroken over you. She understood me. Now I know why."

"She's married."

"I already told you, I didn't know that. Three years ago I was in Miami and stopped by her office. She was out, but I met Alex Goldstein. The man was delightful. You can't believe the remorse I felt when I discovered he was Tasha's husband."

"I'm surprised Alex even spoke with you." I was equally shocked that I never even knew he'd met Greg."

"Alex didn't know about Tasha and me."

"Don't flatter yourself. He knows. He always knows when she cheats on him and who she cheats with. Son of a bitch. How could you do that to Alex? How could you do that to another man? How could you sleep with his wife? You fucking bastard." I started to hit him, hard. I had more fight in me than I'd ever had.

He grabbed my wrists. "Tasha used both of us, Liz."

We sat in silence, both shellshocked by the most bizarre night of my life.

"Why would she do that?"

"Control. It's all about control, isn't it?"

"That's nuts. I moved to California. I made my own life that has nothing to do with hers."

"Maybe she's a romantic and wanted to see our love story continue."

"No."

"Her husband is in love with you."

My brain spun. I wanted to cry but as usual nothing happened.

"Alex isn't in love with me. I'd know." I couldn't even spit out the words I really wanted to say.

Greg brushed my hair off of my face and kissed me. Everything was wrong. He kissed me again.

"Kiss me back," he said. I kissed back for fear he'd do something to me. "Nice," he said.

"Have you had sex with Alexander Goldstein?"

"No, of course not."

"Are you sure?"

"I would have remembered if I'd been with Alex."

"You're extremely close to him. Were you ever tempted to sleep with him?"

"He's married."

"So are you, Liz, and that hasn't stopped you from sleeping around."

"I'm legally dead. I can sleep with anyone I want."

He jerked me up to a sitting position again, his hands on my forearms like a vise. I braced myself to be hit again. "You want to sleep with Goldstein, don't you Liz?"

The thought had crossed my mind over the years, more than once.

"You want him, don't you?" he yelled in my face, so angry I hardly recognized him.

Holy mother of God, I thought. Greg was going to kill me.

Chapter 76

My cell phone rang. It was in the pocket of my sweats. It was Alex's ring tone again.

Crap.

"I have to get that. It's Alex again. It might be important."

Greg took the phone out of my discarded sweats and gave it to me. "Make it short."

I answered, "Hi."

"Shannon…"

"The party was great tonight. Oh my God, we tore up the stage. Royal was a crazy man and the crowd was insane. Wish you could have been here."

"Greg Atkinson knows you're Liz."

"I'm already aware of that. All work no play Alex, will make you a dull boy."

"What are you talking about?"

"I signed the papers for the new gallery yesterday and faxed them to your office. Didn't you get them?"

"You aren't alone. Are you with Laurence?"

"No. It's the first one you mentioned."

"Greg is there?"

"Yes of course. As always you're right. No secrets here."

"Are you alone with him?"

"Yes. You are correct as usual."

"Has he hurt you?"

"Yes, of course, but not much."

"What do you mean, not much? Shannon, how bad did he hurt you?"

"On a scale of one to ten on the ugly scale, I'd have to say seven, but it could easily get to ten if we're not careful about using too much tropical color. This isn't Florida. You know, let's talk about this later. I have to go."

"Don't let him touch you."

"Too late for that."

"Shannon what…"

"I'll call you tomorrow."

"Do you want me to call Laurence?"

"No, that deal is off. I'm not doing business with him anymore. I have to go. Bye Alex."

"Don't hang up…"

"The color I picked out reminds me of the time when we at the Victoria and Albert and saw that landscape by Gainsborough with the incredibly blue sky. Remember? It was a perfect blue. That is the blue I want to cover the walls." I didn't add, "And you almost kissed me and we never mentioned it again and I hope you can fill in the blanks because I might never see you again."

"Shannon, get as far from Greg as you can."

"Sorry. I can't. Bye, Alex. I love you too."

Greg took the phone out of my hand and put it in his pocket. "Do you love him?"

"It's just a saying. We're just friends," I lied. I'd never been so close to anyone in my life since my brother Steve died.

"Goldstein can't have you. Not now, not ever." He put his hand under my shirt and pulled it over my head. Then he pulled me into a kiss. I could fight or I could save myself. I went along with Greg. I didn't have to make any excuses. It was either do that or be beaten to a pulp.

When I woke up, it was dark. I was in my bed, my legs wrapped around Greg. He lay quietly with his eyes closed. Sometime during the night, he'd slipped my wedding ring back onto my finger. My right hand was zip tied to the headboard.

Greg opened his eyes then cut the plastic on my wrist. When I tried to untangle myself off of him he held tight.

"I won't ever let you go," he said, as he expertly rolled on top of me. His mouth met mine. I wanted to say no, but I didn't stop him. I found myself wrapping my legs around him and moving with him. I kept saying no in my mind but forced my body into doing everything I could to please him while plotting my next move in my head. Giving an acting performance of a lifetime, I gasped and told him not to stop.

Now what? I could kill him or go back to him or I could run away again. Or I could come clean and tell the world what happened.

Or I could tell him that I'd go back to him. I'd blame it all on Darren. I'd say he'd caused me to lose my mind. I'd tell him that I loved him then I'd vanish. In Asia or Eastern Europe there had to be someone who could transplant fingerprints from another woman, desperate woman needing money would give me her fingerprints or I'd get them from a dead woman. Maybe someone could do microsurgery on my fingertips. I could go to a place where nobody cared who I was. I had passports from four countries. I could change my hair, my face again if I had to, my accent. My money was under a corporation name. Nobody could trace it to me. Only I knew the passwords to my accounts. I'd have the ultimate revenge. He'd lose me again and never find me. He'd be left standing empty in the ruins of his current marriage, with Tasha biting at his heels.

I thought of Tasha. Why after all this time had she betrayed me? The thought made me sick.

Greg moaned, "You like this. Did you miss it?"

I snapped out of my thoughts and dug my fingers into his hair. "Yes. Oh my God, yes. Don't ever stop," I moaned, still plotting.

There was a noise, a bang from below the deck.

"What was that?" Greg looked up.

"Raccoons," I said, pushing him off of me and going to the window. I watched a shadow go behind the trees. Greg walked over to me. "Raccoons come by almost every night and play." My heart was pounding. I thought I saw someone near my deck, near a group of Aspen trees.

Greg put his hands on my breast then squeezed my nipples until I cried out in pain. Roughly probing and pushing into me from behind, Greg then put his hand on the back of my neck to get me to bend over the windowsill. "I know what you want, baby."

After Greg assaulted me at the window seat, he tied me to the bedpost again. Greg was obviously exhausted physically and emotionally and finally fell into a deep sleep. I looked at his face, like an avenging archangel sleeping before the next battle. I ran my finger over his profile and then my hand across his chest. I could kill him. Stab him with a kitchen knife. Or better yet, strangle him with a guitar string. I'd dump his body in a deep mountain ravine and be home by dawn. He'd be like one of the Donner Party, when the Spring thaw came nothing would be found but a few bones and maybe his watch and the wedding rings he'd worn around his neck for so many years. What a tragic ending it would be for poor Dr. Gregory Atkinson. I lay for hours, watching the clock go from 1:00 a.m. to 4:00 a.m. in a tired blur, trying not to fall asleep, trying to plan my next move. The man was still a machine, so I had to think fast.

He stirred. "I want you again." He cut me down and pulled me close into his arms.

I whispered a lie, "I never really stopped loving you, Greg," and let him do whatever he wanted.

Chapter 77

Unfortunately, I did fall asleep and woke up around 6 am.

Greg had left a note:

My love, my wife, my every desire,

I've gone to speak with Laurence about Candice. I will be back this afternoon to start our new life together. Last night was a wonderful dream.

Your loving husband,

~ G

The plastic zip ties were gone, but left scratches on my headboard and welts on my wrist. I put the sheets in the wash after spraying stain remover on the various bloodstains, and then vacuumed around the bed. Despite the pain that ran through every cell of my body, I quickly wiped down the bathroom, door handles and banister - anything with a sign that Greg had been there. After a long, hot shower, trying to rid my body of any trace of Greg and any blood that might set on the drain, I threw on my robe and went downstairs to make coffee. I needed it badly after last night. A little caffeine always seemed to make painkillers work better. My left eye was almost swollen shut. I needed ice.

On the way down the stairs, I smelled coffee. He was in the kitchen, his back to me, looking out the window. The highlights in his blond hair looked more pronounced in the morning sun. I put on my glasses and turned on the light. They sat on my nose like a thousand pound weight.

"I thought you'd gone."

Tom Mather turned around with a cup in his hand.

"Tom? What are you doing?"

"Making coffee. What does it look like?" he said, without so much as a good morning. "What happened to you?" he asked, shocked.

"A misunderstanding between two adults."

"Consenting?"

"No, not exactly. I consented after he hit me. Otherwise I'd have two black eyes."

"I saw him with you in front of the window."

"That was you banging around under the porch?" I took some ice out of the freezer and wrapped it in a dishtowel. "You didn't take photos, did you?"

He leaned back on the counter, looking at me in obvious disgust.

"Why didn't you call the police after you were assaulted?"

I put the ice on my eye. "I wasn't dressed for company."

"What's going on, Shannon?"

"It's complicated."

"You act like you're used to this sort of thing."

"I am. What are you doing here?"

"Business. Is your friend coming back?"

"Not if I can help it," I said, grabbing a cup. I poured myself a cup of coffee then added my usual half-cup of milk and sugar to it.

"Who is he?"

"Greg Atkinson."

Tom gave a rare show of emotion. "Dr. Gregory Atkinson? The marriage advice guy? Yantz's client?"

"That was him."

"The guy with the dead wife?"

"The To Elizabeth With Love guy himself."

"He hit you?"

"Yes. I already told you he did."

"How'd you get hooked up with him?"

"I knew him a long time ago. It just happened, so just drop it. Okay?"

He was still looking at me with utter disgust. "Where's Laurence?"

"We broke up."

"I thought you were engaged."

"It didn't work out."

"So you get involved with one of his clients?"

"It wasn't like that. I didn't ask for this to happen." I lashed out at him.

"Did Atkinson rape you?"

"Of course he did. I already told you that. It's what he does when he's around me." If I'd had the ability to cry right then I would have been sobbing, but I just whispered it in a hoarse voice.

Tom wasn't about to show any signs of going easy on me. "What do you plan on doing about it?"

"Nothing, and I want you to drop it. It never happened, okay. I think Laurence is having an affair with Tasha Alexander. Know anything about that?"

"She wouldn't touch Laurence. He's not her type. Is that why you broke up with him, because you thought he was cheating on you?"

"Is this a social call or what? I mean, why are you here?"

"Business. How do you know Greg Atkinson?"

"Laurence has been working on Candice Atkinson's murder case. I popped into Laurence's office on Tuesday morning, our usual coffee date, and Greg just happened to be there. Greg has been me stalking since then."

Tom pulled the ice off my face and looked at my eye again.

"Tell me what happened last night. I'm an attorney. You can tell me in confidence."

"I appreciate that, but I just want to forget it, okay."

He took my hand and looked at the red marks on my wrists and swore under his breath. "Greg Atkinson raped you and beat you up."

"I guess."

"What do you mean you guess? Did he or did he not beat and rape you?"

"He hit me and to prevent him from hitting me again I had sex with him and I pretended I liked it. He was rough. Yes, he raped me. He forced himself on me. He did vile things to me. I was cuffed to my bed and he hurt me and I didn't like it. This isn't the first time," I said flatly, pouring more coffee and refilling Tom's, my hand shaking so hard I could barely hold the pot.

He said nothing, but put his gun on the kitchen counter and stared at me.

"Okay," I looked at the gun, "Are you here to clean your gun or did you have something else in mind?"

"I'm not going to kill you. What do you mean by, 'this wasn't the first time'? When was the last time?"

"Just drop it, Tom. Are you going to kill Greg?"

"I'd like to, but I doubt if I will. Who are you, Shannon?"

"The same girl you went to the Bahamas with ten years ago."

"Twelve years ago, you showed up out of the blue with more money than God and become entrenched in the Goldstein-Alexander clan. You marry Jerry Alexander then divorce him two months later and become Alex's muse and Tasha's silly gal pal."

"I'm entitled to friends."

"What did you do before you married Jerry? Were you a high priced whore? A drug lord's girlfriend?"

"Just drop it."

"Are you sleeping with Alex?"

"No. Why does everyone keep asking me that? Jeeze Tom, just drop it, okay?"

"I won't drop it."

"Where does Atkinson come into to this? Did you become one of his groupies after his wife was murdered?"

"Drop it, Tom."

"Tell me the truth."

"I am telling you the truth. You know, the least you could have done was ask me if I'm okay. You could have given me a hug or something but you just stand there and act like this was my fault. Well it wasn't. Greg came into my house, my home, uninvited, and knocked me around, cuffed me to my bed and forced me to have sex with him. He hurt me. How dare you, Tom Mather, act as if I've done anything wrong."

"Do you want to live, Shannon?"

"Of course I do. Where the hell did that come from?"

"Tell me who you are."

"I'm nobody."

"It takes more than nobody to have Alex Goldstein call you twice a day." He picked up the gun. I thought he was going to put it away. "Alex doesn't have time for anyone he isn't making a buck off of. What's your story, Shannon?"

"Figure it out yourself."

"It's your choice, Shannon. You can tell me now or I will force it out of you later."

Tom took out his phone, put on a wireless headset and made a call. "Showtime," he said, and pointed the gun at me. "We're going to the basement."

"You said you weren't going to kill me."

"Move it Shannon." He grabbed me and handcuffed my arms behind my back.

"You asshole. Let me go, or I'll scream so loud they'll hear it in Nebraska."

"Make any noise and I'll smash your face to a pulp. Do you understand?"

I nodded. He put on rain gear with a hood and roughly took me outside under the house. It was freezing outside. I had bare feet with only my robe wrapped around me. I hurt so bad I could hardly walk as he dragged me down the stairs. Rain was pouring down. I was soaked and slipping on the redwood steps. Tom opened the door underneath the house and pushed me ahead of himself.

He spoke into his headset, "You still there?" he asked, "I'll have more pictures in a minute. Yes, you'll get full audio as agreed."

He pulled the cord off of my robe and pushed it off of my shoulders. It hung open wet and dripping. "I've seen you naked," he said, "Don't pretend to be modest."

He spoke into the phone, "Yes, I've fucked her. It's none of your business when. Hold on, the phone is giving me trouble."

He pulled my robe back off of me.

"What are you doing?" I asked, trying to twist so my robe would cover part of me again. "No. Don't touch me."

"When they find you, they'll know you were raped. Just another random violent act."

He looked at me and furrowed his brow. "Did Atkinson make all those bruises?" he asked, looking at the bruises down my ribs, on the inside of my thighs, on my upper arms and breasts.

"Yes." I barely got the word out.

Tom scowled at me. "Did he use a condom?"

"No."

"That could be a problem."

"Why?"

"Evidence. They'll check for DNA. Have you been with Laurence in the past 48 hours?"

"No, I told you..."

"You broke up. That's right. Anybody else? Your friend Chase?"

"I've never slept with Chase. It was just Greg. Come on Tom, let me go. Please. I won't tell anyone."

He spoke to the unknown person on the phone again, "She was with a guy named Greg. Yes, that Greg. It won't matter after today. No, I'm not going to kill him. Are you nuts? The man is famous. You don't need that kind of attention. Just let me do my job."

A blue tarp had been spread on the floor of the space underneath my house.

"Get on the tarp and lay on your back, it will make it easier. Now." He forced me to my knees and pushed me down. He took out the phone and started the video feed of me.

"Who is behind this? The least you can do is tell me! Is it Laurence?" I heard myself sounding like I was begging. I was begging.

"It isn't Laurence. " Tom said.

"Who is it?"

"Shannon, try to make this easy for yourself."

I closed my eyes and started to recite the Twenty-Third Psalm in my head.

"She's ready," he said to his caller.

"You don't have to do this," I said. By then I was shaking so much from the cold and in so much pain I could hardly get the words out. I thought if there was a God in Heaven, this couldn't be happening to me again. "Tom, please." I tried to get up; he gently put his foot on my chest and pushed me back down. "You're no better than Darren Crawford. You'll burn in Hell for this."

He put two fingers over his lips to tell me to keep quiet. Next Tom took out the gun with the silencer. He pressed something on the phone.

Then Tom put the gun to my head and mouthed the words, "Don't make a sound."

I froze, physically unable to move. He fired the gun twice into the ground about three feet from my head.

Tom was still on the phone. "It's done. I'm having problems getting you images. You heard the shots. Good. Are you happy now? I'll send video of the body." He calmly positioned me, spreading my legs slightly and opening my robe completely, turning my head then poured something round my head. Wine. He got on the phone again. "Sorry, we're breaking up. I'll call you right back."

He said quickly. "Look dead. Open your eyes a little and stare off. Open your mouth slightly. Don't breathe."

He got the phone. "I'm back. It's finished."

Using his phone, he took a video of me lying dead on the ground. He pushed me a little with his foot. I lay there like a dead woman. "Happy now?" he asked into the phone.

"Sure, I'll see you next week. Have the funds wired to my account by tonight, or I'll blow your head off too. Sure, no problem. Just wire the money."

Tom quickly uncuffed my hands and helped me to my feet.

"My client thinks you're dead. Let's go upstairs and clean you up," he said, as if he was asking me to meet him at Starbucks.

I didn't even have words for him.

Chapter 78

In my bathroom I showered, towel dried my hair and put on a pair of jeans and a white button-up dress shirt. When I was done, I found Tom sitting on my bed.

"The gun I was supposed to kill you with is registered to Laurence Yantz. The plan was that he'd be arrested for your murder."

I felt as if all the air had been sucked out of the room. "Who hired you?"

"I can't tell you anything right now."

"Was it one of Laurence's former clients? A pissed off prosecutor?"

"I can't tell you. Stop wasting your time asking."

"Who would want to hurt Laurence?"

Tom shrugged. "I can give you a long list of people who'd like him out of the picture."

"If they found my body it would be headline news."

"Don't flatter yourself. It would be a basic crime of passion. Local attorney kills girlfriend after she cheats on him with another man, that man now being Greg Atkinson. No big deal."

"Do you know who I am?" I said, slowly and deliberately."

"I'm guessing you're Liz Atkinson."

"Yes, I am Elizabeth Hobbs Atkinson. You're such an asshole." I pushed him hard with my hand, almost knocking him over.

"Shannon..."

"Go to Hell."

He just looked at me for a while then a hint of a smirk came over his face. "Greg Atkinson, the happy Christian marriage guy, beat and violently raped his wife on a regular basis. Why didn't you tell me before?"

"I was afraid. Greg emotionally and physically abused me every chance he got. I was his property. Love, honor and obey or I'd be beaten and raped until I passed out."

"What about Crawford?"

"Darren Crawford dropped dead before he could finish killing me, so I faked my own death so I wouldn't have to go back to Greg."

"You changed your face."

"The magic of cosmetic surgery."

"How'd you hook up with Alex? He's obviously in on this."

"I dialed the wrong number. Call it God's will. Divine intervention."
Tom looked stunned.

"Oh don't look so surprised," I said, then took him back downstairs and told him the entire story, including the money. After I'd finished, I asked him, "So, who exactly is this client who wants me dead? Come on, I showed you mine, now it's your turn."

Of course, Tom didn't answer me but asked his own question. "How did Atkinson find you?"

"Tasha told him where I was. And all this time I thought she was my friend."

My phone rang with Alex's ring. I answered, expecting a lot of questions.

"Alex." I held out one hand. It was shaking.

"Is he there?" Alex said, his voice was bordering on anger.

"Who? Tom?" I answered innocently.

"Greg Atkinson."

"No. I don't know where he is. I think he went to see Laurence."

"I've been calling all morning. Are you all right?"

"No, I'm not all right. Someone hired Tom Mather to kill me. In fact, he's here right now. He made me strip naked then put a gun to my head."

"He told me he was going to stage something."

"You knew about it? Did you hire him?"

"No, of course I didn't hire him. How could you think that?"

"You know about it."

"You'll understand in a few days."

"Don't patronize me. I was forced to take off my clothes and lie naked on the ground while Tom put a gun to my head."

"I know all about it. Listen to me, Shannon..."

"What is going on?"

"Listen..."

"Who hired Tom to kill me?"

"I can't tell you right now. Listen to me. I have to tell you..."

"Someone wanted Tom to kill me with Laurence's gun."

"I know." He paused longer than usual. "Shannon, I know you've been through a lot."

By then I was beyond angry. If Alex knew so much he could have prevented last night.

"You don't know the half of it. Did you know Greg was sleeping with your wife?"

He didn't say anything. The line was silent. If I'd hurt him I was glad.

"Alex?" I thought I'd lost him. "Greg told me he had an affair with Tasha."

He answered, "I know all about it."

"Greg is obsessed with the idea that you're in love with me. Are you?"

"Shannon this isn't the time for this."

"Everyone is obsessed with the idea. Everyone thinks we're sleeping together."

"Stop." There was a pause. Tom cleared his throat in a mock way and looked at me surprised. Alex spoke first, "Calm down, Shannon. We don't have time for this. What happened last night?"

Alex was annoyed, and sounding rushed. I felt a wave of nausea.

"Greg stayed the night. I didn't have a choice." There was a long pause. "Don't be angry at me," I said.

"I'm not angry at you," Alex said, "Is Tom Mather there?"

"He's standing right next to me."

"Let me talk to him."

Tom got on the phone. "Alex. Sure. It was Laurence's gun. Good thing I was hired for the job or he'd really be screwed. Sure, she's a mess, but holding up. No tears at all. She doesn't cry? No kidding. Never?

Not good. Nasty black eye and a lot of bruises all over, bleeding. Bastard even left bite marks. She should get it looked at but... sure, I understand, she can't risk police involvement... No, it wasn't mutual. He raped her. He zip tied her to the bed at one point... God knows what all he made her do but he was rough. He hurt her, Alex. It's bad... Right, I know. He'll be back for her. I can guarantee that... No. Had I known he what he was doing to Shannon, I swear to God I would have taken Atkinson out last night... No, I would have made it slow and painful. Sure. I don't think so. She's scared and angry. No surprise there.

I could hear Alex's voice, but couldn't make out what he was saying. He talked for a while.

Then Tom spoke again, "I met Liz this morning. No, she never told me who she really is. Surprised the hell out of me. Not in a million years would I have made the connection until this morning. Sure, it makes sense now. No kidding."

Tom turned his back to me. "So, what's the deal between you and Shannon?" he laughed. "I understand. Sure. They are complicated creatures. On another note, everything is still a go for tomorrow. Sure I have everything in order and then some. I'll take care of everything... I'll be back in Miami tonight. I'll drop by when I get in. Sure, yes. Here's Shannon." Tom handed me the phone.

Alex spoke slowly and deliberately. "You need to get to Laurence's office right away. Threaten to have him disbarred if you have to, but get him to stop Greg from exposing you. Greg's wife is in Sacramento to meet with Laurence about her trial. Greg told her you're alive. She knows what you look like."

"How do you know this?"

"Laurence called me this morning. He's concerned about you. He wants you to go public."

"Screw him. I'm not going public."

"No, you're not. Get out to Laurence's office as soon as you can. I'll call him and try to talk some sense into him, in the meantime do what you can to keep him away from Greg or Candice Atkinson. If you feel like you're in trouble, I can have a private plane ready at the Executive Airport for you within the hour. Try to convince Laurence to go with you. Tell him about his gun being used for your murder if you have to."

"Okay. I'll call you. Do you know who wants me dead?"

"I'm pretty sure, but it isn't about you."

"What do you mean it..."

Alex cut me off. "Listen, you have to get to Laurence. Call me after you talk to him. Take your US passport with you and your British and Cayman Island IDs as well."

"What about Tasha?"

"I'll take care of Tasha. Get your ass downtown to Laurence's office, right now, or it will be over for all of us. Do you understand?"

"Where is Tasha?" I asked, wondering if she was with Laurence.

"I don't know. It doesn't matter. You need to see Laurence now."

"Okay, I'm going."

"Call me after you've talked to Laurence."

"Okay. I'll talk to you soon."

"Shannon, be careful."

"When can I see you?"

"Soon. Go."

I hung up. Tom was sitting on my bed again.

"You need to see a doctor about your eye," he said.

"No, a doctor would want to report it to the police. Does your wife know you get paid to kill people?"

"I met her when we were both hired to eliminate the same pedophile."

"Holy crap, Tom."

"I'm an avenging angel, Shannon. Haven't you figured that out?"

Chapter 79

Even though I was half blind and in a lot of pain, I wouldn't let Tom drive me downtown or go with me. I thought about the times Laurence and I had traveled with Tasha and Alex. I thought of the times when Alex and I went to a museum, a hike or to lunch without the other two. They always had an excuse of being tired, or paperwork or a traveler's illness. They were back at the room, together, making love and laughing behind our backs. The trips to Miami when I'd always end up doing something with Alex, while Tasha and Laurence stayed behind. I wondered how long Alex had known. All the while Alex and I traveled together, two perfect travel companions, the hikes, the outdoor markets, the shops; the long walks on the beaches watching sunsets. Talking for hours talking for hours on end. I thought of the times he'd taken my hand or when I'd hugged him, imagining his bare skin next to mine. I pulled over in the rain before I got to the freeway and threw up on the side of the road. He never thought of me like that. God, crying would have been so much easier.

Arriving at the law office, I ran past the receptionist and up the stairs to Laurence's office. I called out as I reached the door, "Laurence, hurry. We need to go."

Laurence wasn't there. Tasha and Greg both turned.

Tasha looked shocked and lost whatever composure she had. "You're alive."

"You hired Tom."

If Greg reacted, I didn't even notice.

"No." she said, then hesitated. "Alex said he thought you were suicidal and couldn't find you."

"Stop it with the lies. You hired Tom to kill me."

"Fine. I hired Tom. I'm tired of the whole mess. I'm tired of you. I'm tired of Laurence." She sat on Laurence's huge antique desk and crossed her long legs. "Greg and I are a lot alike. We keep what's ours. The only difference is that you betrayed Greg and left him for stolen money and promise of an easy life. I've kept Alex."

"You cheat on Alex every chance you get," I said.

"But I stay with him, through his substance abuse and alcoholism, his obsession over his work, and his obsession with helping everyone except himself. I've even stayed with him over his obsession to you."

Greg started to speak but was interrupted by a deafening sound. Tasha's head exploded.

"You're dead now, bitch."

I turned around to see Candice Atkinson holding a gun.

Greg turned in shock, then recoiled from the impact of a bullet.

"Liz is really dead now. I loved you Greg. I gave you my heart. I thought we were soul mates," she said, sobbing, as she fired three more shots into his body.

Candice thought the beautiful blonde standing next to Greg was Liz. The cost of her mistake was Tasha's life.

Candice turned in my direction, seeing me for the first time. "Who are you?"

"I'm Liz," I said to her. I should have just kept my mouth shut.

Candice aimed at me and pulled the trigger, but the gun didn't fire. I don't know if it was jammed, if she was just inept or if it was out of ammunition. Maybe someone up there was looking out for me after all. She hit me across my forehead with the gun, turned and fled.

I ran to Greg. He was breathing but bleeding out. I put my hands over the worst part. It was just a few seconds but it seemed like forever. All I remember was yelling for someone to call 911 and that Greg was still alive. Others had come into the room after hearing the shots.

Greg's eyes met mine and he said, "I love you, Liz." Or I think that is what he said. I kept saying comforting things that I don't remember. Later, I was told that I kept telling him that it would be okay.

All I remember was hearing Greg's gasping breath, squealing brakes, a loud crash that shook the building, and the wail of sirens. I blocked out everything except Greg until he stopped breathing.

A few minutes later, paramedics gently helped me up and sat me in a chair.

What seemed like an entire day was in reality about twenty minutes, from the time Tasha was shot until someone led me out of the room.

Candice Atkinson would never stand trail for the murder of her first husband, or of her second husband. Laurence had driven across town to my house. There, he was told by Tom Mather to get back to his office. He arrived in time to see Candice flee the building. She ran in front of his car. Unable to stop, he slammed into a tree, pinning her. She died instantly.

Chapter 80

After the bodies had been taken away, most of the police had gone, I stood with Laurence on the porch of his beautiful Victorian office. He was in shock, but had the wits to make sure his assistant had called the insurance company and arrange for his office to be cleaned and repaired after the crime scene was cleared. He told his staff to go home and that he'd call them to come back.

An associate of Laurence's had spoken to television and the media, asking them to please respect the privacy of the grieving families, friends and witnesses. Members of his staff were told not to speak to the press. They understood and followed orders.

Laurence and I had both been questioned at the scene. I told the police that I'd come for coffee and the rest was almost exactly as it happened, except they didn't know Greg's relationship with me or with Tasha. I didn't tell them how surprised Tasha was to see me alive. They never learned that I was the woman Candice had come to kill.

The story went down as friends meeting for coffee. Candice Atkinson, upon hearing her husband Gregory Atkinson was filing for divorce, shot and killed him and attorney Tasha Alexander. Mrs. Atkinson attempted to shoot Laurence Yantz's girlfriend, Shannon Gables. After fighting off Mrs. Atkinson, Ms. Gables valiantly tried to save the life of Gregory Atkinson, but he died in her arms, his last words expressions of love to his first wife Liz, who was murdered years earlier.

Nobody knew that Candice had actually found out Liz Atkinson was alive and had mistakenly killed the wrong woman. There was only speculation about the delusional crazy wife who shot her husband and an innocent bystander.

Laurence and I were both sent to the hospital for a brief time. I was questioned about my eye and other bruises. I told them I had tried to stop Candice and she beat me back. Being a good liar comes in handy.

For my trouble, I got a butterfly bandage on the cut on my cheek where Candice had hit me with the gun and a pharmacy bag full of painkillers and sedatives. Laurence sat with me the entire time and held my hand. It was the first time I'd seen him since he'd run over Candice. He didn't say much, just yes and no answers to the medical staff. He came away with a prescription for sedatives to help him sleep.

Alex had been informed of Tasha's death while we were at the hospital. The police had called him. He had called Tom. Then Tom had called me. Then I spoke to Alex's brother Phil.

Laurence had driven my car to the hospital, and by 2:00 pm we were back at Laurence's home. He was shaken but had no idea the kind of day I'd had.

In an attempt at affection, he put his arms around me. "Shannon, if she'd killed you I..." his voice cracked, "I love you."

I pushed myself away from him. "Tasha hired someone to kill me this morning. I mean, she didn't hire them this morning. What I mean is, I was supposed to be killed this morning. I had a gun to my head."

Laurence looked shocked. It wouldn't be the first or last time that morning.

"What are you talking about?" he asked.

"A hit man was at my house this morning. We went to the basement, he made me take off my clothes then he put a gun to my head." I paused and took a breath to keep my stomach from knotting up.

"Someone was in your house. Did you call the police?"

"He didn't kill me."

"But..."

"I know him. He's a friend of mine."

"You said he tried to kill you."

"He faked it so Tasha would think he'd killed me."

"You're not making sense."

"For five years, you never questioned a word I said and now you don't believe anything."

"You lied to me for five years. Can you blame me?"

"Hear me out."

"Fine. What happened?"

"My friend came into my house and set up the murder scene then called Tasha. She listened on the phone and saw pictures and video until right after he shot the gun. He shot into the ground so it would sound like he'd killed me. He made me lie down on a tarp with my eyes half open and my mouth open like I was dead. He faked it. Just like the huntsman in Snow White."

"Who is this guy, the one you said Tasha hired?"

"He's an old friend. That's why he didn't kill me. Tasha had an affair with him a long time ago so she thought he'd do anything for her."

"Who is he?"

"Are you asking as my attorney?"

"Yes, as your attorney. I won't tell anyone."

"Tom Mather."

"Tom's a divorce attorney."

"Tasha hired him to kill me. You can't tell anyone about him. You can't, Laurence."

"Tasha would never be involved with anything like that. I know Tasha."

"You don't know Tasha. The gun that was supposed to kill me is yours."

"What?"

"Where's your gun, Laurence?"

He left the room to check in his safe. Seemed like forever before he came back. He checked the nightstand drawer.

"The one I kept by the bed is missing. Did you take it?"

"Didn't you hear anything I said? Tasha hired Tom to kill me with your gun."

"Tasha wouldn't have framed me for your murder."

"The last thing Tasha said to me this morning was, 'You're supposed to be dead.' She looked like she'd seen a ghost when I walked into the room. Then Candice blew Tasha's face off."

Laurence was visibly shaken by the visuals.

"She wanted me dead and she wanted you to spend the rest of your life on death row for it." I barely got the words out. It felt like my brain was shutting down.

Laurence stared at me in horror. We stood for a minute staring at each other. He was soaking wet and bruised. My face was a mass of bruises and my hair was matted with Greg's and Tasha's blood.

"Where is my gun now?" Laurence finally asked.

"I don't know." The conversation was getting surreal. "Maybe he'll mail it back to you."

"Are you absolutely sure it was Tasha he was talking to?"

"I have her phone." I pulled her phone out of my pocket and showed him the video and photos. Laurence saw the text, photos and video.

"Oh God. Why?"

"I don't know. If they'd found me dead, they would have identified me as Liz Atkinson. I don't know why she would have risked that? It doesn't make any sense."

"You didn't stage this?"

"Why would I do something like that?"

"You've staged your own death before."

"Fuck you, Laurence. I came here this morning to save you."

"Save me from what? Shannon, what the hell is going on?"

"Alex called and told me that Candice was going to kill me, and Greg's attorney, meaning you. I came here to warn you because wouldn't answer my calls."

"I wish I'd never met you."

"I hate you too, Laurence, but right now I have Tasha's brains in my hair and Greg's blood under my fingernails. I'm going to go use your shower, then I'm leaving and you'll never see me again," I said. I think Laurence was in too much shock to say another word. As I walked up the stairs to the bathroom I yelled back, "I can't believe that you, of all people, would be mad at me because Tasha wanted send you to prison for a murder you didn't commit. You should be thanking me for saving your sorry ass!"

In the bathroom, I stripped off my clothes, spotted with blood from both Greg and Tasha. I lost it and threw up in the toilet, my empty stomach knotting up in pain. I couldn't breathe. I sat on the floor, gasping for air.

Laurence came in and helped me up. He didn't say everything would be okay, because he knew it wouldn't be.

He started the shower for me. He brought in clean clothes of mine that were still in his dresser, my favorite jeans and a black tee. He even brought in my matching cobalt blue French bra and panties he gotten for me in London. I'd never gone back to clean out my things. He'd never bothered to pack his things up at my house.

I couldn't get Tasha out of my mind, or the look on Candice's face when I told her who I was. Most of all, I couldn't forget Greg, his head cradled in my lap, taking his last breath. Numbness overtook my entire body. I grabbed the shower door to keep from falling. I looked at the pale white scars on my arms. Some thick and prominent, some thin and barley visible. I heard Darren's voice saying, "Welcome back to Hell."

Laurence came back into the bathroom and got into the shower with me.

"Don't," I said, crossing my arms over my chest.

He looked tired and lost. "You need help with this. Any bone or other matter lodged in your skin could become infected."

"Oh God," I said, wanting to tear my skin off.

He helped me wash my hair and scrubbed my nails until the water ran clear. He cleaned the drain of bone and hair and clumps of unidentifiable chunks of Tasha's head, mixed with Greg's blood. He checked my neck and ears, looking for traces of my former best girlfriend and husband. He gently ran his hands over my body with citrus scented soap, his touch so familiar. He kissed my hands, my shoulders, he washed my legs and feet then embraced me, stroking my hair.

He said, "I'm sorry. I'm so sorry for everything." Then he held me, the hot water running over us, mixing with the tears that ran down his face.

Bruises were on his shoulder and arm from when he lost control and slammed his car into the tree. I kissed his bruises and scrapes to make them go away, but the pain would never go away. It would never be right between Laurence and me but maybe we could make it work again.

His hand went to my face. My eye and cheek were swollen and blackish purple from the night before.

"Candice hit you pretty hard," he said, gently cradling my face near my swollen and bruised eye.

"This is from her." I touched the butterfly bandage. "Greg hit me last night. The eye and the rest are from him."

"Greg was with you?"

"Uninvited. Greg knows, knew, who I was. He thought I'd go back to him, be his wife again, forget the past. When I refused his offer, he hit me. Just like old times. I'll tell you all about it later, okay." My voice cracked and my breath shortened in my tearless cry.

"Shhhhh," he said, "Baby, it will be all right." He held me again.

"That day I came over and Greg was in your office, I was going to tell you that I'd marry you. That's what you wanted, wasn't it?"

"More than anything. Shannon, I never stopped loving you."

He kissed me like we used to kiss.

"I can't. Last night, Greg did more than hit me."

A horrified look came to his face.

"I'll be okay. I just need some time."

He left the shower and let me stand under the water a little longer.

Chapter 81

I bagged up my bloody clothes and saved them in case the police wanted them.

Going back to the bedroom for socks, I flicked on the light. I made a dead, cold stop. On the floor by his bed were two condom wrappers. I didn't use condoms with Laurence. In the corner of the room was Tasha's signature turquoise and yellow bag. Her 2 CT yellow diamond engagement ring and diamond studded wedding band, and sapphire earrings were on the nightstand. Black thong panties, and Tasha's favorite black stiletto pumps on the floor next to the condom wrappers.

Son of a bitch, Greg had told me the truth.

Laurence had been having an affair with Tasha. There she was, like a ghost in his bed where I'd made love to him just a week ago. I slipped Tasha's rings and earrings in my pocket then went back downstairs where Laurence was waiting with a pot of coffee. He motioned for me to sit next to him on the couch.

I sat in a chair and told him about Greg's visit, not sparing any of the graphic details.

He looked at me in sort of a catatonic, shocked way, like he couldn't take in any more information. Funny, how he discussed crime and evil all day but couldn't take it when he was on the receiving end.

"Why'd you bring Greg to the club last night?"

"I wanted to see you play. It was just supposed to be for a few minutes."

"You left Greg alone with me at the club so you could be with Tasha."

"It wasn't like that."

"You knew if I was with Greg I wouldn't show up at your house. You sacrificed me for your own selfish desires."

"Don't even go there. I'd never do anything to hurt you."

"You didn't even have the decency to pick up Tasha's panties and the condom wrappers."

"Do you have to bring that up now? Tasha is dead."

"How long have you been having an affair with Tasha? How long, Laurence?"

"Two years. Shannon, you have to believe me when I say I didn't intend for this to happen. Tasha loved me. She offered me something perfect. You wouldn't understand."

"No, I don't understand perfection, especially if it means cheating on someone who loves you."

"Don't blow this up into something it isn't. Her marriage with Alex was over years ago."

"What about us? If what you had with Tasha was so perfect, why'd you ask me to marry you?"

"I loved you. Why didn't you trust me enough to tell me who you really are?"

"Don't turn this around on me. Don't you dare turn this around! I'd planned on telling you I was Liz Atkinson. Alex and Tasha said they'd be there with me, and we'd tell you together so you'd understand. They both knew how much I love you."

We sat in uncomfortable silence for a few minutes. A tear rolled down his cheek. He closed his eyes and slumped back in the chair.

Chapter 82

There was a knock on the door. I glanced out the window and saw a van from a local TV station.

"Don't answer!" Laurence snapped.

I turned on the news. It was all over the local and cable stations: Greg Atkinson murdered. Tasha Alexander murdered. It showed the office building in Miami with Alexander and Goldstein on the door. Photos of Tasha and Alexander together, film clips of Laurence, a quick shot of Laurence and his girlfriend Shannon Gables, the innocent bystander, walking through his front door.

After they left, I put a *Please Do Not Disturb* sign on his front door made out of a piece of yellow paper off of a legal note pad.

A couple of detectives named Cameron McGill and Laurel Greenside finally showed up at the house about five minutes after I put up the sign. We spoke to them in hushed, shocked tones, together and separately. Laurence fought back tears. I couldn't stop shaking and had to excuse myself to get sick, again, when I told the detectives about Tasha's head exploding all over me.

Laurence kept saying, "Tasha was so beautiful." I don't even think he knew what he was saying when he described in graphic detail Candice running in front of the car then hitting her and pinning her against a tree.

I told McGill and Greenside I'd be home with Alexander Goldstein and his brother Philip in a few hours. They were free to come by but they had to expect Alex would be in shock.

After the detectives left, I figured it was time for me to go. I didn't need to stay with Laurence anymore.

"Alex and Phil are staying at my house. I have to go," I said, standing up. "Where are my keys?"

"Stay. We need to talk. It isn't over between us, Shannon."

I saw my keys on the table by the front door. I picked up my purse and walked toward the door.

"Don't walk away from me, Shannon. I killed a woman today. Two people I cared about were shot down in my office in cold blood. You have no right to judge me, Shannon."

"No, I guess I don't. Goodbye, Laurence."

"You shouldn't be driving."

I didn't answer and fumbled with my coat.

Laurence followed me to the door. "Shannon, I'm sorry."

"Tasha would never have left Alex for you. She'd get more from keeping your affair going forever. She had too much power in Alexander and Goldstein to throw it all away. She enjoyed the rush of making love to you or some other man, then flying home to a night of vicious fighting and hot, nasty make-up sex with Alex. It was what she lived for." I opened the door and started out, not planning to turn back.

"Get back in here," said Laurence, grabbing at my sleeve.

I slapped his hand away and stepped away from him. "You're such a stupid idiot and I will never ever forgive you for that!"

Chapter 83

I called Winter Knight on the way home and she said she'd come to my house. By 5:00 p.m. I was home in bed, the same bed I'd been in with Greg the night before. I pulled a blanket over the top of me, but couldn't bring myself to get under the covers. Winter had said something about Sean and Erin being on their way but I didn't catch most of it. I glanced at my phone and saw a message from Phil Goldstein, Alex's baby brother. I fell asleep with my last conversation with Alex on my mind. I closed my eyes with a wave of nausea and fell into a deep, drug-induced sleep.

Winter picked Alex and his brother Phil up at the airport and brought them to my house. I was in no shape to pick them up or drive anywhere.

I woke from my drugged stupor in pain again. Every cell in my body ached. It was 1:23 am. I had been asleep when Alex and Phil arrived. I put on my robe and made my way to the kitchen. I glanced over to the front door and saw five pairs of wet shoes in the entryway next to mine. It was still raining.

Alex was alone in the kitchen, drink in hand, leaning against the counter. He wore jeans and a black hoodie, unzipped without his shirt on. He looked like a haggard male model, just come from a photo shoot and heroin fest.

I wanted to hug him but folded my arms. I didn't know what to expect from him.

"Phil is asleep," he said.

"I'm so sorry. I couldn't stop it. It happened so fast. Tasha… she was just gone. Alex…" I couldn't get out the rest of the words. I didn't even know what words to say.

Alex put down the glass and came to me. His hand went to my eye and the bandage on my forehead. He took my hands and checked the ligature marks on my wrists.

"I should have insisted you divorce him and press charges." His eyes glistened but no tears, not yet.

I shrugged my shoulders and poured myself a glass of bourbon from the bottle Alex had set on the counter. "Greg died… he died in my arms, telling me that he loved me."

"I know."

"'Til death do us part."

"I keep thinking of Jean Valjean."

I had to smile at that one. "Sort of like that."

261

"Where's Laurence?"

"Home. His sister is staying with him tonight. I'm so sorry Alex, about Tasha."

He crossed his arms. "It's cold here. Do you mind turning up the heat a little?" I turned up the heat. Alex zipped up his sweatshirt. "Shannon, I don't know what to say. I don't know what to think. I'm going to the morgue in the morning."

"You don't want to see her."

"I've seen dead people before."

"Alex, half of her face is gone."

He closed his eyes, and then wiped a tear with his hand.

I reached in my pocket and pulled out her rings. Alex didn't ask me if I'd pulled them off her dead left hand or found them in another man's bedroom.

He put the rings in his pocket and wiped his eyes again. "I've hated Tasha for so long but I never wanted it to end like this."

He might as well have told me he'd been abducted by aliens with that statement. I didn't say anything. What could I have said? Oh sure, I know that, Alex. I didn't know he hated her.

We were both still in shock. I mean, how is anyone supposed to feel in a situation like this? It's confusing.

I let him talk. "I could put up with a lot. We were always so bust and under so much stress. It was what happened with my brother Rob that sealed the deal."

"Rob? What did he have to do with it?"

"Rob wanted you to go back to Philadelphia, back to Greg. He didn't believe your story. In his medical opinion, you were mentally ill. Tasha blackmailed him into doing your face."

"I thought he wanted to do it. I don't get it."

"He slept with Tasha. My brother slept with my wife. Tasha told Rob she'd tell me if he didn't do your surgery. Their affair started a few months after my sister-in-law Ava died. It stopped a few months ago."

"When did you find out?"

"Remember when you asked me to send your music binder a couple months ago? You were writing some songs for Royal and you left them there."

I knew where this was going. I'd left it in my condo in Miami. Both Tasha and Alex had keys.

Alex continued, "The door was open when I got there. They were in bed, in the act. Rob saw me. I didn't say a word. I took the binder and left. It took him a week to call me about it. Didn't have the heart to tell you. I didn't want to tell you. Makes me sick to think about it. And you thought your family was twisted." Alex leaned back against the counter and closed his eyes for a few seconds. "I was going to leave her. Tom was going to have papers served on her tomorrow, I guess that would be today, now."

"Alex, I am so sorry."

"Don't be sorry about anything. Tasha played you with Laurence and Greg the same way she played me with anyone she could, including my own brother. I don't know what her motivation was, except she was a bitch. I honestly couldn't tell you. I've been dealing with criminals, liars, and psychopaths for years and never would admit to myself that Tasha wasn't any different. No, actually she was worse than any of them."

"You loved her."

"I wanted to keep loving her. I really did, until Tom told me she paid to have you killed with Laurence's gun. It was over a long time ago, but..." he trailed off and poured another shot of bourbon and downed it.

"Now what?" I asked.

"A large stylish funeral and then I don't know. What about you?"

I shrugged. "I'm not sure. Maybe a nervous breakdown."

We talked and compared notes. It was difficult.

Laurence had been pressing Tasha to leave Alex. She decided she could get rid of him and me all at once and gave Tom Laurence's gun.

She'd led Greg back to me then feared Greg, with all his charm, would convince me to go back to him. After she'd slept with Greg she never believed what I'd said about him. He was too sweet. He loved me too much. She thought I'd imagined it all when I was with Darren. She wanted Greg for her own.

Alex was going to serve her with divorce papers. She couldn't handle it. She told him he'd be nothing without her.

Through the kitchen door came Erin, in a red flannel robe she'd taken from my closet. She gave Alex a big hug and fussed over him. Then she mothered me and held me. I held her back like the mom I never had.

Sean and Winter came downstairs a few minutes later. We talked and sat and supported. Nothing was new here and nobody had to hide anything.

At 6:00 a.m. Phil came downstairs and looked at all of us piled up on the couch around his brother. I sat curled alone in a chair. He smiled and gave all of us hugs.

Despite the tragedy and confusion, this was the first time I'd ever felt like I had a real family.

Chapter 84

A beautiful portrait of Tasha graced the front of the cathedral. Her body was in a closed white casket covered in yellow roses. More yellow roses and orchids graced the isles and podium. Music from a string quartet calmed the mourners, who were each given a small bouquet of yellow and white daisies.

Jerry sat shocked and red-eyed with his wife Heather next to him clutching his hand. Alexander never told him about Tasha and Laurence. It didn't matter anyway because Jerry had known about it all along.

Sean and Erin sat next to me, all three of us holding hands. I felt like looking around to see if any other known criminals or maybe some side show freaks were sitting in the row with us.

Tasha's oldest girlfriend, a cousin, and colleagues all spoke of the beautiful, brilliant woman.

After a sweet poem from Tasha's cousin, I went to the front with my acoustic guitar, the first Royal had made for me, and sang Amazing Grace. Then Jerry's small girls came to the front with me and we sang *This Little Light of Mine.*

Next, in tiny voices, the girls said, "We love you Auntie Tasha."

Next, Jerry spoke about his sister. My heart broke as he made us all laugh with his stories, then his tears. I wanted to cry, not for Tasha but for my brother Steve. It all came back, ever sick and twisted memory. I still missed my brother.

Mourners gave their condolences to Alex, who was gracious but unusually distracted. He loved her but she had tortured him. I knew what it was like, to love someone who hurt you day after day and you never knew why you stayed, or made excuses why.

I learned later that Laurence had called Alex about the service. Alex calmly told Laurence that if he showed up at Tasha's memorial, he would end up as shark food somewhere between Cuba and the Florida Keys.

I was invited to Greg's funeral by his family. I was the woman who had comforted him and attempted to save his life. They were grateful. I received gracious notes from my former mother-in-law and from my former sister-in-law.

I didn't respond back.

Laurence attended the funeral. I accused him of milking it for everything it was worth. He said he was "Doing the right thing." I supposed he was. I refused to go with him. I think my final response was, "What part of no way in hell don't you understand?"

Greg was buried under a double monument that shared my name. Our children lay next to him with their own tiny little markers.

Alexander and Jerry took a boat out into the Atlantic Ocean and scattered Tasha's ashes.

Chapter 85

I looked down at the gravestone.

Gregory Randolph Atkinson

In Memory of Elizabeth Ann Hobbs Atkinson
Loving wife and mother
Love never dies.

Mother. My stomach cramped like I'd been stabbed with a knife.

I put flowers on the three small graves. My children: Emmiline, Andrew, and Ethan. They would have been 14, 15 and 16 years old. All born theoretically early enough to survive but not really, only little Ethan attempting a breath on his own for three hours then deciding not to live in the world of his parents.

My babies. They never existed to anyone but me. I thought about them every day.

For the first time since I was a child, I cried.

I had that funny feeling someone was there. I looked up after wiping my eyes with my sleeve.

There stood my brother Brad, looking older with gray temples, hair brushed back. The bump on his nose was still there from when I busted it. He didn't recognize me. We looked at each other with the same blue eyes and the same black mold on our souls that we'd never scrape away.

"Sad situation," he said, nodding toward my grave.

I dug in my purse and found a napkin from the morning's coffee. I nodded, wiping my eyes and blowing my nose.

"You knew them?" Bradley asked. Listening to his voice was like listening to a ghost.

"Yes," I nodded and crossed my arms.

"You left flowers for my sister's babies. Liz never showed anyone how much she was hurting over them. God, I felt bad for her. I don't think she ever got over them."

He squinted up his eyes like he'd always done and gave me a sideways look. "You were the one who was with Greg when he died."

I held up my hand. "Listen, I'm not looking for any attention. I just came to say goodbye."

"I can respect that. Did you know her, my sister?"

"I did. Greg too. It was tragic what happened to Liz. I mean everything, her brother Steve and her horrible life with Greg, and then what happened with Darren Crawford. I guarantee you she's much happier now."

"It kills me every day, knowing what happened to her."

"You never told anyone that Greg used to beat up Liz, did you?"

"What are you talking about?"

"You knew Greg was physically and mentally abusing Liz. But like a typical Hobbs kid, you shrugged your shoulders and kept your mouth shut. She called you and left a message the day before she vanished, but you never called her back."

He looked like he was going to speak but nothing came out of his mouth.

"Brad, you could have prevented it if you'd just called her. If you'd let her come stay with you for a few days, none of that would have ever happened. She would have left Greg and avoided being picked up by Darren Crawford. Liz would still be alive, if you'd only taken the effort and listened to her."

"Hey, I didn't... How'd you know my name?"

"Did you ever tell anyone about the time you and Liz beat the crap out of each other and told everyone it was an attempted robbery? You almost killed her. You know, defending the family honor and all. You still have the bump on your nose, and the scar where she smashed you with a bottle."

He put his hand to the scar on his cheek then put it down quickly. "You don't know what you're talking about. We were attacked."

"You can still keep a secret, Brad. All of the Hobbs kids could, especially Mark and Kathy. Are you going to tell anyone that Mark killed Steve? We all know he did."

"What do you want, lady?"

"Are you ever going to tell anyone that Mark is the father of Kathy's kids? I mean, it's obvious two of them are his."

"Hey..."

"Remember that night all of us were sitting around doing homework and Steve said other people didn't live like us? We all agreed but none of us changed anything. We just sat there and laughed about it. Have you broken the cycle yet, Brad? Do you hit your own kids? Do you hit your wife? Do you belittle them and make them live in fear like Belinda and Douglas did to us?"

"What do you mean, us? Who are you?"

"You're such an idiot. There was no reason for you to treat Liz the way you did."

He face started to get red and blotchy. I'd made him mad. "I loved my sister."

"Well, you sucked at showing me that, Brad. You're so clueless. If you'd been there for me, I'd still be alive."

He backed away from me. "What do you want? Who are you?" His voice was shaking.

I looked him in the eyes and put my hands on his arms and spoke in my old voice, "I want you to tell me that you've broken the cycle. I want you to be Scrooge to my Marley and admit it isn't too late to change. Okay?"

"I have changed. Oh God, no."

"Do you know who I am, Brad?"

"You can't be. You don't look like yourself."

"I still have the same eyes as you. We have the same smile. I escaped. How about you Brad? Have you escaped yet?"

"But you couldn't have survived. Your blood was everywhere... they said you were dead."

"I am dead."

"I should have helped you."

"I'm fine, Brad. Just take care of yourself. By the way, I hear you're a good dad. I hope I'm right."

"Liz."

"Brad."

"Don't just walk away."

"Are you going to tell anyone?"

"No. Are you kidding? Who'd believe me? Where have you been?"

"You know I was with Greg when he died, so figure it out yourself."

"It's been twelve years, Liz. What the crap happened?"

"I'll tell you all about it later. Love you too, Bro. I'll see you around." I gave him a big hug and a kiss on the cheek.

I walked away. Brad started to follow. "Don't follow me, Bradley. I'm a ghost. I don't exist."

"Come on, Liz. Don't do this."

"I'll be in touch."

Chapter 86

About eight months after Tasha's death, Alex started dating. It wasn't so much dating as women aggressively pursuing him. It was one beautiful and accomplished woman after another. He didn't talk to me much about it. I didn't ask. But I'd hear about it. The whole thing reminded me of what happened to Greg after I died.

Alex didn't tell me about the one who called herself his girlfriend but she showed up all over the Internet with him. Nicole Mendoza was a well-known local Florida news media personality, a curvy, smart and successful woman with stunning looks and a sassy attitude.

I asked Alex about her.

His response was, "She pursued me looking for an interview. I told her no to the interview but she wouldn't take no for an answer on anything else. That's how they get into my schedule." Not his life, or his bed or his heart, but his schedule.

Photos continued to show up on the Internet. Alex looking handsome and healthy, Nicole looking beautiful and flawless, like a luscious brunette version of Tasha.

Jerry called one night to tell me Alex was in the hospital. He'd been in a car accident. It was raining a Florida downpour, and several cars were involved. Alex had suffered a broken arm and had been knocked around pretty badly. Jerry and Alex's brothers Phil and Rob decided it would help if I showed up. Alex had asked for me, not Nicole or anyone else, just Shannon.

When I arrived in Miami, Alex had already gone home with a pin in his left arm and a cast from his hand to his shoulder. Phil opened the door and looked happy to see me.

A beautiful young woman in tight jeans and a tighter pink shirt stood beside Phil. It was the girlfriend. I wanted to ignore her but Phil introduced us anyway.

Nicole took me aside, looking at me with mock concern. "What exactly is your relationship with Alex?"

"Alex is my best friend." It came out so fast, I was surprised I even said it.

"You were married to Jerry."

"For about five minutes."

"Why Alex? Did you have an affair with him, or what?"

"Of course not. Alex was married to Tasha. She was my friend."

"Alex said you weren't sleeping together. I just wanted to make sure."

"Nicole, I'm not your rival."

"Then what are you? Men like Alex don't have women for best friends. "

"I am a ghost, Nicole. I come and go from his life like a phantom in the dark. I am the darkest depths of his soul and the blackest parts of his heart. And when all is lost and the world turns away from him, I will always be there for him as a light in the darkness."

Nicole stared at me, flustered by my answer. I knew she'd be. Her eyes brimmed with hate. "His life is with me."

"Good for you."

"I'm going to marry him."

"Congratulations. Wait until Tasha's body is a little bit colder before you start picking out your dress." I refrained from rolling my eyes and went back in with Alex. How could he shackle himself with such a shallow piece of fluff?

I kissed Alex on the cheek and told him I was leaving for the night. "Nicole is lovely. She told me she is going to marry you."

Alex smiled a little to be polite through the painkillers and hugged me with his good arm.

Then he grabbed my hand and whispered a rambling monologue in my ear, "Sometimes when we're in bed, Nicole talks to me in Spanish but she isn't very good at it. She took a few classes in high school but never spoke it at home. Alejandro is what she wants to call me but I keep telling her my name is Alexander. My mom said Alexander sounded romantic, like a prince. She likes epic romantic fantasy tales. That's how I got my name. Did you know that, Shannon?"

"Yes, I did. But thanks for telling me again, Alex." I squeezed his hand. He was higher than a kite.

"Nicole thinks because I'm fluent in Spanish that she needs to be too. When I tell her to speak English, she pouts."

"Nasty habit, pouting."

"You think that is nasty, she shaves her crotch and has a prickly 9:00 shadow down there."

"Okay. Alex, that is way too much information. I'll see you tomorrow. Try to get some rest and don't talk too much."

"I love you, Shannon Amelia Gables."

"Love you too, Alex."

"I'm serious. I love you, Shannon."

"Good night, Alex." I gave him a quick hug with a kiss on the cheek. My head started to ache.

I checked with Phil about Alex's medication. The painkillers were talking up a storm.

Rob, who'd also showed up, had expert advice. "How are you?" he asked, as if we were the best of friends.

"I'm putting my condo up for sale. A couple of sleaze bags were using it as a love nest. I don't feel comfortable there anymore."

"I'm so sorry, Shannon."

"You're sorry you were caught. I trusted you with my life and now I can't even stand to be in the same room with you."

"Don't talk like that, please. I didn't plan it that way."

"Alex looked up to you, Rob. You could do no wrong in his eyes. But I guess it's okay if you were sleeping with your baby brother's wife. Tasha was sleeping with my boyfriend Laurence too, and Greg Atkinson, to name a few. So pick a number, Rob, and I'll eventually forgive you for what you did to Alex."

"Tasha blackmailed me. She said if I stopped seeing her, she'd give up you and Sean and Erin."

"You were screwing Tasha before you ever met me, so you can go to Hell."

After speaking with Phil for a few minutes more about Alex's condition, I went back to my condo. I sat on the balcony overlooking the ocean, thinking about what I was still doing living a quarter of each year in Florida. Maybe it was time to move on. I didn't want to spend the rest of my life hearing about Nicole's crotch or anything else about her. I didn't want to see Alex with anyone yet. He wasn't ready. I wasn't ready.

It was Friday night, so I called a few old friends and met for drinks and dancing to get my mind somewhere else. It didn't work. They ended up talking about Alex and Tasha and all of the gossip about Nicole. They asked me again about the day Tasha and Greg died. The next morning I headed back to Alex's house to try to make my peace with the situation.

Chapter 87

Alex was in the den watching football. He was wearing pajama pants with no shirt, a blanket over his shoulders, and his left arm in a sling. In the light I could see a greenish yellow bruise on the side of his face and more bruising on his shoulder. I wondered how someone who drank so much and was so banged up could still look so good.

I noticed several of Greg's books; To Elizabeth with Love and Grieving were on the table by a bottle of vodka and a couple of empty beer bottles. He'd started earlier than usual. A bottle of painkillers was on the table as well. Great, an overdose was just what he needed.

I'd only been in the living room and bedroom the day before. The furniture in the den was new. Last time I was at the house there had been a modern yellow leather sectional that Tasha had been so proud of. Now it was cozy tropical print couch and two matching chairs. Comfortable, but a little on the tacky side. Actually, it was a lot on the tacky side. Indoor furniture should never have pink and orange parrots on the upholstery. A large lamp with about twenty bulbs in a cluster of multicolored glass flowers overhung the couch. It looked both expensive and vulgar.

"Um, having Jimmy Buffet over?" I asked.

"Nicole picked it out. She insisted I needed a change. Do you like it?"

"Not really. It's kind of garish. How are you feeling?"

"Pretty good, now that the drugs have kicked in."

"Should you be drinking with that?"

"I'm not going to be driving." He closed his eyes and put his head back. I would have been surprised if he'd fallen asleep. Instead he put his hand on my wrist. "I'll have a scar on my arm when the cast comes off. We'll match."

"Regular twinsies," I said. "What are you doing with these?" I picked up the copy of To Elizabeth With Love, then put it back down."

"It is ironic in a way that Greg's introduction of To Elizabeth with Love parallels my life right now."

"Don't identify with his grief. It isn't the same thing."

"How would you know? You've only run from men, never to them."

"That isn't true."

Alex gave me a look that could kill. "I can't believe you actually loved that worm Laurence. He called you a liar and all the while he was fucking my wife at the same time he was fucking you."

It was the first time I've ever heard Alex use the F word. It sounded strange and out of place in his voice.

"It doesn't matter anymore. They're both gone from our lives," I answered calmly.

"Tasha was fucking Greg Atkinson too. She knew all about him but she couldn't stay away from him. What did Tasha know that you didn't know? Why was she so attracted to your men?" I could hear the anger in his voice was directed at me, not Tasha or Greg or Laurence.

"Stop," I said, trying not to get angry.

"You know Shannon, if you'd slept with me, maybe my wife would have stopped fooling around. Think about it."

"If you're going to be rude I'll leave."

"No, don't leave. I need to talk to you, Shannon, dear. Women have been coming in droves trying to comfort me. Listen to this." He read from the book. "After Liz was pronounced dead I was bombarded by the attentions of women, each wanting to be the next Mrs. Gregory Atkinson. These women proclaimed they wanted to rescue me from my heartbreak. Most of them wanted to take advantage of my situation and cash in on my grief. Most had the false hope that they could comfort me. Each thought she could be a replacement for my lost wife, like a new puppy or a shiny new car.

These women, who lined up to tempt me with home cooking, sex and sympathy, only coveted what Elizabeth had. My disgust in them grew but I also pitied them in their ignorance of real love and the real meaning of marriage. To them I was a possession to be had, the big catch, a great opportunity. I would be the man who would make their lives complete.

I didn't need a wife. I needed Liz. I needed her laugh, her understanding, her touch and her love."

"Stop it Alex."

"I needed Liz. I needed her laugh, her understanding, her touch and her love. He missed you. I can understand that. I know exactly what Greg was feeling."

"Stop it. You need to deal with your grief over Tasha's betrayal and death, but not like this."

"Tasha? I've been comforted by quite a few women lately wanting to be the Next Tasha Alexander Goldstein. Don't tell Nicole."

"You don't need to tell me this."

"In fact, I've been comforted by six, no seven different women since Tasha passed to the great beyond. Or was it eight? I can't remember. No, it was six. That makes for an even dozen for a lifetime total. I bet you thought I'd been with more women than that. No, just Tasha for years and years and..." He trailed off and closed his eyes.

I scowled at him. "When was the last time you had anything to eat?"

He shifted and straightened up on the couch. His expression changed, eyes narrowed, a mean smile came to his perfect lips. "You could comfort me, Shannon. I've been thinking about how you looked the first night you stayed here, in your transparent purple camisole, trying to beat the life out of Jerry with a gun handle. You were so lost and alone. I could have had you that night. That time I almost kissed you in the museum. I should have. I should have taken you away and..."

"Stop it."

"I wanted you so bad. You wanted me more than you ever wanted anyone. We should have said to hell with everyone else. I can't get it out of my head. I was in court the other day and completely lost my train of thought because I was thinking about how it would feel to fuck you silly."

"Stop it, Alex, now."

"Slide off your panties and come sit in my lap. We could do it before Nicole gets here. She'd never know."

I didn't know the man in front of me anymore. I felt the unfamiliar sting in my nose and watering in my eyes from the tears I was trying to hold back.

"What is the matter with you?" Alex asked, anger in his voice.

I didn't bother to answer him. I turned and left, the same way I left Laurence the day Tasha and Greg died. It was over. I could hear him calling my name and yelling something else I couldn't understand but I didn't stop.

When I got to my car in Alex's driveway, Nicole was getting out of her car.

She glared at me. "What are you doing here?"

I didn't answer.

Chapter 88

The next day, Sunday, my answer box was filled with apologies from a sober Alex. A box was delivered from a local estate jeweler with an opal and diamond bracelet. It was one I'd admired in the window the last time I'd been in town with him. I closed the box without even trying it on. I doubted if I'd ever be able to wear it without feeling sick. That afternoon I signed papers with a real estate agent to sell my condo and started to pack up the few things I wanted to ship home.

Monday morning Alex stopped by, to my surprise. I'd fixed coffee but was still just wearing the long tee shirt I'd slept in. Alex was in a white shirt with a loose tie around his neck. He held gold cufflinks in his pocket. His casted arm was in a sling. Aside from the cast and sling he looked great. Not a hair out of place, not a wrinkle or scuff, his mouth turned into a smile and eyes sparkling under long thick lashes. Maybe I should have let Kyle Rutledge take a belt sander to him.

"I need help," he said apologetically. Any number of people could have helped him.

"Where's your girlfriend?" I snapped.

"Girlfriend? You mean Nicole? Work. She's interviewing Erin's ex. The Congressman. Kind of weird and ironic, our connection and now Nicole is interviewing him. The bastard is running for office again."

Peas in a pod, I thought. "Lovely. If you tell Nicole about Erin, I'll kill you."

"Who's Erin?" He smiled like a movie star on the red carpet. "Don't worry, we still have a stash of exceptionally nasty photos Erin plans on sending out tomorrow." He held out his hand with the cufflinks. "I need help with these and the tie. Only my left hand works at the moment."

I straightened his collar and did an expert job with the tie. Next was the cuff links.

He seemed so happy. Happy wasn't something that was in my current vocabulary. He rattled on about his agenda of the day. Today was his first day back at work after his accident. He wasn't supposed to go back to work. He said it was only for a few hours, to meet with his staff and check his schedule. Rachael and Trevor would be helping him at home for the next few weeks.

"I'm so sorry for the way I behaved on Saturday. I'd like to say it was because of the drugs and pain, but there is no excuse. I was cruel and vulgar and... I'm afraid you'll fade out of my life. I've hardly seen you since Tasha died. I thought it would be easier if it ended badly."

"It did end badly, Alex. You should go now."

"Finish up with my tie."

"Alex."

"Talk to me. I'm ready for some changes. I need you here with me. Nobody understands me like you do."

"I'm selling the condo. I don't think I'll be coming back here much anymore. Phil told me you had an offer on your house," I said, making uncomfortable small talk. "I have coffee. Do you want some?"

"Sure. Coffee would be great. Um, there is a good offer on my house. I have another place picked out. I want you to take a look at it."

"I'm leaving tomorrow morning."

"Change your flight. There is so much going on right now. The accident. Trying to deal with the business without Tasha. I'm still taking care of all of that. To top it off, Jerry has been a basket case. I love the guy, but he is driving me nuts. And I'm in love."

"Love? Good for you," I snapped at him but decided quickly to calm down. "Nicole is a beautiful and successful young woman," I said. It was the best lie I'd ever told. I wanted to say, The bitch will ruin your life worse than Tasha ever did. But I remained cool and pleasant as I tried not to resort to physical violence.

He smiled. "Yes, Nicole is quite beautiful and successful."

"How old is she?"

"Twenty-seven. Just a baby compared to us. How old are you now? Thirty-four?"

"I'm thirty-four on paper. Thirty-six in real life."

"That's right, we're six years apart." Then he dropped the bomb. "I want to get married again. My marriage with Tasha was over long before she died, but out of respect I'll wait at least a year after the date of her death."

I was going to try to talk him out of it but I knew if I opened my mouth I'd throw up on his expensive shoes.

"I want a family. I'm not getting any younger."

"I don't know, Alex. Maybe this marriage thing is overrated."

"This time I'm going to do it right."

"How?"

"I've loved her from the first minute I set eyes on her. She feels the same about me."

"Oh, come on Alex, life isn't like a romance novel. Are you sure you want to marry Nicole? It would be Tasha all over again. Have you asked her yet?"

"No I haven't." He took a box out of his pocket and gave it to me. Inside was a flawless emerald cut diamond, 3 ct., shimmering in a perfect platinum setting. "Do you like it? I picked it up on the way here this morning."

It was a shock but I told him calmly that he'd made a good choice and that he'd be happy for the rest of his life. Nicole was a lucky girl. I wouldn't attend the wedding but I'd wish him happiness. Well, not really. I went to the kitchen, poured coffee and fought off the tears. He followed me in to talk.

"I have to clarify a few things. Sit down," Alex said as he watched me shovel more sugar into my coffee. "How do you drink that?" he asked, as he'd asked so many other times over the years.

So we talked over coffee while I tried not to run to the bathroom and get sick, and my life changed again.

After we talked, for at least an hour, Alex held me with one arm for what seemed like forever. "You're the best friend I've ever had."

I listened to his heartbeat as I always did when he hugged me and tried to blink away the tears. He kissed my eyes and cheeks. "I love you, Shannon. Nothing will ever change that."

I didn't say a word and let him go. He had to get to the office and his driver was waiting. I sat down, feeling as if I'd faint, trying to adjust my feelings.

I'd always loved Alexander Goldstein, from the first night in the pool house when he held me in his arms and told me that I'd be safe. I'd talked to him almost every single day for ten years. Now I'd move on again. From battered wife, to hostage, to fugitive, to realizing that I was always the same person because no matter what, I'd have to live with myself.

Chapter 89

After Alex left I called Brad. It was finally time to take care of family business.

I sat on the balcony and curled in a chair. God, I'd miss that view of the ocean. Brad picked up the phone.

"Brad, it's your sister."

"Liz? Where are you?"

"On a balcony overlooking the Atlantic Ocean."

"Oh wow. Is it really you?"

"Of course it is. Listen, Brad, after Steve died I hid my diaries from when we were kids and the disk with the photos from that night under the floorboards in the basement under where the old desk was. I wrapped it all up with plastic, in a cardboard box marked Bible Verse Flash Cards. With any luck, you'll be able to print the photos."

"You're shitting me."

"I shit you not, dear brother. Get Jordan, get the stuff and turn it over to the police. Have Steve's body exhumed. It was murder. Mark slammed Steve's head into the wall six times or more. Jordan saw it all. The cause of death wasn't from the fall. Mark threatened me several times after the murder. That is all written in the my diaries."

There was a long silence.

"If you don't want to do this, I'll contact the police with an anonymous tip but I'd rather not do that."

"Why are you coming out with this now?"

"It's the right thing to do. You and Jordan deserve justice. Jordan is considered mentally ill, so he won't be charged with any crime, plus Mark threatened to kill him and rape and kill me if he ever said anything. I wrote that down too.

Okay, we know Mark is running for the State Senate. He fathered at least two children with your twin sister and killed our brother. Do you really want to see Mark go to Washington? He has been rewarded in life over and over with good things. It is time to stop him and reward him with what he deserves."

"Mark is still having sex with Kathy every Tuesday and Thursday, plus holidays."

"Still? They're disgusting. Completely immoral and disgusting."

"You're not telling me anything new. What about you, sis? Are you still going to hide?"

"For now, yes. I want to see you again. I have a lot to tell you. I'm going to help you with this, Brad. I'm going to help you and Jordan with a lot of things."

Mark stopped his campaign for State Senate. He was investigated but never arrested for the murder of our brother Steve, but it ruined any political career he might have had.

Kathy's husband left her and demanded custody of the children. All three of them decided to stay with their father, who moved the family to Chicago. Kathy claimed she was raped and threatened by Mark to hide the facts of Steve's death. Brad, Jordan and I knew she was lying but we said nothing. Eventually her husband believed her lies and she moved to the windy city.

My parents, Douglas and Belinda, separated after the news of their children's bad behavior hit the fan. Dad blamed it on Belinda. Belinda said she never wanted any children after Mark was born, so it was all her husband's fault.

Our brother David is still a doctor in war-torn regions of the Earth. He never married or had children. Brad said he is still a self-serving jerk and other doctors don't like him. They only put up with him because he is so good at facial reconstructive surgery. Go figure.

I still keep in touch with Brad and Jordan. They never told anyone my story. They're no longer speaking to Mark, Kathy or our parents.

The Law Firm of Alexander and Goldstein became Goldstein and Mather. It was time to expand the business, as divorce often came with criminal defense cases.

Sean and Winter got married and are expecting their first child. Or should I say children – a boy and a girl.

Erin stayed in Napa with her own life, only seeing Sean and I occasionally. She and her girlfriend Maddie are engaged. Sean and I love Maddie like another sister. Maddie is expecting their first child. Sean donated the secret ingredient.

Laurence's daughters Beckka and Brynn stayed in touch with me. I couldn't blame them for their father's actions. Laurence sold the Victorian house he loved and moved his law practice to San Francisco. At first he'd send me weekly emails. I never responded to him, so after four months the messages stopped. He never told anyone that I had been born Elizabeth Hobbs.

Chapter 90

There were always those days when I thought, what will I lie about today? Who will I invent, to what picture will I give a past, what will I make up about my own past?

On my fortieth birthday I sat on the beach, wrapped in a blanket, watching the surfers in the morning waves. I looked over and saw Laurence, walking along the beach, as I'd seen him on so many romantic weekends. I used to smile when I saw him.

I guess he expected me to be glad to see him. I wasn't happy or angry, just well, it just seemed so weird to see him there. It had been almost four years since I'd talked to him. After he'd relocated his practice in San Francisco, I never returned his calls. I never returned the calls of his friends.

"Hi," he said simply. Nothing more. Nothing less.

"Laurence," I said back. I didn't stand up to greet him or give him a hug. "You can take off your mask if you want." We were still wearing masks, thought I wasn't wearing one because practically nobody else was on the beach.

"You look good. I like the new hair color. It's long now."

"It's my old hair color, you know, the one I was born with." My hair was indeed brown with strands of gray near the front.

He smiled. "I'm visiting Beckka. She said you had lunch yesterday. She told me you were staying at the beach house, so I thought I'd stop by."

I had indeed had lunch with his daughter. They'd reached out to me after everything hit the fan. "It was great seeing her. You've been a great dad. I really love her. I love both of your girls."

"They love you too. Thanks for keeping in touch with them. It means a lot to me."

"They're part of my life. If they need me I'm not going to just vanish." I waited to see if he'd make a remark about that one. He was playing it safe. "The past year has been hard on everyone. Any bit of contact with others helps."

"Beckka said you have a lot of changes in your life but she wouldn't tell me anything. You know how she is, a flair for the dramatic."

I changed the subject from me to him. "I hear good things about your office in the big city."

"It's great. Business is booming."

"Good. I hope you're happy. I really do."

A small flock of terns flew overhead. Terns are one of my favorite beach birds. I glanced at Laurence and thought about that day I jumped off of the bridge after watching a flock of chickadees. Then I thought of Mae West... I laughed. I hadn't slept much lately and couldn't keep myself thinking straight.

"Do you ever watch birds, Laurence? You should."

"Shannon. "

"You should have called me before you came here."

"You wouldn't have answered my call. I miss you. Not a day goes by when I don't think of us."

I bet you didn't miss me when you started sneaking away to screw Tasha, I thought, but said, "I thought about it a lot too."

"Shannon," He looked so sad. "I loved you. I still love you."

This was getting uncomfortable. I looked out at the ocean. I watched a man in the distance walking the beach. He let the waves lap over his bare feet.

"We can start over," said Laurence.

"No, we can't. It's over. Done. I've moved on."

"Shannon, I don't care who you were. I only care about who you are now."

"You don't know who I am now."

"You can show me who you are."

There was a mewing sound. I looked under my blanket. "Shhhhh, kitten," I said.

"You brought your cat to the beach?"

Pulling up the blanket, I adjusted my shirt and stuck myself back into my bra before I put my baby on my shoulder. "My child, Laurence. Her name is Ione. She is just fifteen days old. By the way, I've been married for three years. Our anniversary is tomorrow." I lifted up my daughter. She was so tiny. "Ione, meet Laurence. Beckka's daddy."

"She is beautiful." Ione took Laurence's finger in her tiny hand as infants do. "Did you adopt her? You said you couldn't have children."

"Would it have made a difference where she came from?"

"Well, no..."

"Ione was a surprise. I didn't think I could carry a pregnancy to full term but here she is, absolutely perfect and healthy."

Laurence glanced at my hand and saw my emerald cut diamond. "What is her full name?" he asked. It was more polite than asking who the father was.

I looked down the beach and saw my husband walking in the distance, still keeping an eye out for interesting shells. I waved. He waved back. Laurence looked as if he'd seen a ghost.

"Ione Elizabeth Goldstein. I think you should go now."

And Laurence went away.

A word from the author

Thank you to everyone who has helped me along the way in so many ways. I'd like to give a special call out to my friends at WPaD (Writers, Poets, and Deviants) for all of their support and love. Thank you to all of my other friends and family who have been reading my work forever and cheering me on. I'd also like to give a special thank you to my husband Steve, my and daughter Charlotte for their patience and love.

Thank you dear readers for taking the time to read *Exceptional Liars.* If you enjoyed this book (or even if you didn't), please take a moment to leave a review on Amazon.com to let other readers know what you thought of it.

~ Marla Todd

About the Author

Marla Todd is an artist and writer based in California.
Marla also writes short stories and the parenting/urban fantasy blog https://vampiremaman.com/ under the name Juliette Kings.
Marla is a founding member of WPaD (Writers, Poets, and Deviants) and has contributed numerous stories to their themed short story and poetry anthologies.

Other Works by Marla Todd include:

Morning at the Vineyard (with Juliette Kings)

WPaD (Writers, Poets, and Deviants) Anthologies as Marla Todd and Juliette Kings
- Goin' Extinct Too! Apocalypse A Go-Go
- Weirder Tales: An Omnibus of Odd Ditties
- Strange Adventures in a Deviant Universe: WPaD Science Fiction
- Creepies: Twisted Tales From Beneath the
- Bed Creepies 2: Things That go Bump in the Closet
- Creepies 3: Nightmares on Deviant Street
- Goin' Extinct: Tales From the Edge of Oblivion
- Dragons and Dreams: A Fantasy Anthology
- Passion's Prisms: Tales of Love and Romance
- Tinsel Tales 2: Holiday Hootenanny
- Tinsel Tales: A Holiday Treasury
- Nocturnal Desires: Erotic Tales for the Sensual Soul

WPaD books are available worldwide in paperback and ebook. For more information, please visit our website:
http://wpad.weebly.com/ Find WPaD Publications on Facebook for updates on our upcoming projects.

Exceptional Liars is a work of fiction.

Unfortunately abusisve relations are real. Jealousy and abuse both mental and physical is not a healthy or normal part of any relationship.

Is your boyfriend or husband unreasonably jealous or controlling?

Fact: Every day 3 women die at the hands of an abusive partner in the USA.

Fact: Physical abuse often goes hand in hand with jealousy.

Many people mistake jealousy for an endearing display of affection without realizing it can be a sign of something more sinister. How do you know when jealousy has crossed the line from simple affection to unhealthy obsession?

A jealous partner isn't doing out of love – he/she is doing it for control.

I recommend **"The Jealousy Game" by Mandy White**, for all parents and teens and anyone (of any age) who might be at risk for staying in unhealthy relationships.

"The Jealousy Game" by Mandy White is available FREE to everyone and is available on Smashwords and Amazon.

If you feel you are in danger call 911 or seek out help from your nearest shelter.

~ Marla Todd

www.ingramcontent.com/pod-product-compliance
Lightning Source LLC
Chambersburg PA
CBHW060357180626
46817CB00007B/2456